Secret Sisterhood

Secret Sisterhood

Monique Miller

URBAN
CHRISTIAN

www.urbanchristianonline.net

URBAN CHRISTIAN is published by

Urban Books
10 Brennan Place
Deer Park, NY 11729

ISBN-13: 978-1-60162-947-0
ISBN-10: 1-60162-947-8

First Printing October 2007
Printed in the United States of America

10   9   8   7   6   5   4   3   2

This is a work of fiction. Any references or similarities to actual events, real people, living, or dead, or to real locales are intended to give the novel a sense of reality. Any similarity in other names, characters, places, and incidents is entirely coincidental.

Submit Wholesale Orders to:
Kensington Publishing Corp.
C/O Penguin Group (USA) Inc.
Attention: Order Processing
405 Murray Hill Parkway
East Rutherford, NJ 07073-2316
Phone: 1-800-526-0275
Fax: 1-800-227-9604

Dedication

This novel is dedicated to all the Secret Sisters;
Past, Present and Future.
I hope it gives you hope and inspiration.

Acknowledgments

The writing of this novel has been a long time in the making, therefore there are many I need to not only acknowledge, but thank for many reasons. Bear with me everyone; this will be pretty extensive.

First I have to thank God for using me as a vessel and allowing me to take the storm and turn it into lemonade and for in the process, blessing me with my beautiful daughter, Meliah.

Next I'd like to thank my parents, Mr. William H. Miller and Ms. Gwendolyn Miller, for giving me support and providing inspiration to me for as long as I can remember, especially with the writing of this book. Mama, thanks for burning the midnight oil with me and Meliah for this book! Thank you also to my Grandparents, Mr. William S. Frederick, Sr. and Mrs. Caroline H. Miller, you've both been and continue to be an inspirations to me. I'd like to thank my sister, Penny Miller, for her assistance throughout the writing of this novel.

Many thanks also to the following people for your assistance, support and words of encouragement throughout the past few years: Family—Denita, Erma, Giovanni, Valeria, Tiffany, Sheila, Lauren, LaQuita, LaTricia, Sherika, Tonya and Jonica.

ALIBC—Bishop Aubrey G. Mullen Jr. and Co-Pastor Vanessa Mullen of the Abundant Life International Baptist Cathedral in Jacksonville, NC.; Debra Willis for your assistance with my computer. The Stewardship of ALIBC—Mr. Adams, Doug, Deacon Taylor, Deacon Washington, Myra, Deacon Woods, Sonya and last, but certainly *not* least, Deacon Monk.

Circle of Friends Book Club IV Jacksonville, NC—Kim, DaDonna, Denna, Tiffany, Angela, Tammy, Dee and Talaisha.

Friends—Clitondra & Darlene, Elizabeth, Lori, Halona, Diedre, Lorrie and Kenydra. Thank you for your encouragement during the book's infancy into its maturity. You don't know how much it meant. Thank you for believing in me.

Sorors—Thanks, Crysta, Tracie, Marie, Sonya, Renee, Darneise & LeKaja. Tau Omega Omega, Jacksonville, NC.

New Vision Writers Group—Jacquie, Angela, Suzetta, Sandy, Cassandra, Titus, Lesley, Karen, Pansy, Tonya and Valderia. Thank you all for being such a wonderful group in which I am proud to be a part of.

WIC Chicks—Jacksonville, NC: you Christine, Bea, Ellen, Judy, and Kavitha for all your support.

Cheryl Underwood—Wake County Public Library in Holly Springs, NC. Thank you, Cheryl, for giving me the chance to officially promote my book for the first time (Even though the book hadn't even been printed yet).

WOCC: Thank you First Lady LaShawn Thompson of World Overcomers Christian Church for your feedback on my novel.

Readers: Thanks also to Sandy Dowd, Shamir Faison, Nancy Ferguson and Michelle Cooper for taking time out of your busy schedules and providing your tips and comments for the book.

Authors—Thank you to authors Toschia and Jacquelin Thomas. Toschia, your belief and support has been priceless. Jacquelin, your guidance has been, and still is, much appreciated. Without you two ladies I wouldn't have gotten as far as I have in such a timely manner. I feel blessed to be able to call you my friends. Since starting to write I have met many authors who have been blessings not only to me, but to so many others. Keep on doing what you are doing. Thank you Suzetta Perkins, Kendra Norman-Bellamy, Sherri Lewis, Stacey Hawkins Adams, Tia McCollars, Angela Benson, Dorothy

Pettis, Vanessa Davis Griggs, Victoria Christopher Murray, Cassandra Darden Bell and Monica P. Carter.

Editors—From my first editor to the current, thank you Theresa Greenwell, Annette Dammer and Joylynn Jossel, you are all phenomenal women.

Agent—To my agent Sha Shana Crichton, thank you for seeing enough in my writing to take interest years ago. Thank you for all the edit points, which helped to make Secret Sisterhood a success.

The UC Family—Thank you to Carl Weber, Kendra Norman-Bellamy and Joylynn Jossel for embracing me into the Urban Christian Family and giving me the opportunity to share my novel with the world-Literally speaking ☺

Prologue

"Ten . . . nine . . . eight . . . seven!" the doctor pressed. "Come on, you can do it, push!"

"Six . . . five . . . four . . ."

"Hughhh," she let out a low moan. The contractions were excruciating; the pain medication had worn off.

"Push a little harder. Come on! Three . . . two . . . one," the doctor finished the countdown for what seemed like the hundredth time in an hour. "Alright, you can rest now. Breathe, try to relax and get ready for the next contraction."

She allowed her arms and legs to relax. Her mouth was dry, and she wanted something to drink, but knew it wasn't possible. The ice chips were not doing the job and the stir-ups her feet rested in didn't help at all.

"These stir-ups aren't helping," she panted. "Can I take my feet down?"

"Sure, try it without the stir-ups next time. Use your hands to hold your feet. The nurses can help you," Dr. Evans replied.

She closed her eyes and took deep breaths. She felt someone place a cold cloth on her forehead and face. She didn't bother to look at who it was. It really didn't matter. She was just glad they'd done it. The room had gotten hotter and hotter with each contraction.

She was ready for the next contraction. More ready than anyone in the room could ever imagine. She had come a long way to get to this point. It was an end to a long journey.

Pain shot through her abdomen again. But she wouldn't let it get the best of her. With strength from God, she would pull through it. She had to bear the pains the gift of life brought.

She removed her legs from the stir-ups, grabbed the heels of her feet, and pulled them closer to her body.

She held her breath and pushed with all the strength she could muster as the doctor began the count down again. "Ten . . . nine . . . eight . . . seven . . . six . . . five . . . four . . . three . . . two . . . one. Okay, breathe again, and try to relax until the next contraction."

She fell back onto the pillows of her hospital bed, attempting to relax again. The cool cloth returned to her forehead. Her mouth was even drier than it had been only a few minutes earlier, but she didn't have the strength to reach or ask for the ice cup.

It had taken her twenty-eight hours to get from the first contraction, to her cervix being dilated ten centimeters. It had never taken that long on *A Baby Tale*, the television series she had been so fond of during her pregnancy. It only took those women thirty minutes, with commercials!

She imagined how many babies could have been delivered within the hours she'd been there. With two shows an hour, times the twenty-eight hours of labor, that would be at least fifty-six babies, not counting those women who had twins and triplets! And here she lay after hours of labor and still no baby. She wasn't having twins or triplets. She only expected one. *That show sure was misleading*, she thought.

"Ugh!" She pulled herself up to the baby bearing position. Back to reality, it was time to push again.

"Ready?" the doctor asked her.

She took another deep breath, nodded, and began to push.

After a couple of seconds Dr. Evans said, "I can see the head. This is it—push, push! You can do it. It is finally time to meet this baby. It is finally time."

Chapter 1

Shelby Tomlinson

Shelby's trembling forefinger traced her husband's lips on the enlarged 4x6 photograph she held. She had used the same finger that very morning on his lips. The tender touch she gave caused him to stir awake with a smile. Just as she had wanted and expected, he pulled her into an embrace and kissed her.

Now she held the picture, which usually sat on her office desk, in hopes to simulate the feelings she'd had earlier that morning. She needed to pull from her "happy place." That is what her psychotherapist called it. Holding the picture of her husband and thinking about their morning kiss helped her to relive the feelings.

Thankfully, she didn't have to use the psychotherapy technique often since the anxiety attacks were inconsistent. They usually happened when she was highly stressed or if she was pondering over something with worry for too long.

Staring at the picture, Shelby remembered what their early morning kiss led to and the tightening in her chest and rapid heartbeats slowly subsided. She smiled as the pain subsided.

Beads of sweat formed quickly. The sweat was predictable with the hot flashes she experienced after each anxiety attack. One second she was cool—the vent in her office blowing directly down on her—then the next second she felt as if she was back outside in the ninety-five degree North Carolina heat. Taking the lid off the soda cup left over from lunch, she pulled out a piece of ice and wiped it on her forehead, cheeks, and neck.

It had been a few months since she'd had an attack. The cause of that attack was the same as the one this afternoon—she had been stressing about wanting to get pregnant.

She'd found that the best relief from the anxiety attacks was to practice the psychotherapy techniques her childhood doctor taught her. Shelby's mother had taken her to see the doctor on her first day of junior high school. That was when Shelby had her first attack. She'd been stressing over the first day at a new school. Just before leaving to go to school that morning, her monthly cycle started for the first time. Even though Shelby had been scared and excited at the same time about the transition into womanhood, her fears of going to school and being embarrassed about her clothing getting messed up overtook her. Her panic attack happened in the girls' bathroom before she made it to her first class.

She hated referring to the techniques as psychotherapy, so she called them her mini-vacations instead. During her mini-vacations, she focused on something that brought her joy. Over the years she found that pictures of her loved ones helped the most. So as a result, in her office, purse, and home, there were many memorable pictures scattered about.

Attempting to take a deep breath, Shelby focused on the photo. It was taken two years prior during their annual family vacation in Mexico. Each year for as long as she could remember her family had taken a family vacation. Since she had gotten married, her husband Phillip was now a part of the tradition.

She stood next to her husband as they exited their cruise-ship. They were wearing matching sombreros, which shielded them from the hot Mexican sun. She could barely see his beautiful hazel eyes because of the shadow cast by the hat. Her tawny-colored skin had started turning bronze during the first couple days of their vacation.

Their vacation turned out to be wonderful. Upon their return, Shelby's mother asked if she could expect grand-children soon. Sadly, Shelby hadn't been able to give her mother an answer that day or since. Shelby often asked her-self the same question, to the point of stressing. This nag-ging question as well and the influx of prenatal patients she saw before lunch caused her to have her most recent attack.

Suddenly Shelby heard a knock at the door. She placed the picture back on her desk and pulled out a Kleenex to wipe her hands and face. Her mini-vacation was over and it was back to reality—work.

"Come in," Shelby said, clearing her throat.

The door opened. Shelby could hear the talking from the lobby full of patients echoing. Her co-worker and friend, Rachel, stepped in, closing the door behind her. Rachel's face was flushed. She sat back in a patient chair opposite Shelby and fanned herself with the medium-sized Post-It Note she was holding.

"Can I sit for just a second and catch my breath?" Rachel asked. "Is the air working? It seems like it's over ninety de-grees in here," she let out a sigh and rubbed her temples. "It's been such a mad house today."

"I know, that power outage yesterday wasn't good," Shelby said, nervously dabbing the Kleenex on her neck. She always felt embarrassed by the attacks, but was relieved Rachel had walked in and not one of the other nurses. "You know we have the patients we couldn't finish seeing yesterday, plus our regular schedule. Being closed Monday for the upcoming Labor Day holiday doesn't help either."

Shelby glanced at the picture she had just held. "I was in the middle of taking a mini-vacation from today's reality."

"Are you okay?" Rachel asked.

Shelby smiled. "Yeah, I'm fine. It was just a little attack this time." Shelby had confided in Rachel about the attacks just after she had witnessed one.

"Are you sure? What do you think triggered it?"

"I guess pondering too much on when and if I'm ever going to have a child. That, coupled with the influx of all those prenatal patients we had this morning." *The fact that my husband avoids me like the plague when I want to talk about my feelings and concerns really doesn't help either*, she thought. Shelby's face darkened as she thought about all the times her husband changed the subject or conveniently found a way to wriggle out of talking to her. She saw the look of concern on Rachel's face. "But don't worry, I'll be fine." She straightened her face and smiled to reassure Rachel and herself as well.

Rachel leaned forward and touched Shelby's hand. "It's me you're talking to. You don't have to put up any false pretenses."

"I know, and I thank you. But I assure you, I'll be fine." Her lips felt dry, so Shelby picked up her purse and rummaged through it for lip-gloss.

Rachel rolled her neck around her shoulders. She slipped her hands under her curly auburn hair to knead her neck. "I need a mini-vacation. You always look so refreshed after you take one."

Shelby loved her friend for showing her obvious concern and then backing off the subject of the attack. "You should try it sometime. It's economical and you don't need a pass-port," Shelby said.

"I might have to take you up on that someday."

Shelby glanced at her watch. It was one o'clock in the afternoon.

Rachel placed the Post-It on Shelby's desk in front of her. "Do you still have Ms. Cline's chart?"

Shelby rolled her eyes. "You're kidding me right? It's been so busy I haven't had time to complete any of my charts. Of course I still have her chart."

"I figured you did. Anyway, Walter Reed Hospital called, and they need Ms. Cline's recent lab results faxed to them A.S.A.P."

Shelby sighed. "One more thing to add to my long list of things to do. Do you have their fax number?"

Rachel perked up, standing immediately. "It's right there on the Post-It." She pointed to the fax number. "I need to tend to my patients, you know you should do the same thing," Rachel said playfully.

Shelby grabbed her stress ball and threw it at Rachel. "Funny, very funny." She snorted as she laughed.

Just before running out of the office, Rachel picked up the ball and threw it back, leaving the door ajar. Sounds of in-coming patients filled the lobby.

Shelby stood slowly and took a deeper, almost painless breath this time. *How nice it would be if I didn't have to see any pregnant patients this afternoon*, she thought.

When she first began working at Silvermont Women's Center as a registered nurse, Shelby had loved working with all the patients, especially the prenatal ones. She'd secured the job just two months after graduating from Carson State University, a local college. Shelby considered herself blessed to get the job. Silvermont Women's Center was known through-out the state of North Carolina for being one of the best OB/GYN and infertility offices.

Over the years she had seen women of all types and ages come through the office for one reason or another. The first couple of years Shelby actually had an affinity for working with the pregnant patients. Most of them seemed to have a joyous radiance about them, especially when she told them the positive results of their pregnancy tests. She loved giving the good news.

The euphoria about other women getting pregnant vanished after two years of trying to become pregnant herself. Shelby eventually got to the point where she dreaded sharing the positive test results with her patients.

She began to envy many of the women, especially the ones who bragged about easily getting pregnant after only a month or two of trying. Then there were times when she felt angry towards the women who hoped they weren't pregnant. Shelby would deliver the good news of their pregnancies and they looked horrified—as if it was the worst thing in the world. Shelby knew differently. There was nothing worse than praying for months and months to become pregnant—but to no avail.

Lately, the only time she felt solace was when she was working with the women who were having trouble conceiving. She could relate to them. They, to some degree or another, were in the same boat as she. Shelby felt like she was in a secret sisterhood with these women. Her "sisters" knew exactly how it felt to long for a child day after day. They knew the emotional ups and downs.

Often when her sisters needed a listening ear, they confided in Shelby. Whenever time allowed during their appointments, Shelby spent extra time talking with them about their grief. She listened attentively, knowing these women needed to vent.

There were many times Shelby wished she had someone to confide in, especially her husband. Often she wanted to tell her *sisters* that she had many of the same concerns and longings. But it wasn't professional to talk to them about her personal problems, even if they seemed to be similar. Nor did she want to confide her longings to her closest friends or family. She felt too embarrassed to talk to them and didn't think they would truly understand. No one close to her seemed to be having any problems having babies. All of her married friends either already had children or were pregnant. So she kept all of her thoughts to herself.

Now after four years of working at Silvermont OB/GYN, overall, she continued to enjoy her work. But some days the longing to have a child coupled with the flood of prenatal patients, got to her so much that she started stressing. She stressed to the point that the anxiety attacks, which had ceased her freshman year in college, returned.

Before she left the comforts of her office, Shelby checked her appearance in the full-length mirror behind the door. She finger-combed her shoulder length hair, putting out of place hairs back. She checked her clothing to make sure her make-up still looked fresh. Once she was presentable enough to face the world, she plastered on a smile and left her office, ready to see the patients.

She checked off the next appointment. The patient was new, a young girl only 15-years-old. She was five foot, nine inches and weighed 125 pounds, which meant the girl had been underweight prior to the pregnancy.

It wasn't a big surprise anymore for Shelby to see someone so young, pregnant. The youngest had been 12, which wasn't so common. It was common for most of the teens to come in the office late in their pregnancies, usually after the girls couldn't conceal their swelling stomachs from their parents anymore.

She shook her head wondering again why this 15-year-old was pregnant instead of her. Inwardly Shelby scolded herself. It was negative thoughts like that which caused her to have attacks. She took a deep breath, remembering the smile on her husband's face in the photograph, counted to ten in her head, and pushed the negative thoughts out of her mind.

She opened the door to the waiting area. Just as it had been earlier that morning, the lobby was packed with patients. All types of women sat waiting to be seen by the doctors. A woman of Asian decent sat with her hands folded staring out of the window towards the parking lot. Another woman who looked of African American decent read a novel while twirling one of her dreadlocks between her fingers. A Caucasian woman, who looked to be about 65-years-old, sat reading the Silvermont Times.

Shelby knew some of the women were there for obstetric appointments. Others for gynecological needs and still others were there for their infertility appointments. Except for the women with obviously swollen bellies, you really couldn't tell why each woman was there just by looking at their faces.

In the corner of the room she saw a young Caucasian girl with her head down. Shelby figured it was her patient from the height and weight recorded on the chart.

Shelby called the name, "Allison Smith."

When the girl stood, Shelby took a double take. Allison's face was caked with makeup, which made her look to be at least 25 years old. The face paint consisted of heavy eye shadow, burgundy rouge, matching eyeliner, thick mascara, and burgundy lipstick. Her nails looked like claws; at least an inch long in an array of neon colors. She wore navy overalls with a blue tank top. The top was too small and showed the sides of her engorged stomach.

The perfume the girl wore didn't mask the cigarette smoke, which reeked from her hair and clothing. The stench was so strong, it made Shelby want to sneeze. If she had driven by Allison on the street, she'd have thought the girl was a prostitute.

Shelby smiled as warmly as possible, hoping the smile made it to her eyes. As Allison followed her back to the exam area, she smacked on a piece of gum. Her eyes widened as she looked around the unfamiliar setting.

"Right this way," Shelby said as the teen trailed slowly behind her into the examination room. "Allison, Dr. Evans will exam you in here. You'll need to put on this smock and cover your legs with this sheet." Shelby pointed to the items already laid out on the exam table. "Do you have any questions before I leave?"

Allison continued to smack on the gum. "Yeah, can the doctor tell me when the baby is gonna come?" The voice was indeed that of a 15-year-old—hesitant, whiny, and insecure.

"Yes, Dr. Evans will be able to give you a due date based on your LMP and the ultrasound."

The girl stopped smacking, her face contorted into a frown. "LPM? Ultra what? What's that?"

Shelby had momentarily forgotten she was speaking with a 15-year-old. Allison's choice of words and facial expressions brought her back to reality.

Shelby spoke precisely, pacing each word. "The L-M-P is the first day of your last period. The ultrasound is going to take a picture of your uterus to see how big the fetus, your baby, is at this time. With these pieces of information the doctor will give you a due date; she'll tell you when the baby will be born."

The girl's face lit up. "You mean the doctor can take a picture of my baby right now, and I can see what it'll look like?"

Shelby had to bite the insides of her mouth to keep from looking amused. "No, it's not that kind of picture. It won't even look like a baby to you when the doctor shows you the ultrasound. Dr. Evans can explain more to you when she comes in."

The girl's frown turned to fear. "Will it hurt?"

"No, the ultrasound won't hurt. We will have to do some blood work before you leave, that will only hurt a little, for a few seconds."

The girl started rubbing her hands together nervously, her eyes darting around the room as if she wanted to escape. She shrank back from Shelby. "I don't wanna have that done. Y'all can do that ultra thing, but I don't want y'all putting any needles in me. My mama says I have a low tolerance for pain. Y'all ain't gonna put no needles in me."

"I understand your concerns. I assure you the doctor will only do what is necessary to make sure you and the baby are doing well. Dr. Evans will explain more to you when she comes in." Shelby walked towards the door. "I am going to step out so you can get undressed. Do you have anymore questions before I leave?"

The only reply Shelby got was the humming of the overhead florescent light. With reluctance, the girl started undressing. Shelby took this as her cue to leave and headed out the door.

Young girls like Allison gave Shelby so many mixed feelings. On one hand, she felt sorry for Allison being so young and about to undertake grown-up responsibilities of becoming a parent. On the other hand, she often felt angry. She couldn't understand why God allowed girls so young to become pregnant when they obviously didn't need to be. This particular girl burned her up because she was more concerned with the pain of a needle than the health of her baby.

Shelby sighed thinking how the girl would react when she found out how much pain she'd be in for labor. Shelby shook her head.

"Why are you shaking your head?" Rachel said startling her.

"Oh, nothing." Shelby said and shrugged it off.

A sheepish grin sprawled across Rachel's face. "I've got something for you. This will really make you shake your head."

With hesitance Shelby asked, "What?" and braced herself. She knew Rachel pretty well. After four years of working closely together, they didn't have much of a choice. Even though Rachel's Northern-Irish upbringing was totally different from Shelby's southern, African-American one, it had only taken them a couple of months to become friends.

"Your favorite patient is here." Rachel said.

"My favorite patient?" Shelby's eyebrows furrowed as she thought. "I have plenty of patients I like."

"Not that kind of favorite." Rachel's grin grew wider.

Shelby's thoughts shifted from positive to dread. If Rachel hadn't meant her favorite in a good way, then she was being sarcastic. There were a couple of patients who quickly came to mind, patients who had rubbed Shelby the wrong way more than once. Their number was minimal, especially since a couple of the patients had transferred to other doctor's offices. She'd known the women's reasons for leaving weren't totally her fault. They were just women who were not going to be satisfied even if Jesus himself had been the actual doctor.

Shelby glanced over Rachel's shoulder at the mountain of charts waiting in the basket. "Help me out here," she pleaded.

"I'll give you three guesses."

Shelby proceeded to guess in order to minimize the delay. With her own sarcasm she said, "One, it's a woman, two she is pregnant, and three she doesn't want me for her nurse."

"Two out of three ain't bad." Rachel walked away from Shelby towards her own office.

Shelby's mouth dropped open. "So you're just going to leave me hanging?"

"No, just check the 'In' basket. She's the next chart. And

knowing how much you care for all our patients, I told everyone else to leave her for you."

Proceeding to the basket she pulled out the worn thick chart. Her eyes widened, and her head immediately started to hurt. She rubbed her temples wondering if the day could get any worse.

She flipped the chart open hoping that it was a different Melva Lewis. But there was no such luck. Ms. Lewis was her most dreaded patient who only came in for two things: her yearly annual exam and whenever she was pregnant. Shelby knew she wasn't due for an annual exam because she had just had it a couple of months prior.

Maybe, just maybe, she was in for something else, Shelby hoped. With a deep breath she walked to the waiting area to call Melva back.

"Ms. Lewis," Shelby said with a forced smile. "You can come back now."

The woman's face lit up as soon as she saw Shelby. "Oh, Shelby. What's up girl? I was hoping I'd see you." She walked right past Shelby as she spoke. Melva had started calling Shelby "girl" during her third pregnancy. She acted as if she and Shelby were long time friends from then on.

"Well, you got lucky," Shelby said, thinking it was really she who had the luck; bad luck.

"Ms. Lewis, what can we do for you today?" Shelby asked.

"Shelby," she said, slowly looking down at her feet, "it's happened again. I'm late. I think I'm pregnant."

Shelby clearly recalled the last time Melva had been in the office for her postpartum appointment. Shelby had tried to stress the importance of birth control, especially so soon after having a baby. Melva told Shelby she didn't like taking "none of that stuff". Then Shelby mentioned abstinence, and Melva looked at Shelby as if she had lost her mind.

Melva's acting surprised about being pregnant wasn't any-

thing new either. In four years, Shelby had already seen
Melva for three pregnancies, although this would actually be
her sixth child.

"Shelby, I got a good man whose gonna stick by me. I already told him I might be pregnant, and he didn't even tell
me to get rid of it, like that last no good jerk!"

"So you have a new friend?" Shelby asked with slight curiosity. Melva's life was like an on-going soap opera when it
came to her baby's daddies.

"I sure do, and Freddy is the best man a woman could
have. He so kind to all my kids. He even buys them books
and toys. And you know he ain't all that bad looking either.
Looks real nice when he puts on a dress shirt," Melva rambled on. "Yeah, he a good man. I know he'll take care of his
baby. He says he takes care of all his other kids."

"Well, good for you," Shelby said, wondering what could
have happened in the woman's life to cause her to have such
low standards.

The woman was only two years older than Shelby. The
first time Shelby saw her she thought Melva was one of the
prettiest women she had ever seen. Today Melva's jet-black
hair was fixed in a bun with glossy finger waves. Except for
brown lip-gloss, she wore no other make up. She didn't need
any. Her skin was flawless. Melva always lost all of her pregnancy weight within a month after each delivery so nobody
would ever guess she already had five children.

"I just want to make sure before I tell Freddy, I don't want
to get his hopes up if I'm not," Melva continued to ramble
on.

Shelby didn't think this Freddy would be the "One,"
Melva's knight in shining armor, just as none of the others
had been. Shelby was sure Melva wouldn't realize this until
it was too late.

The pregnancy test came back positive. Shelby took her

vital signs and drew blood for further tests. Afterwards, she showed Melva to the exam room.

"Shelby you don't have to tell me what to do. I know what to do from here," Melva said, hopping up on the exam table. "Girl, when you gonna get started on having some children?"

It was the question Shelby was hoping Melva would skip this trip. Every time Melva came in, she asked the very same question and each time Shelby gave her the same answer.

"Oh, when the time is right, we'll add to our family. I'll be sure to let you know." Shelby looked at her watch. "Melva, I'd really love to talk to you a little longer, but you saw that waiting area. We're swamped."

Without waiting for the woman to come up with another question or comment, Shelby grabbed the doorknob and quickly left the exam room.

The rest of the afternoon was just as hectic as the morning. Patient after patient, Shelby became more depressed about all the prenatal women she was seeing.

God smiled on her at the very end of the day. Her last patient turned out to be a breath of fresh air. It was April Henderson, a member of Shelby's Secret Sisterhood.

She had known April for over a year and a half, ever since she had started coming to see Dr. Evans for infertility treatments. Shelby remembered April's first visit—she had been an excited newlywed. From day one, she and her husband had wanted a child badly, but after a year of trying on their own, they sought professional help. Dr. Evans started seeing April as an infertility patient at that time. Since then, both April and her husband had undergone a battery of tests to find out what the problem might be.

Dr. Evans had found the problem to be a simple one in terms of infertility and costs. April's monthly cycles lasted on the average of about thirty-eight days, which caused her

to ovulate on day nineteen of her cycle, instead of the normal twenty-eight day cycle in which most women ovulate on
day fourteen. During their year of trying, April and her husband had done some of their own research on getting pregnant and tried month after month to conceive on day
fourteen of her cycle only to find out that they had been focusing on the wrong day.

Shelby saw a dazed look on April's face as soon as she
saw her in the lobby. After calling her in from the waiting
area, Shelby said with concern, "Mrs. Henderson, I didn't
know you had an appointment today. What's going on?"

"Shelby," she said almost in a whisper, "I think I'm pregnant. I'm so nervous. I'm late, and I can't believe it might be
true." She quivered as she spoke.

Shelby began to smile, now understanding the look on
April's face. "April, sit down for a second. You're shaking
like a leaf."

"I really have to go to the bathroom. I didn't want to use it
until I got here for the test."

"Okay, what are we waiting for? Let's find out." Shelby led
her towards the bathroom, giving her a cup to collect a urine
sample. A few minutes later, Shelby saw the positive result
and could hardly contain her excitement. She gave April the
good news and a hug. She then happily set the date for
April's first prenatal appointment.

After April left, Shelby walked back to her office and
closed the door. She had renewed hope that there was still a
chance for her. She made up her mind. She would attempt to
bring up the subject of getting pregnant to her husband
again. It was eating her up inside, and she had to confront
him about it. Somehow she'd have to make him talk.

Shelby eased into her SUV. The leather seats were warm
so she turned on the air conditioner. North Carolina was ex-

periencing an Indian summer. Even though it was almost Labor Day, the temperatures were still reaching ninety and above. The heat and humidity were something she had been used to all her life, so they didn't really bother her.

As she headed out of the parking lot, Shelby thought more about how afraid she was to talk to her husband. She couldn't let the fear get the best of her. She knew if she didn't try to face the fear head on, it would continue to haunt her. It was time for her and Phillip to talk and as far as Shelby was concerned, this would be the night. This time she would stand her ground and not let his evasiveness deter her from talking about wanting to have a child. Thoughts of her past failed attempts to broach the subject, made her heart quicken. Her husband would often change the subject or make up lame stories about having to go somewhere or do something. But not tonight. She wouldn't allow it.

The forty-five minute commute home would give Shelby time to figure out exactly how and when the conversation would take place. She turned the radio to 1520 AM to listen to the traffic report for possible delays on the interstate. Traffic was already pretty heavy. Silvermont had its share of accidents during rush hour. And she didn't want to be hindered trying to get home.

After listening to the traffic report, she turned on the CD player. This evening she felt like listening to contemporary Gospel. The music would help her relax and think of a good way to broach the subject with Phillip.

While listening to the soothing melodies, Shelby devised a plan, which included having dinner ready when Phillip came home. With no time to cook, she stopped by Mama Lula's restaurant. Mama Lula's had the best southern cooking in Silvermont. Anything her appetite could desire could be found at Mama Lula's. From Chitterlings to fried catfish, Mama Lula had it. Both she and Phillip loved eating there.

Shelby's hope was that after some good food and TLC, they'd both be relaxed enough to talk.

With her plans made, Shelby's mind wondered again to the times she had tried to talk to Phillip. It baffled her. Why was he being so evasive? He had always been supportive when it came to everything else. Usually they could talk about anything.

Not wanting to relapse into another attack, she focused on positive memories instead of the negative. She reminisced about the days when they first met and dated in college.

Thoughts of their meeting and dating always brought a smile to her face. The first time she laid eyes on Phillip had been on the secluded third floor of the library, when she was studying for an anatomy exam. Shelby thought he was one of the most gorgeous guys she had ever seen, standing at least, six foot three inches. His hazel eyes were mesmerizing even from where she sat. Glancing at his jet-black curly hair, she wondered if it felt as soft as it looked. His skin was the color of chocolate mocha—a compliment to her tawny-colored skin.

She saw him on several occasions in the library, but never spoke to him. She just admired him from afar—until one evening when he surprised her by coming over to speak. After taking the seat next to her, he introduced himself. Nervously she introduced herself. As they made small talk, the nervousness soon passed. They talked until the library closed. Before parting, they exchanged phone numbers.

He called her a couple of days later and that same night they went on their first date. They had gone to Mama Lula's. For a month straight they talked every day on the phone and went on several more secluded dates. After a month and a half they became an official couple. These thoughts always brought a smile to Shelby's face.

It wasn't until after they were officially dating that she found out Phillip was very popular on campus. He had kept secrets about his being in a fraternity, his star status on the football team and his family's wealth. Phillip explained his reasoning for withholding the information. He was looking for a girl who wanted him for him and not for the popularity or money. He promised from then on he wouldn't hold anything back from her.

It was true. They had been able to discuss anything. Shelby had even confided to him about her problems with anxiety attacks. They had been open about everything the first couple of years of their marriage—that is until the subject of children came up. And for the life of her, Shelby couldn't understand why Phillip was acting the way he was. It baffled her, and she wanted to finally get to the bottom of it.

Shelby pushed the button on the garage door opener and waited for it to fully open before rolling into her parking space. She was careful to avoid hitting the boxes of automobile memorabilia her husband stacked there for their newly built, unattached garage. His hobby was restoring cars and the unattached garage was his on-going pet project.

His parking space was empty; she was glad to have beaten him home. After closing the garage behind her, she grabbed the containers of food and entered the house through the side door that led directly into their kitchen. She set the food down on the counter and quickly turned to disarm the security system. Hearing the pitter-patter of paws rounding the corner, she looked down to greet her dog. "Goldie." She bent over and stroked the cocker spaniel's head. "Have you been a good girl today?"

The dog panted rapidly, her tail wagging furiously. She licked Shelby's hand.

"Goldie, I'm going to have to put you in the backyard for a couple of hours. I've got some business to take care of."

Shelby led the dog to the back yard making sure she had fresh water in her bowl, then proceeded with the preparations for Phillip's arrival. She pulled a bottle of sparkling red grape juice from the wine rack and put it in the ice bucket. She opened the larger containers of food and placed hearty helpings on two lead crystal plates and then put them in the oven for warmth. Then she placed the smaller containers in the refrigerator.

Next, she moved into the dining room where she prepared two place settings and put two new candles in the crystal holders. Feeling everything downstairs had been taken care of, she ascended to the second floor, headed for their master bathroom where she started running bathwater. She poured in strawberry scented bubble bath, lit the candles that sat around the garden tub, and turned the lights off.

In the closet of her bedroom she pulled out a plastic container, which held artificial rose-petals she had been saving. She dropped the petals on the floor, making a trail from the master bath to the garage. She figured Phillip's curiosity would get the best of him, allowing the petals to lead him directly to her arms.

Again she ascended the stairs and entered the recreation room, selecting three of their favorite soft jazz CDs. After starting the first CD, she punched a button so that the music could be heard throughout the house. She did one last check of her mental list, making sure nothing was forgotten. Pleased with all she had done in such a short amount of time, she smiled.

She returned to their bedroom so she could look out of the window. She was in just enough time to see Phillip's SUV entering the security gate of their sub-division. Quickly she returned to the master bathroom, removed her clothing, and turned the water off in the tub, which was now full. She tested the water with her foot—it was hot and inviting. After immersing her body up to her neck, she allowed herself to enjoy the rhythmic sounds of the soft jazz. The smell of strawberries, from the strawberry bubble bath, permeated the room and made her stomach growl.

Shelby closed her eyes and said a quick prayer. She prayed that the night would go well without any anxiety attacks and that her husband would finally open up and talk. Then she waited patiently for him to appear in the bathroom.

After a few minutes, Phillip peeked his head around the corner then filled the bathroom doorway. "Shelby, you are something else. May I ask what is going on?" his smile was longing.

Answering him seductively, Shelby said, "Baby, do you really have to ask? You're a big boy, and I'm sure you can figure it out."

"Well, I bet if I don't figure it out, you'll help me," he said, removing his tie and shirt.

After getting completely undressed, Phillip stepped into the tub and sat down in front of her. Shelby massaged his neck and shoulders in hopes to relieve any tension from his day at work. He in turn massaged her feet. Then, they joined as one, relieving any mutual stress from their hard day at work.

An hour later, they were famished. Shelby held Phillip's hand as she led him into the dining room.

"Baby, can you light the candles for me please?" She handed him the lighter.

Phillip did as he was asked. "The candles are lit, the music set for romance and the sparkling juice is chilling," he said looking at the bottle of juice. "What do you have in mind *now*?" Phillip asked. "Hold on a second." He put his nose up in the air and sniffed. "I know that's not what I think it is. I'd know that smell from anywhere. You went to Mama Lula's, didn't you?"

"Phillip, just have a seat and pour the juice. I'll go get the food, since you think you know so much." She retrieved the plates and hummed along with the music as she sauntered back towards the dining room.

Phillip poured the sparkling juice in their crystal long-stem glasses. "Baby," Phillip said, "that bubble bath was right on time. We just closed a deal today, and my team is number one again this month. All those long hours I've been putting in are about to come to an end, for at least a week or two. I couldn't have asked for a better celebration than this."

Shelby returned, balancing a plate in each hand. "Here you are my dear; all of your favorites."

"Whew, baby, you really know how to take care of your man, don't you?"

Once her hands were empty, Phillip took them into his and pulled her down onto his lap. He then placed both of his hands on the small of her back to embrace her tenderly.

Shelby wrapped her arms around his neck, touching her forehead and nose on his so that they looked directly into each other's eyes. She kissed him for what seemed like forever.

When they stopped for a breather, Phillip said, "I am the luckiest man in the world. You are my angel. You are not only beautiful on the outside, but on the inside as well." His muscular hand stroked her hair gently as he spoke.

"I love you so much." She let her hands massage his broad muscular shoulders and arms. She kissed him again until his stomach growled loud enough for them both to hear. They busted out laughing simultaneously. "I guess we'd better eat," Shelby said and continued laughing as she took her seat.

Phillip gazed down at the collard greens with pieces of country ham, baked macaroni and cheese, stuffed pork chops, and candied yams heaped on his plate. Two big pieces of broccoli-cheese cornbread sat atop the collards.

"Umph, my mouth is watering." Phillip licked his lips. "Mama Lula's, I told you. You know these are all my favorite foods. The only thing missing is the banana pudding."

"It's in the refrigerator," Shelby smirked and gave him an air kiss.

"I should've known. What on earth are you trying to do to me? It's a good thing I don't have to work tomorrow. And even better, I'll have three days to rest from the work out you just put me through," he said, taking her hand into his again.

"It's still early. I might let you have a little rest later on tonight." Shelby winked.

They held hands while Shelby said grace. Then they dug into their food as if they had not eaten in days. Once finished, their stomachs were too full to eat their banana pudding. They made their own dessert after returning to their bedroom, before drifting off to sleep.

"Baby. Baby. Wake up," Shelby said in a whisper as she shook Phillip's exposed muscular shoulder. She could hear his soft snoring as he slept peacefully next to her in a semi-fetal position.

He stirred a little and returned to snoring. She then took her index finger and lightly traced his lips.

Finally he woke, twitching his mouth and nose, then smiled up at her. His voice was husky. "That tickles."

"Wake up. I've got a taste for some of that banana pudding."

"Yeah, what time is it?" he asked without looking at the clock.

"It's almost eleven o'clock."

"Is that all? It feels like I slept for more than a couple of hours. Ummm!" He uncurled his body, stretching the full length of the bed, and let out a deep breath. "Banana pudding, would hit the spot right now."

Shelby's face beamed. "Good! I'll go get it." She crawled out of bed and headed for the kitchen. Once she was downstairs, she leapt for joy. Her plan was working so far. Her heart beat was nervous anticipation. She hugged herself with glee and tried to calm her nerves. Regaining her composure, she pulled the containers of banana pudding out of the refrigerator and returned to their bedroom.

She could still feel the pounding of her heartbeat as she ascended the stairs. Once she was on the landing outside their bedroom door, she paused and said another quick prayer to God asking for His favor and for things to continue to go smoothly. Once finished, she took a deep breath and entered the room.

"Here you are," she swiftly closed the door, returning to their bed.

After handing Phillip his banana pudding, they both dug in, devouring their dessert.

"Umph, umph, umph, that was good," Phillip said, rubbing his washboard stomach after eating the last drop.

Nervousness began to set in again for Shelby. "Do you want something to drink?" She felt her mouth start to go dry, thinking about what she had to do next.

"No, I'm fine," he said, snuggling back under the down covers for warmth.

"Well, I'm going to get some water." She hopped back out of bed and headed for the kitchen again. She couldn't believe she was starting to lose her nerve. Her mouth was so dry. But she knew it was now or possibly never. Plus there was nowhere he could possibly say he had to go to at almost 11:30 at night, and he was full and rested. She took two huge gulps of the cold water.

With all the courage she could muster and remembering the prayer she had said just a few minutes before, she returned to bed to talk with her husband.

After fluffing her pillows and taking another two gulps of water, Shelby took a deep breath before speaking. "Guess who came into the office today?"

"I don't know, who?" Phillip snuggled up against her and caressed her neck as he spoke.

"Do you remember when I told you about the Hendersons, April and her husband? We saw them at Ginny's the night we were celebrating your promotion."

He was silent for a moment, pausing to think. "Oh, yeah. What about them?"

"She came in to have a pregnancy test, and she's finally pregnant!" Shelby said excitedly.

"Oh. That's good," Phillip said, his voice flat—almost inaudible.

Shelby immediately noticed the change in Phillip's tone as well as the stiffening of his body. He pulled away from her slightly. She was at a loss for words. Then Phillip started wiping his forehead and she could have sworn she saw little beads of sweat forming there.

After a minute or so of silence, he finally spoke. "Yeah, that's real good for them. I know they must be happy." He threw the covers off and jumped out of bed. "You know what? I think I do need some water." Without waiting for a response, he left the room.

Shelby's jaw dropped open. She couldn't believe it was happening again. He had found a way to finagle his way out of the conversation again. She had no idea what to do.

Her eyes began to water just before she felt stinging tears stream down her cheeks.

Looking up to Heaven, Shelby spoke to God.

"God, I don't understand what is going on. Lord, I just can't take this anymore. I need your help. I need You to give me some kind of answer. Lord, I need some release from all of my pain. What am I supposed to do?"

She sat in the silence of the room. The other parts of the house were silent. Minutes passed as she waited on an answer from God. Then she thought, how silly it was to think God was going to answer in some kind of loud booming voice.

She was tired, and even though she didn't want to, she was ready to give up the fight. She made up her mind, she wasn't going to push her husband into something he didn't want to do. She cried harder as she felt all of her hope was slipping away.

* * *

Phillip realized that the twelfth hour had come, and he couldn't avoid discussing the subject he most dreaded. He headed for the downstairs' bathroom and splashed cold water on his face. He looked in the mirror and hated the reflection of the man staring back at him.

As soon as Phillip realized Shelby wanted to talk about having children, their normally large and roomy king-size bed seemed to shrink into a twin-size. And the walls felt like they were closing in on him too. He started to get hot and felt beads of sweat forming on his forehead. He was burning up and his mouth had become dry. He'd had to get out of the bedroom and get some air.

Each time Shelby brought up the subject of children, Phillip couldn't talk about it. He wanted children with his wife just as much as she did, but knew his past wouldn't allow that to happen. Phillip had skeletons in his closet that were trying to break free. He wanted to confide in Shelby, but he couldn't. It was the one subject he just couldn't bring up. Phillip knew he might lose his wife because of his deception, but he was tired of running, tired of hiding the truth.

He no longer wanted to hurt Shelby by his elusiveness and dishonesty. He wiped his face. He had to talk to Shelby, had to tell her the truth. He hoped she would understand

and forgive him. He prayed God would give him the strength he needed to come clean. Even though he had asked God for forgiveness years earlier, the past still ate away at him. Phillip turned to go back upstairs.

He would finally tell her the truth.

Chapter 2

Crystal Shaw

BEEP! BEEP! BEEP! . . .

Crystal heard the alarm clock but wasn't ready to get up. She pulled the pillow over her head. "Ugh!"

She felt her husband moving to turn the alarm off.

Good, she thought, *a few more minutes to snooze.*

"Crystal, honey, it's time to get up," her husband, Warren, said.

She was so tired. Her eyes were heavy and her body ached. It was Saturday morning, the only day of the week in which she could actually sleep in late. "What time is it?" she asked groggily through the pillow.

"Six o'clock."

"Why on earth did you set the alarm for six?"

"I've got to set the items up for the youth church. The kids are leaving at eight for their trip."

Crystal slid the pillow slightly off her head exposing one eye. She watched her husband as he searched for a shirt. "So, why must I get up now?"

"You said you wanted me to wake you up when I got up.

Don't you still need to prepare the potato salad for the cookout today?" he said.

Flatly Crystal said, "Oh yeah, the cookout."

"I'm going to set up the items for the trip and I should be back here by eight-thirty."

"Okay, I'll get up. I just want to snooze for a few more minutes. Can you set the clock for six-thirty?" she asked.

"Sure, honey, but don't over sleep. You know how your mother can get sometimes. We don't want to be late for the cookout."

"I know, I know. I'm just so tired. Six-thirty, I promise."

Just as Crystal was about to dose back off to sleep, she felt Warren pull the pillow back and kiss her on the forehead. "I love you sweetheart."

"I love you too," Crystal mumbled back.

When the alarm sounded again at six-thirty, Crystal slid the pillow away and turned it off. Then she counted to one-hundred in her head, and eased out of bed. She walked haphazardly into the bathroom trying to get her bearings. Upon looking in the mirror she wasn't surprised to see that her eyes were puffy from crying the night before. There were dark circles under her eyes. She had awakened around 2:30 a.m. from the recurrent nightmare she'd been having for weeks.

In the dream, she was at the hospital holding a baby in her hands—her baby. It was a beautiful baby boy. He looked just like her husband Warren; baldheaded with thick, bushy eyebrows and full lips. The baby's complexion was a mixture of her mocha complexion and his medium brown complexion.

The first part of the dream was always the same. A nurse would come into the room telling her the baby needed to be fed, then Crystal would go down to the nursery and look through the window, at a room full of newborns. Crystal was always on the outside looking in. The babies' faces and names changed with each dream, but one thing that remained constant was her insistent tapping on the glass to ask the nurse which baby was hers. The nurse would check all the names and then shake her head indicating to Crystal that she didn't have a baby.

Crystal's hospital gown would then disappear and was instantly replaced by street clothes. At this point in the dream, Crystal would start screaming and wake up. Each time she woke from the dreams, her heartbeat was rapid and she always had an uncontrollable need to cry. Even now, just thinking about the nurse shaking her head, negatively, made Crystal want to cry.

Each day as she worked with the children at her daycare center, Crystal's longing for her own child grew stronger. Sometimes she wished she could find a desk job in a corporate setting so she wouldn't have to see children every day.

Crystal turned on the cold-water facet and splashed cool water on her face. After a few moments when she felt calm enough, she brushed her teeth and took a lukewarm shower.

Once she was out of the shower, she looked in her closet for something to wear. The weather forecast had called for the temperature in her hometown to be sunny and breezy. It was late summer and still pretty hot on most days. The temperature the day before had climbed to over ninety degrees.

She pulled out a couple of outfits, trying them on. Many of them didn't fit as comfortably as they used to. *Had they shrunk*, she wondered; but knew they hadn't. The additional weight she had put on over the past year was showing in her face, arms and thighs.

Crystal had never been what most consider small. Her mother had to shop for her in the hefty section when she was a little girl. Crystal hated it. Back then they didn't have Lane Bryant or other stores close by that catered to larger size girls and women. Her clothing never quite matched the stylish clothing of the popular girls. So Crystal never made it to the *in* crowd. She'd worked hard over the years trying to lose weight but never seemed to make it down to the model size most commercials portrayed.

Crystal wanted to look nice but also wanted to wear something comfortable for the two and a half hour ride to her hometown. The annual neighborhood cookout was always held the Saturday before Labor Day. Each year the cookout got bigger and better with more people and more activities. Since leaving home Crystal had trekked back annually for the event. And each year it seemed as if more people would ask her the same old questions and make the same old comments. Comments like, "Little Crystal, girl you ain't so little any more. You gaining some weight? Are you pregnant?" It would always make her cringe inside.

It was just like some people to be so bold. Just because she had put on a few extra pounds, they assumed she was pregnant. *Everyone gained weight as they got older*, she thought, but she didn't hear them asking everyone else if they were pregnant. She hated the questions and snide comments. She always did her best to ignore the comments and held her head up. Even though she dreaded going each year she continued, not wanting to let her mother down by not showing up.

She ended up choosing a sundress with vertical lines. She was pleased with the choice. The dress with its matching jacket would help conceal her pooch of a stomach. After laying the outfit on the bed, she slipped on a housecoat to wear, until she finished making the potato salad. She walked to the kitchen at the opposite end of the house and pulled the potatoes and eggs out of their respective bins in the refrigerator.

Over the years she had put on weight. Starting with college then leading to the comforts of being married and settled. She didn't have any time to exercise with her full schedule.

The daycare she worked for, took up most of her time and energy. She usually worked twelve hours a day. Most days she arrived as early as six in the morning to let the cooks in and often stayed late until the last child and employee left in order to lock up.

Crystal had been acting as the interim director of Little Angels Daycare Center, as well as the teacher for the 2 and 3-year-olds. She was certified in "birth to kindergarten," so she was qualified to run the center and teach.

She had been tired enough before taking on the dual positions, but now she was truly exhausted at the end of each work day. It took every ounce of her strength to get up each morning. As a result, exercising wasn't a current part of her daily routine.

When she was offered the director's position, Crystal declined, telling the board of directors she had too much on her plate. She told them she would help in any way possible until someone could be hired. It was now six months later and the position still wasn't filled.

She couldn't complain so much about the positions and hours, since her paycheck showed an ample increase. The difference in pay was enabling her to speed up the process of opening her own day learning center. She'd dreamed of opening her own center every since she graduated from college. But with the costs and intricate details of starting one, she had been unable to. The dream had to be deferred.

Now twelve years later, she was finally going to be able to open her own center. The extra money helped so that she and her husband would not to have to scrape by in order to make ends meet. The cost of renovating the older building they had come across, had virtually depleted their savings and checking accounts. They also had to take out loans to meet unexpected building requirements. The Grace of God and the extra money in her check sustained them. So even though Crystal was often exhausted, it was still a good feeling because after twelve years her dream of having her own center would be realized. In a little over five months, her day care would be renovated. She couldn't think of a better Valentine's gift.

Crystal thought about another dream she'd had since childhood, the dream of being a mother. She had often envisioned getting married and becoming pregnant when the time was right. She pictured herself with at least three children—just like her parents. So far she had no idea when or if that would happen. Crystal and Warren had been actively trying for over five years to get pregnant. They had put off trying to have children in their first six years of marriage feeling they needed to enjoy time alone with each other.

Crystal met Warren in the fourth grade after her parents moved back to their hometown of Warsaw. Being the new girl in school, Warren took the opportunity to pick on her by calling her names like "Short Girl" and "Brownie".

When he sat behind her in class, he would poke her with his pencil when the teacher wasn't looking. Crystal was too scared to say a word to him or the teacher to complain.

There were many school days when she'd run home to tell her parents but they only laughed saying that he probably liked her. She couldn't understand how name-calling and poking could mean that a boy liked her.

One day later on in that year, while on the playground, some of the fifth-grade boys started picking on her. They called her chubby and fat. Warren saw what was happening and even though he had been smaller than them, he took up for her, telling them to leave her alone. The boys actually backed off and did as Warren told them. This display of kindness on Warren's part bewildered her.

From then on he stopped calling her names. But then he went to the other extreme and wouldn't talk to her at all.

That had confused her even more. She concluded that she would never understand the strange actions of boys.

When they got to middle school she often noticed him staring at her, even though he still wouldn't talk to her. Whenever she caught him looking he would try to turn his head quickly as if he hadn't been looking her way. She remembered what her parents said; *maybe he did like her*.

By the time they were in high school, Crystal was tired of wondering about his strange behavior. One afternoon while she was talking to her friends, she saw him staring at her out of the corner of her eye. When she turned her head quickly in order to catch him, surprisingly he hadn't averted his eyes.

After her friends left, she walked over to him and asked him why he always stared at her but never spoke. He told her because he thought she was pretty. She felt her cheeks getting hot and knew she had to be blushing. Warren confirmed the fact when he asked why her cheeks were turning red. Crystal was so embarrassed, she ran from the building and didn't stop until she got to her bus.

At the end of their ninth grade year, Warren asked her if she was going to the end-of-year dance. She said yes and he told her that he looked forward to seeing her there. For a reason she couldn't explain, Crystal was ecstatic.

During the school dance, he was the perfect gentleman when he asked her out onto the dance floor. Later he offered to get her a soda and saved her seat when she went to the bathroom. He had even stood with her by the door while she waited to be picked up by her parents. Their being together at the dance had made Crystal feel like she was on a real date, and every time she thought about being with him, she got a warm tingling feeling in her heart.

They dated throughout the rest of high school and even through college. They married the year after graduating from college. And now eleven wonderful years of marriage had passed.

Crystal sighed with dread. She wasn't looking forward to the cookout. And definitely wasn't looking forward to the insensitive comments and questions from her family and friends alike. She wanted to stay home and take a mental and physical break from the world, spending Saturday doing absolutely nothing.

The phone rang, jarring Crystal out of her thoughts. She picked the cordless up off the kitchen counter, "Hello, Shaw residence."

"Crystal, baby, that you?" the voice on the other line asked.

"Yes, Mama. Good morning."

"Crystal, you know what time you need to be here, don't you?" Crystal's mother, Willie Mae's voice, was rushed.

"Yes, we'll be there at noon. It doesn't start until three, right? We'll be there in plenty of time to set up."

"Can't you get here any earlier, Crystal?" her mother's voice rose in disappointment.

"No, I'm just finishing up the potato salad. But I promise you, we'll be there in enough time."

"Is Warren going to be able to come? Doesn't he have to go on some church trip with the youth?"

"No, he will be coming. One of the youth ministers is going to take his place."

"Well, hurry up and finish so you can get here. I always end up preparing everything by myself and I need some other hands. You know your sisters got to get them kids ready. You only have to get yourself ready, so I need you here, Crystal."

"Okay, Mama, okay. I know. We'll see you in a few hours," Crystal said, ready to end the call with her mother.

"Oh Lord my pot of greens is boiling over. I need to tend to it. Love you, Crystal."

"Love you too, Mama." Crystal hung up the phone. Her mother was really working her nerves. She always knew just the right things to say to push Crystal's buttons.

The phone rang again.

"Hello, Shaw residence," Crystal said.

"Hey, Crystal," the caller said.

"Hey, Marcy. What's up, sis?" Crystal asked. She was relieved to hear her sister's voice. Her sister understood how nerve racking their mother could be.

"Have you talked to Mama this morning?"

"Yes. I was just talking to her. She was pressuring me about what time I could make it down there. She seems so worried about how things are going to turn out."

"You know how Mama can be. I don't know why she acts the way she does sometimes. We've had this neighborhood cookout for years and its always turned out fine," Marcy said.

"All I know is that she is already starting to work my nerves." Crystal replied.

"What do you mean?" Marcy asked.

Crystal thought about the comment her mother had made about her sisters having to get their children ready. She knew that was just another way for her mother to remind her she was childless. She often confided things to her sister, but her concerns about having children were not one of the things she had fully confided to Marcy.

"Oh, nothing. Forget about it. Did you finish the baked beans yet?"

"Yeah, they're done. And don't worry, I already took some out for you and Warren. What about you? Did you put some potato salad aside for us?" Marcy asked.

"Not yet, I'm waiting for the eggs to cool down now. I just need to mix them in and it will be done. I won't forget to set aside some for you, Mama and Shanice."

"I thought you were going to make it last night?" Marcy asked.

"No, I was too tired. These long hours are really getting to me. To tell you the truth I wish I could just skip the party, stay home and rest."

"Well, I hope it tastes good," Marcy said, not hiding her disappointment. "You know it needed to have chilled overnight for it to taste right. Man, it won't taste right."

"It'll be just fine. And if its not, then oh well. Nobody will die. They probably won't even notice," Crystal said in a snippy tone.

Ignoring her sister's snippiness, Marcy continued. "That's what you think. I'll notice. That's great-grandma's recipe. Mama and Shanice will know too."

Getting slightly frustrated Crystal said, "Like I said, you won't die. Besides, you don't have to eat any. You can wait until tomorrow and let yours chill overnight that way you won't have to taste today's monstrosity if it is so important to you," Crystal said. "I don't mean to cut this short, but let me go so I can finish getting ready. Mama already thinks that we won't be there in enough time."

"Okay, I'll see you soon. I hope you're feeling better by then." Marcy said.

"I'll be fine. Sorry for being so curt. Give my niece and nephew hugs for me."

"I will. And I love you anyway," Marcy added quickly.

"I know, I love you too," Crystal replied before hanging up the phone.

Crystal checked the eggs again. They were cool enough to chop and mix in. She took out four plastic containers in order to put potato salad aside for her mom, sisters and herself. That way she wouldn't have to cook more after church the next day. She knew whether they liked it or not, the potato salad would all be eaten up. She placed the larger bowl and the smaller containers in the refrigerator. She found a cooler and put ice packs in it for the transport to her mother's house. Then she went to prepare for what she hoped would be a pleasant reunion.

About twenty minutes into their trip, Crystal remembered she'd forgotten something. "Oh, no. I forgot the cookbook I was supposed to return to Mama."

"Do you want me to turn around and get it?" Warren asked.

"She looked at her watch. "No. I guess it's okay. If we turn around now it will put us forty minutes behind. I think it will be more important to her that we arrive on time without the book as opposed to being late, with the book. I promised her we would be on time."

"We can just take it the next time. I am sure she'll understand. It's not like she really needs it, you know," Warren said. "Your mother is one of the best cooks I know. She can cook anything she wants."

"It is still amazing to me how my mom can cook something with the recipe once and then never need to read it again. It's like she has selective photographic memory. So unless she wanted to cook something new, it shouldn't be a real big problem.

"You know, she probably has the whole book memorized by now."

"Probably," Crystal said. "Yeah let's just keep going. If we turn around, I just might be tempted to stay home."

"Stay home? Why, Crys? What's wrong?" her husband asked with concern.

"You know how much I dread this thing. All those people coming up to me asking why we haven't started having children yet. People are always comparing me to my sisters, reminding me that I am the oldest. I know Shanice is one up on me and Marcy two."

"I know how it is. People also ask me when we are going

to start our family. First, I remind them that you and I are a family. Then I tell them when the time is right God will add to our family as many children as *He* wants. God *will* bless us with children, Crystal, but we have to be patient. We just have to ask God for the strength and guidance to get us through this day and the days to come. In the meantime, we can't hide from people."

"Warren, I know what you're saying is true, but it just doesn't make it any easier." Crystal started admitting feelings she had been holding in for a while. "I feel like I'm on an emotional roller coaster when it comes to my feelings about us having children. Most of the time I am up, I don't let the things in life get me down. But other times I get to this peak and something will make me plummet down hill physically and emotionally. It's just so hard, Warren. I can't really explain it with words. It's so very hard."

Warren looked as if he didn't know what to say. Crystal had gotten quiet; she needed time to herself. He didn't say anything else and Crystal was glad, it would give her some time to think.

Crystal sat quietly wondering why they had not yet been successful in getting pregnant. She knew there might be something wrong, but couldn't think of what it might be. She had thought about asking her doctor to check her out ever since she had seen a documentary about the biological clock as it relates to women over thirty. But for some reason she was just too embarrassed to bring it up.

She had seen couples on television and in the movies that had problems conceiving. Many of those couples were able to get pregnant with the assistance of fertility medicine. A few people she had seen even had multiple babies after the fertility treatments. But Crystal didn't know anyone personally who was having the same problem. It seemed as though most of the people she knew were getting pregnant left and right. Even if she did know someone with the same problems, she couldn't imagine talking to anyone about it. She wasn't even comfortable talking to her husband about what was really going on in her head.

She wanted to ask him how he would feel about seeking professional advice. She didn't know how he might respond. Her husband had always been very strong in his spiritual walk. Her faith, when it came to having a child, was not as strong. Warren believed that for everything there was a season, and for everything there was a reason.

She continued to think as they drove, focusing on getting through the day ahead. She'd be glad when the day came to an end, so that they could return to the warmth and comfort of their home. It was her place of solace.

"Crystal, wake up. We're here." Warren pulled into Crystal's mother's driveway.

"Ummm, that was a good nap." Crystal stretched. "I actually had a good dream."

"What was the dream about?"

"I dreamed we were home relaxing instead of going to this cookout."

"Do you want me to pull back out and head home?"

She smiled at her husband. "Don't be silly. We're here now."

"I will honey, if that's what you want. I'll pull right back out of this drive way." He shifted the car into reverse. "We could stop at Hardees and get a sandwich. We can eat it along with all those pounds of potato salad we have in the cooler," Warren joked.

"You are so cute when you are trying to be funny. Park this car." She pinched his cheek. "What time is it?"

Warren looked at his Timex and answered, "Eleven fifty-five."

"Good, we are a whole five minutes early. That'll make Mama happy. Can you get the cooler please?"

Crystal got out of the car and walked to the screen front door and knocked. "Knock, knock is anybody home?" She let herself in before her mother had a chance to respond.

"I'm in the kitchen," her mother called. Crystal walked to the back of the house and into the kitchen. "Crystal baby, come give me a hug."

She hugged her mother tightly. Even though her mother had a knack for often getting on her nerves, Crystal still missed her very much.

Her mother pulled away. "Let me look at you. It's been two months since I last seen you. You shouldn't stay away so long. Looks like you put on a few pounds. Is there anything you want to tell me?" her mother asked, finally stopping to take a breath from the barrage of questions.

Crystal realized it was already beginning, "No, Mama, there is nothing that I have to tell you."

Warren stepped into the kitchen with the cooler of food. "Hey, Ms. Willie Mae." He sat the cooler down and gave his mother-in-law a hug.

"Hey Warren baby. How you doing today?"

"Fine. And I can see you are doing fine also. Looking just as young as you did when I first met you years ago."

Crystal watched as her mother smiled and blushed.

"Oh stop now Warren. You know I don't look that young anymore."

"Ms. Willie Mae, you might want to go visit your eye doctor and get some new glasses because obviously you don't see what I can see."

Willie Mae playfully hit Warren's shoulder. "I know you Warren. You are just trying to make sure you get an extra piece of my pineapple cake."

Warren smiled and nodded his head in agreement.

"I've got your back son. Don't worry about it." She looked out of her kitchen window towards the backyard. "Warren can you tell Joe to move that grill away from the tree before he burns down the neighborhood?"

"Yes, ma' am." Warren pecked Crystal on the cheek before heading for the back yard.

Without missing a beat, Crystal's mother returned to the subject they had been talking about. "I had a dream about fish last night. And I ain't talking about no fried fish either. I'm talking about fish swimming in a flowing brook of water. You know what that means don't you?" Her mother asked. "It means somebody's pregnant."

"Mama, that's nothing but an old wives' tale and there's nothing to it. And don't worry, when we do have some news, we will make sure you are one of the first to know." Crystal said, not knowing how she was going to get through the next five minutes—let alone the next few hours. She had only been there two minutes and her mother was already asking the questions that always ate away at her. She wanted to jump back in the car and leave. Now she wished more than ever they hadn't come.

"Whew, it's almost three o'clock, and they still haven't gotten here with those extra chairs. Marcy can you call and find out where they are?" Crystal's mother asked.

"Yes, Mama," Marcy replied.

They stood in the back yard finishing up the preparations. Families had already started congregating in various spots in the adjoining backyards. Crystal's mother's home bordered the homes of five other families. All six backyards were used for the neighborhood to congregate. Each had tables with food for everyone.

"Shanice, wipe off those tables and put the tablecloths on them. The staple gun is in the shed if you need to tack them down. It's a little windy out here," Willie Mae said.

"Sure, Mama," Crystal's youngest sister, Shanice, replied.

"Crystal, do we have spoons for all the food? I asked everyone bringing something to label their containers and bring a serving utensil. But you know how these folks are sometimes. They do what they wanna do."

Crystal did a once over of everything around her. "Yes, Mama. I put names on each dish as they came in. So don't worry about that. We'll know who everything belongs to at the end of the night. And each dish has a serving utensil. Some people didn't bring their own, so I used some of yours. But don't worry, I put green tape on them so none of them will walk away," Crystal reassured her mother.

"Good, Crystal. We need to make sure we give the right bowl and pans back to their rightful owners," her mother said loudly so anyone listening could hear her. Then she dropped her voice to a whisper so only Crystal could hear. "You know I need to know who cooked what, cause I ain't even eating everybody's cooking, especially Martha Davis'. That woman's got the filthiest house I have ever seen!" Willie Mae made a face, which looked like she just bit into a lemon. "Ain't no telling what might be crawling in them greens she makes every year. And don't eat none of Sadie's cooking either. She got all them cats around her house. I'll just bet those cats jump up and eat out of the pots when she ain't looking. Can't trust no cat Crystal. Cats are just as sneaky as they come."

"I know, Mama," Crystal chuckled. "You know I only eat the family's cooking. The labels are right on the front so we'll know what to and what not to eat." Knowing how her mother could be at times, Crystal had brought her label maker and placed labels on each dish of what the food was and who prepared it. Everyone loved her mother's turnip greens and she knew that dish, as well as a few others, would go quickly. Sadly, others would end up sitting untouched.

"I taught all you girls so well," her mother said with satisfaction. "Now if they would just get here with the rest of those chairs everything will be ready."

"Don't worry, Mama. You know most of the people will be late getting here anyway. That's why I left the potato salad, coleslaw, deviled eggs, and crab salad in the refrigerator. It's not too hot out so everything else should be fine."

"Thank you, Crystal. What would I do with out you? You always think of everything. You'd think that after fifteen years of having this thing I'd remember how late these people can be." Her mother frowned, looking at the unsecured tablecloths blowing in the wind, "Shanice, girl, what is taking you so long?" she yelled across the yard. "That girl is slow as molasses. I don't understand why she don't have no common sense like you and Marcy. I raised you all the same way. Can one of you please go help her with those tables?"

"Yes Mama," Crystal said. "Why don't you sit down and rest for a few minutes? We'll take care of the rest of things. Get a glass of iced tea or something."

Crystal didn't know how her mother did it. She could cut a person down in one sentence and in the next she would build an altar underneath them. Crystal did as she was asked and helped her sister wipe the tables and secure the tablecloths. Then she put mini fish bowls filled with water in the center of each table. She placed three floating candles in each bowl so that they could be lit once it got dark out. She hoped the wind would die down by then.

As they finished the tables, Warren and Marcy's husband drove up with the extra chairs. They placed them throughout the yard and were ready for the party to begin. There was nothing left to do but wait for the people to arrive.

At around four o'clock, the D.J. finished setting up his equipment. Since it was a multi-cultural neighborhood, they requested he have a variety of music. The D.J. had most of what the people wanted—R&B, Jazz, Rap, Latin Rhythms, Pop, Reggae, slow jams, and oldies from the 60's, 70's, 80's, and 90's. The D.J. had been highly recommended, and said he could make it blend.

The music started around 4:15, and by 4:30 more people started to migrate to the center of the neighborhood for the party. By five o'clock the front and backyards were packed with people. It was like a family reunion. Children who had grown up and left the neighborhood came back yearly for the gathering. Even many of the families that had moved out of the neighborhood often returned.

The D.J. rotated different kinds of music, a little something for everyone. Except for when the gospel music was playing, the dance area was always full. Most of the people used the gospel songs to eat and catch up with people they hadn't seen in a while. Others used the time to simply take a rest from their non-stop dancing.

After two rotations, the D.J. handed Crystal's mother the microphone.

"Everyone can I have your attention?" She had to repeat herself three times before she got their attention. "As everyone is aware, we always celebrate Ms. Janie's birthday at the annual cookout. Ms. Janie turned 90 yesterday." Everyone clapped. "Ms. Janie, stand up so everybody can see that pretty dress and hat you have on."

The elderly woman slowly stood up, leaning on her walker. Everyone sang "Happy Birthday" to her. She stood there shaking nervously and smiling, showing all of her false teeth. Crystal sat motionless, almost holding her breath, thinking the feeble woman might fall at any moment. Once they finished singing, the old woman thankfully took her seat again.

The neighborhood adopted Ms. Janie after her husband, Mr. Otis, died twenty years earlier. The couple never had any children, so the neighbors decided they would help her in any way possible. So far, she had been well taken care of, and with the neighborhood support, Ms. Janie didn't have to go into a nursing home.

As the music resumed, Crystal looked at the people all around her. Deep down she loved coming home for the get together. She liked the food, folks and usual fun. She also looked forward to seeing people she hadn't seen since the previous year. So far the evening had not been as bad as she feared. No one had approached her or Warren asking any of the dreaded questions. Finally, she allowed herself to relax.

Crystal sat and talked with her husband and sisters. They tried to catch up on all the time they missed since they'd last seen each other. Marcy told them that her son was starting to take karate and her daughter started peewee gymnastics. Crystal had not seen her niece and nephew in over six months, and they seemed to be growing quickly. She admired her sister for being a stay-at-home mom. Marcy sometimes told her how tight money got for them. She was frugal and looked for bargains all the time. Crystal knew her sister wouldn't trade the experience for anything in the world.

Crystal's other sister, Shanice, was a totally different story. Sometimes Crystal wondered where she truly came from. Shanice didn't work and wasn't planning on working any time soon. She depended on all the public assistance she could get and her "Man of the Quarter." She always said she wasn't going to work as long as she could help it. Crystal noticed Shanice didn't care about the fact that she was living in a one-bedroom low-income apartment with her two-year-old daughter, Malika.

Shanice swore all out that the baby belonged to her ex-boyfriend, Malik. She said the baby looked just like him and that she knew he was the father because she counted the days from the last time they had been together. When she tried to get child support and took him to court the blood test showed that by a 99.9% chance, Malik was not the father. She never said after that who the father might be and never sought anyone else for paternity.

Shanice was smart when it came to the books, she was valedictorian of her high school class. But when it came to common sense, she must have been too slow getting in line because she had completely missed out.

Crystal's sisters were as different as night and day. Marcy seemed happy with her American dream but Shanice, on the other hand, was just living in a dream. Crystal wondered how Shanice with all of her issues was the mother of a beautiful little girl, while she was childless.

"So, Crystal, do you get any donations from those diaper companies?" Shanice asked. "Malika is going through training pants like they are going out of style. They are expensive."

"No, Shanice. We don't get any donations from any companies for anything. The parents have to provide their children with diapers, clothes, formula, shoes, socks, pacifiers, bibs, wipes, grooming supplies, baby food, and especially their own breast milk. The parents have to provide all those items and more.

Crystal made sure she listed all the other things so Shanice wouldn't start asking further. She hoped Shanice would get the point that it was her responsibility to provide for her daughter, not everyone else's.

"Well, they sure are getting tight these days. They should give a single mom a break and not be so stingy," Shanice said with disgust.

Crystal could clearly see that her sister had not gotten the point at all. She looked at Marcy for help. Marcy just rolled her eyes.

As the party progressed, Crystal felt more and more relaxed. She and Warren were actually having a good time. They enjoyed listening to the contemporary gospel music. They also talked about past cookouts. They reminisced when they heard the first song they had danced to at their ninth grade dance. The D.J. played many of the songs that were popular when they were in college. Memories of their wedding surfaced when they heard a couple of songs that had played at their wedding reception.

Crystal had almost forgotten her apprehension about coming to the party when someone tapped her on the shoulder. She turned around and saw Annette, one of her good friends from high school. Crystal was surprised to see her.

She quickly stood up and gave Annette a hug. They had not seen each other since right after graduation. Annette had gotten married and moved to Germany with her husband when he joined the Army. Crystal had gone on to college. They called each other a couple of times and wrote each other once or twice, but it had been over thirteen years since their last correspondence.

"Annette! Oh my goodness. I can't believe it's you. It's so good to see you!" Crystal hugged her again. "Warren, look, it's Annette."

Warren stood up from the picnic table and gave Annette a light hug. "Wow it's been a long time. How's your husband?"

"He's fine. He's at his parents' house taking a nap. He drove through the night, so we could get here. Fourteen hours of driving really took a toll on him."

"Tell him I said hello," Warren said as he sat back down.

"I'll be sure to tell him," Annette told him before turning back towards Crystal. "Crystal, it is so good to see you too! How have you been? Where have you been? What have you been doing? We really have to catch up." Annette smiled warmly.

"I'm fine. Warren and I got married. We decided to stay in Silvermont when we graduated from Carson State. It's a really a nice city. I've been working as a pre-school teacher since I graduated. We are in the process of having a building renovated, so I can open my own day-learning center. In a nutshell, that's about it," Crystal said excitedly. "What about you?"

"I am doing just fine. As you can see, it seems like we have just been in the business of making babies over the years," Annette said rubbing her stomach.

Crystal hadn't noticed Annette's slightly protruding stomach. With all the excitement she hadn't fully looked at her. She looked down and could tell she was indeed pregnant.

"I . . . see," Crystal said very slowly, almost stuttering. She stared at what Crystal thought was one of those perfect-pregnancy stomachs—round like a basketball, only smaller.

"Yeah we're in the baby making business. I thought I was finished, but then here pops this one. I told my husband no more. I am getting my tubes tied after this."

Crystal returned her gaze back to her friend's face. "So how many children do you have?" Crystal asked, not sure if she really wanted to know.

"We have a 12-year-old daughter and an 8-year-old son. That daughter of mine is about to drive me crazy. I don't know whose hormones are worse, my pregnant ones or her pre-teen ones. And my son is hyperactive. I don't want him on any medication, so I have to watch certain foods he eats so he won't drive me crazy. I am ready for this baby to come on out already.

"What about you?" Annette asked.

"Me, well, Warren and I are, well, we haven't had any children yet. We're waiting for the right time. You know we want to spend as much quality time together as we possibly can. We will probably start soon though. You know I am not getting any younger," Crystal said, trying to convince herself the more she spoke.

"I don't blame you, Crystal. I wish we had waited until now. My husband and I really didn't have much one-on-one time before our daughter was born. I love my kids, don't get me wrong, but believe me, I wish I had waited a little longer. You just take your time. But like you said, don't take too much time. I heard somewhere that as you get older the chances of conceiving decrease. I guess that didn't work for me though." Annette patted her swollen stomach.

"Yeah, we have been talking about having children lately," Crystal said, trying to convince Annette their waiting was by choice.

"Well, let me know, cause I can save as much of these baby things as possible. That way you wouldn't have to buy as much."

"Okay, I'll do that," Crystal said.

Annette continued. "Girl, I thought I was finished changing diapers, cleaning spit-up, and breastfeeding every one and a half to three hours. My kids are old enough to dress themselves and fix something to eat. Now I have to start all over again. This just isn't a good time for me."

"Annette, you have to remember that everything does happen for a reason. Whether it seems good or bad."

"I guess you're right. I'll have to keep that in mind when I am changing all those diapers." Annette smiled patting Crystal on the shoulder. "We have so much catching up to do. I'll have to get your number before the party's over."

"That would be great. My business cards are in the house with my address and phone number." Crystal said.

"Don't let me forget, okay? Pregnancy has done something to my memory."

"Don't worry I won't." Crystal said.

"Do you think your mom will mind if I use the bathroom?" Annette asked.

"No, she won't mind. She just walked in the house. Go ahead on in."

"Thanks, I'll talk to you later. It was good, seeing you both again!" She looked down at Warren and hugged Crystal, just before making her way into the house.

Crystal felt the depression setting in. She and Annette were the exact same age. In fact, she was five months older than Annette. She was already on her third child and Crystal still had none. She knew Annette was only being kind when asking how many children Crystal had. She wouldn't mind changing diapers and she'd love the opportunity to deal with teenage hormones.

She knew people like Annette meant well when they told her to take her time and have children. People were always giving her advice about taking the time to be alone with her husband. But all of those people had children. They didn't know anything about wanting to have a child so badly, but having to wait. All the other childless couples she knew were not giving out the same advice.

The surprise reunion with her old friend had been bitter-sweet. She didn't want Warren to know that she was shaken by the further realization of their childlessness. She had to be strong and hold her head up. She wouldn't show any emotions—at least not until she could do so in private. She plastered a fake smile on her face.

"Crystal, are you okay?" Warren asked.

"I'm fine," she quickly replied.

"Are you sure?"

"Yes, I said I'm fine!" Crystal snapped.

Crystal's mother came and sat down at the table next to them. "Ooooh, I'm having so much fun. That was my song, "Cooling Water," by the Williams Brothers. I wish your father could have been here for this."

"Me too, Mama," Marcy said as she sat down with a plate of dessert.

Looking past her mother, Marcy said to no one in particular, "What is Shanice doing?"

Everyone at the table looked up to see Shanice walking up to the D.J. She whispered something in his ear and then took the microphone. "Hello everyone."

Everyone got quiet, knowing it was possible for almost anything to come out of Shanice's mouth.

"Can I have everyone's attention?" she said again not realizing everyone was already quiet. "I have an announcement. I just wanted to let everyone know that Malika is going to soon be a new sister, I mean a new big sister. I am pregnant!" Shanice said with excitement.

Everyone looked around at each other wondering what they were supposed to do next. Shanice continued to stand, waiting for a response; some people started to clap.

"Thank you," Shanice said and dropped the microphone down on the D.J. table.

"What did she just say?" Crystal's mother said in a daze.

"I think she just said she was pregnant, Mama," a stunned Marcy replied.

"I know that ignorant girl didn't just stand up there, with that microphone, and tell all of these people, with her unwed butt, that she is pregnant! Please tell me I am dreaming. Please!" Willie Mae pleaded.

"Mama, you aren't dreaming. She just stood up there and said she was pregnant," Marcy said again.

"I knew somebody was pregnant when I dreamed about them fish. But why on God's green earth did it have to be Shanice? She don't need another baby. She can barely take care of the one she's got. Lord, that child is crazy. I believe she is really crazy," Willie Mae said. "Crystal, that should be you, not her. I just can't believe that girl is pregnant again and stupid enough to think that was a good reason to get up in front of all of these people and tell the news."

Crystal couldn't believe it either. Her sister was pregnant again. She didn't really care about the fact that Shanice had made a complete fool of herself. What did matter was that Shanice was now two up on her. She wondered why God would allow Shanice to get pregnant again, but not her.

Chapter 3

Vivian Parker

Vivian Parker sat at her desk looking over the plans for the Whitman project. She had a meeting with the CEO of Whitman and Associates later that afternoon to review the construction plans for the building.

Vivian had designed the Whitman Building according to all the requests Whitman wanted. The ten-story building would accommodate his entire legal staff as well as the staff of all his associates. Each floor would have its own unique scheme.

Vivian was the head planner with ten people working under her. She gave the people working under her the overall picture of what their clients ultimately wanted. Then the assistants would fine-tune the plans for Vivian's approval.

She looked the plans over and was pleased. She always planned everything down to the tiniest details. Her company prided itself in having a reputation for "one stop" shopping when it came to building and renovating. Companies were able to have all their construction, renovation, landscaping and design needs taken care of in one place. They employed professionals who were the top in their fields. The company was known for its five-star service.

She looked down at her watch. It was two hours before the meeting. She wanted to drive to the building site to have one last look. That way it would be fresh in her mind for her meeting with Trace Whitman and his associates.

Vivian loved her office, because she had designed it, as well as the entire building. When the ground had been broken, Vivian knew every nook and cranny of the thirty-story building. She had planned where her office would be, knowing what a beautiful view it would have.

She walked to the window to see if any clouds were forming in the direction of the site. From her office, she could see the majority of Silvermont. She could tell when the traffic was heavy or when there was an event at the convention center. She could even see the top of New Hope, a church she visited a couple of times.

The atmosphere of New Hope reminded her of her church back home in Mississippi. The couple of times she had attended brought back too many painful memories. Vivian remembered kneeling and praying so many times at the altar of her family's little Mississippi church. She had so many hopes of God coming through for her but, He hadn't. She ended up learning how to depend on herself and not ask God for anything.

Her eyes blurred with tears. She took a deep breath and blinked, allowing her vision to refocus on Carson State University. The view of the campus from her office was beautiful, with its sprawling rolling hills and verdant green lawns. The trees were just starting to turn, signaling the beginning of autumn. Vivian had attended CSU, majoring in Architecture and Design. Right after graduation, she secured a job with a firm in the mid-west for the first five years. Then she moved back to Silvermont and landed a job with the previous owners of the company.

When she first started working for the company she was given smaller projects like churches and doctors' offices, then she moved on to bigger projects like banks and schools. Vivian had been working with the larger projects for over ten years and was a valuable asset with her expertise. She could draft the plans for the exterior of the buildings and also sketch the interior décor.

Vivian was pleased with the way her career was turning out. She smiled to herself, satisfied with all of her accomplishments. After years of diligent work, her portfolio was extensive, and she was highly spoken of in all of the architectural circles.

Vivian heard her phone beep. "Mrs. Parker," her receptionist, Nikki said.

"Yes, Nikki?" Vivian continued to look out of the window.

"Mrs. Parker, you have a phone call on line two from a Dr. Evan's office," Nikki informed her.

Vivian quickly turned around and returned to sit at her desk. "Thanks, Nikki. Send it through."

She took a deep breath and picked up the phone, "Hello, Vivian Parker speaking."

"Hi, Mrs. Parker, this is Shelby Tomlinson, one of the nurses at Dr. Evans' office. We got a message that you wanted to speak with someone further about getting an appointment."

"Yes. I wanted to see if I could get an appointment with Dr. Evans."

"Will you need a gynecology appointment or an obstetric appointment?" the nurse asked.

"Well, I don't know. I guess both," Vivian said, not really sure how to explain what she needed.

"Are you pregnant, Mrs. Parker?"

"No. But my gynecologist does not practice obstetrics, and he suggested I call Dr. Evans for that service. My husband and I want to start having children. I am also currently due for my annual exam. So that's why I said both," Vivian explained.

"Oh, okay I understand. Let's set you up for your annual

exam first, then at the same time you'll be able to talk to Dr. Evans directly. How does that sound?" the nurse asked.

"That sounds good to me," Vivian told her.

"Our first available appointment is on the fifteenth of this month. How's that date for you?"

Vivian looked at the calendar on her personal organizer. "No, the fifteenth is a bad day. My *friend* will be here."

"Your *friend*?" There was a pause on the other end. "Oh. What date would be good for you?"

Vivian counted the days on the calendar, "The nineteenth."

"We don't have anything on the nineteenth, but what about the twenty-third at 9:30 a.m.?"

"September 23rd at 9:30 a.m. sounds fine," Vivian said as she double-checked her calendar. "What do I need to bring?"

"Bring your insurance card along with your co-payment. You will also need to come about fifteen minutes early to fill out some paperwork."

"Okay, thank you. What is your name again?" Vivian asked.

"I'm Shelby Tomlinson, one of the nurses."

"That's a pretty name. Thanks again Shelby. I'll see you on the twenty-third."

"Thank you," the nurse replied. "We'll see you then."

"Okay," Vivian concluded and then hung up.

She was glad she hadn't left the office and missed the call. Vivian and her husband were eager to see a doctor before trying to having a baby. Now, they were one step closer with the appointment set. She couldn't wait to let her husband know.

Leaning back in her chair, Vivian steepled her fingers beneath her chin. She looked at her Bachelor's and Master's degree on the wall as well as various awards and plaques she had received over the years. Before marrying her husband, with hard work and self-determination, she had managed to build a comfortable nest egg. It was all part of a plan she had devised just after her grandma died.

As a child growing up, Vivian had promised her grandma that she would do well in her classes, graduate from high school, and go to college—something no one else in her family had done. She promised her grandma that she would learn as much as she could and make her proud. Vivian's Grandma Eva told her often that once a person learned something, no one could take the learning out of their head.

Vivian loved and respected her Grandma Eva and would never let her down. When her grandma passed away, Vivian was the tender age of 13, and she vowed to keep the promises she made.

She had gone above and beyond the promise to her grandma. Not only had she graduated from high school and gone to college for her undergraduate degree, she'd gone on to get her masters. She didn't seriously consider the idea of getting married and having children until after receiving both degrees.

By her original calculations, she'd be married by the age of 30 and have her first child a couple of years later. Instead, her plan had been altered. She hadn't gotten married until the age of 38.

Now at 40, she and Roland were ready to have a child. She had spoken with her previous gynecologist who told her that because of her age she needed to see an OB/GYN doctor that also specialized in fertility problems. When Vivian asked what her age had to do with anything, the doctor told her probably nothing, but if she did have any problems, at least she would already be seeing a specialist. So after she spoke to her husband about what her doctor suggested, she called Dr. Evans' office.

She picked up her keys to leave the office for the work site. Just as she reached the door, she bumped into the president of the company as he was entering her office.

In a deep voice he said, "Hello, Mrs. Parker." He always looked and sounded so astute to Vivian.

"Well, hello Mr. President. How may I help you?" Her voice was coy. She looked the president up and down. Vivian thought he was one of the most handsome men she had ever seen. He stood six-foot-two and looked as if he had come straight from African royalty. His hair was cut close with a sprinkle of gray throughout. The hair extended down his cheeks and face into a neat goatee. His skin was the same color as his dark brown eyes and he always walked with an air of sophistication.

She stepped back into her office. He followed and closed the door behind him.

"Mrs. Parker, I must say you look very lovely this morning. Royal blue is your color," he said, as his eyes traveled up and down her body.

"Excuse me, sir?"

"Yes, Mrs. Parker your husband is a lucky man to have an absolutely beautiful woman like you. I'll just bet he hates to part from you each morning. Heck, he probably doesn't even know what a lucky man he truly is." He moved closer, backing Vivian up against the desk until she could no longer move. His soft manicured hand caressed her ear and cheek.

"I think you had better stop right now," Vivian said, her breathing was heavy.

"Oh, I don't think you really want me to stop. Now do you?" He moved his hands to her waist and then down to her hips. "Now do you?" he repeated forcefully.

Vivian liked it when he spoke with strength. It was just one of the things she admired about him. "I don't think my husband would like this," she said, placing her arms around his waist.

He moved closer to her, his smooth lips brushing her ear lobe. "Well, what he doesn't know won't hurt him, will it?"

"What if I tell him?" she challenged. She felt his hot breath on her neck.

"Tell him. I don't care," he whispered arrogantly. "What's he going to do?"

Vivian shivered. "What can I do to get you to stop?" her voice pleaded.

He pulled back, his brown eyes looking directly into hers. "You could join me for dinner tonight," he suggested.

Vivian moved her face closer to his, their noses touching. "Where?" she asked, giving in. She could smell his cologne and knew she'd be able to smell it on her clothing long after they parted.

"2583 Greyson Way."

"2583 Greyson Way? Isn't that your address? You want me to come to your home? Hummm, that sounds pretty risky. What time should I be there?" She said, accepting his invitation.

"Let's say eight o'clock."

"Eight o'clock. I think I can swing that."

He kissed her lightly on the lips. "Don't be late." He squeezed her hips tightly.

Vivian pulled an arms length away from him. "Give me two good reasons as to why I should meet you tonight, Mr. Parker."

"First, we need to finish what we've started here. And second because, I love you so much, my absolutely beautiful wife," he said pulling her back into his embrace. He kissed her again. "And I do realize what a lucky man I am."

After a long kiss, Vivian finally pulled away from her husband and started to fan her face and neck with her hand. "Whew, Roland. What was that for? Keep it up and we can finish everything here and now!"

"We got the Frederickson account. Tonight we are going to celebrate," he said, his teeth gleaming as he smiled.

"You told me we'd get the account."

"I knew we would. Frederickson knows our company is the best in the business. The meetings were just a formality as far as I was concerned."

"Good, that makes two things we can celebrate."

"What else are we celebrating?" He asked, his right eyebrow raising.

"We are celebrating the start of our family planning process. I made an appointment to see Dr. Evans on the twenty-third of this month. It's a start, so I think we should celebrate that also!"

"That's great sweetheart. I guess we'll be celebrating two events then. I've already spoken to the cook. The menu for tonight is Caesar salad, beef burgundy, garlic-sautéed spring vegetables, fresh yeast rolls, and our favorite red wine. Dessert will be a surprise," he said.

"Sounds good, but do you think William will want to eat beef burgundy and garlic vegetables?" Vivian said, referring to her stepson. "You know how picky he is when it comes to trying new foods."

"Not to worry, sweetheart. William is spending the night with a friend. They have a field trip tomorrow and his friend's parent, just happens to be one of the chaperones."

"How convenient. Oh, alright. So, a surprise dessert, huh? I never know what to expect from you with your surprises Roland. Don't get too outrageous," she said with a grin.

"Don't worry I didn't. But you know with me, nothing is mediocre. I do promise you'll love it." A grin covered his face.

He looked at her keys and purse and asked, "Were you getting ready to go somewhere?"

"Yeah, I was about to go over to the Whitman site to give it a last look before the meeting today. Do you want to go with me?"

He looked at his watch. "Sure, I've got a few minutes. My conference call isn't for another hour. You know I wouldn't turn down a chance to spend time with you."

"Roland, you can see me anytime you want. All you have to do is walk over to this end of the building. Don't you ever get tired of being together all the time?"

"No, I don't," he said, taking her back into his arms. "I waited a long time for you to come into my life, and I am never going to let you go. I could never get tired of seeing your beautiful face."

"Roland, I love you so much. I am the luckiest woman in the world to have you as my soul mate. I could never get tired of seeing you, either." This time she kissed him and didn't want to let go, but stopped herself. "Okay, let's get a move on. We can finish this tonight at eight. Then we can pick up right here in this position." She placed her hands around his waist.

"It's a date," Roland said, and they headed to the door.

"Mrs. Parker, these plans are great. Everything is just the way we envisioned it," Trace Whitman said. "We are very pleased with your work thus far. The reputation that preceded your company was correct." Trace Whitman's associates who were also gathered for the meeting, shook their heads in agreement.

"Thank you, Mr. Whitman. Thank you all." Vivian said.

"You can call me, Trace," he said.

"Trace, as you know we aim to please. Our clients mean everything to us."

"How early can renovations start? I know originally we asked for March, but we are eager to begin as soon as possible. Is there any way the date could be moved up?" Trace asked.

"I'll check with the builder to see if they can start any earlier. It may not be a problem since things are slow in construction right now. I'll let you know what I find out."

"That would be great. If not, I understand. I just didn't think these preliminary plans would be ready so soon," Trace said.

"Like I said before, we aim to please, so I'll see what can be done."

"Let me just say again that we are truly pleased with the presentation today," Trace said as all of his associates shook their heads in agreement.

"As soon as the start date is finalized, I'll have the completed contract with the changes we discussed couriered over," Vivian said, standing up to signal the meeting was over. She shook hands with Trace and the other associates.

"Thank you again," Trace said.

Once everyone left the room, Vivian turned off her laptop and collected her papers. Now she and Roland would have three events to celebrate.

Vivian left work at five-fifteen. She opened the sunroof on her Bentley for some fresh air for the drive home. It was a beautiful, late-summer day. The temperature had gotten up to 83 degrees. Vivian liked the weather in the central part of North Carolina during September—normally it was never too hot or cold. The only downfall were the months of hurricane season. Luckily, this year they hadn't had any hurricanes and none were currently brewing off the African coast.

As Vivian drove, she reflected on the prosperous day she and Roland were having. She was happy about the deals they were about to close, but she was most happy about the appointment she had been able to get with the doctor so they could add to their family. It had been one of the best days of her life.

She looked forward to the night ahead, the celebration dinner, and the surprise dessert Roland had planned. Roland's surprises were just that. He came up with the most unusual ideas and she had always loved every one of them. She smiled thinking about the biggest surprise he had ever given her.

She had been working at the company for five years as an interior designer. When one of the architects was fired due to a drinking problem, Vivian's hard work was recognized, and she was moved up into his position. Soon after, the president of the company was so impressed by all of her accomplishments, he started giving her larger projects.

Roland had bought the company after Vivian had been working there twelve years. He'd done some house cleaning and reorganization, weeding out the essential and nonessential employees and departments. Roland didn't leave the decisions of who stayed and who didn't up to one of his employees, he did all the interviewing himself, determining the employees' strengths and weaknesses.

When all was said and done, the hard-nosed Roland kept Vivian on as a valuable asset to the company. She was quickly promoted to management with two architects and three interior designers under her. Her new position gave her a twenty-thousand dollar a year salary increase.

Even though she was pleased with the new position and raise, she'd been more delighted to work under the new president and CEO. Roland Parker was one of the best in the architectural and design business. His name was known worldwide.

Vivian learned through a co-manager that Roland was single. Curious as to why this handsome man was unmarried, she was told his wife had died of an inoperable brain tumor only two years after they were married. He was left as a widower and had a 13-month-old son to take care of. She felt sorry for his misfortune.

She couldn't help but notice how attractive he was. He was tall with a dark brown complexion, almost the exact Hershey chocolate complexion as hers. On the outside she saw a handsome and distinguished man. On the inside, she felt he was hiding his true feelings behind a mask. The smiles he wore didn't hide the sadness in his eyes.

One morning she walked into his office and caught him staring off into space. Figuring he might need someone to talk to, she boldly asked him what he was doing for lunch. He told her he'd bought a sandwich and was going to sit at his desk and eat it.

She knew his lunch patterns well. If he wasn't scheduled for a business lunch, he would sit in his office and eat a sandwich. She knew he *had* to be sick of sandwiches, especially since he hadn't had a business lunch in two weeks.

Vivian told him she was about to go to one of her favorite places for lunch and wanted to know if he would like to join her. Surprisingly, he had said yes. They went to an ice cream shop within walking distance of the office.

During lunch, they made small talk. Vivian was surprised by how different her boss could be when he wasn't in the office. Not once did he bring up the subject of work. He asked where she was from, what kind of hobbies she liked, if she liked to read, and if she had ever been married.

She asked him what he liked to do, where he was from. Near the end of lunch, she asked what his favorite flavor of ice cream was. He told her strawberry cheesecake. She told him it was her favorite, too.

Not once during their lunch had his eyes turned sad.

When they got ready to leave, Vivian picked up the check. He told her she didn't have to, but she insisted since she had extended the invitation to him. She offered him a chance to pay the next time. He told her he would.

As they walked back to the office he continually shook his head. Finally Vivian asked him why. He told her that in all of his life he had never had a woman buy him lunch or any other meal. He said he was touched by her gesture.

He thanked her again for lunch. She told him that it was no problem. Being bold again, she told him that she looked forward to their next meal together.

She didn't have to wait long. Two days later he asked her what she was doing that Saturday. She told him that she didn't have any major plans. He invited her to a play that was tour-

ing the city called *Count It All Joy.* Without the slightest
hesitation, she accepted his offer.

He'd told her he wanted to re-pay his lunch with a dinner
instead. So, prior to going to the play, they had dinner at
Ginny's. Ginny's was a five-star restaurant that Vivian never
imagined she would be going to any time soon, especially
with a fine gentleman on her arm.

The night was like a dream. She wore a black, floor-length,
A-line dress, cut low in the front and back. He wore a black
tuxedo with a silver tie. She wasn't sure if she was over-
dressing and sighed with relief when she saw him in the
double-breasted tux.

He picked her up in a Rolls Royce limousine. Vivian
couldn't believe her eyes. She didn't know what to think or
how to act. She was very nervous at first, but she finally relaxed in the company of the gentleman who had asked her
out.

She looked at her watch thinking that at midnight the
limo might turn into a pumpkin. It was silly, she knew. The
evening was elegance at its best. She hated to see it come to
an end. Once she was back home, she peeked outside and
watched the limousine drive off into the moonlight.

The cologne on her skin and dress let her know the night
had not been a dream. The night would be etched in her
memory forever. She knew she would never experience anything like it again. Roland had gone all out to top her little
hamburger and banana split lunch.

Over the next year, Vivian and Roland had grown closer
through their special dates. Vivian found herself spending
many nights like the first. Each night became more special
than the one before.

One day Roland came to her with a project he wanted her
expertise on. He told her they had obtained a new client
who just happened to be an old friend of his from college

named Sebastian. Roland's friend wanted them to design a new home for his family.

Vivian asked him why Sebastian had not gone to a regular builder. Roland explained it was because of a bet he'd lost in college during a card game their freshman year. He told Sebastian he would repay him one day by designing a home, free of charge. The friend was finally collecting.

Vivian agreed to help with the designs. Before they started on the project, she asked what the friend wanted in a home. Roland shared the plans with her. The house was to have three stories in which the family of six, would have enough room for ample comfort.

Vivian felt like a child in a candy store. Roland told her to think and plan as if she were planning for herself. So Vivian tried to keep everyone in mind, not only the husband, but the wife and children also. Roland had done a good job but his plans needed a woman's touch. She offered ideas to change many of the aspects, adding features she was sure any woman would truly appreciate.

The second level of the home would have four bedrooms suites, each with their own private baths and walk-in closets. Also on this level would be the computer room, a bonus room with a window seat and its own powder room, as well as a sewing room equipped with workable storage areas.

On the main level there was to be the formal living room, the two-story family room, a foyer with a circular staircase and granite floor. This level would also have a master suite with trey ceilings, a sitting area, fireplace, and his and her walk-in closets. The master bath was to be equipped with a garden tub with Jacuzzi jets, a separate shower stall with three showerheads, along with his and her sinks, and his and her toilets.

Other main level features included the cherry-wood library with fireplace, a gourmet kitchen equipped with custom cherry cabinetry, an island, beverage center, wine cooler, and icemaker. A secondary staircase would be located off of the kitchen next to a laundry room leading down to the lower level. All of the formal areas of the house had fireplaces.

If need be the lower level could function as a house by itself. It featured the family recreation room, kitchenette, bar area including an icemaker with a refrigerator, temperature-controlled wine cellar, and a state-of-the-art media room with elevated theater-style seating which would accommodate six couples.

There was also a nanny's suite, which would have its own full bath and sitting area. Other features included an exercise room, billiard room, full bath with shower, and a covered patio with a hot tub.

In all, the home was over 9,000 square feet with two three-car garages on the main and lower levels.

Roland was pleased with all of the work Vivian put into planning the home and Vivian was pleased with the work they had done together. It gave her a chance to spend more time with him. She really enjoyed not having to think about a budget and wondered if she would ever be able to afford anything half as extravagant, one day.

Vivian asked Roland to let her know when the home was completed. She looked forward to seeing it before the owners moved in. Roland said he didn't think his friend would mind. He also told her that Sebastian and his wife were happy with the plans thus far.

After another year of dating, Roland told her the home was built and ready to be seen. He'd asked if she'd like to go by and see it. Excited, she wanted to view it as soon as possible. They went the next Saturday for the tour.

The house was even more beautiful than she could have ever imagined. The landscaping was immaculate. Roland opened the front door and Vivian was breathless. She had never seen anything so stunning. The home was already fully furnished. As soon as they walked into the foyer, she saw a black and white baby grand piano. Her jaw dropped.

As a bonus to the family, she'd suggested furniture ideas for each room. The piano was the exact one she'd suggested. It complimented the granite floor and spiral staircase.

All of the rooms held the furniture Vivian had suggested down to the monogrammed towels matching the color scheme in each of the bathrooms. The wine cellar held some of the finest wines money could buy.

After they finished touring the house, Roland suggested they celebrate the masterpiece they had created together. Roland went into the wine cellar and pulled out a bottle of champagne. For all the planning they had done, he'd said he was sure his friend wouldn't mind.

He then went into the kitchenette and pulled out two champagne glasses. After pouring the bubbly into the glasses he handed Vivian one for a toast. "To new beginnings." He had said. She remembered smiling, thinking about the wonderful new beginnings the family was sure to have in their new home.

Closing her eyes, she took a sip of the champagne. When she opened them back up she noticed something in the bottom of her glass. A closer look revealed that it was a diamond ring. She looked at Roland in confusion.

Roland took her glass and drank the rest of her champagne. He then dropped down to one knee. He took her hand in his and asked the four words that completely changed her life.

She was speechless at first. Then, with tears of happiness, she said, "Yes!"

Roland again asked her if she liked the house and she remembered wondering why he was back on the subject of the house. He had just asked her hand in marriage and now he was asking about the house again. She also wondered why he had chosen to ask her to marry him then and there.

"Yes, Roland. I like the house."

He told her, the answer to her earlier question was, "Yes."

Confused she had asked, "What question?"

He said, "You asked me if my friend's wife liked the house."

Still confused she said to him, "Yeah, and you said that you didn't know if she liked it." He couldn't know for sure until he asked her to marry him.

Slowly, she began to realize there never was a friend. She realized the house she had helped to plan was actually going to be hers. Then it dawned on her; the letters on the monogrammed towels, in all the bathrooms, were all "RP" and "VP". With all the awe she felt touring the house she hadn't noticed none of them had an S on them for Sebastian's name.

Thoughts about Roland's many surprises brought a smile to Vivian's face and heart. Some of the surprises over the years were extravagant, while others were just creative and thoughtful. She knew she was a blessed woman and was eager to see what Roland had in mind for later that evening. She pressed the accelerator and exited the beltline.

Chapter 4

Shelby Tomlinson

"Shelby," Phillip said, returning to their bedroom.

She looked up at Phillip, her eyes were red and puffy.

"Shelby, don't cry. What's wrong? Are you okay? Are you having another anxiety attack?"

She didn't want to discuss it anymore. Talking about it further would only upset her more. *What was the use?* She thought, *he'd probably run out of the room and avoid me again. Then I'll probably have another attack.*

"Shelby, talk to me. Please, baby," Phillip pleaded. He had rejoined her in bed wrapping his arms around her shoulders. He caressed her cheek and wiped tears as they trickled down her face.

Shelby hoped he would take her silence as a cue to leave her alone, it was okay now. He wouldn't have to come up with another excuse to avoid her. She wasn't going to put either one of them through that ordeal again. But the more she thought about her lost hope, the more she started to cry.

"Shelby, talk to me. I'm here and I'm not going anywhere. Talk to me please baby."

Before she knew it, she blurted out, "Phillip, I just can't

take it anymore." She sobbed harder. "I want to talk about us having children, but every time I try to bring up the subject you hide. I mean you literally run and hide from me. I have concerns, but you don't even know what they are because you are always hiding." Tears streamed down her cheeks.

"What kind of concerns? I'm here, talk to me, baby."

Phillip continued to hold her. She'd noticed he hadn't shrunk away this time when she mentioned wanting to have children.

"I think something might be wrong with me. And whatever it is, is causing us not to conceive. There must be something wrong with my body." She wiped the tears forcefully with her tightly-balled fists.

"Shelby, I am so sorry. Baby, I love you. I know I've been avoiding the subject, and I want to apologize. I'm sorry I haven't been there for you emotionally. I am here for you now. I won't run or hide anymore." Phillip pulled her closer and held her tight.

He will never leave you or forsake you, Shelby thought. The scripture came to her as if someone had whispered it in her ear. God had answered her prayer just that quickly. Was it possible? After almost two years of waiting, just that quickly her prayer of being able to talk openly with her husband was answered. She allowed herself to sob into his chest with relief.

He still wasn't tense and hadn't moved away from her. He stayed and held her tightly.

"Phillip, what's wrong?" she asked, sniffing.

"What do you mean?"

For a second she felt him tense but then he allowed himself to relax.

"Phillip, I really think something is wrong with me and that's why we haven't been able to conceive. I want to ask

Dr. Evans if she can run some tests to see what the problem may be. Is that alright with you?" She pulled herself out of the tight embrace and looked into his eyes earnestly.

Phillip inhaled, then let out a long breath. "Yes, baby, I think we've waited long enough. I'll stand by you in whatever you want to do. Whatever you think is right."

"Thank you." She paused, wiping her eyes with the satin sheet. "I know together we can get through this."

"Yes, baby, together we can." Phillip smiled at her with love in his eyes.

Shelby was glad and hugged him again. She got the feeling that something about Phillip's demeanor wasn't right. Was it something in his eyes? She couldn't quite put her finger on it. She put it out of her mind, thinking it was probably just her nerves. The whole day had been a long, emotional, roller coaster, and she was just glad to have it over with. Exhaustion hit her hard and she slid under the covers snuggling as close to Phillip as she could. Sleep overtook her before she could say a prayer to thank God for coming through for her.

Shelby rocked her head from side to side as she listened to the Sunday morning Gospel music on K97.5. She had felt like a burden had been lifted off her shoulders. She reflected on her conversation with her husband the previous Friday night. Finally, it seemed as if they would now be able to move forward to find out why she wasn't getting pregnant.

Shelby popped a tortilla chip in her mouth and thought she heard the doorbell ring between crunches. She was expecting her parents to visit.

She looked out of the kitchen doorway to the foyer. Through the opaque glass she saw the shadows of two figures just outside the door.

"I'm coming," she called out. She opened the door wide. "Hi, Mom and Dad!" Shelby stepped out and hugged her mother and father as soon as she saw them. "Where have you all been? I just got back from picking up the broccoli cheese corn bread for you Dad."

"Hello, baby," her mother replied as she entered the foyer. "We stayed after church and spoke with the Bishop for a little while."

"How's my little girl doing?" her father asked as he looked down at her. "You got me some broccoli cheese cornbread?"

"Of course Daddy."

"Thank you baby."

Shelby noticed a few more gray hairs on his partially bald head. "I'm fine and I'm not a *little* girl, Daddy."

Touching her nose with his index finger he chuckled, "You'll always be my little girl and don't you ever forget that."

"Yes, Daddy," Shelby said, feeling like Daddy's little girl again.

"Shelby, you know how your father is when it comes to you. I don't know why you always try to change his mind." Her mother walked toward the kitchen.

Shelby agreed, "I should have learned by now."

Her father removed his hat. "Where's Phillip?"

Shelby took her father's hat and jacket. "He's in the game room. I think the game started about ten minutes ago." She walked towards the hall closet. "Are you two hungry yet?"

Shelby's father patted his gut. "You know I am. It's been hours since I ate anything."

She hung his jacket and hat. "We've got a few snacks for you. They should hold you until dinner's ready."

"Good, baby. That communion juice and tiny cracker just teased my stomach."

Shelby heard a smack before turning to see her mother hit her father on the arm. "Don't say that."

"Ouch, woman!" Rubbing his arm, Shelby's father said, "Well it's the truth."

"Don't play like that." She shook her head furiously. "Don't play with God like that!"

He looked at Shelby for help while speaking to his wife. "Sorry, sweetheart, I know how sensitive you can get."

"I'm not sensitive. I just don't want you playing with God like that. Don't apologize to me, repent to God." Shelby's mother was dead serious.

"Dad," Shelby said, trying to change the subject. Her mother was usually easy-going until it came to two subjects: one, Jesus and two, her sorority. "I've got your favorite snacks."

"Hot salsa and chips?" he asked. Her father looked at her thankfully for changing the subject.

"Just the way you like them. Right this way." Shelby led her parents into the kitchen.

"Daddy, do you mind taking the snack upstairs? I was just on my way up there when you got here."

"Gladly." He took the ceramic Sombrero containing the salsa and chips. "Ladies, I'm going up to join Phillip before I miss any more of the game." He kissed his wife and exited as quickly as possible.

Immediately regaining her composure, Shelby's mother asked, "So Shelby, how have you really been?"

"I'm fine, I told you." Shelby had actually been happier than she had been in a long while. "How was church?"

"It was wonderful. I've wanted to visit New Hope for a while. I was delighted when I found out our pastor was coming to be a guest preacher. It's like a two for one special: to be able to visit the church and my baby girl, all on the same day."

"That's really good." Shelby washed her hands in the sink, drying them on a dishcloth.

"Have you and Phillip had a chance to visit New Hope yet?" Her mother took a seat on one of the bar stools.

"No. But I've been to the church down the street a few times. The preaching there is okay, but the choir is awesome. Phillip went once, but he says he wasn't really feeling the church thing, so he hasn't been back. He always says that if he needs to get any words from God, he can just turn on the T.V. and listen to one of those evangelists. He doesn't see the point in getting all dressed up to go to church."

Her mother nodded as if she understood. "You should really visit New Hope, I think you'd like it. Their pastor is truly anointed and so is their choir."

"One of the patients from the clinic invited me to New Hope also. Maybe the next time I go to church, I'll check it out," Shelby shrugged.

"I really think you'll like it Shelby."

"Okay, Mom. I might check it out next weekend. I'll let you know." Shelby moved quickly trying to finish up the dinner preparations.

"Are you sure you're okay?" Her mother pressed again.

"Yes, Mom I'm fine. Why do you keep asking?"

"Have you had any anxiety attacks recently?"

"Yes, but don't worry, I'm fine. I'm not worried about the anxiety attacks right now." Shelby left it at that.

"Sooner or later you'll tell me what's really going on with you."

Shelby didn't say anything. She walked over to the refrigerator and pulled out the ingredients to make the salad. Her mom could always tell when something was wrong with her. Normally she could talk to her mom about anything. They were more like best friends than mother and daughter.

Her mom rolled up her sleeves. "What do you need me to do?"

"Can you slice the mushrooms for me?"

Her mother walked to the sink and washed her hands. "How thin do you want them?"

"As thin as you can get them."

Shelby prepared the rest of the ingredients for the salad. After her mother finished slicing the mushrooms, Shelby used them to garnish the top of the salad. Then she covered the bowl with plastic wrap and placed it in the oven.

"Shelby!" her mom shrieked.

Startled Shelby turned around. "What mom?"

"Why on earth did you put the salad in the oven?"

"The what? I didn't, did I?" Shelby turned back and peered through the glass of the oven door. She opened it quickly, pulling the bowl out just before the plastic wrap had a chance to melt. She chuckled with embarrassment, "I guess my mind was somewhere else."

"I guess so." Her mother smirked.

Shelby decided to confess. There was no use in trying to hide the fact that something was wrong. "You're right, something has been bothering me."

"Put the salad in the refrigerator. Let's sit down and talk. The game won't be over for a while. The men will be preoccupied until it's over," her mother said.

"I can't, I still need to make the dessert." Shelby protested weakly.

"Everything else is ready right?" Her mom asked.

"Yeah."

"What were you planning to make for dessert?"

"I was going to make a cake," Shelby said, pulling the flour and sugar containers out of the cabinet.

Her mother squinted her eyes thinking quickly. "Stop. Wait a second. Do you have any cookies?"

Shelby nodded her head, "I think we do."

"What about ice cream?"

"We have French vanilla."

"Good, don't worry about making a cake. Consider dessert done. After dinner we'll have ice cream. We can sprinkle some crumbled cookies on top. Do you still have your food processor?"

"Yeah."

"Good all we have to do is finely crumble the cookies in the food processor and then sprinkle them on top of a couple of scoops of ice cream. Phillip and your dad will think it's some kind of new dessert. They'll never know the difference."

"Sounds like a plan to me." Shelby smiled with relief.

"I know it is," her mother said. "Now come on in the den so we can talk."

Shelby wiped her hands and did as her mother requested. They moved into the den. Shelby nervously picked up the remote for the stereo to search for some soothing music. After turning the volume on low, she sat next to her mom on the couch.

Shelby looked down, nervously twirling the remote in her hand. She didn't know how to start. The aquarium bubbled—the fish were happily swimming around.

Her mom placed her arm around Shelby. She could feel her mother's love. "Tell me what's on your mind sweetheart."

Shelby sighed. "Mom, I don't know where to start."

"Just start as close to the beginning as you can."

Shelby looked up into her mom's caring eyes. She admired her so much and wished one day she would be as wise as her. "How do you do it? You've known something was wrong with me for a while now haven't you?" Her mom smiled and squeezed her arm encouraging her to go on speaking. Feeling the comfort, Shelby continued, "Phillip and I have been going through some communication problems, but I think we've resolved them. At least, I feel pretty sure we have." Shelby paused.

"I'm listening," her mom continued squeezing Shelby's hand.

"You know how you and Dad are always asking when we're going to make you grandparents?"

"Yes."

"And I always tell you that we're not ready yet. Saying when the time is right we'll have children."

"Yes, baby." Concern covered her mother's face. "What about it?"

"Something is wrong, Mom. We've been trying for two years and nothing has happened. There's something wrong with me, I just know it, and Phillip thinks so too, because until the other night we couldn't even talk about our not getting pregnant." She paused again.

Her mother took a deep breath. "Go ahead baby, I'm listening."

"Like I was saying, I think there is something really wrong with me. Deep down he probably thinks I can't give him any children."

Her mother pulled back a little. "Did Phillip tell you that?"

"No, but I just have this feeling." Shelby sighed.

"Did you ask him if that's the way he's feeling?"

"Not specifically. I told him I thought something might be wrong with me, but I didn't say anything about him thinking it was my fault."

"You've been holding these feelings in for how long? Almost two years now?"

"A year and a half or so," Shelby said, trying to make it sound not so bad. "It wasn't that bad at first. It wasn't until after the first six months that I started getting concerned. It was after the first six months that I really started trying to talk to Phillip about my concerns. The next thing I knew it had been a year, then a year and a half. I'd try to bring up the subject, and he would conveniently find an excuse to avoid talking with me. It didn't take long for me to get the hint.

"From then on, I'd only bring the subject up periodically, when I could build up my nerve. But most of the time, I didn't have the courage or the energy to push the subject." Shelby started crying after she finished revealing her true feelings.

Shelby's mom wrapped her arms tighter and pulled her closer. "Here, honey, lean on me."

It was a few minutes before either of them said anything. Shelby was the first to speak. "Mom, what's wrong with me?"

"Shelby I'm sure there's nothing wrong with you. Don't speak so negatively. You and Phillip need to talk. Don't let this tear you apart. Stand your ground and talk to your husband. Let him know how you really feel. Don't keep these feelings bottled up. It's not good for your health."

Shelby perked up slightly. "The other night I let him know I was on the verge of falling apart. We talked about my getting checked out."

"What did he say?"

"He responded in a way that I couldn't believe. He admitted he'd been avoiding the subject. He agreed with my idea to speak with the doctor and to have some tests done."

"That's a good start. Now you must continue the communication process. Continue to let him know how you feel. You've got to be honest with him. Communication is the key. It can make or break any relationship."

"I know we need to communicate and so does he. We're going to work through this together. He said he'd be there for me. And I'll need him for comfort if the test results are negative."

"Stop right there," her mother said. She cupped Shelby's cheeks into her hands and pulled Shelby's face so that it was looking directly into hers. "I've known for a while that something was bothering you. I just couldn't put my finger on it."

"How'd you know?"

"I'm your mother, and I know. One day you'll understand when you have your own children." She paused and smiled with love at her daughter. "And you will have your own children.

"Now you listen to me. Like I said, I've known for a while that something was bothering you. There were so many times when I wanted to ask, but I knew in time you'd talk to me. I'm glad the time has finally come.

"I am here for you whenever you need me. I just don't want you to continue to speak negatively about problems you don't have. I am not going to sit here and let you do that. Have the test done. Be positive and don't look for anything bad to happen. If you look for problems, you'll find them."

Shelby sniffed, wiping her face with the palm of her hand. "I know what you're saying, Mom, but I've already waited so long, and it just seems like I'm never going to get pregnant." Hearing herself say the words, made Shelby start to cry again.

"Be patient. Pray and work on the communication with Phillip first. It will happen for you in due time," her mother assured her.

Shelby listened to what her mother said. Even though she knew her Mom was right, she still felt there was little hope for them to conceive.

"I'm just concerned for you. I don't mean to pry. You know me better than that, but just let me know how things turn out when you go for the tests. And if you need a listening ear, you know I'm always here for you."

Shelby wiped the tears from her face again and shook her head in agreement. She gave her mother a hug. "I will Mom. I'll keep you updated. I promise."

"Now go wash your face so we can set the table. The men should be down soon. We've got some cookies to crumble."

"Shelby, you have really outdone yourself this time." Shelby's father sat back in his dining room chair and patted his belly. "It almost tasted like your mother's cooking." He smacked his lips. "Umph, that roast was tender. Keep it up little girl. What's for dessert?"

Shelby looked at her mother, and they both laughed, "It's a new recipe."

"So are Phillip and I your guinea pigs?" Her father looked between the two women wearily.

"You'll like it. And I promise it will taste better than those mud pies I use to make when I was little," Shelby winked at him.

"I hate to break the news to you, but I never ate your mud pies," her father said, winking back.

"I know, Daddy, but you pretended and that's all that mattered to me."

Phillip raised his eyebrow. "So, what kind of new recipe is this, Shelby?"

"Hold on guys, just a minute. We'll be right back."

Shelby and her mother walked into the kitchen and prepared the bowls of ice cream with crumbled cookies.

"I think we have some cherries," Shelby said, finding the jar. She opened it and spooned some cherries on the side of each bowl.

"It looks great. You don't have to slave over a dessert for it to taste good." her mother said. "I can't wait to try it!"

They slapped each other a high five and returned to the dining room.

"Here you are, gentlemen. This is a special dish called Helado de Galletas."

"Hela what?" her father asked.

"It's a Spanish dessert." Shelby told him.

"Spanish Shelby?" Phillip raised the other eyebrow. "Since when is ice cream with cookies on top Spanish?"

"Since I just said the name of the dish in Spanish, smarty pants. Would you prefer it in French?"

"Whatever it is French, Spanish, Chinese or Vietnamese, who cares? It looks good to me!" her father said as he spooned a mouthful. "And it tastes good, too."

As Shelby's parents prepared to leave, the men argued about which one's favorite team was going to the Super

Bowl. Shelby's mother took the opportunity to pull her to the side. "Let me know how everything turns out."

"I will, Mom." She gave her a long hug. "And don't worry about me so much, I'll be fine."

"I know you will, honey." Her mother pinched Shelby's cheeks with love.

"What you two women doing over there?" Shelby's father asked. He stood holding the front door ajar. "Didn't you have enough time to talk earlier?"

"I'm coming honey," her mother quickly replied.

Shelby gave her mother another hug then hugged her dad before she followed them down the front steps. Once they were in the car she shouted, "Call us when you get home, so we'll know you got there."

Shelby's parents nodded their heads affirming they would. She watched them off as they pulled out of the driveway and down the street. She was glad they'd come and hated to see them leave.

Shelby walked back to the kitchen. Phillip had already started loading the dishwasher. He had changed into a sleeveless red and white fraternity T-shirt and baggy red shorts. From the doorway she admired his muscular arms and legs and the grace with which he moved around the kitchen.

"It was good seeing your mom and dad again. It's been a little while," Phillip said.

Smiling, Shelby replied, "It sure was."

"What's that look on your face all about?"

"What look?"

"You look so serene. I haven't seen you look this peaceful in a while. Is this the old Shelby I'm used to?" Phillip said

"Life is just good, that's all." She reflected on the conversation she'd had with her mother. "I'm just happy about my parents' visit. It was good to talk to Mom in person. Plus, I am looking forward to talking with Dr. Evans on Tuesday."

"Oh, that's all?" Phillip said with dejection. His mouth

curved into a frown, making his face look like a sad puppy dog. "I thought it might have been for some other reason."

"What reason would that be?" Shelby asked.

"I thought maybe you were thinking about us practicing." A sheepish grin appeared on his face. "You know, making our children."

"If that were the case, then I wouldn't be standing here with just a little smile. I would be grinning from ear to ear," she said her smile actually turning into a wide grin.

"Like you're starting to do right now?"

"Yep, just like this."

"What else would you do?" Phillip asked, drying his hands on a dishcloth.

Shelby lifted her index finger and said, "I'd take this finger and motion for you to follow me."

"And where would I be going?"

"I guess you'll need to follow me and find out, now won't you?"

He dropped the dishcloth like it was a hot potato. "I guess I will."

"Please come this way, sir." She motioned him to follow her out of the kitchen, through the foyer, and up the stairs. Once they reached the landing, he then walked towards their bedroom.

Shelby stopped him by pulling his shirt-tail to draw him back. "Excuse me, sir just where do you think you're going?"

He tugged. "To the bedroom for our practice session."

"You're not following my finger, are you?"

He gestured his head in the direction he was originally headed. "No, but the bedroom is this way. The only thing that way is the game room."

"I know. Isn't that the best place to practice? It's where we practice everything else: pool, darts, ping-pong?"

"Yeah, but how . . . and where in the world would we . . . ?" His voice kept trailing off.

"Use your imagination. We haven't played pool in a while, have we?"

"No I guess we haven't." He shook his head, finally getting Shelby's hint.

He laughed, "You know, you are really something else. There's never a dull moment with you."

Shelby continued to pull him into the game room and on to the pool table.

"Good, now let's get to practicing, Mr. Crazy Eight."

"Whatever you say, coach!"

Back at work the Tuesday after Labor Day, Shelby was so full of excitement that she'd sung with the radio all the way to work. She had hardly been able to sleep a wink the night before. Today she would speak with her boss about possibly having some fertility tests done. She arrived at work early in hopes to catch her boss, Dr. Evans.

Shelby had been lucky. The first person she saw when she pulled into the parking lot was Dr. Evans, who was just stepping out of her silver Jaguar. She was carrying a briefcase and a bag of bagels from a local bakery. The doctor strutted towards the building. Even though the woman was 50-years old, she didn't look a day over 40.

There were only a few sprinkles of gray hair in the top of her head, and she moved with the speed of someone at least 20 years her junior. From the pictures Shelby had seen of the woman in her younger days, it appeared as if the college years, being married, and having three children hadn't influenced the doctor's weight at all. Shelby admired her and hoped she would look and feel as good when she hit fifty.

Shelby got out of her SUV in time enough to open the door for her boss. "Good morning, Dr. Evans."

"Good morning, Shelby. How are you doing?"

"I'm doing just great. How was your Labor Day weekend?"

"Totally uneventful. It was relaxing though, and I feel so rested. No medical emergencies." The doctor had a habit of speaking with her hands. "My husband and the kids took me to dinner."

"How was your weekend?"

Shelby had a professional as well as personal relationship with her boss. She knew Dr. Evans was the best infertility specialist in the city and one of the top in the nation. The doctor also had a bedside manner, which kept patients coming back, even after they didn't need infertility services.

The people Dr. Evans chose to employ in her practice were all very much like her. She only wanted people who were caring and who truly enjoyed working with people.

"My weekend was very good actually. We spent some time with my parents Sunday and went to a cookout at a friend's house yesterday. It was quiet otherwise."

"That's good."

As other employees were starting to arrive, Shelby decided not put off the reason she had come in early in the first place.

"Dr. Evans. I want to know if I can speak with you this afternoon about a personal matter."

"Sure. There isn't anything wrong is there?" Dr. Evans asked, her eyebrows furrowed with concern.

Shelby was nervous and figured it must have shown. "Oh no, not really. Not anything that's dire anyway. I do have some questions that I hope you won't mind helping me with."

"Sure, no problem. We can talk at the end of the day. Just let me know what time our last appointment is scheduled."

Shelby stepped over to the receptionist's desk and picked up the appointment printout. Scanning to the bottom she said, "Three-thirty."

"We can talk at about four-fifteen. How's that sound?"

"Sounds good to me. And thanks, Dr. Evans."

"No problem."

* * *

The entire day Shelby felt like she was on top of the world. Not once had she gotten depressed or envied any of her prenatal patients. And in all her excitement, she hadn't even had an appetite the whole day.

The clock seemed to move in slow motion. It was taking forever for four o'clock to arrive. Shelby hoped there wouldn't be any high priority walk-ins or emergencies for the afternoon.

By the time the last scheduled appointment of the day arrived, Shelby felt home free. The last patient was a woman Shelby considered to be one of her secret sisters. Shelby was very familiar with the woman's case. This particular patient had been seeing Dr. Evans for over two years. The woman had experienced three consecutive miscarriages prior to becoming a patient of Dr. Evans.

Dr. Evans was able to determine that the woman's uterus wasn't able to hold the fetus causing the miscarriages. To prevent it from happening again, the doctor stitched the uterus shut to keep the baby in until it reached full-term.

The woman was now 38 weeks gestation with only two more weeks to go until her actual delivery date. By the doctor's standards, the baby was now full term. Today the stitches would be removed.

"Hi, Shelby!" the patient gleamed with excitement.

"Hello, Mrs. O'Brien, it's almost time."

Shelby couldn't help but beam too. She led Mrs. O'Brien from the lobby to the scale. "Let me get your weight. Hop on up."

Mrs. O'Brien did as she was asked. "I'm getting so nervous. I've never been this far along in a pregnancy before."

"You'll be fine," Shelby reassured her. "One sixty-six. Okay let me get your blood pressure and temp."

Mrs. O'Brien waddled off the scale. "I hope so. I just can't believe it is really going to happen this time."

"Well it is. Do you have the baby's room ready?"

"Yeah, we sure do. We're using Noah's Ark as the theme since we're still not sure if it's a boy or girl."

"Do you have the hospital bag packed?"

"Not yet. I still need to pick up some slippers and a robe." She touched her micro-braids. "I did manage to get my braids done though. I don't want to have to worry about doing my hair for the first month or so."

"I like your braids. I was going to tell you so," Shelby said.

"Thanks."

"Your blood pressure and temp are good. Let's go back to the exam room." Mrs. O'Brien held the bottom and side of her stomach as she waddled behind Shelby. "You might want to pick up the items you need, when you leave the office today. The baby could be here next week. You never know. Once Dr. Evans removes the stitches, things could start rolling pretty quickly." A look of concern washed over the woman's face.

"But don't stress, it could be another couple of weeks. But at least you'll be ready either way."

Mrs. O'Brien let out a huff of relief as she climbed onto the exam table. "I don't know why I keep procrastinating about getting those last few items. I guess because it doesn't seem real to me yet."

"Well, when you leave here, just go get the things you need. That'll give you time to choose what you really want without having to rush."

The woman fanned herself with her hand. "That makes sense. I should do that."

Shelby smiled at the anxious woman, "Let me leave so you can get undressed. I'll be praying for you, and I look forward to seeing your bundle of joy in a few weeks."

Closing the exam room door behind her, Shelby saw Rachel as soon as she stepped out into the hall.

"I'm done for the day," Rachel said.

"I'm almost done. I've got a few more charts to write. Mrs. O'Brien was our last patient."

"I'm going to head on out. I still need to finish packing for my trip." Rachel said.

"Did you ever figure out where Todd's taking you?"

"I have no idea. He won't even give me a hint. I tried to trick him into telling me by asking if I should pack a bathing suit. When he told me yes, I figured we were going some place warm. But then he added, 'Pack a snow suit too.'"

Shelby laughed at her friend.

"It's not funny." Rachel rolled her eyes.

"It's cute, kind of romantic really. Your man is taking you on a surprise vacation. Don't you think it's romantic?"

"What I think is that I'll be carrying more bags than I need to. If he would just give me a better hint, I wouldn't have to pack so much."

"Stop fussing Rachel. Just a year ago you were whining because you didn't have a man. Now you've got one who treats you like the Queen of Sheba, and still you find something to whine about."

Rachel let out a sigh. "You're right as always, Shelby. I need to be thankful. Live for the moment and enjoy it while it lasts."

"You sound as if this is some kind of short-term thing or something."

"You never know. I've dated enough men to know not everything is always what it seems. Plus I know he's getting tired of me saying no to him. I made a vow to myself before I even met him. I vowed that I'd never sleep with another man until we were married, and I meant it. So I hope he is not trying to take me on some romantic whirl-wind trip to try and get some, because he'll be sorely disappointed."

"Where on earth did that come from? Your boyfriend is

one of the most polite men I have seen in a long time. I'm quite sure he's not taking you on this trip, just to try and get some. He doesn't seem that shallow."

Rachel sighed again.

"Face it, you've got a good man this time. Don't let all of those past relationships mess this one up for you. Go and have fun!"

"I know he's a good man. He is everything I could've asked for, even though he does already have two kids." Rachel shook her head disbelievingly. "I can't even believe I am dating a man with kids, but I guess at my age I can't have everything I want."

"At your age? Thirty? You act as if you're elderly or something—ready to collect social security benefits." Rachel chuckled. "And those two little boys adore you."

"I know. I really love the boys too. It's not them or Todd, honestly, I think I'm just PMSing or something. Hopefully my hormones will behave in more ways than one, on this trip, if you get my drift."

"You'll be fine," Shelby assured.

"I'll call you when I get back, unless of course he has got me packing for a trip thirty miles down the road to Raleigh or something. If that's the case, you'll get a call from me telling you to come and pick me up!"

"Stop it. He's probably taking you to the islands or something. Now go ahead and finish packing. We'll talk when you get back."

Shelby gave Rachel a goodbye hug then returned to her office to complete the rest of her charts. It was just past four o'clock when she finished. Dr. Evans was wrapping up her last appointment for the day.

A few minutes later, Shelby knocked on the doctor's office door. Dr. Evans looked up from a chart. "Come on in, Shelby. Have a seat. I need to run to the bathroom. I'll be right back."

Shelby sat in one of the patient chairs.

When Dr. Evans returned, she sat down and gave a warm smile, "So, what's going on? What did you want to talk about?"

"Well, I want to talk to you about a personal problem."

"I'm listening."

"It has to do with my husband and me trying to conceive. We've been . . ." Shelby's voice trailed off upon hearing Dr. Evans' pager go off.

"Hold on just a second," Dr. Evans said, picking up the phone to call her service. "Hello, this is Dr. Evans. Yes. Did she say how far the contractions were apart? Three minutes! They're on the way to the hospital now. I'm on my way." She hung up the phone.

"Shelby, I guess you heard that. It's Mrs. Wilson; she is about to deliver. You know she's the one with triplets. Her scheduled c-section wasn't supposed to be until Friday. I need to get over to the hospital and meet them. I'm sorry, we'll need to continue this conversation tomorrow," Dr. Evans said, grabbing her car keys and purse.

"I understand. Be careful," Shelby said as she watched her boss leave. Shelby rose and returned to her office to pick up her purse and keys.

Before she knew it she was on the expressway, the traffic was moving at a slow pace. She hadn't checked the traffic report, although this evening she didn't really care. All the excitement she had earlier in the day had been deflated like a helium balloon punctured by a needle.

All she could think about during the ride home was the interruption in the doctor's office. She was disappointed about not being able to finish talking. The more she dwelled on her thoughts, her spirit plunged.

She wondered why she was taking it so badly. After all, it was only to be a short delay. Shelby thought about what her mother said about being patient and scolded she herself.

She also knew she'd have to calm down. If not, she'd be a basket case and her anxiety attacks might continue to recur.

Deep in her heart she knew God had already answered her prayer, and it was just a matter of time before everything would be resolved. She would just have to practice patience.

She pushed the button for her gospel CD, needing to hear words of encouragement. She knew just the right song. Turning the volume up she listened to the soothing words of "My Heart Knows" by gospel artist Doreen Vail. This particular song always helped lift her spirit.

The traffic grew more congested, but she didn't mind. Shelby focused on the words to the song. She wasn't going to let the small setback continue to depress her any longer.

By the time she arrived home, she felt the same optimism as she had driving to work that morning. Her hope was renewed, and she was thankful to God for it.

Chapter 5

Crystal Shaw

Crystal sat in church the morning after the cookout. Instead of focusing on what was being said, her thoughts lingered on her sister's announcement and the reunion with her long-lost friend Annette. The thoughts were depressing, so much so that she didn't feel like talking to anyone, not even her husband. He hadn't pressured her to talk, even though she had a feeling he knew something was bothering her.

When she allowed her focus to return to the service, the choir was ending a song and her pastor, Victor Jordan, was starting his sermon. "Today, congregation, I want you to turn to Hebrews 11:1. We will be continuing our series on faith." Pastor Jordan waited for them to turn to the Scripture. "When you have the Scripture, say, 'Amen.'" After a chorus of amens, the pastor continued. "And it reads, 'Now faith is the substance of things hoped for, the evidence of things not seen.'"

"Today our faith can be used in so many ways. The title for today's message is 'Believe, You've Got to Have the Faith.' You can hold your finger or place a book mark on that scripture, but we'll also be looking at several other Scriptures to illustrate this message."

Crystal turned to the Scripture and read it silently. *Faith* she thought to herself. She had faith, but it was wavering. She'd had faith for five years that one day, she'd become pregnant, but to no fruition.

"Faith is believing in God. Believing that God can do what seems impossible," the pastor said, his baritone voice rising and falling with inflection on the words he wanted to stress. "Faith needs to be unwavering. You can't have it in one instance, then doubt in the next. If you add belief with unbelief, it equals nothing. The equation just doesn't balance. This is what happens when you start having doubts about the things that are Godly. Remember, it is not the size of your faith, but the quality of your faith, even if you only have mustard-seed faith."

Crystal listened intently to what Pastor Jordan was saying. She knew it to be true enough, but still had her doubts about whether she was ever going to have a child. So according to the pastor, this made her own equation of faith equal nothing. She opened her notebook and jotted down other Scriptures as the pastor gave them, each illustrating examples of people in the Bible who demonstrated faith.

When Pastor Jordan asked them to turn to 1 Samuel 1 and 2, Crystal's ears perked up as she read along silently listening to the pastor. "Hannah exercised faith in wanting a child. In this Scripture you'll find that Hannah, the wife of Elkanah, wept year after year because the Lord had closed her womb. She prayed and prayed, even though she had bitterness in her soul. She prayed in her heart and poured out her soul in the Lord. She prayed with faith while having anguish and grief from not having any children.

"One morning the Lord remembered Hannah and in the course of time Hannah conceived and gave birth to her son, Samuel. If you read on, you'll see how Hannah dedicated

Samuel to the Lord. You can also read the prayer she prayed in 1 Samuel 2.

"Hannah had faith while praying year after year. Some of us don't even have faith after praying for a few hours or days. It wasn't the quantity of her faith but the quality. Faith the size of a mustard-seed moving mountains.

"There are other women in the Bible with similar situations like Hannah's, all praying and keeping the faith. Elizabeth in Luke 1, Rachel in Genesis 30, and Sarah in Genesis 18. Even though Sarah laughed at the words from God saying that she would bear a child, God still blessed her well into her years.

"With faith nothing is too hard for God. You just have to believe. You must have confident assurance and believe that you have already received what is rightfully yours," Pastor Jordan preached, his baritone voice booming now. " Believe and keep the faith when you have trials in your life. Many times we see others getting blessed before we do. Do not fret. Remember Matthew 19:30, it says: 'But many that are first shall be last: and the last first.' God is just saving your blessing for last. He is saving the best for last."

Crystal especially took note of the women in the Bible her pastor had spoken about—Hannah, Elizabeth, Rachel, and Sarah; especially Sarah. This message was for her. It had been exactly what she needed to hear. She felt renewed faith.

She closed her notebook and said a prayer thanking God for the sermon. After she finished praying she looked directly at Warren in the choir stand. He was looking at her with a knowing smile. He knew the message had been for her also.

Warren pulled out of the church parking lot and headed for their home. Crystal sat in the passenger seat thinking about the powerful sermon.

"What's on your mind?" he asked.

"I was just thinking about Pastor Jordan's message. I really needed to hear it; it feels like it was especially for me."

"It was a powerful sermon. I got a lot out of it also. I need faith to be able to deal with some of my tenth-graders; faith that God will move in many of those children's lives. So many of them are going down a path that won't lead them anywhere positive."

"You're right. I guess it touched many people in many different ways," Crystal said.

"Yeah, that's the way God works. Different strokes for different folks."

"I'm going to study all the Scriptures before Bible study this week."

"We can study together. Like we used to do," Warren said, placing his hand on hers. "We've been so busy, we haven't studied together in a while. We need to make a conscious effort to start again. This is an area where we can't fall short." Warren said.

He paused for a moment as if choosing his words carefully. "That's not the only subject that needs to be looked at again."

Realizing what he meant, Crystal said, "I know, I'm sorry. I've been pretty quiet the past few weeks and especially since yesterday. I don't do it intentionally. I've just been needing a little time to myself."

"Sweetheart, I know you're going through a lot, but you're not the only one. I am, too. We have to work through this together. I love you, and I don't like to see you in the state you've been in."

"It's not just yesterday. Day in and day out I have questions about what God's plans are for us having children. Sometimes I really think God doesn't think we need any children." Crystal became quiet as tears welled in her eyes.

She turned her head, looking out of her window so that Warren couldn't see. "It's like God sends me daily reminders of our childlessness, and it feels like He's taunting me for some reason. It's really been getting to me lately." She wiped a tear that had fallen.

"I do apologize for making you worry about me and my problems. It's just that I've been trying to work things out myself, emotionally. I also have to remember that you're also affected."

"Do you want to talk about yesterday?"

"Truthfully, not really, but I know I need to. I just... I just don't understand why things happen the way they do. Like for instance, Annette, she's on her third child and she's basically complaining because she is pregnant. Then there is Shanice who can barely take care of Malika. Now she's pregnant with her second child. Why in the world would God bless her like that?"

"I understand what you mean, but what you have to realize is that God does not always do things the way we think they should be done. God does things for His reasons the way He wants and in His season."

She turned back to face her husband. "I know Warren, but Shanice. Come on now, what reason would He possibly have for that?" She shook her head. "I can't understand that one at all."

"Me either, I have to agree, but it's not always for us to understand."

"It's not just yesterday," Crystal continued trying to get her point across. "Day in and day out I have questions about why God blesses some people with children." Crystal got quiet again. Tears continued to well in her eyes. She turned her head again, looking back out of her window.

"What do you mean?" Warren asked, coaxing her to talk.

"All week long I am in contact with children and their parents. Don't get me wrong, I love my job, especially working with the children. You know if I didn't love it so much I wouldn't be trying so hard to open my own center."

"Okay?" Warren asked, trying to understand what she was saying.

Without looking towards Warren, Crystal said, "Day in and day out I look after and take care of other people's children. When their babies are tired, it's me who rocks them to sleep. When toddlers hurt themselves, I'm the one who helps make the pain go away. I often find myself wondering when I'll get a chance to experience those things with my own child. Warren, it's so hard sometimes."

"I know it's got to be hard, honey." He placed his hand on hers and squeezed it. Trying to lighten the subject Warren said, "Why don't we trade jobs? You can work with the hormonal teen-agers, and I'll work with those sweet little timid toddlers."

She turned to him and wiped her tears. "Very funny, don't tempt me; I need a mental break." Crystal said in all seriousness.

"I was just trying to lighten things up a little. Just joking."

Crystal failed to see any humor in her husband's comment and continued to speak, "Then there are some parents who, for the life of me, I can't understand why they do some of the things they do. For instance, some moms will come in looking like they just stepped out of the cover of *Essence Magazine* but their children look as if they have washed and dressed themselves and picked out their own clothes. There is one little boy in particular that I feel so sorry for.

"Don't get me wrong, I have a lot of very good parents. Many of the children come from single-parent households. But there are many I feel should have had to pass a test or something before being blessed with a child.

"That is sad," Warren nodded his head.

"It really is, Warren. Then there are some children who I

can tell don't get any real affection at home. They act as if they don't get hugs of any kind until they come to the center. They thrive on the love and attention we provide. It's sad when I think about them going to their non-affectionate homes."

"You've never really told me this before. Those poor children."

"Then there are those parents who literally don't take care of their responsibilities. Like the two children I have in my three and four year-old classes. It's a sister and brother in foster care. They're so adorable. The foster parent told me their grandmother put them in foster care because she couldn't take care of them any longer. She'd gotten too old. And where are the parents? God only knows."

Warren shook his head.

"Now do you see what I have to go through each day?" she asked. "And the events from yesterday didn't help either."

"Just have faith, Crystal. Like you said, the message today was for you. Use it as a means of encouragement. Pray for the families of the children in your daycare. And I know it can be hard sometimes, but try not to judge anyone. That's God's job, not ours.

"I hate that you think God is taunting you. Honey, He isn't; He loves you too much to do that. Think of it all as a test. We are going through a test, and if we put our faith in God, we can get through this. Just continue to pray and God will give you the strength you need to endure."

"I have been praying," Crystal paused. "And I'll continue to do so."

Warren pulled the car into their driveway.

"You know what?" Crystal said, realizing they didn't have anything to eat for lunch.

"What?"

"All we have to eat is potato salad. I wasn't in the mood to pack food yesterday, and I really hadn't thought about lunch until now."

"So what do you want to do?"

"I don't feel like cooking now either. Unless you want to cook," Crystal offered.

"Not really."

"So what are we gonna to do?"

"Why don't we go to Mama Lula's? I am in the mood for some down-home southern cooking."

"Is she open this early on Sunday?" Crystal looked at her watch. It was almost 11:15 in the morning.

"Mama Lula is open everyday for breakfast, lunch and dinner. By the time we get to the other side of town, she should be serving lunch."

"Sounds like a plan to me," Crystal said.

Warren put the car in reverse, "I think it's a great plan. My mouth is watering thinking about those hot cheese and butter biscuits."

"Let's go then."

"Hi, Mr. Shaw," the young waitress said as she approached Crystal and Warren's table.

Warren looked up from the menu the hostess had given them. "Rose, how are you doing?" Warren smiled at the young lady.

"I'm fine, Mr. Shaw."

"Crystal, dear, this is Rose, one of my former students."

"Hi, Mrs. Shaw." Rose said to Crystal.

"Hello Rose; nice to meet you." Crystal gave the young lady a smile.

"What have you been up to?" Warren asked.

"Nothing much," Rose shrugged. "I've been working here for the past month. It's a whole lot better than the job I had working late nights at the gas station. Now I can spend more time with my little boy."

"How old is he now?"

"Three, he'll be 4 in a couple of weeks though."

"So did you ever get a chance to get your GED?"

"No sir." The waitresses' eyes turned sad. "It's really hard trying to work and go back to school. And it costs a lot to pay a babysitter. Maybe I'll get it one day."

"You should; you were one of my brightest students. I'm sure if you take a little time each day to review the materials, you'll pass the test with flying colors."

The young waitress' face perked up. "You think so?"

Crystal looked up from the menu when Rose's voice perked up. She had to smile at the excitement in the young lady's voice and face.

"I know so," Warren said. "If you need any help or have any questions, you can give me a call. Our number's listed."

The girl's face lit up even more. "Thanks, Mr. Shaw. I am really going to think about it, because Ms. Lula is nice, but this is only a small step up from the gas station."

"You've always wanted to be a lawyer, right?" Warren asked.

"Yeah, I used to," the girl said with doubt in her voice.

"If that's still your dream, then don't let it die. Where there's a will, Rose, there's a way. Always remember that, okay?"

"I will, Mr. Shaw." The girl smiled broadly. "I guess I need to go ahead and take your order; it's not much, but I don't want to lose this job."

Crystal closed her menu. "I think I'll have the fried chicken dinner. For the sides, let me have the collard greens and candied yams. And to drink, I'd like sweet tea."

Rose looked to Warren. "What about you Mr. Shaw?"

Warren shook his head at the choices. "It all looks so good. Let me get the meatloaf with rice. For the other side I think I'll try the okra with stewed tomatoes. And I'll also take an iced tea."

"Will there be anything else?" Rose asked taking both their menus.

"Yes, I'd like some extra lemons for my tea," Crystal added.

"Okay, will do, and I'll be right back with your drinks and basket of biscuits." She took their menus and walked away.

"Maybe I should have gotten the stuffed pork chops instead," Crystal stated, rethinking her decision. "No, I guess not. I don't want to risk the pork giving me a headache."

"Keep eating that pork." Warren said.

"There is nothing wrong with it. My grandmother ate it until she was 105-years-old."

"You know people are still debating her age."

"She was a hundred and *something*, and she ate pork her whole life," Crystal said, defended her grandmother.

"I'll bet she had headaches and a few bad dreams also," Warren replied.

Not wanting to continue the subject of pork, Crystal changed it. "If we're lucky, they'll be pulling our biscuits straight out of the oven."

Crystal looked over at the table next to them. The biscuits in their basket were steaming. She smelled the soulful cooking of Mama Lula's. The restaurant bustled with customers. The walls held pictures of Mama Lula with her family and many of the celebrities that occasionally stopped by the restaurant.

Their waitress returned with the drinks and hot biscuits. "These biscuits just came out of the oven. Do you need anything else?"

"No thanks," Crystal said.

Rose handed them a couple of straws. "Your food should be out soon." Then she turned to disappear back into the kitchen.

Crystal picked up one of the biscuits, broke off a piece, and popped it into her mouth. "Umm, it just melts in my mouth."

Warren did the same, placing a little extra butter on his.

"She's a nice girl." Crystal commented, referring to the waitress.

"She really is. She was always on the A-B honor roll."

"What happened for her to be here working as a waitress?" Crystal wondered out loud.

"She got pregnant in the eleventh-grade. From what I understand, she didn't have any help from her family, so she dropped out of school in her senior year."

"That's terrible." Crystal said.

"It sounds like she's had odd jobs, here and there, trying to support herself and her little boy." Warren took a sip of his tea.

"See, there is another example," Crystal said, continuing the conversation from earlier. "I don't understand why people have children in the first place if they can't help the child when he or she makes a mistake. It's like they want the baby at first but when it hits the terrible twos and the terrible teen years, they forget these children are their responsibility."

"I know what you mean." Warren said.

"It just really makes me mad, Warren. More people who don't deserve the gift that God has given them. It's a parent's job to raise their children. They should care for them physically and emotionally. They need to nurture them. She was in her senior year. They could have at least helped her get her diploma. She won't have many opportunities without it."

"I know. I guess there are a lot of people out there who don't think like we do."

"I guess they don't." Crystal said.

"Don't you have some of those old GED study books at the house? Maybe you could give her a few so she can start studying. At least that way she'll know that someone cares about her education," Crystal suggested.

"That's a good idea. I'll talk to her about it before we leave."

"Speaking of former students, I saw Brandice the other day. She came to pick up her little brother."

"How's she doing?" Warren asked.

"She seems to be fine except for her Algebra II class; she has an F in it but straight A's in all her other classes."

"Brandice with an F. That is hard to believe," Warren said.

"I told her you tutor and to give us a call at home. She doesn't want to ruin her scholarship eligibility with that F. She said she'd speak with her parents first."

"She was my best student in geometry. I don't know why she is having such a hard time in Algebra II."

"I think she'll probably end up calling you. She really doesn't want an F in that class."

"I know she'll be able to grasp it. She probably just needs to focus a little harder. Brandice isn't use to having to study hard. So this class is probably just a challenge, which will be good for her. It'll prepare her for college."

"She'll probably call. She wants help and I am sure her parents will bend over backwards to help their daughter, unlike some parents," Crystal said sarcastically.

After they consumed another biscuit, Rose returned to their table with plates of steaming food. "Do you need anything else?"

"No, we're fine. Thanks," Warren said. "Rose, I've got some GED study books at home. My wife suggested I give them to you. It will enable you to start studying."

"Wow, that would be great." Rose's eyes and eyebrows lifted. Her voice rose an octave. "And you know I'll take care of your books Mr. Shaw."

"I know you will. When do you work again?" he asked her.

"I'm off tomorrow but I work again Tuesday from nine to six."

"I'll drop the books off here after school on Tuesday then. Will that be alright?"

"That would be great. Thank you, Mr. Shaw, and thank you too, Mrs. Shaw."

Crystal smiled. "You are more than welcome." It warmed Crystal's heart to see the smile on the girl's face and hear the joy in her voice.

"And I'll do exactly what you said, Mr. Shaw. I'll make time to study each day," Rose assured him.

"Like I said, Rose, if you need any help let me know. I also tutor students."

"Wow. Thank you so much."

"You are more than welcome."

Tears filled Rose's eyes. She hugged Warren and Crystal.

Tears filled Crystal's eyes too. "Don't cry, Rose, you're going to make me cry."

"Sorry," she wiped her tears with her hands. "It's just that I've been praying to God to be able to go back to school. I pray every day that He'll help me so I can get my GED. Just last night I told God I knew there had to be something better for my life. I don't want to work these odd jobs, never being able to spend any quality time with my son. I want so much for him. If I get my GED, then I know it'll open more doors for me. Then maybe I could be a lawyer one day."

"Yes, Rose, you can. Through Christ you can do all things," Warren said.

Rose was overcome with joy as she smiled with newly sparked hope. "I just can't thank you both enough."

"Don't thank us, thank our mighty Father. You prayed to Him and He is the one answering your prayer. We are just His yielded vessels." Warren said.

"Thank you again. I really better get back to work. Ms. Lula is looking over here." Rose left to take orders at another table.

Warren smiled. "Umph, God is so good."

"Yes He is," Crystal agreed.

He looked down at his plate of food. "We didn't say grace yet, did we?" They held hands, bowed their heads and said grace.

"I wish we could take Mama Lula home with us. I'd never have to cook again," Crystal said after taking a bite of her fried chicken. "Of course after a while I wouldn't be able to move around with all the weight I'd gain!"

"There you go again talking about your weight. What will I hold on to if you lose weight? You'll be skin and bones. As your husband I should have a vote in saying that I happen to like meat on your bones. So what if you put on a couple of pounds in the last few years? You are as beautiful to me as you were the first day I met you. You're my beautiful, milk chocolate queen."

"Stop before you make me blush." Crystal could feel her cheeks getting warm.

"Too late."

"Is it getting hot in here to you?" Crystal waved her neck and face with her napkin.

"No, the air seems to be working just fine. It's probably just you, my hot little mama," Warren said lifting his hand to caress her cheek.

"Whew it is getting hotter by the second." Now Crystal waved her face with both hands to cool down. "Obviously we're going to have to take our dessert with us. I think we've got some business to take care of at home."

"I was thinking the same thing. We can't put our important business off for too long. Let's get a doggy bag for the rest."

As soon as Warren saw Rose emerge from the kitchen again, he called her over, "Rose, can we get containers for our food? And we'd also like to get two pieces of sweet potato pie to go."

"Coming right up Mr. Shaw." Rose returned to the kitchen.

Warren took Crystal's hand in his and kissed it. "I can only give you a kiss on the hand for now. One on the lips in the car, and when we get home I'll give you all my kisses. So I hope the one or two kisses until we get home will hold you."

"I don't have to wait you know. There's a hotel on the way home," Crystal said, grinning with anticipation.

"Yeah, you're right. We could stop," Warren said calling her bluff.

"No, on second thought, you, my king, will have to learn to be patient. You'll have to wait until we get home."

They waited for Rose to return with the boxes for their food and dessert. Then they left a generous tip of ten dollars before paying their bill at the register. On the way out, Crystal thought she saw someone she recognized.

"Shelby?" Crystal said.

The woman waiting at the counter turned around. "Crystal. Hi!"

"Hey, I thought it was you. You look different without your lab coat on. How are you doing?"

"I'm fine."

"Shelby, this is my husband, Warren. Warren, this is Shelby; she's one of the nurses at my doctor's office."

Warren shook Shelby's hand. "Hello, nice to meet you."

"Nice to meet you too," Shelby replied.

"What are you up to today?" Crystal asked.

"I had to run over here and get some broccoli cheese cornbread. My parents are coming over after church for dinner. My dad loves that cornbread."

"I didn't feel like cooking. We came over right after church." Crystal said.

"I should have gone to church this morning. What church do you go to?"

"New Hope. It's off of Yonkers Road," Crystal said.

"Oh, I know where that is. My mom and dad are visiting there today. My mom really loves your church. She's been trying to get me to go for a while. One of these mornings I will."

"When you do decide to come, call me, that way I'll be on the look out for you."

"Okay, I'll do that," Shelby replied, she looked at her watch. "I can't believe you all are out of church already. That means my parents should be at my house at any minute. I'd better get going."

"We went to the eight o'clock a.m. service." Crystal looked at her watch. They probably won't be out of the second service for another thirty minutes or so."

"Good. How many services do you all have?"

"Two. Eight and Eleven o'clock." Crystal said.

"Okay. I'll have to remember that." Shelby looked back at her watch. "Well thanks. It was nice to meet you, Warren. You both take care."

"Nice meeting you too," he waved as he and Crystal headed out of the door.

In their bed Warren held Crystal in his arms stroking her now tangled hair. "It's too bad we haven't been able to spend more time just relaxing in each other's arms like this," Crystal said.

"We've both been so busy. It's been hard lately with the end of grade testing, and the church committees," Warren replied.

"I'm thankful for our Sunday evenings. It helps me to relax before the long week ahead." Crystal snuggled closer to her husband.

"It won't be like this forever. Sooner or later they'll hire someone for the director's position. Then not too long after that your center should be opening."

"I can't believe it's actually going to happen; my dream is finally coming true. And I'm so ready for it to happen. Deep down I do know all things happen in their own season. Especially when I think about how God is working everything out. I guess God just wanted me to get some experience in a center before He blessed me with my own."

"Yeah, that's how you have to look at it. God is about order. When the time is right, and if it's in His will, He'll allow us to do and have the things we want."

"Slowly but surely, I'm starting to understand what that means." Crystal said.

"Think about it honey. First He allowed you to get your degree, then you were able to get hands on experience. And as a bonus, He put you in this director's position so that you'll know the ins and outs of running an entire center."

Crystal nodded. "I hadn't really looked at it like that before."

"And when God sets things up, He always sets them up right. Notice how He timed it so that you're getting experience in the director's position and at the same time you're getting a higher salary. A salary that's right on time, since we've had so many expenses with opening your center."

"I don't know how we would have handled it if we hadn't had the extra money. Not to mention the people who've helped us with monetary donations as well as other things like furniture and equipment. We're going to have to make sure we invite all those people to the grand opening. Especially your parents. They have been a Godsend," Crystal said.

"Don't forget your sister, Marcy. She donated that pick-up truck full of toys and baby things."

"It wasn't a truck full."

"It was so, at least a small pick-up truck full." Warren laughed at her. "They've all been such a big help. I can't believe we've almost depleted all of our savings. I hope we don't have too many more unexpected expenses."

"Don't worry about it, Crystal. Everything will turn out fine. God set all of that up. He has placed people in our lives who love us and are willing to help us in our time of need."

"I'm glad we have most of what we need. The only things left are the refrigerator and dishwasher."

"It's a good thing your mother is donating a refrigerator," Warren said.

"Is there enough room left in the storage unit for it?"

"It's almost full. We might have to store it in our garage. You'll have to remind me to hook the trailer up on the truck so we can bring the refrigerator back next time."

"Clear your calendar for whatever day we go. It will have to be a full day trip. Most of the day will be spent moving junk out and then back in. Mama said it's in the back of her garage. I don't know why she doesn't throw all of that trash away."

"When will the inspector be back to check the building?" Warren asked.

"There's still a great deal of work that needs to be done according to the construction supervisor I've been speaking to. He says an inspection won't be scheduled until everything is complete, probably another three or four months. To tell you the truth, he seems like he doesn't really know what he's doing. I know this one girl who opened a center and it took her almost six months after the projected opening before she passed her inspection. There was a great deal of miscommunication with her construction company and the inspector."

"We'll just have to pray that doesn't happen to us."

"She did say it was worth it in the end though."

"You'll have to keep that in mind. Just in case we do have some sort of set back, remember you just said it yourself, it will all be worth it in the end," Warren reassured her.

"She did start from the ground up. At least we started with a building that we're having renovated."

"You know God's hand was in that too. We were blessed to find out the building was for sale even before the sign even went up. And it's in such a prime location. We won't have any problem filling it with children. You know that was nothing but the workings of God." Warren shook his head in awe. "Man, God is awesome."

"He worked it out perfectly. That old community building already had separate classrooms, bathrooms and a kitchen. Even the study room equipped with a sink was a bonus. As soon as I saw it, I could picture it as the infants' room," Crystal said.

"Like I told you earlier, when it's the right time, God will work it all out so that things just seem to fall into place. In the meantime, we just have to continue praying that things will go well. And by keeping God first, we can't go wrong."

Crystal pulled back from Warren slightly. Her thoughts trailed to her other dream. "At least one of my dreams is coming true."

The telephone rang. "I'll get it." Warren pulled the cover off and slipped out of the bed.

Crystal thought about her last statement. Tears welled in her eyes. She slid out of the bed quickly heading for the bathroom. By the time she reached the mirror the tears were streaming down her face—just as they had so many times before in the previous weeks. She couldn't help thinking about the news segment she saw about the biological clock. It talked about women over 30 and their decreasing chances for conceiving—Crystal was now 33.

The closer she came to her dream of opening her own center, the more depressed she became about not having her own children. It wasn't like she could just snap her fingers and say, "Today the daycare is open and in nine months, I'll have my baby." The realization was hitting her hard.

Warren tapped on the open bathroom door. "Crystal?"

Crystal saw him through the mirror. She turned and faced him while wiping the ever-flowing tears from her face.

"What's wrong? You were fine just a few minutes ago. You want to talk?" he asked with slight apprehension.

"Yeah," Crystal said. Her voice was raspy and almost inaudible. She felt like she was on an emotional roller coaster.

He walked over to their bed and motioned for her to sit next to him. She did as he requested. "Come here," Warren said, pulling her even closer. "Don't let the fact that we have not conceived yet get you down. Patience my dear, you've got to have patience and faith."

"How do you know that's what I am crying about?" Crystal chuckled.

"Give me some credit. How long have we known each other? And how long have we been married?" Warren hugged her. "And let me confess something else to you, I've heard you crying before. I just never let you know. I knew in time we'd talk about it. And I am glad we are starting to discuss our feelings. I've seen the look of caring and longing on your face and in your eyes when you see other people with children, especially babies."

"Is it that obvious?" Crystal was embarrassed.

"Only to me because I know you so well. Have faith and everything's going to work out fine. We are good people and we are God's children. He knows the desires in our hearts."

"I am trying hard not to be so depressed and emotional. The message from the pastor today actually helped lift my spirit somewhat."

"Good, I don't like it when you're down. When you're feeling bad I feel bad. I like to see you happy and smiling. You know, like you were when we got home earlier."

Crystal pulled back farther so that she could look into her husband's eyes while she spoke. "You know, Warren, I've been thinking."

"What have you been thinking about?" Warren asked.

"I haven't used contraception in years. You'd think I'd be pregnant by now. Maybe I could have the doctor check me out and see if there are any problems. I know we haven't really talked about it much, but maybe there's a problem."

"Maybe you're right. I think that's a good idea. Why don't you make an appointment with your doctor?"

"Too bad tomorrow is a holiday. I'll call Dr. Evans' office first thing Tuesday morning." Finally Crystal felt they just might get to the bottom of what could be preventing them from having a child.

Chapter 6

Vivian Parker

Vivian pulled her BMW into the lower level garage of their home. It was six o'clock. She had two hours before the dinner celebration with Roland.

As soon as she walked into the house, she pulled out a bottle of water and walked to the laundry room where she changed into her workout clothes. Once she was dressed, she headed to the exercise room for her nightly workout session. Today, she'd focus on cardio and muscle toning.

She clicked the remote turning on the television and VCR. Her exercise tape was ready. Her personal trainer, Clea, was on vacation and had left tapes for Vivian to use. She hit play on the remote. After warming up slowly, she picked up to the fast pace of her personal trainer.

Today she was doing the quad step. It was her favorite routine. Vivian liked the challenge of trying to keep up with her personal trainer. Vivian hoped one day to have a body as sculpted as Clea's. And after two years of training, she wasn't far from it. She completed her muscle toning exercises after her cool down. Once she was finished, Vivian ascended the stairs to her bedroom for a shower.

She was fondest of their master suite with its strategically placed amenities. It was functional as well as beautiful. The television and stereo system were accessible throughout the master bath's mirror. She picked up the remote to turn the television on. The evening news still had a few minutes before it was due to go off.

Vivian especially loved the doorless circular shower, which was big enough for four people, with its three showerheads and stone seats. The design was perfect in every way, and Vivian was proud of the work she'd done.

Once in the shower, she turned on all three showerheads. The steaming water pulsated down her neck and back. It soothed her recently stretched muscles. She closed her eyes, enjoying the water massage. Feeling a hand on her back only a few moments later, she opened her eyes with a smile knowing her husband was ready to join her in the aquatic pleasure.

In their formal dining room Vivian and Roland ate their celebration dinner. "This dinner is good. I guess I was hungrier than I realized."

"Honey, we did expend a great deal of energy in the shower."

"First my workout and then you, no wonder I was so hungry. The cook did an exceptionally good job on dinner." Vivian took another bite of her beef burgundy and sipped her wine.

"These shitake mushrooms are succulent."

"Umm they are. What year is this wine?"

"1908."

"That was a good year for this wine."

"I knew you'd like it," Roland said, shaking his head matter-of-factly.

"I sure wish I didn't have to get up early tomorrow morning. But I can't complain; this week has been hectic but very productive. With all these workouts tonight though, I'll need a little extra rest in the morning."

"So don't get up early. You *are* the boss, you can make your own hours."

Vivian rolled her eyes at her husband. She was a workaholic just like him and she would probably make it to work before he did the next morning.

"I'm just saying, sweetheart, you do have that option."

"Thank you for reminding me, but you know I'll be up bright and early as always. I didn't get this far in life by sleeping in each morning. My grandmother did teach me how not to be slothful."

"And she did an excellent job."

Vivian smiled. "I am looking forward to next week being even more productive as we start the process of adding more members to this family. You remember this house was originally planned for four children. You remember don't you? A certain someone told me about a fictitious friend with a fictitious wife and their four fictitious children."

"Okay, Viv, I get the point. I'll have you know that my friend is very real and so is his wife. They now live in this beautiful home with their son. We just need to complete the rest of the story."

Vivian's eyebrows rose. "Meaning I am supposed to have three children?"

"Unless my math is wrong, yes, that would bring the number to four."

"Roland Parker, one yes, two, a weak maybe. But three, no sir. I'll be 50 before I finish changing diapers."

"I'll help you," he chuckled. "We can do it together."

"I'm not getting any younger you know," Vivian said.

"You could have fooled me earlier in the shower. You look younger and younger each day to me. And your body looks like that of a 20-year-old."

"Thank you sweetheart for all your compliments, but your

sweet talk will not get three babies from this twenty-something-looking body."

"We'll see about that won't we? You never know, fate might work it out so that you get pregnant with triplets. Bam just like that one, two, three."

"Let me let you in on a little secret," Vivian whispered. "I had a little talk with fate and fate is on my side."

"Okay, okay, you win. I'll leave the triplet scenario alone. I'll be happy if it's just one. I'll be happy with whatever we are blessed with, boy or girl."

"I'm already starting to get a little nervous just thinking about the appointment." Vivian said.

"You'll be fine, don't worry."

"Will you come with me?"

"Of course I will. This is about our having children. I want to be there for everything. Be sure to let my secretary know, so my schedule will be cleared," he said in support.

"I am so excited about having a child. Everything is in place just as I've always wanted; my education, career, marriage and home. And now I'm going to have a baby."

"Don't you mean we're going to have a baby? You said I," Roland asked for clarification.

"I'm sorry. You know what I mean—all those years of hard work to get to where I've wanted to be. And putting myself through school, working all those odd jobs just to scrape by, was hard. I remember all those years of seeing others handed things while I had to make my own way. Many a day I wished I had it as easy as they did.

Then there was all the waiting and watching I did while my friends were getting married and starting their families. But with hard work and determination I've achieved just as much as the others and more. Now I don't have to wait any longer to have children. It feels like a dream come true," she said, closing her eyes.

Roland reached over and pinched her arm.

"Ouch, why'd you pinch me?"

"To let you know you weren't dreaming. This is all real, sweetheart."

"How do you think William will feel about all of this?" Vivian asked.

"He'll be fine, believe me."

"But, Roland, he has been an only child for so long. I know he doesn't remember his mother, so my coming into your lives wasn't very traumatic, but a new child could affect him differently."

"I know he'll be fine. I never told you this, but William has actually asked me if he'll get a little brother or sister. He thinks it'll be cool. He wants to be like his other friends."

Surprised Vivian asked, "Roland, when did he say this?"

"He's said it a couple of times—usually after one of his friends gets a new brother or sister."

"You never told me this."

"I didn't want to tell you until we seriously talked about it. So he'll be fine."

"Good, I can put that worry out of my mind," Vivian smiled. "Did you save room for dessert?"

"I sure did. The dinner was great; how are you going to top it?"

"Believe me I can *top it*. Wait and see. Let's clear these dishes first. I sent the cook and maid home early," Roland informed her. "William called me earlier from his friend's house. He's having a great time and his friend's parents assured me he was in good hands for the night."

"Oooh, I'm scared of you." Vivian snapped her fingers. "What do you have planned for dessert?"

"Wait and see."

When they finished loading the dishwasher, Vivian returned to the dining room table ready for her dessert.

"Why are you sitting there?" Roland asked.

"I'm waiting on this spectacular dessert you have planned. I saved room and I've been waiting all day."

"Oh, I didn't tell you?"

"Tell me what?"

"We're not having dessert in the dining room tonight."

"We're not having dessert?" Vivian asked, frowning with disappointment.

"We are having our dessert. It just won't be in here."

"Where then? I really don't feel like going back out to-night." Vivian looked down at her jogging suit. "I'll have to change into something else."

"Shhh, my darling. Close your eyes. And you have to pro-mise me you'll keep them closed."

"I promise." She did as she was told.

Roland took her hand. "Come with me please." He led her out of the dining room, through the kitchen, family room and past the study towards their bedroom.

"Roland why are we in the bedroom?"

"Did you peek?"

"No. I know this house like the back of my hand. So what's the dessert? You?"

"That will be entirely up to you. If you want me to be your dessert, I can be. Keep your eyes closed."

They walked a little further into their bedroom.

Vivian stopped and sniffed the air. "What's that smell? It smells like something sweet. Like strawberries or cherries."

"You've got sharp instincts." Roland said.

He led her a couple more steps into the room. "You can open your eyes now."

Vivian slowly opened her eyes. She was facing the sitting area of her bedroom. In front of the window stood an ice cream cart with a pink and white canopy. Painted on the side of the cart was a large ice cream cone with multi-colored ice cream scoops.

As she walked closer to the cart she saw the labeled fla-
vors of ice cream. Her favorite, strawberry cheesecake, was
the first label she read. She also saw containers with cherry
vanilla, French vanilla, cookies and cream, and her second
favorite flavor, brownie fudge. Then in the condiment bins
she eyed hot fudge, cherries, strawberries, whipped cream,
nuts, sprinkles, silver balls, hot caramel, raisins, walnuts,
pineapple, and bananas.

"Do you like your surprise?"

"Yes, I love it. I never would've guessed. I can make any
kind of sundae or banana split I want."

"Or you can make a Roland split."

"I most certainly can. You can be my first dessert," Vivian
said, picking up the container with the strawberry cheesecake ice cream.

September 23rd rolled around quickly. Vivian and Roland
arrived thirty minutes early for their appointment with Dr.
Evans. They easily found the building and parked in the first
available parking space.

Vivian nervously stepped out of the car. Roland took her
hand as they walked through the large wooden door leading
to the office.

"May I help you?" one of the receptionists asked.

"We have an appointment this morning. The nurse I spoke
with said to come in a little early to fill out preliminary paperwork," Vivian answered.

"What's your name?"

"Vivian Parker."

"Okay, Mrs. Parker. Please take these." The receptionist
handed her a clipboard with a pen. "I'll need you to fill out
these forms."

Vivian took the clipboard and sat down next to Roland.
After she finished the required paperwork, she returned it
along with her insurance card.

After sitting back down, she whispered, "I don't know why I am so nervous." "I'm a little nervous also," Roland admitted.

"But you look so calm."

"Inside I'm shaking. It's not everyday I get to come to the OB/GYN."

Only a few minutes passed before the nurse called, "Vivian Parker."

Vivian squeezed Roland's hand before standing up to follow the nurse.

"Hello, Mrs. Parker, I'm Shelby, one of the nurse's here. You're here for a pap smear and your family planning consultation, right?"

"Yes, that's correct."

"The first day of your LMP was last Tuesday on the eleventh?"

"Yes."

"And your last pap smear was last year?"

"Thirteen months ago actually."

"Have you ever had a mammogram?" Shelby asked.

"No."

"Alright let me check your vitals."

The nurse checked Vivian's vital signs. "We received a copy of your medical records from your previous doctor. All of your vital signs look good, although your pulse is a little elevated."

"That's probably because I am a little nervous."

"We don't bite around here, don't worry," Shelby teased.

Vivian laughed in spite of herself.

"Let me show you to the exam room." Shelby walked her into the examination room. "You'll need to disrobe. Here are exam capes to drape your top and bottom. Dr. Evans should be in shortly."

"Thank You," Vivian said as the nurse left her to undress.

She was still shaking nervously as she undressed. Looking down at her toes she was glad her manicurist had been able to squeeze her in the day before. The platinum color she had chosen went well with her skin tone.

She removed her clothing, placing everything in a neat pile on a chair in the corner. Then she quickly climbed onto the exam table not wanting the doctor to walk in while she was bare.

After a few minutes the doctor knocked on the door and entered the room. "Hello, Mrs. Parker. I am Dr. Evans. How are you doing this morning?"

"I'm fine. Just a little nervous, that's all."

"Nervous? We don't bite around here?" the doctor chuckled.

"I know, Shelby just told me the very same thing. No, I'm just a little nervous about the family planning part of this appointment."

The doctor's demeanor turned serious. The doctor had ceased smiling. "Yes, I did see the note for family planning."

Vivian watched the doctor as she flipped through the chart and thought, at one point, she had seen the doctor frown. But as quickly as she noticed it, the frown disappeared. It happened so quickly Vivian thought she must have imagined it. Out of nervous habit Vivian fingered the scar on her chin.

Finally looking back up, the doctor said in a pleasant tone, "Alright, Mrs. Parker, let's go ahead and complete your exam and afterwards we can go into my office to discuss some family planning options."

"Okay," Vivian said, wondering why the doctor said the word, "options" when referring to their family planning. She wondered what kind of options she could be talking about. Gradually her nervousness started to fade as she became comfortable. She couldn't put her finger on it, but it was something about the doctor's demeanor.

The doctor examined Vivian's lungs, breast and performed the Pap smear. "Alright, Mrs. Parker, we'll send the cells off for testing. I'll contact you if any abnormalities are found. Your lungs were clear and I didn't detect any lumps in your breasts."

"I do a self breast exam each month. A friend and I have a buddy system so we can remind each other."

"That's really good. A lot of women don't see the importance in doing the self-breast exams. But if you ask any woman who has detected a problem early, they can attest to the importance. I see here you've never had a mammogram." The doctor said, pointing to her medical chart. "I'd like to schedule you for one."

"To tell you the truth doctor, I've heard it hurts and I guess I've been putting it off. I do understand how important it is to have it done."

"Good then, I'll have the nurse schedule you for one before you leave. Please go ahead and get dressed. When you are finished, you can come across the hall to my office so we can discuss family planning options."

Vivian heard the word "options" again and didn't like the sound of it. Each time the doctor said the word, it was as if it had a negative connotation.

"My husband is in the lobby. Can I get him for the consultation?"

"Sure."

"I'll be right across the hall." The doctor left the room.

Vivian gingerly stepped off the exam table, her feet touching the cold floor. The chill from the floor shot through her body. It bothered her that the doctor had frowned a second time when she looked back at Vivian's chart. The second frown she was sure she had seen. The other thing that nagged at her was the nonchalant way the doctor kept mentioning family planning options.

Vivian was relieved Roland came with her for the appointment. Her nervous anticipation had now been replaced with dread because of the doctor's words and actions. The appointment had not gone the way she imagined it would. She had envisioned the doctor examining her, giving her a clean bill of health. Then she was supposed to receive a prescription for prenatal vitamins and the go-ahead to start making a baby.

Instead, the doctor had a fake cheerfulness and kept mentioning family planning options like there was some sort of problem. She wondered if by options the doctor meant which kinds of prenatal vitamin she should take. One of her employees had to try three different kinds before she found one that didn't make her sick.

After dressing, she headed to the lobby to get her husband. He was reading a magazine and hadn't noticed her come out of the door. She took his hand in hers and squeezed it. She pulled him back towards the door not saying a word until they were just inside the entrance.

As if sensing a problem, Roland asked, "Vivian what's wrong?"

"The doctor wants to talk to us about our family planning options."

"Options? What do you mean?"

"I don't know."

"There is only one way to find out. Let's go see." Roland said.

They walked to the doctor's office.

"Come on in Mr. and Mrs. Parker," Dr. Evans said, after seeing them appear in the doorway. She then stood and shook Roland's hand. "Please have a seat." Dr. Evans walked over to the door and closed it behind them.

"I understand you want to discuss your family planning options."

Vivian squeezed Roland's hand even harder. Roland began to speak as she did this. "Yes, we're here to start discussing what type of prenatal care my wife will need. We're ready to have a baby."

"Umm, I see," the doctor said.

"My wife's previous doctor didn't practice obstetrics and referred us to you."

"Mrs. Parker," the doctor said, speaking directly to Vivian. "Did your previous doctor say anything about why he referred you to me?"

"No, not specifically. He said you were good, and if there were any problems, you are one of the best."

"Did he happen say what kind of problems?"

Vivian was slow to answer fearing that something might actually be wrong. Maybe her previous doctor had put something in her chart that was negative and never told her about it. Vivian thought the appointment wasn't going well at all. And for some reason, the doctor wasn't cracking a smile as she spoke.

"No, Dr. Evans. My previous doctor said I was healthy. He didn't mention any problems with our decision to have a baby. He was really quite positive about our decision." Vivian was hoping the doctor would get the hint and stop acting so indifferent. Vivian added, "I did stop taking my birth control pills recently. I know sometimes it takes a while for the hormones to get out of a woman's system. So I expect a short delay there, but I don't see where my husband and I would have any other problems."

Vivian stared at the doctor. She could tell Dr. Evans was trying to form her words carefully.

"Mr. and Mrs. Parker, you may not like what I am about to say, but I'll say it, because I am a doctor who deals in facts."

The doctor paused again and Vivian wasn't sure what the doctor was about to say, but she had a feeling she wasn't going to like whatever came out of her mouth. Roland said nothing as he continued to hold Vivian's hand.

"I'm sorry no one has explained the facts about age and fertility. You are forty years old, soon to be 41; Mr. Parker how old are you?"

"Forty-three," Roland said stiffly.

"To put it simply, your age is working against you. You've heard about the biological clock haven't you?" Even though the doctor asked the question, neither Vivian nor Roland answered. Dr. Evans continued. "The biological clock is very real. Like I just said, I deal in facts. The fact is that your chances of conceiving naturally, with your own eggs, are slim. It's actually less than 8%. If you do conceive at this age the chances of birth defects for a child would also be higher. Studies show that over half the eggs you have at this age, would be chromosomally abnormal. There is also 35% chance of miscarriage. Less than 1% of babies born in the United States are born to women 45 years of age or older."

Vivian and Roland sat in their seats not knowing how to respond to what they were being told.

The doctor continued. "That's what the biological clock really means. I'm just sorry I have to be the first one to give you this information. I wish more doctors would make women aware earlier in their childbearing years.

"Many women don't know that by the age of 27, the decline begins for conception. By age 35 the percentages for conception continue to decrease and the percentages of miscarriage, ectopic pregnancies and chromosomal abnormalities, rapidly increase.

"By no means is it my intention to scare you. But I know you want a child so I must give you all of the facts. Then, I can give you some options, which can help you achieve the goal of having a child. You may be able to have a child that is biologically yours. If that is not possible, there are options to assist you with birthing a child that may not be both of yours biologically."

Roland found the words to speak. "Now hold on, what exactly do you mean?" He was visibly trying to control his building anger.

"Mr. Parker, please calm down. Let me say this, I want you to conceive naturally. However, if that is not possible, through modern technology there are options that can help you conceive a child that would biologically be yours. If that doesn't work, there are still other options in which you can have a child you'll be able to call your own.

"I *am* on your side. Professionally and morally, I must give you all the facts so everyone involved knows what the game plan will be," the doctor assured them.

"I'm sorry," Roland apologized, "I really don't mean to get angry. It's just that we've never heard anything like this before. I've heard of older couples having children. Like that actress, you know the one, Elizabeth Mantanelli. She just had twins."

"Yes, you're correct, Mr. Parker. She did have twins with the help of in-vitro fertilization. She used donor eggs to get pregnant. That's one of the options I want to discuss with you. Many older couples use donor eggs for the woman. Men don't have the same biological clock as women do."

Vivian stared at the doctor, stolid in her seat. Her facial expression frozen in a state of disbelief.

"How long has it been since you stopped taking your birth control pills?" Dr. Evans asked Vivian.

Vivian remained motionless not answering.

Roland answered for her. "It's been six months."

"And for six months, you've had unprotected sex?" the doctor asked blatantly. She was direct and to the point.

"Yes." Roland said.

"I see." The doctor jotted notes in Vivian's chart. "Normally we like to wait at least twelve months with a couple having unprotected sex before we deem them infertile. In your case, because of the age factor, I would really like to go ahead and start trying some of the options I mentioned. I don't want to waste any time.

"Of course first we'll see how viable your eggs are Mrs. Parker and Mr. Parker, we will need to do a semen analysis to see if there are any problems there."

Roland shook his head acknowledging what the doctor was saying. Vivian continued to sit in her motionless state.

"If the egg quality is poor and sperm is fine, then the first option I'll suggest is called Intracytoplasmic Sperm Injection or ICSI as it is called for short. We'd use your eggs and your sperm," she said, looking at each of them respectively as she spoke. "If there are any eggs of good quality we will take a single sperm and literally inject it into an egg. We'll do this for as many good eggs as we can obtain. After a couple of days we'll see how many fertilize and grow into embryos. Then we can transfer one to three of the embryos into your uterus. Hopefully the process will yield at least one full-term pregnancy.

"The second option is donor eggs. This option can be used if we find your eggs are of poor quality. If the sperm is good, we can fertilize donor eggs and place them in your uterus, and then hope for the some results as option one. The thing you have to remember with this option is that the child will biologically be Roland's but legally and emotionally, it will be both of yours."

"So if my wife's eggs are not good and we use someone else's eggs, she can still carry a pregnancy?"

"Yes, Mr. Parker, even if the eggs are not of good quality, your wife's uterus should be able to carry a pregnancy." She continued on. "The third option is adoption. If the other two options don't work for you, I can assist you with finding a child to adopt. You could give a deserving child a good, loving home.

"Those are the options." Dr. Evan's concluded. "Each option entails different sets of circumstances and different amounts of money to make them happen. The ICSI process is the most expensive. One cycle will cost about $15,000.

That is without donor eggs. The adoption would be a lot less costly but has more paperwork and legal issues."

"Dr. Evans, money is *no* object for us," Roland quickly interjected. "Those are the options?"

"Yes, ICSI, donor eggs, or adoption. I know I have given you a lot of information to digest in a short amount of time. Why don't I let you discuss this together before we start anything? Do you have any questions?" Dr. Evans asked.

"No, not at this time. If my wife and I have any questions, we'll call you."

"Please, let me say again, Mr. and Mrs. Parker how sorry I am to have been the bearer of all this obviously unpleasant news. As I said before I deal with facts and I want you to be informed so we can work together for a common goal. I want you to make informed educational decisions."

"Thank you, doctor." Roland said, reluctant to thank her for the bad news.

Dr. Evans handed Roland a handful of pamphlets. "Here are few booklets on IVF procedures and adoption. Please feel free to call me if you have any questions and when you decide what you want to do."

"We'll do that," Roland said, quickly standing up and almost knocking the chair over.

Vivian stood up as Roland did but didn't say anything. She walked out of the office in front of Roland.

In the car, Vivian sat in a slumped position on the passenger side. Roland drove them back to their office. Neither said a word during the entire trip. Once they reached the office parking garage Roland finally spoke. "Vivian, sweetheart, talk to me. I need to know what's on your mind."

He pulled into his reserved space and turned towards his wife. It wasn't until then that he noticed the tears trickling down her cheeks. With alarm he said, "Vivian sweetheart, don't cry. What's wrong? Talk to me."

Vivian wanted to speak but couldn't find the right words. All she could do was shake her head. She didn't know how to put a voice to her feelings so she started sobbing.

"Vivian." Roland attempted to say more but stopped short, not knowing what to say for comfort. Vivian had never shown her weak side to him before. Except for during a sad movie, he had never even seen her cry. He'd only known her to be strong and confident. At a total loss for words, he placed his arms around her, hoping it would somehow comfort her.

After what seemed like an eternity, Vivian finally spoke. "What just happened? I feel like I've had the wind knocked out of me. I don't understand how this morning I was on top of the world ready to have a baby, and now I just feel like I've been hit by a Mack truck. I don't understand." She paused to take in a deep breath. "I should be feeling good right now. We should be on our way to pick up a prescription for prenatal vitamins. Tonight we should be making a baby not discussing options as to why we can't."

"Vivian, don't talk like that."

"You heard the doctor, Roland. I'm too old! My eggs are too old! My biological clock is about to tick midnight," she said sarcastically." I waited too long without even knowing it."

"Vivian, I know you're feeling bad right now, so do I."

"Mother nature is so cruel. It's daylight savings time and the clock has sprung forward without giving me any notice. So, that's it. We can't have our own children. I'll never be able to give you a child." Vivian said.

"Don't say that. The doctor gave us the facts. That's all. She didn't say we couldn't have a child; she just gave us the odds. It's still possible that God could bless us with a child of our own, one we may be able to conceive in the traditional way."

"But you heard the doctor just like I did. The odds are stacked against us. Even if I do get pregnant, there's a risk of miscarriage and birth defects. The chances of having a healthy child of our own are slim to none."

"Look, I think we should take some time and digest all this information. We need to consider all the information the doctor gave us. Then we can talk about it later."

Roland pulled the cell phone out of his suit pocket. "Hello, Renee, this is Mr. Parker. Vivian and I won't be back in this afternoon. Please call Vivian's secretary and let her know also. Thank you."

He restarted the car and drove them both home.

Chapter 7

Shelby Tomlinson

As she drove back to work the next morning, Shelby listened to another inspirational gospel CD. It was a Wednesday, the designated office workday. The office was closed for scheduled appointments.

Shelby arrived twenty minutes earlier than usual for work but, decided to remain in the car listening to inspirational music until it was time to go in. She also took the extra time to pray to God for the right words to say to her boss. She prayed for the strength not break down in tears while discussing her concerns.

At about three minutes to eight she got out of her car and headed into the building.

Just after placing her purse in the file cabinet, Dr. Evans poked her head into Shelby's office. "Shelby, I hoped you were here. I'm ready to talk whenever you are. I promise you'll have my undivided attention. And let's pray there won't be any interruptions this time."

They both went into Dr. Evans office and sat down. Shelby felt weird sitting there again in the chair as a potential infertility patient.

Dr. Evans sat intently, her hands folded, ready to listen to whatever Shelby had to say. "What's on your mind?"

Shelby took a deep breath and sat straight up. Even though she hadn't meant to, she spoke in rushed words, "In a nutshell, my husband and I are ready to have children. Actually, we've been ready and trying for about two years now but I haven't gotten pregnant. Truth is, I feel like it's somehow my fault. Like there must be something wrong with my body."

Putting her hands up in a halt position, Dr. Evans said, "Slow down. Why are you saying it's your fault?"

"I don't know for sure. It's just that I have this feeling, that's all. There must be something wrong with me." Shelby felt the tears well up in her eyes. "Maybe I'm not eating right or maybe there's something wrong with my reproductive system. My husband is so healthy and I just feel like it has to be me. So that's the reason I'm here. I want to find out if you can run some tests to see what my problem is." The tears released from her eyes.

Dr. Evans handed her a tissue.

Shelby dabbed her eyes, then wiped her cheeks and neck. Finally, she laughed. "Sorry, Dr. Evans. I tried my best not to get so emotional."

"It's okay Shelby. The subject is an emotional one. You know I, of all people, know this."

Shelby continued to dab her eyes to keep more tears from streaming down her face. "I'm just glad I was able to finally tell you. So there it is, out in the open. I didn't know what to do next so I came to you."

"Are you saying you want to be seen as an infertility patient?"

Shelby could see the sincere concern in her bosses eyes. "Yes, I guess that's what I'm saying."

"As you know, I classify women as infertile who've actively tried to get pregnant for a year or more; therefore, you would actually fall in the infertility category. There very well may be something going on. But don't jump to any conclusions," Dr. Evans said quickly. "It may be a problem with you or your husband. It may not be a problem with either of you. It may just be timing."

Shelby nodded her head. "After working here so long, I, of all people, should know this. But it is so different when the shoe is on the other foot—my foot to be exact."

"I'll tell you what I can do. Since it would be awkward for you to be seen in this office with me and your co-workers, I'd like to call a nearby infertility specialist I know. His office is in the next building, Suite D. I think that'll be best. And don't worry, he went to school with me, and he's one of the best in the city. Let me call him. I'll explain the situation to him. How does that sound?"

Shelby perked up. "It sounds great!"

"Let me call him right now." Dr. Evans picked up the phone and hit her speed dial. "Hello, this is Dr. Evans. Is Dr. Silva available? Yes I'll hold." She held for a few seconds, tapped her fingers on the desk and smiled warmly. "Hello, Dr. Silva. I'm doing fine. Yes, the kids are fine also. Yes, said he can't wait to beat you in golf again." Dr. Evans laughed. "The reason I am calling is I have a referral. One of my nurses is concerned about her fertility status. She wants to look into reasons why she and her husband have not yet conceived. They've been trying for about two years now."

Shelby listened attentively.

"I wanted to see if you had any slots available in your program. Good, that'll be great. I'll have her do that. Thanks again and I'll tell my husband what you said. Take care. Bye," Dr. Evans said, hanging up the phone.

"It's done. He said for you to call and set up the initial appointment."

"Thank you so much, Dr. Evans," Shelby said jumping up to hug her boss

"You're more than welcome. Like I said, Dr. Silva is one of the best. We graduated together from medical school."

Shelby breathed another sigh of relief. "I really appreciate this. Now I can find out what the problem is. I'll give them a call to get an appointment set up right away," Shelby said, standing to leave.

"Keep me updated on how things go. I'm sure everything will turn out fine. If you have any questions, don't hesitate to ask."

"Thanks. I'll keep you updated," Shelby said and then headed to make the phone call.

After making the appointment, she called Phillip to tell him the good news. The receptionist told her he was in a meeting and would probably be in meetings for most of the day. She decided to wait and tell him in person at home.

The rest of the day went smoothly. She finished all her paperwork, then helped the receptionists file charts and make appointments. Not once did she get depressed about the prenatal patients.

As soon as Phillip walked in from the garage, Shelby lunged from behind the kitchen door and grabbed him, giving a bear hug. "Hey, baby!" She kissed the back of his neck and cheek.

"Whoa, what's going on?" Phillip stumbled forward. "You're in an extremely good mood." He turned and embraced her.

"I've got some really good news. I tried to call you as soon as I finished talking with Dr. Evans, but your receptionist said you would be in meetings all day. So I decided to tell you in person."

Phillip loosened his tie. "Meetings and more meetings—the company is downsizing in some areas." Shelby looked at him with concern. "Don't worry, I'm not going any where. My boss and the company know what an asset I am. My department brings in record-breaking numbers, and it's because of my leadership. They can't afford to lose me and wouldn't dare think of letting me go." Shelby sighed with relief. "So what's the good news?"

"It's done. I made an appointment with Dr. Silva. He's one of Dr. Evans' friends who also specializes in infertility. He's going to run some tests to see what's going on."

"That's great, honey," he said, his voice was void of excitement.

Noticing the lack of enthusiasm, Shelby asked, "Honey is everything alright?"

"Yeah, I just had a hectic day. I'm sorry I don't sound more excited." He looked down into Shelby's eyes. "When's the appointment?"

"It's in three weeks. Dr. Silva's office is close to our office, so it's perfect. I really hope the next three weeks go by quickly." Shelby beamed with excitement.

With a little more enthusiasm Phillip said, "That is really great. Hopefully the doctor can find out what's wrong and put both our minds at ease."

"I feel so much better already just with the appointment being set. But most of all I am happy because you and I are finally talking about all of this. I know everything's going to be fine as long as we continue to communicate." She buried her face into his chest and gave him another tight hug.

"It'll be fine. I promise. We are in this together." Phillip stroked her hair reassuringly.

Shelby looked back up at him. "You do look tired. Why don't you go upstairs and take off those clothes. I'll start the jets in the Jacuzzi. When you come back down I'll be ready to massage those tired muscles of yours," she said, her voice dropping an octave seductively.

"I like that idea," Phillip said, loosening his tie.

"Hurry up now. I'll meet you in the Jacuzzi. I'll be the one wearing my birthday suit."

"You don't have to tell me twice. I'll be back in a minute," Phillip said unbuttoning his shirt.

The next Monday morning, Shelby and Rachel sat in Rachel's office as they spoke. "So . . . don't keep me waiting! Your tan is beautiful. Where did Todd take you?" Shelby asked. Rachel had returned from her surprise trip.

Rachel's face beamed.

"Come on now. Patients will start filing in the lobby at any moment. Where'd you go?"

"It was hot!" Rachel proceeded to fan her face with her left hand.

"You're always hot." Shelby noticed Rachel's left hand and shot straight up in the chair. Her mouth dropped open, and she moved closer to Rachel, and grabbed her hand. "What's this?" Shelby admired the pear-shaped diamond glistening on Rachel's finger.

"He proposed! It was so beautiful. He took me to a resort in Negril. I couldn't believe it. You know how I've always said I wanted to go to Negril. The man remembers everything. The food we ate was all my favorites. Plus our room was accented in my favorite colors. He had even brought my favorite music CDs along for the trip. Everything was planned to a tee!"

"Rachel, I am so happy for you. Todd is such a good man. And I have never seen you happier." Shelby jumped out of her seat and hugged Rachel. They both started crying.

"Shelby, you act as if I said yes."

Shelby pulled away. "You aren't going to tell me you said no, are you?" Shelby looked at her in horror.

"No way. I ain't stupid. God sent me my Prince Charming and I am not going to let him go!"

"I am so happy for you," Shelby smiled and looked closer at Rachel's ring again.

"We came back and immediately told the boys. They were

happy. The oldest one pretty much understands what's going on and I think the four-year-old does too, since their mom recently got remarried."

"Did Todd's ex-wife say anything?"

"I don't know. We told the boys at Todd's house. I haven't seen or talked to her. What can she say?"

"Nothing, but you know how those ex's can be. Whether she is remarried or not you just never know. My best friend, Kara, has a time with her husband's ex-wife. And not to mention the battles they have over visitation and money when it comes to her stepson." Shelby said.

Rachel looked at Shelby with concern. It was the first time she had stopped grinning.

"Rachel, I'm sorry. I didn't mean to put a damper on your good news. Todd is great. Your soon to be step-sons love you; you love them and that's all that matters. I'll help you with any plans you need to make."

Rachel started to smile again. "Thank you, Shelby. I know you didn't mean anything bad."

Shelby hugged her friend again. "Have you set a date yet?"

"Yes. February 11th."

"That only gives us about four and a half months to get ready!" Shelby said.

"I know. It's fine. I don't want anything big. Just close family and friends."

"Just let me know what I need to do, and I'll do it."

"Thank you so much, Shelby. You're such a good friend."

"So are you. And if we don't get to work, we will be good jobless friends. Let's have lunch together, then we can talk more."

"Okay," Rachel replied.

The weeks flew by swiftly, and before Shelby knew it she was sitting in the office of Dr. Jose Silva for her first infertility appointment.

"Hello, Mrs. Tomlinson. I'm Dr. Jose Silva; good to meet you." The doctor spoke with a heavy Spanish accent that reminded her of her college Spanish teacher. He shook Shelby's hand. "Please have a seat on the exam table."

"Thank you," Shelby said, getting up from the chair in the exam room.

"Your GYN records have been sent over. I've had a chance to look at them and your vital signs from today. Everything looks fine so far. You seem to be very healthy."

Shelby smiled nervously. "It seems that way, but I still fear something is wrong since so much time has passed and we haven't conceived yet."

"We'll see. I'll run a battery of tests starting with the simple ones and then moving on. Believe it or not, there are some patients who test well on everything but still don't conceive. Many of my patients have been trying for longer than you and your husband. Sometimes it's really just a matter of timing. Of course I am sure you know more about what I mean than the average person would, since you work with Dr. Evans."

Feeling like she was just the average person, Shelby shifted on the exam table uneasily. "So what happens if you do find something wrong with me?"

"It will depend on the actual findings. It may be something small that can be corrected with surgery, or if needed, the use of some type of assisted reproductive technology."

Shelby listened to the doctor and liked his demeanor. He was warm and friendly, which made her feel more comfortable than she had imagined she would.

"If we don't find anything wrong with your tests, then we will do some tests on your husband. Then we'll see if there is a problem that lies with him." The doctor paused.

Shelby let what the doctor was saying sink in. "Okay so what happens first?"

"I will run a CBC on you. You are familiar with the acronym, right?"

"Yes, of course, a Complete Blood Count."

The doctor chuckled. "I'll have to keep in mind you are a nurse. It's out of habit that I explain everything in layman's terms."

"I understand. I do often work with Dr. Evans' infertility patients. I am most familiar with the BBT charts and their blood work for the CBCs. I'm sure there's a great deal I still don't know."

"Good then, I'll explain everything like I would for any other patient. When it comes to the reproductive system and infertility, unless you are a specialist, there is a lot many people don't know."

Shelby felt very good about the way the visit was going. She knew the decision to come here was one of the best she'd made in a while.

"If you have any questions, don't hesitate to ask."

"Don't worry I won't," Shelby assured him.

"Do you have any questions about what I've said so far?"

"No, none yet."

"Alright, like I said before, we'll do the CBC, which will test your red and white blood cells. It will also test your DHEAS and Prolactin levels. We will also do a Thyroid profile, and test for Chlamydia."

Shelby's eyes grew wide. "I know I don't have Chlamydia."

"Good, but we will test anyway. My tests are thorough, I'll leave no stone unturned along the way."

"Dr. Evans said you were one of the best in your class. Sorry, I didn't mean to interrupt you like that," Shelby apologized. "But I know I don't have any venereal diseases."

"I'm not saying I think you do, but these are the tests I do for everyone," Dr. Silva said.

"I understand."

"Are you taking prenatal vitamins?"

"No. I've been taking an over-the-counter vitamin with extra calcium."

"I want you to start taking the prenatal vitamins. They have the extra folic acid which will help prevent neural tube birth defects. The folic acid is most effective prior to pregnancy. I also want you to start charting your basal temperature." The doctor opened his file cabinet and pulled out a blank BBT chart. "You said you're familiar with the charts?"

"Yes." Shelby said.

"Good, I want you to take your temperature each morning, preferably at the same time. You'll need to take it as *soon* as you wake up, before you start moving around and get up. Start charting on the first day of your next cycle. I want to see if your temperature has the spike around day 15 or if your temp spikes at all during your cycle."

"How long do you want me to do this?"

"I want you to do it for at least two months. I may have you do it for three months depending on how the first two months look. The chart should tell me whether or not you are ovulating. If you're not, I may need to do a Clomid Citrate Challenge test."

"That's a long time," Shelby said with discontent. "I was hoping we could find out pretty quickly what the problem might be.

"You'll find patience will help you during this process. If your problem is simple, there will be no reason to rush into more complex and expensive testing," the doctor explained.

Shelby nodded her head in understanding. "I've guess I've waited this long for answers, I should be able to wait a little longer."

"Yes, be patient. I promise my staff and I will do everything in our power to find out what the problem might be."

Shelby looked down at the blank BBT chart. "So just take my temperature for two cycles, and call you when I'm done?"

"I'll check the results of the blood test and if there are any problems, I'll contact you. If there aren't, then we'll sched-

ule you to come back at the end of the next two cycles.
Make sure you buy a basal temperature thermometer, if you
don't already have one."

"I'll pick up one up this evening."

"I'd also like to do a sonogram now, before you have your
blood drawn. I want to see if I can detect any abnormalities
in your uterus and ovaries."

"Okay," Shelby said, ready for her first, official infertility
exam.

"Go ahead and disrobe from the waist down. I'll be back
in a few minutes."

Shelby took a deep breath; she couldn't believe she was
about to have a sonogram performed. It sounded funny after
assisting with so many sonograms for her patients. She undressed from the waist down and covered her lower half
with the drape sheet.

After a few minutes, Dr. Silva returned. "As I said earlier,
I'll be checking your uterus and ovaries for any abnormalities."

As he proceeded to perform the sonogram, Shelby saw
the ultrasound on the monitor. "Wow, you know it's weird to
finally see my own sonogram, especially since I'm so used to
seeing them with a baby present." She stared at the ultrasound, which was hollow. Her spirit plummeted. "It looks so
empty."

"Don't worry about that. One day, hopefully, we will do a
sonogram and we'll see a baby. That's the goal, right?"

"Right," Shelby sighed.

The doctor continued to perform the exam. "Everything
looks good. I don't see any abnormalities."

"Good," Shelby said with a bit of relief.

"It's a good start. I'll see you in about two months, if there
aren't any problems with your blood work."

Still lying down, Shelby felt awkward. "Thank you Dr.
Silva."

"You can get dressed now. Take care, and we'll see you later."

She sat up and redressed so the nurse could draw her blood for the CBC.

It was four o'clock by the time she finished, time enough to get home before the rush hour traffic began. She decided to stop at the drug store to buy the basal thermometer. Things were starting to look up.

Beep, beep, beep, beep, the thermometer made its high-pitched sound. Shelby pulled it from her mouth. "It's 99.98 humph, at least I know it works," she said to herself as she walked to the bathroom to rinse it off.

"Are you talking to yourself?" The deep sexy voice of her husband came from behind her.

Shelby spun around to see him framing the bedroom doorway. "I guess I was. Don't have me committed."

"I'd never do that," he said, giving her a hug and kiss.

"Good, cause the only thing I am crazy about is you," Shelby admitted.

"The feelings are mutual." He kissed her again. "How'd your appointment go?"

Shelby was slightly surprised that he'd asked about the appointment on his own. He had barely said a word about it in the weeks prior. But she was glad he'd asked, nonetheless. "It was pretty good. I liked Dr. Silva's bedside manner."

Shelby recapped the events of the day, explaining why she had been talking to herself.

"You have to take your temperature every morning for the next two months?"

"At least," Shelby said halfheartedly.

"Better you than me," he joked.

"Keep making wise cracks; if all my tests go well, your turn will be next."

Phillip pulled back suddenly. "My turn for what?"

"Dr. Silva said he would run some tests on you also, especially if all my tests come back good. He doesn't want to leave any stone unturned."

"There is nothing wrong with me," he said adamantly. "I'm healthy, and I can swim like a fish, so I know my little friends can swim like fish too."

"What little friends, Phillip?"

Phillip gestured to show her what he was talking about. "All the little friends that visit us in bed and in the Jacuzzi. They are the same little friends that visited us in the game room last month—the ones that look like tadpoles. Do I need to go on?"

"Oh, those little friends," Shelby said, finally getting the point. "Well, we'll find out, especially if all my tests come back good. They may be swimming in the wrong directions or maybe just treading water. And Lord knows, I hope they're not doing the dead man's float."

"Hey, that's enough," Phillip said defensively. "I assure you, they're all fine."

"Stop being so defensive. Can't I make a joke?"

"I'm not being defensive." Phillip said.

"Yes, you are, and edgy too. If I didn't know any better I'd think you were afraid of being tested."

"Me, scared? Nah."

"Are you scared the doctor is going to—"

Phillip cut her off. "Hold up, stop right now. I don't think the doctor is going to do anything. I'm not scared of any doctors."

"I'll leave you alone. You're too edgy for me. You asked me how the appointment went, and I was just telling you. I'm just trying to keep you updated to keep our lines of communication open."

"And I thank you for that. I just don't need graphic details on what the doctor will want to do to me." Phillip pulled away completely. He turned on the water faucet and splashed his face with the cold water.

"Sorry, I didn't know you'd be so squeamish."

He pulled a hand towel off the rack and dried his face. "I'm not squeamish, Shelby."

"I hope you're not, because when it's time for me to go into labor, I won't need you passing out on me."

Phillip poked his chest out and hit it with his fists. "Don't you worry your pretty little mind about that. I'll be just fine."

He turned to look in the refrigerator. "What's for dinner?"

Shelby noticed how quickly he'd changed the subject and decided she'd let it go. "I hadn't thought about it. We could order a pizza."

He quickly closed the door and said, "That'll work. I'm going to go out to the garage and strip the rest of the paint off the old Chevy. Let me know when the pizza gets here."

"Didn't you just strip the paint off last week?"

Phillip stuttered, "Uh yeah, that's right. I do need to check on which engine parts I'll need to order."

"Okay, whatever," Shelby said, shrugging her shoulders. "I'll order it when you are about finished."

"That's fine," Phillip said and left hurriedly to change out of his suit.

After Phillip was gone, Shelby stared out of the kitchen window thinking about his reactions. Now she was pretty sure she knew why he had been so distant—he was scared of seeing a doctor. It actually seemed like he had some type of phobia. She giggled to herself thinking about how cute it was. He was doing a poor job of covering up his fears.

She had finally found something her Mr. Macho was afraid of. She hoped in the end that he wouldn't need to see the doctor. And if he did end up having to be tested, she'd have to pray he'd be able to get through it. She could only pray for the best.

*   *   *

Outside in his detached garage, Phillip sat on a lawn chair and tried to collect his thoughts. He had done his best to keep his composure while talking to Shelby a few minutes prior. Deep down, all he really wanted to do was scream. He wanted to scream out the fact that it was his fault that they couldn't have children. He knew it deep down. God was punishing him in his marriage for his shameful, sinful past. It was a past full of partying, drinking and a long trail of women. Over the years he'd kept these secrets from Shelby because he was ashamed of the way he'd acted during his college years—before he met her.

Before his leg injury, Phillip had been one of the biggest players on campus. Not just a football player but also a player of women and their emotions. He had a girl in just about every one of the dorms on campus. This was in addition to his still dating his high school sweetheart, who still lived in his hometown of Raleigh.

He had always been good at keeping secrets from all of his women. Most of them never knew about the others and most times he used football as an excuse for his secret getaways. Whenever one girlfriend would find out about another, he'd just drop her and pick up another one to take her place.

He was also ashamed because there were times when he hadn't used any protection during sex. He gauged using protection with a girl by her background and hygiene status. His system worked, not having caught any diseases during his promiscuous reign. He had also been lucky enough to only have gotten one girl pregnant during this time.

Jeana had been one of his freshman conquests. As soon as he found out about the pregnancy, he told her she'd have to terminate it. He gave her enough money and told her to take care of it. He had only seen her once after giving her the money for the procedure. Later a friend told him Jeana had dropped out of school.

Jeana's pregnancy had been the only close call he had, and he felt fortunate. But now he felt his fortune had run out. Phillip knew God had to be punishing him for his promiscuous lifestyle.

Now he was sorry for the way he acted in the past but knew there was no way for him to change it. It haunted him daily, especially when he looked at the longing in his wife's eyes to have a child. He knew he'd have to come clean with her. He needed to tell her that his past irresponsibility was the reason for them not being able to have a child.

He sat in the garage for almost an hour, trying to figure out a way to tell her. He loved her so much and was afraid once the truth came out, he might lose her.

Phillip didn't have to worry about what would happen if it came down to him having to have tests run, because he knew the tests would come back good. He had never tested positive for any sexually transmitted diseases, plus he knew he could father a child, because he had already done so in the past.

Trepidation over came him as he thought about the next couple of months. In the end, he hoped Shelby would understand and forgive him for holding such important information from her. He could only hope.

"Are you about ready for Thanksgiving?" Rachel asked Shelby as they finished with two of their patients.

"As ready as I am ever going to get. We are going to my Mom and Dad's. How about you?"

"Pray for me. I am cooking for Todd and the kids. It'll be my first time, especially with the turkey." Rachel looked glum.

"Don't look so grim. What else are you planning to have with dinner?"

"Stuffing, gravy of course, umm, corn, cranberry sauce, rice," Rachel paused thinking for a moment, "and rolls."

"That doesn't sound so bad. But you do have a lot of starchy foods on the menu."

"You think so?"

"Yeah." Shelby said.

"You got any suggestions?"

"How about instead of corn you do some green beans. There is a brand called Glory green beans which are already seasoned, all you really have to do is heat them up."

"Thanks, good idea."

"What about dessert?" Rachel asked.

"I hadn't thought that far."

"Why don't you go over to the Cheesecake Factory at South Point Mall in Durham. You could get some cheesecake or a regular cake, then you won't have to cook a dessert."

"Great idea! Thanks, Shelby."

"No problem. It'll turn out fine. Oh yeah, get one of those turkeys with the thermometer already in it, that way you can better gauge when it is completely done," Shelby said, but noticed Rachel was looking behind her at someone. Shelby turned her head back and saw one of the patients who had been in a couple of months prior. She turned back to Rachel. "Earth to Rachel. What's up?"

Rachel's attention returned to Shelby. "I thought that was the lady who was in here a couple of months ago."

"She does look familiar."

"She looks like the one who almost knocked me down when she and her husband left." Rachel thought for a moment. "Vivian something."

"Parker," Shelby said. "I called her to set up the initial appointment. That lady could pass for her twin."

"Yeah, she and her husband left out of here like there was a fire or something. I checked on Dr. Evans after they left to make sure everything was okay."

"What happened?" Shelby asked with concern.

"She got upset when they discussed trying to get pregnant. The couple hadn't liked the information Dr. Evans gave them about infertility relating to age." Rachel shook her head. "From the look on their faces, I was pretty sure we'd never see them again. That's why I was so surprised at first. But it isn't her."

Shelby looked back at the woman who bore a striking resemblance to Vivian Parker. She had remembered Mrs. Parker coming in and how excitedly nervous she was about wanting to have children. Shelby knew her age was a factor before the woman even stepped into the office. She had not been the first woman to find out late that her age might prevent her from having children naturally.

Shelby shook her head. Mrs. Vivian Parker was now a member of the secret sisterhood.

Chapter 8

Crystal Shaw

"Mr. and Mrs. Shaw, do you have any questions?" Dr. Evans asked.

"No, not really. You've answered all of our questions so far," Crystal said.

The phone in Dr. Evans' office rang. "Hold on just a second please," Dr. Evans said.

Crystal and Warren were sitting in Dr. Evans' office for their second infertility appointment. Crystal had been there once before to have a few tests done. For this appointment, Warren joined her.

Crystal had been blessed to get her first appointment as quickly as she did. Someone had canceled just before she called. Things were moving quickly, and it was all exciting.

Dr. Evans hung up, completing her call. "Sorry about that. Normally I have them hold my calls, but I was expecting that one. Good, now where were we? Oh yes, I've already ordered the semen analysis and other tests for you, Mr. Shaw. I'm just waiting on the results from your Clomid Challenge, Mrs. Shaw. Once I get those in, we'll take it from there."

"Thank you, Dr. Evans," Crystal said with a beaming smile.

"You're welcome. I'm glad when my GYN patients come in with the news that they are ready to have a child."

"We figured it was time for us to get some professional help," Warren said.

"You're in the right place for that. We'll see how all the test results turn out. If there are no problems, there are a few other tests I'd like to run."

"Sounds good to us," Crystal said, looking at Warren.

Nodding his head in agreement, Warren said, "Yes, that'll be fine with us."

"Don't lose any sleep over these tests, alright? As soon as I get all the results, I'll call you to see where we stand."

"I do have one question," Crystal said. "Are all the tests you are running included under my insurance?"

"Yes, all you have to do is pay the co-pay. These are the basic tests to rule out infertility. Most insurance companies cover these tests."

Happy for the reassurance, Crystal said, "I thought so, but I just wanted to make sure."

"It is good your insurance covers them because the tests and the lab work you had done today alone, would have cost you about two-thousand dollars without insurance."

"Wow, that is a blessing to only have to pay a co-payment of thirty dollars," Warren said.

"Being infertile can be very costly," Crystal said.

The doctor nodded her head in agreement. "Did you have any other questions?" she asked.

"No, we are just glad that we were finally able to get in here and get all of this testing started," Crystal uttered.

"Okay then. That's it for me today; you'll be hearing from me in a week or so," Dr. Evans said and stood up to shake Warren's hand. "It was really nice to finally meet you, Mr. Shaw. Crystal has been coming to this office for years."

"It was nice to meet you also. I just wish it had been under different circumstances. But God knows what He's doing. He has got a plan. We just have to follow it," Warren said.

Dr. Evans agreed. "Amen to that. You both take care and I'll talk with you soon."

"Thank you again, Dr. Evans," Crystal said before they left the office.

As Crystal stopped at the reception area to pay her co-pay, she heard her name being called. She looked up. It was Shelby. "Shelby, hi, I was looking for you when I came in but I didn't see you."

"I know, I had a doctor's appointment of my own. How are things going?" Shelby said.

"Pretty good. I think we're making some progress." Crystal said.

"That's good."

"We'll be back after our test results come in."

"Good. I'll see you then." Shelby said.

"Don't forget, the invitation for church is still open."

"I haven't forgotten. I am going to come, I promise. I still have your number."

"I'll see you later," Crystal said and soon joined Warren in the car.

"I feel so much better about this whole situation already," Warren said.

"I feel pretty good too."

"Things are working out so well. Can you believe those tests would've been almost two-thousand dollars?" Warren asked in amazement. "It's a blessing we didn't have to pay that much. God is so good."

"I guess He knows we couldn't afford that right now." Crystal said.

"Of course He knows. He knows all of our wants and needs, even though at times we may not understand what's in His plan. But I don't know if we would've ever been able to afford that kind of money."

"I just really have a good feeling. This must be the track God wants us to follow," Crystal said. She had renewed optimism.

"You're probably right, honey."

"It's just got to be, with everything I've been through emotionally; He must be giving me a break."

"God won't put anymore on us than we can handle," Warren said.

"He knew I couldn't handle much more. I felt like giving up so many times—even started getting to the point where I thought I was going to have a nervous break down," Crystal said, revealing more of her feelings.

"I didn't realize it had gotten that bad for you. Why didn't you tell me this before?"

"I didn't want you to be worried."

"What are you talking about?" Warren asked.

"I just didn't want to worry you."

"If you're upset or depressed, you shouldn't have to go through it alone. I just need to know what's on your mind so I can give you encouragement. We need to talk about things together, especially the things bothering us. That's what I'm here for."

"I know and I'm sorry. But I think I'm fine now. Like I said, there's a feeling of renewed hope in my spirit. I have a really good feeling about our appointment today. I know everything is going to be just fine," Crystal said with a smile that was genuine.

"It will, honey. You just have to have faith and trust in the Lord."

Crystal stepped into the dining room. "Warren honey, I'm sorry to disturb your tutoring session, but do you know where the dust pan is?"

"Sorry, honey, it's out in the shed. I was using it when I cleaned it out yesterday. I'll get it for you," Warren said and stood up. "Brandice, I'll be right back," Warren told the student he was tutoring.

"Hi, Brandice," Crystal said to the teen.

"Hi, Mrs. Shaw." Her voice was dull. "How are you?"

"I'm fine. It's been a while since you've come to pick your brother up from the daycare," Crystal said, trying to make small talk. Brandice was normally happy and bubbly, but not tonight. She was sullen and quiet—that beautiful smile of hers was nowhere to be found.

"I'll be glad when I can get a car of my own. I don't usually pick him up unless my mom lets me drive the car for the day." She spoke the words, but her tone was indifferent.

Trying to change the subject to something that might interest her, Crystal said, "Are you ready for the big game with the Tigers this Friday?"

"Yeah, my boyfriend, Antwan, says it'll be an easy win. I hope so. They beat us the last three years," Brandice said with little more enthusiasm. "I'd like to see them win before I graduate from Silvermont."

"The game against the Silvermont Stallions and the James Kenan Tigers is always such a big event. I remember when they first moved it over to Carson State University because of the crowds," Crystal said.

Warren returned with the dustpan. "Sorry, honey. Here you go."

"Thanks. I'll let you all get back to your session," Crystal said.

"We're actually about done. Oh yeah, if Deacon Cooper calls, please let me know. He's supposed to call me tonight."

"Okay," Crystal said returning to the kitchen to sweep. After she finished emptying the dustpan, the telephone rang.

"Warren, telephone." Crystal walked back into the dining room and handed him the cordless phone.

"Hello? Oh yes, it's all been settled. Great. So Deacon Green will be there to unlock the doors. Hold on just a second," Warren said, putting his hand over the receiver. "Brandice, I'll see you next week. I need to finish this call."

"Okay Mr. Shaw," Brandice replied. With that, Warren left the dining room.

"So how did your session go?" Crystal asked Brandice.

"Good." The girl spoke absentmindedly, her eyes not meeting Crystal's. "It was good."

"Would you like some pie? I've got lemon pie in the kitchen."

The girl's face contorted into a grimace. "No thank you. I think I'll pass."

"If you don't like lemon pie, then we've got some peanut butter cookies."

The girl's face contorted more. "No, no thanks I'm not hungry." She looked up quickly saying, "May I use your bathroom?"

"Of course, you know you can," Crystal said, but before she could finish, Brandice was already moving.

This wasn't the first time Crystal noticed the strange behavior in the teen. It wasn't anything Crystal could put her finger on, but she had a nagging feeling something was very wrong. In the beginning she thought it might have been the Algebra class pre-occupying Brandice's thoughts. But she knew Brandice was one of Warren's best students and normally liked to tackle hard math problems head on. Then she thought it might be troubles with Brandice's boyfriend until she realized the girl's actions seemed different than mere heartache. Crystal hoped sooner or later Brandice would find resolution to whatever was bothering her.

Returning to the kitchen from the dining room, Crystal cut a piece of pie. She sat at the kitchen table and picked up the newspaper. She read an article about the birth of triplets in the local section of the paper. She had just completed the article when she heard what sounded like gagging sounds coming from the bathroom.

Putting the paper down, she wondered if her mind was playing tricks on her. Listening harder, she heard the sound again and walked toward the bathroom.

Concerned, she tapped lightly on the door. "Brandice? Are you okay?" She listened at the door and heard sniffing and soft crying. "Brandice, what's wrong? Are you okay, sweetheart?" She waited for a reply but heard nothing. Everything was still for a few moments. Trying again Crystal said, "Brandice, I need to know if you're alright. Did you hurt yourself?"

Crystal listened, but no sounds came from behind the bathroom door. The house became so quiet that she could hear the kitchen clock ticking. Then, after what seemed like an eternity, Brandice finally said, "No, I'm fine. I'll be out in a few minutes."

"Alright," Crystal sighed with some relief. "I just wanted to make sure." Glad Brandice had finally spoke, Crystal took a deep breath and returned to the kitchen to wait for the teenager to come out.

After a few minutes, Brandice crept around the corner of the kitchen to join Crystal. Head held down, the teenager rubbed her stomach with one hand. Crystal saw dried tear tracks on her cheeks.

"Come on in, Brandice. Have a seat." Crystal pulled a chair out from the kitchen table, and Brandice slowly slid down into it. "Are you sure everything is alright? Do you want to talk about what's bothering you?" Crystal asked with trepidation.

"No, Mrs. Shaw. I just have a lot on my mind right now. I'll be fine. I must have eaten something earlier that disagreed with my stomach. I feel a little better now." She fiddled with the zipper on her jacket, still not meeting Crystal's eyes.

Crystal got the feeling Brandice was trying very hard to be

convincing—not only to Crystal, but also to herself. "I understand," Crystal said, not wanting to close the door for the possibility of communication at a later time. "Brandice, I just want you to know if there's anything you need to talk about, big or small, I'm here to be a listening ear. Okay?"

"Okay. I'll remember that."

"Let me get a washcloth so you can wipe your face. Your mom will be here soon. I don't want her thinking my husband tried to beat the math into your head," Crystal said, trying to get Brandice to laugh a little.

"Thanks, Mrs. Shaw." Brandice finally looked up, offering a slight smile at the joke.

Relieved, Crystal said, "Hurry up, before your mother gets here."

By the time Brandice left to go home, Crystal had formed a number of questions in her mind, trying to figure out what was really bothering the girl.

Brandice was a beautiful girl inside and out. She came from a very good home with two parents who loved her very much. She was a straight A student and her boyfriend was the quarterback of the high school football team. Crystal knew the girl had so many wonderful things going for her. She didn't think trouble with one class would be enough to have upset Brandice to this degree.

Crystal sat at her kitchen table sipping her now lukewarm coffee. She didn't realize how much time had passed until Warren came in to ask if she was coming to bed. She didn't hear him the first time he spoke.

"What's on your mind?" he asked.

"Huh?" she said.

"I said what's on your mind? You look pretty dazed sitting there."

"Oh, I was just thinking." She didn't know if she should voice her concerns about Brandice.

"What are you thinking about?" he asked.

"Brandice just doesn't seem like herself lately. I'm concerned with the way she's been acting." She wasn't sure whether she should tell him about the crying episode or not.

"Don't worry about it, honey. She's probably just concerned about her class. Worried she won't get a full understanding, but she will. She's a very smart girl who, like I said before, never really had to deal with these types of problems in math."

"I know but . . ."

Warren gently cut Crystal off, "Honey, don't worry about her. I promise everything will turn out fine. Now we've had this conversation before, and I know it's not happening overnight, but everything will turn out fine. She will pass her class with flying colors."

"Okay, I hear you, but at least hear me out on this."

Warren leaned against the kitchen door-frame, patiently waiting for her to continue.

"She seemed the same way the last time she came to pick her brother up. She used to be so talkative. Lately she barely says a word. Her glow seems to have faded. Warren, I really think something is going on with her. And I don't think it has to do with just her grades." Pausing for a moment, Crystal spoke her next words carefully. "And she was crying earlier in the bathroom."

"Oh honey, you know how emotional young teenagers can get. She might've been crying because she passed the pop quiz I gave her."

"That's not the feeling I got. Tears of joy come with a smile not a sad frown," Crystal countered.

She was trying to get Warren to understand her point. But after talking with him for a few more minutes, she realized her efforts were futile. Her neck was tense, her eyes were getting heavy, and she was drained from her hard day at work. She was losing the strength to continue the conversation.

"Crystal, I'm tired. Can we talk about this tomorrow?" Warren asked.

"Yeah, that's fine. I'm tired, too and ready to get some sleep."

They retreated to the bedroom and prepared for bed.

"Do you want me say the prayer or do you want to?" Warren yawned.

Even though Crystal was tired she replied, "I'll say it."

They kneeled down on the side of the bed, held hands, and bowed their heads.

"Dear Heavenly Father we come to You this night in prayer, once again to thank You for allowing us to see another day blessed by You."

"Yes, Father," Warren said in agreement.

"Father we thank and praise You for the awesome miracles You perform on a daily basis. We thank You so much, Lord."

"You're so awesome, Father," Warren said echoing Crystal.

"Father we pray that You will continue to give us grace and mercy, as two of your children coming humbly in prayer."

"Yes, Lord."

"Father, we also come to You in prayer for our family and friends. Bless them all, Father. We pray that You will take care of all the children who are neglected and abused. We especially pray for the children in the center. Cover them with Your blood, Lord Jesus."

"Cover them Lord." Warren said.

"Father, we pray that our family members and friends who don't know You will come to know You soon and that You'll have us be an instrument in their salvation. We yield ourselves to You Lord. Use us as you need, as tools in the building of Your Kingdom." Crystal prayed.

"Use us, Lord." Warren said.

"Lord, I have a special request tonight. I want to make this request because there are some heavy feelings on my heart, Lord. I pray that You will give Brandice guidance in whatever she is going through. Lord, I feel she really needs You right now. Speak to her, Lord. Let her know You are there for her always." Warren squeezed Crystal's hand in agreement. "Thank you again, Lord, for allowing us the opportunity to come to You together in prayer. We thank and praise You. In Jesus' name, amen."

"Amen," Warren repeated.

Crystal awoke, sweat pouring down her face. She'd had the nightmare again. The clock on her nightstand read two o'clock in the morning. She slipped out of bed, padded her way to the bathroom in the dark closing the door before turning on the light. The sudden brightness caused her to quickly shut her eyes.

In the mirror, she looked at the bags under her eyes. The nightmares haunted her night after night. She feared they wouldn't cease until she had a child. She splashed cold water on her face, dabbed it dry with a hand towel and returned to bed.

She flipped her pillow over to the dry side, placed her head back down, closed her eyes tight, and willed the dreams to stop. Crystal fell back into a fitful sleep.

"Crystal, welcome back. I have some good news and bad news," Dr. Evans told her.

Crystal was back in the doctor's office to find out the test results from a few weeks earlier. She and Warren had gone through a battery of tests in hopes to find out what their problem might be for not conceiving.

Crystal didn't know what she wanted to hear first. She shifted with nervous anticipation. "Good and bad news?"

"Well, actually, it's the same news, it just depends on how you look at it."

Crystal raised her eyebrows. "Okay?"

"Okay, let me explain. Over the past few weeks you and your husband have undergone various tests to find out what kind of problems you might be having in conceiving. So far, the tests show your ovaries are fine. The HSG test revealed that your fallopian tubes are clear. There are no abnormal growths in your uterus. Your cycles are steady, and your levels show that you are indeed ovulating on the typical day fourteen. The analysis for your husband doesn't show any abnormalities. The same goes for all of his other tests."

"Sounds like good news to me," Crystal said, feeling a little relief.

"Yes. Overall it is very good news. And I'm glad you're looking at it that way."

"So how can it be considered bad?" Crystal wondered.

"According to the tests neither one of you has any problems, if that is so, then you should have already conceived by now. But for some unexplained reason you haven't."

"So what you're saying is that there is no reason at all, for me not to have gotten pregnant by now?" Crystal asked making sure she understood what the doctor was saying.

"Bingo. What you and your husband are going through is what we call 'unexplained infertility'."

"Unexplained?"

"Yes. For some reason, even though physically you are both fine, a pregnancy hasn't occurred. It could be something that hasn't been detected in the usual tests. Or it could be stress, heat sensitivity to your husband's scrotal area, or even timing."

"Timing?"

"Yes, timing. Even though you ovulate on day fourteen, if

the elements of conception are not set forth in the right place at the time of ovulation, then a pregnancy will not occur.

"Believe it or not, even couples without health problems, still only stand a 25% chance of becoming pregnant during each cycle."

"Stress can be a factor also?" Crystal asked.

"Yes, stress can affect our health in many different ways."

"So some or all of those factors could be reasons why we haven't conceived?" Crystal asked again for further clarification.

"Yes. As far as the tests are concerned, neither you or your husband have any medical problems. I'm not sure why you haven't gotten pregnant after all these years," Dr. Evans said.

"I guess I still need to look at it as positive news. I've been pretty stressed lately but not for the whole past five years. And I'm not really sure about the timing part. I haven't paid attention to the dates in my cycle."

Dr. Evans added, "Considering how long you have been trying, you could get pregnant next month or maybe not until three or more years from now."

"Or never?" Crystal looked at the doctor in frustration. The realization of what the doctor was saying had sunk in, her head started to hurt. "So what are we supposed to do, Dr. Evans? Are we just supposed to wait patiently? Am I supposed to wait every twenty-eight days to be let down each month for years to come? Finding for some *unexplained* reason, we won't be able to have any children?" Crystal grew more and more upset with each question she asked.

"Crystal, I understand what you're . . ."

Crystal cut the doctor off. "Are you sure you understand? Have you been in my shoes?" The more she spoke, the higher her voice became.

"No, Crystal, I can't say that I have," the doctor said, looking at her with obvious concern.

Crystal took a deep breath and counted to ten in her head in order to calm down. "Look, I'm sorry. I really don't mean to get so upset and raise my voice. I'm not mad at you. I'm just so frustrated. For five years we've been trying to conceive. Since I was a little girl, I've known that I wanted to be a mommy. Each month for the past five years, I have been so hopeful. But lately it doesn't even faze me when my cycle rolls around."

Dr. Evans looked at her. Crystal could see the sympathy in the doctor's eyes. But for Crystal, sympathy wasn't enough. She felt the frustration from the previous weeks returning. She wanted to lash out at someone. She wanted to run away and be alone so she could cry.

"Dr. Evans, do you know what I do for a living?" Crystal continued without waiting for an answer. "I work at a daycare center. My husband and I are in the process of opening our own center. Do you know how hard it is for me to go to work with all those beautiful children? Helping them learn? Nurturing them? I give so much of my love to all of those children. Other people's children get the abundance of love I am unable to give to my own child. It's so frustrating, and it hurts me so much."

She paused, tears welling up in her eyes. Dr. Evans handed her a tissue. Crystal rubbed the tears off her cheeks.

"It's been so hard. I've tried to be optimistic, and I've tried having faith. Seeking professional help was like the last straw. Now it seems as if we've hit a dead end."

She stopped again to wipe the tears, which quickly escaped her eyes. "So even though I do see our news as being good overall, it would have been better if there was a reason. I thought coming to an infertility specialist would be the answer to all of my prayers, but now it feels like I am back to square one. And it makes me feel so helpless." Crystal ended up sobbing in front of the doctor, not really caring that the woman saw.

When Crystal's sobbing let up, Dr. Evans said, "I am so sorry you feel the way you do. I don't know exactly what you're going through, but I'm here to listen. Sometimes talking to someone can help get us through.

"I do want you to know that as an infertility specialist, I will do all I can in my power to help you and your husband conceive," Dr. Evans assured her.

"But you already said all the tests came back stating we were healthy. There is no reason for our infertility."

"That's right. And you could still get pregnant naturally."

"Which takes me back to the waiting game—the game I lose horribly every month," Crystal said with dejection.

"There are some things that can be done to help you medically."

"More tests?" Crystal asked unenthusiastically.

"No. No more tests. Since all of the tests came back saying you are both healthy, it can be to your advantage."

"In what way?" Crystal asked with doubt.

"Your eggs and uterus are fine, and so is your husband's sperm."

"Okay so?"

"With these factors in your favor, you and your husband would be very good candidates for IVF."

"IVF?" Crystal asked, vaguely familiar with the medical term.

"Yes, in-vitro fertilization. In short, it is the process in which we extract some of your eggs and mix them with your husband's sperm. Hopefully, the process will produce an embryo. If an embryo or embryo's form then I can place them into your uterus, and after a couple of weeks, we would do a pregnancy test to see if you are pregnant."

"Do you think something like that would work for us?" Crystal asked with a sliver of hope.

"Yes it could work, but you still have to keep in mind there is always the chance that you'll get pregnant on your own. But of course, no one knows the future."

"I know, but there is still a chance that we may never conceive naturally for some unexplained reason," Crystal said. Her voice sounded facetious, even though she hadn't meant it.

"I just wanted to reiterate that IVF is an option. It would be a risk. I must also tell you that with the IVF procedure, you could become pregnant with twins or even triplets. The chance for the possibility of multiples increases due to the possible effects of the fertility medication."

"Fertility medication. What fertility medication?"

"I gave you the short version of the process a moment ago. In order to extract more than one egg, we will need to give you medication to stimulate your ovaries, thus making you release more than one egg. The process can be costly and we want as many usable eggs as we can extract the first time."

"It really isn't an easy solution is it?" Crystal asked.

"It is a solution, but you're correct Mrs. Shaw, it isn't an easy one. The procedure can be costly and stressful, too."

"I was hoping this was going to be a simple appointment. Now I wish my husband could have made this appointment with me."

"Why don't I give you time so that you and your husband can discuss things? If you have any questions, call me back, and if you decide to go through with the IVF, we can schedule another appointment. Then I can go over the process with you in detail from A to Z."

"I think that's a good idea," Crystal said, nodding her head in agreement. "Wow, you've given me a great deal to think about."

"I know, but at least now you have options. And Crystal, just pray about it first, don't worry."

"You know, that is a good idea. I do need to pray on this. Thanks, Dr. Evans."

"I got the idea from you. Just follow what your key chain clearly says."

Crystal looked down at her key chain and read it. "If you're going to pray, don't worry." It was ironic that even though she'd had the key chain for years, she hadn't heeded the key chain's advice in this particular aspect of her life.

Crystal returned home from her doctor's appointment with what seemed like a million thoughts and questions in her head. She laid the mail and her keys down on the kitchen table.

"Honey, is that you?" Warren called from the den.

Startled, Crystal answered, "Yeah. You scared me. What are you doing home?" She turned the corner and greeted her husband.

"Teacher workday. I took a half day."

"I didn't see the car outside."

"It's at the shop. I had to get an oil change and tune up. I walked back."

Impressed, Crystal said, "You walked all the way back home?"

"It was only two miles. I need the exercise any way."

"Are you going to walk back?" Crystal wondered.

"No, now I don't have to."

"I don't know, maybe you want to rack up two more miles."

"No, that was enough exercise for me today. That short walk let me know I need to start working out again."

"I need to start going with you. Maybe we can start working out together. I really need to be doing something."

"For what?"

Crystal pinched her waist. "Look at me, Warren. I've gained so much weight since we got married."

"And?"

"And I think I need to shed some pounds."

"If you want to shed a few pounds fine, but don't ever say I make you feel like you have to. If I remember correctly from seeing your beautiful body just last night, you still look fine to me. If you lose weight, we might be walking one afternoon and the wind will start blowing and you'll blow away."

"I'd have to lose a lot of weight for that to happen. Maybe I'll make that my goal," Crystal said, playing along with him.

"Go right ahead. I'll keep you in the house to ensure I can keep you. Especially through hurricane season, you know how it can be here on the east coast."

"You're going to keep me in the house all the way from May to November?"

"Yep."

"Very funny," Crystal said.

"Seriously, you look fine to me. I love you, and I don't care if you've gained a couple of pounds."

"Thanks baby. You saying that to me means so much. I don't want to add another twenty pounds of baby weight if I ever get pregnant."

"Speaking of getting pregnant, what did the doctor say?"

Crystal wished she had kept the last comment to herself, especially the part about getting pregnant. She'd wanted to think things through before she talked with him. Plus, she wanted to pray about it first. Now it was too late—she'd have to tell him.

"She had good-bad news," Crystal stated.

"Good-bad news? Don't you mean good and bad news?"

"No, let me explain." Crystal recapped her meeting with the doctor. Warren listened without interrupting.

Once she was finished, he said, "Good-bad news, you were right."

"Guess what the doctor said just before I left her office?"

"What?"

"She said for me to pray about it."

"We'll do that right now. Let's give it to God right now and ask Him for guidance in what should be done. We need to pray before we make ourselves crazy by racking our brains."

"I agree. Let's pray."

Chapter 9

Vivian Parker

Vivian moaned, tossing and turning restlessly until she awoke with her heartbeat racing; she tried to get her bearings. It took her a few moments to realize she was in her king-size bed, safe and secure. Bright sunlight, from the open curtains in her bedroom, beamed on her face. *Roland probably opened them before he left for work*, she thought.

She had no idea what time it was but figured it was somewhere around lunchtime because of the chicken noodle soup she smelled coming from the direction of her nightstand. The maid had left another tray of food for her. She hadn't had an appetite in days and had no intention on eating the food.

A month had passed since Vivian's appointment with the doctor. Since that afternoon, her emotional state had spiraled into an abyss. The depression she felt about her biological clock had overtaken her. She didn't want to talk to anyone and hadn't been back to work since that day. She had been moping in her bedroom for weeks now.

Having the doctor treat her so indifferently and hearing that she wouldn't be able to conceive naturally brought back feelings of being a poor, helpless, little black girl back in

Mississippi—the girl she had tried desperately to leave in the past.

Since the appointment, Vivian had been having recurrent nightmares of the days when she was a little girl in Mississippi. The dreams never contained any good memories, because so many of the bad memories outweighed the good. They made her wake up feeling just as she had as a child. *She wasn't good enough and would never amount to anything*—these were the words her mother often told her and her baby brother, Daniel.

Vivid memories were flooding back to her in her dreams. Memories of her mother often telling her and Daniel they were going to grow up just like their father and his side of the family—a bunch of no count, good for nothing drunks. She told them they would end up dying at a young age. Vivian often awoke from the dreams having a hard time bringing herself back to reality—separating the past from the present.

She accepted it was a dream when she realized she was lying under her 1,000-thread-count sheets in her king-sized bed and not a twin bed with the dank, pee-smelling quilt. It was then that she knew she was safe.

Vivian couldn't understand why her mother chose to abuse her and Daniel. She was called the "knee baby," the second to the youngest. She had five older brothers and sisters who never received the same abuse. The difference in how the older children were treated caused a rift between them; a rift that still remained until this day. The only one she had been close to was her baby brother, Daniel.

Vivian figured she and Daniel had been treated differently because they had a different father than their older siblings, and because she and Daniel were the spitting image of their father. Their mother developed an irreversible hate for the man after he left her for another woman. So whenever their mother wanted to get back at him, or when she was having a bad day, she took it out on Vivian and Daniel. Almost on a daily basis she verbally and physically abused them—especially when she was on her way to drinking herself into a stupor.

Vivian often rubbed the right side of her chin and elbow unconsciously. Scars on those two places of her body still lingered from the last night she lived in the same house with her mother. The memory of that night was always the most vivid in her dreams.

On that night, Vivian's mother stumbled into the house from a party in the wee hours of the morning. Her clothes reeked of smoke and her breath of alcohol. Vivian hadn't heard her come in. She had fallen asleep on the couch exhausted from the list of chores her mother had given her earlier in the day.

Vivian's mother slapped her awake, ranting and raving about how she could have had a life if she didn't have all the kids. The screams woke Daniel, causing him to run in to their little living room. When their mother saw him, she glared and called him by his father's name. Yelling "How could you do this to me? Why did you leave me?" After shaking her head and refocusing her eyes, Vivian's mother realized Daniel was not his father.

Seething with anger, she picked up the picture of their father and threw the frame towards Daniel. Vivian jumped in the way to shield her little brother, causing the corner of the frame to hit her chin and then ricochet off her elbow. The skin tore in both places, causing them to bleed profusely.

Vivian grabbed her little brother and pulled him out of the house. They ran a mile to their maternal grandma's house to hide. Vivian knew their mother wouldn't dare come to their grandma's home raising such foolishness, which is what Grandma Eva called it.

Her grandma took them both in. She cleaned the wounds with peroxide and alcohol, then covered them with bandages. That night Grandma held Vivian in her arms, allowing her to cry until she couldn't cry any more. She always felt safe being held in Grandma Eva's bosom.

She remembered her grandma talking about the devil doing his work through Vivian's mother. Her grandma prayed for Vivian's mother for hours that night.

In her grandma's protection, no one could hurt her; not even Vivian's mother. Even though Vivian's mother was a force to be reckoned with, she came second when it came to her mother, Eva. Vivian and Daniel stayed with their grandma until the day she died—never returning to live with their mother.

Vivian had always been thankful to her grandma for taking them in. In Vivian's eyes, her grandma, Eva Shepard, was invincible. Eva didn't take any mess from anyone, and everyone in their small town knew not to get on the old woman's bad side.

Too bad her grandma wasn't here now. Vivian shivered in her king-sized bed and pulled the comforter up over her head, then wrapped her arms around herself. She knew it couldn't be cold in the room, yet thoughts of Mississippi brought a chill to her spine.

It hadn't taken long for Vivian to realize that her grandma wasn't invincible. Eva was human like everyone else. On Vivian's 13th birthday, her grandma had come down with pneumonia. Because she couldn't afford to get the proper treatment from the doctor, one week to the day of getting sick, Grandma Eva went on to Glory to be with the Lord.

The passing years hadn't diminished the amount she missed her grandma. It felt as though she had just died. Before Vivian knew it, she had fallen back to sleep.

At 7:05 that night, she awoke again to see a tray sitting on the night stand. She slowly pulled herself up into the sitting position in order to look more closely at the food. On a plate sat a hoagie with turkey, tomato, lettuce, and a pickle on the side. On a saucer next to the plate was an apple sliced into four pieces with an orange sliced the same way. The tray also held a glass of juice and a mug with spiced tea. For the first time in days, Vivian's stomach rumbled and her mouth watered in anticipation of the meal.

Vivian pulled the covers back and gingerly stepped off of the bed. She crossed the room to the bathroom. There she looked in the mirror. Her eyes were dark and puffy. Her skin, which normally held a healthy glow, was dry, as well as her lips. She looked like a mess. She couldn't believe she had allowed her body to get to this point. Again she was reminded of the days when she lived back in Mississippi with her mother. The thought repulsed her. For years she had tried to push the bad memories of Mississippi out of her head. Except for the loving thoughts of her grandma and younger brother Daniel, there was nothing she could think of fondly. Now that her grandma and Daniel were gone, there was no reason to think of the past.

Vivian turned on the cold water in her bathroom sink and splashed some onto her face, then patted it dry with one of her beige and gold monogrammed hand towels. She pulled her toothbrush out of the medicine cabinet and brushed her teeth. The bristles felt good as they massaged her gums and tongue. She didn't look much better afterwards, but at least she felt a little better.

Vivian returned to the bed and climbed back in. She placed the tray from the nightstand over her lap. After eating only half of the sandwich, the apple slices, and the cup of lukewarm spiced tea, Vivian was full. Her full stomach caused her to want to sleep again. She placed the tray back on the nightstand and snuggled back under the covers.

The next morning Vivian awoke, startled by something in a dream she'd just had. The clock on her nightstand read

9:41. There wasn't any food on the nightstand, so she figured the maid had already taken the breakfast tray away.

She pulled herself up into a sitting position and adjusted the pillows for comfort. She thought back to the dream, trying to remember what had jarred her awake. The feeling had been different than when she'd had the nightmares. She wrapped her arms around herself and closed her eyes, trying to picture whatever she last saw in her dream. It was the smell of jasmine. Her grandma always smelled of jasmine. The memory flooded back. This time she was having a good dream about her grandma.

In the dream, Vivian was being held in her grandma's bosom again. The dream had been clear. Vivian had been elated to see her. Grandma Eva looked just the way she remembered her before she got sick—vibrant and glowing.

Vivian was excited. In rushed words she tried to catch her grandma up on the events of her life. She was proud to tell her grandma she had kept the promises she'd made to her before dying. She told her about all her degrees, work accomplishments, and the love of her life, Roland.

Her grandma smiled, encouraging Vivian to tell her more. Vivian talked about her feelings and confided the events of her most recent past. She'd even revealed to her grandma that she felt like her life was crashing down around her. She told her that she was a wealthy woman who could buy almost anything imaginable and that she had influence with people in high places. She told her how badly she felt about the wealth coming much too late. If she had been wealthy all those years ago, her grandma could have seen the best of doctors and not died of pneumonia.

She also told her grandma how bad she felt. Even though she had so much money, the money couldn't buy the thing she wanted most in the world—to have her own child. She couldn't buy back the years needed for her own eggs—time could not be tempted monetarily.

Grandma Eva took Vivian's face into her hands and smiled. It was then that she finally spoke, telling Vivian, "I'm so proud of you for keeping all of your promises and making a name for yourself. Don't cry. Be thankful for God's love because it is more than sufficient."

Then she told Vivian, "Have faith , God will take care of you, just like He did when you were a little girl." Her grandma paused, looking lovingly into Vivian's eyes. "Vivian, baby. I didn't die because I didn't have any money. I died because God wanted me to come home to Him.

"Make me another promise," her grandma asked. "Promise me you will not let the troubles of this world depress you. Stop shedding all these tears over what can't be done in your strength. Remember God is the source, not just a resource."

Vivian hadn't understood what her grandma meant and asked for further explanation, but the radiant glow started to fade. Her grandma started vanishing before her eyes. Vivian yelled, pleading for her not to go. But a few moments later she had faded completely. The next thing she knew, Vivian was awake.

The feeling of her grandma holding her, lingered. She could still smell the jasmine. She hugged herself tightly, remembering the promise she made only a few minutes ago in her dream, and she vowed not to cry again. The state of depression had to end. She needed to take back control of her life.

She threw her legs over the side of the bed and hopped out. Talking to Grandma Eva was just what Vivian needed. She crossed the threshold of her bathroom and headed for her garden bathtub for a long hot bath. She turned on the faucets and poured in jasmine-scented aromatherapy soap, hoping it would continue to take her mind off of the depressing thoughts that had been consuming her.

Once the water was three-quarters of the way to the top,

she turned the Jacuzzi jets on low, stripped her cloths off and stepped in. The steaming hot water embraced her all the way up to the base of her neckline. The familiar smell of jasmine filled her nostrils. The bath was exactly what she needed.

She closed her eyes and listened to the ripples form in the water. Relaxation came gradually, like the sand slowly filling an hourglass. It was as though with each piece of sand her negative feelings and thoughts drained away. A cleansing of her body was taking place not only on the outside but also on the inside. Her heart and soul were getting a jumpstart.

When Vivian opened her eyes, she saw beams of light streaking downward toward her. The sun's rays were bright and peaceful.

She'd take her life back and stopped feeling sorry for herself. She turned the bath jets up as high as they would go. It was time for her to look at all the positive aspects of her life. She needed to be optimistic not pessimistic. She had never been defeated before and wasn't going to start now.

Then she reached for the remote, turning the CD player on. After changing through a few CDs she found the track she was looking for. It was a song by a Psalmist named Doreen Vail. The songstress had sung at New Hope the last Sunday Vivian attended services. The two songs the gospel artist sang touched a part of Vivian's soul which hadn't been reached since her days of going to church with her grandma in Mississippi. She had been one of the first people in line to buy a copy of the CD when the service was over. One of the songs that made her buy the CD in the first place, was now going to be her song of strength in her journey back into life.

She listened to the words of the melody then sang along with the artist. Even though she sounded nothing like the anointed singer on the CD, Vivian's joyful noise gave her strength with every syllable. Each time she sang the chorus, it seemed to pull her further and further out of the valley she had been stuck in. And with God's guidance, she knew she would make it through the trials.

Vivian hit repeat and played the song over and over. The song and its lyrics were embedded in her soul. Her heart pulsed with rejuvenation. By the time she stepped out of the tub she felt even better than she had a month prior.

In her bedroom closet, she looked for her Damonaé silk pants suit. She had a great deal of work ahead of her for the remainder of the day, and she wanted something soft and comfortable to wear. Tomorrow she would return to work, but today she was going to start tackling the beast that had held her down for so long. Vivian was going to spend the rest of her day doing research on the biological clock. She wanted to do as much research as she could on the options Dr. Evans had discussed.

Once dressed, she ascended to the third floor and headed for the computer study. There she pulled out medical CDs hoping they would lead her in the right direction. Looking at the clock, she saw that it was almost noon and she hadn't eaten anything. Her determination to do research outweighed her need for food.

She typed keywords dealing with infertility; words like invitro fertilization, ovaries, eggs, age, women, baby, conception, and biological clock. She also typed acronyms like IVF, ART, GIFT, ZIFT, and ICSI. From past experience Vivian knew the only way to conquer an obstacle was to find out as much about it as possible.

After hours of researching and printing out pages and pages of relevant information, she allowed herself to take a stretch and relax as the grandfather clock chimed five, she couldn't believe so much time had passed. It was almost time for Roland to come home. She knew he'd be delighted to see her back to her old self again—focused and on a mission.

Vivian stretched and was reminded that she hadn't exercised in weeks. A guilty twinge hit her. Her personal trainer was probably going to have a few choice words for her when she finally had a session again.

She shut the computer down, gathered the papers she'd printed, and placed them in a folder. She headed for her exercise room.

Once she was in her exercise room, she placed the beginning step aerobics tape into the VCR. She knew it would be hard at first, but she had to start somewhere before trying to catch back up to her regular exercise schedule. She knew her body would pay dearly for falling behind.

After her workout, she went back to her master bathroom to take a shower. Before stepping into the shower, she turned the water on in the tub. After taking a quick shower she turned off the water in the tub. The scent of jasmine filled the room again. The water was steaming hot, almost too hot to get into. It would be perfect by the time Roland arrived home.

Dressed in a terry cloth, strapless short set, Vivian made her way into the kitchen. She was famished. The cook had left a tray with an assortment of cheeses, crackers and cold cuts in the refrigerator. She pulled the tray out and placed some of the food on a saucer.

As she began nibbling on a cracker, she heard the door from the garage open and quickly turned around.

"Sweetheart, you're up?" Roland said. Astonishment covered his face.

"Yes, I am. I was knocked down for a little while, but I'm back up now. And, honey, I'm going to stay up." Vivian embraced Roland and kissed him.

"I am glad to hear that. I have been so concerned about the state you've been in. I was even toying with the idea of seeking some professional help for you."

"I wasn't that bad was I?" Vivian asked in disbelief. "You wanted to send me to a shrink?"

"I didn't know what else to do. And yes, sweetheart, you were that bad. I hoped and prayed sooner or later you'd come around. God answered my prayer."

Vivian kissed him again and said, "Yes, He has. I'll have to tell you about my day. But first I want to put your mind at ease. I know you've been worrying about me for the last few weeks. I've had a chance to relax my mind and body. Now you need a chance to relax also."

Roland raised his eyebrows as Vivian started removing his tie.

"Please follow me," she said, putting the tie around her neck. She led him with one hand and held the saucer with food in the other.

Once they were in the bathroom, Vivian placed the cheese and crackers on the side of the tub. Then she proceeded to help her husband undress.

"Here you are my dear. Your bath awaits you," she gestured.

"Umm how nice. No let me to help you undress." Roland attempted to pull her strap down.

Vivian stopped him. "Oh no, honey. I've already taken my shower. This bath is just for you. I'm here to take care of all your bathing needs. Whatever you need, the sponge, soap, glove, cheese, crackers, you name it, I got it. My sole objective is to help you relax."

"What did I do to deserve all this?"

"You have been supportive and patient with me over the past few weeks. I want to thank you for not getting frustrated with me. And also thank you for your prayers."

"For better, for worse, through thick and thin, that's what I'm here for," Roland told her.

"I know, and I just want to show you how much I appreciate you."

"I'm glad to have the old you back." Roland grinned with joy.

"I'm glad to be back," Vivian smiled.

* * *

At work the next day, Vivian spent most of her time trying to catch up on the loose ends during the weeks of her absence. Her assistants had done as much as they could without her, but there were still many aspects of the projects which only Vivian could tie up.

Except for a quick sandwich at her desk and two bathroom breaks, Vivian worked eight hours straight. It was now four o'clock and she was tired. The office would not officially close until five, so she decided to wind down during the last hour of the day by reading more information about infertility. She took her palm organizer out of her attaché case. The day before, she had downloaded two books on infertility. And from the little bit she already read, she was finding in-vitro fertilization to be an interesting subject—especially since she would probably be undergoing one or more of the procedures.

There was so much she didn't know about the male and female reproductive systems. She was surprised to learn that men really didn't have the same time on their biological clocks. Where women could have problems at age 35, men could still father a child naturally until the age of 70 if they wanted. Plus, the children would usually turn out healthy. It seemed so unfair.

Vivian's cell phone rang. "Hello?"

"Viv, where are you?" Roland asked.

"I'm here in the office. Where else should I be?"

"On your way home, it's five-thirty."

Vivian looked down at the clock on her palm organizer. "It's already five-thirty? I didn't realize it. The time has flown by. I got caught up reading this book. I'm really learning a lot."

"That's great, honey. Why don't you come home and tell me about it. Better yet, tell me over dinner."

"Dinner?"

"Yes, I'm taking a potential client out to lunch Thursday, and I want to check out this new restaurant."

"What about Ginny's?"

"I took him there for our first meeting. If this new restaurant is as good as I hear it is, I can start using it also."

Vivian closed the palm organizer and started gathering her things to go home. "What time do you want to leave?"

"Seven is good. I'll see if I can get reservations for seven-thirty."

"I'm leaving now. That'll give me time to come home and change."

"Okay sweetheart, I'll meet you there," Roland said.

"See you soon."

"How was your first day back?" Roland asked as they sat at the dinner table.

"It was busy and tiring. But it felt really good being back in the swing of things."

"That's good to hear." Roland smiled, glad to have his wife back.

"This restaurant is really posh. Ginny's had better watch out; it looks like they're going to have some strong competition."

"It has been rated as a five-star. With all the potential business I have on the line, I can't afford to rely solely on a review. So you know I needed to check this place out for myself."

"I'm glad we did. It's nice to have a little change of scenery," Vivian said.

"I hope the food is as good as the service has been," Roland said.

"I wonder what the lunch crowd has been like?"

"I was wondering the same thing. I am assuming it shouldn't be too bad since you need reservations for lunch."

"They were prompt in getting us seated," Vivian said.

The waiter brought the appetizer they'd ordered. For dinner, Roland ordered the lobster on a bed of spinach. Vivian ordered prime rib with steamed seasonal vegetables.

"Smells good," Vivian said, putting a portion of the appetizer on a plate. Then she tasted it. "This appetizer is delectable."

Roland did the same. "It is very tasty. If our dinner tastes this good, I'm sold. They'll definitely see more of me."

The dinner arrived soon after they finished the appetizer. They ate until they were almost full—neither of them could have finished all of their main courses if they'd tried. Plus, they wanted to save a little room to try a sampling of the house desserts. Once they finished the sampling, they were thoroughly satisfied.

"I'm sold. What about you?" Vivian said, dabbing the corners of her mouth with her napkin.

"They've got my business. I'll have Nikki make the reservations for me this Thursday. I hope there will still be some openings."

"Oh, Roland, just make them while we're here. You don't have to wait for the secretary to do it."

"I guess I could do that, couldn't I?"

"Yes, you can." Vivian rolled her eyes playfully.

Roland made the reservations and they returned home, exhausted from their long day at work.

"We were having such a good time, we didn't even talk about your research on the IVF procedures," Roland said.

"I know. Let's talk about it tomorrow. I'm really excited about what I've learned so far, but I'm starting to wind down. I guess coming back so strong after my little break is really starting to catch up with me."

"I'm pretty tired too. We can discuss it tomorrow," Roland agreed.

* * *

Vivian and Roland were again sitting in Dr. Evans' office. Almost two months had passed since their last appointment. Vivian rescheduled the appointment to continue their previous discussion with the doctor—this time on a positive note.

Luckily, she had been blessed to be able to get an appointment within less than a month. As she waited for her appointment date to arrive, it seemed as though the time had flown by. She stayed busy catching up on work, plus she had taken over several of the smaller projects from a project manager she'd had to let go.

In her spare time she researched as much information as possible on the subject of infertility. This time she wasn't going to be caught off-guard, she'd be prepared for their appointment with the doctor.

The same nurse she met on her first visit, led her and Roland into the doctor's office. This time she was calm as they waited for the doctor. Vivian's heartbeat was regular and steady.

Briskly walking in and closing the office door behind her, Dr. Evans greeted them. "Hello, Mr. and Mrs. Parker. I am glad to see you back again."

"Hi, Dr. Evans, thank you for seeing us, especially after the way I was the last time I left here," Vivian apologized.

"Mrs. Parker, don't worry about it. I understand. You're not the first person to have that kind of reaction."

"Thank you," Vivian said with relief.

"Yes, thank you for being understanding," Roland said.

"So what exactly can I do for you today?" Dr. Evans asked.

Vivian spoke first. "My husband and I have been talking over the past month and I've also been doing a great deal of research on the different aspects of ART procedures and IVF."

Pleased, Dr. Evans said, "Very good. I like it when my patients seek more information about their medical needs. Actually, I encourage all my patients to read as much information as they can."

"From my research and the options you gave us last time, my husband and I have decided to try IVF, even though we know it may be a long shot."

With pleasure, Dr. Evans clasped her hands together and said, "That's wonderful."

Delighted with the doctor's response, Vivian said, "That is what we'd like to do, even though I've read the chances are my eggs may not be the best. But after all my research I also now know there is a small chance some of my eggs may be good.

"We both agree we should at least try IVF as an option," Roland said.

"You do know that degenerative eggs could lead to chromosomal abnormalities and because of the age factor there is a higher chance of miscarriage?" The doctor wanted to make the information clear.

"We know. We've also read about the increased chances of ectopic pregnancy."

Impressed, the doctor said, "You have been doing your research—although you won't have to worry about ectopic pregnancy with IVF."

"Believe us, we know about the risks. We want to try it any way," Vivian said.

Roland held Vivian's hand. "We've discussed it extensively over the past month."

"It sounds like you're both pretty firm in your decision," Dr. Evans clasped her hands together again.

"We are." Vivian and Roland said in unison.

"Alright." Dr. Evans rolled her chair back towards the file cabinet and pulled a packet out. "This is the IVF information packet. I know you've done a lot of research on ART and

IVF, but this packet is specific to our clinic and what we do here."

Vivian flipped through the packet, scanning the pages. "This is pretty thick."

"There's a wealth of information on all of the procedures we perform here, along with references and an extensive glossary of terms. As I said before, I deal with the facts. I like it when my patients are well informed about what they'll have to undergo."

"This is really nice," Vivian commented, admiring the graphics and the professional way the packet had been laid out. She flipped to the page outlining costs and then the glossary of terms. She found many of the words she had recently come in contact with, as well as others that were still foreign.

"We'll start running tests and doing blood work for both of you. I want to make sure there aren't any other factors that might be potential problems. If there are none, then we'll move on to the ART procedure called ICSI," the doctor said.

Vivian thought for a moment. "ICSI? I think I remember seeing that acronym. You mentioned it with our first appointment didn't you?"

"Yes. If you'll look on page twenty, you'll find more information on the process. I'd rather use this process instead of wasting valuable time and eggs with regular IVF procedures."

"Aren't the chances of pregnancy better with the ICSI process anyway?" Vivian asked.

"Studies show the chances are a little better," Dr. Evans said.

"Good. When can we get started?" Vivian was anxious.

"Right now. I'll have the nurse start the tests on you both. I'll also need to have a semen analysis performed. We can perform the analysis if you haven't had intercourse within the past 72 hours. Are you able to have the analysis done now?"

Vivian and Roland looked at each other sheepishly.

"Not today. I wish we had known this a few hours ago," Roland said.

"Okay we'll have to schedule the analysis for another day. Make sure you abstain for at least seventy-two hours before the test. Also avoid excessive heat to that area—which means no Jacuzzi until the testing is done."

"If you say so," Roland said reluctantly.

"Please read the contents of the packet, especially the pages on ICSI. Have a seat right outside and I'll inform Shelby which tests I'd like run for you. She can also schedule your date for the analysis, Mr. Parker. Just give her a date which will be safe for the full seventy-two hours."

"That should be in about sixty-five hours," Vivian said jokingly.

"Alright, we can schedule the test in four days. In the meantime, for further information on the semen analysis, look on page eleven."

They each shook the doctor's hand before she exited the room. The two embraced with hope and inspiration.

Chapter 10

Shelby Tomlinson

Shelby yawned into the phone receiver.

"Are you getting enough sleep?" her mother asked.

"Yes, Mom."

"It doesn't sound like it. You've yawned at least five times already. I know I'm not that boring. So you must be tired."

"I guess I might be a little tired. Getting up each morning to take my temperature doesn't allow me to get all the rest I'm used to." Shelby's voice was sluggish as she spoke.

"I know how you like to get your rest," her Mom chuckled.

"My dreams consist of making sure I don't forget to take my temperature and making sure I'm taking it at the same time each morning. Once I take it, I can't get back to sleep."

"How's the charting going?" her mother asked.

"It's still going well, like I was telling you after Thanksgiving dinner. I can actually see a drop in my temperature right before day fourteen of my cycle. I need to take my temp for one more month though. The doctor wants to make sure it happens again."

"How long has it been? Over two months?"

Shelby sighed. "Going on three."

"I know you'll be glad when it's over, so you can get some real sleep again."

Shelby yawned again while saying, "I sure will be. I can't wait to sleep in again."

"I hate to break the news to you, but what you are experiencing is nothing compared to the way it will be when a new baby arrives, especially in the first weeks of life."

"I know Mom, but when that happens I'm sure I won't mind."

"My dear Shelby, you say that now, but after a week of sleepless nights, you might not feel so optimistic."

"I've been waiting so long, I think even if I'm tired I'll continue to thank the Lord."

Her mother chuckled again.

"You sure are laughing a lot. What's so funny?" Shelby asked.

"I was just remembering back when you were born. Your father and I brought you home in that old Toyota Corolla. We laid you down on the couch wrapped in your little pink hospital blanket. You were so tiny and quiet. We stared at you, not really knowing what to do next."

"You've always said I was a handful," Shelby said.

"You were. After that first week we really had our hands full. You had your days and nights mixed up. And on top of that, you had colic. Oh, we had such a time with you."

Defensively Shelby asked, "I wasn't that bad was I?"

"Yes, you were honey. I don't think your feet touched the ground until you were 2-years-old, either. You were so spoiled."

Shelby rolled her eyes to herself. "Mom, stop exaggerating."

Her mother continued to laugh. "Well, it seemed like it. Being the first grandchild and niece, no one wanted to put you down. You were passed from arm to arm."

"Mom." Shelby said, her tone serious.

"Yes, baby?"

"I'm sorry," Shelby said.

"Sorry for what?"

"All I put you through."

"Oh nonsense, I wouldn't change it for the world. You have nothing to apologize for. You just did what babies do." Her mother laughed it off. "Don't get so serious on me."

"But you just said I took you and Dad through a lot of changes."

"Yes, but our love for you was, and still is, unconditional. You could've been a perfect baby, and I couldn't have loved you any more than I did. It's all part of being a parent."

"Maybe one day I'll know that kind of unconditional love," Shelby said, fearing she might never experience what her mother was talking about.

"You will, Shelby. And your child will have all the family love you had. You know your father and I will do nothing but spoil our grandchild."

Shelby smiled at the thought. "Phillip's family will too. I'll be lucky if the child's feet reach the ground before its 5, in time for kindergarten."

"We all learn from our mistakes."

"What do you mean?" Shelby asked.

"Your brother knew how to walk by the time he was 10 months old. I wasn't going to make the same mistake twice. I made sure people put him down after a few minutes."

"That explains it."

"Explains what?"

"For years I've wondered why my little brother can't seem to commit to one woman. I guess he's used to only being in one place for a short time. Then he feels the need to move on."

"You're right. I guess that's my fault also."

"Just kidding, Mom."

"I know, sweetheart."

"What's Dad doing?"

"He is out with his buddies playing golf. I don't see what they get out of chasing a little ball around all day long."

"It's pretty fun actually. Plus you can get a lot of exercise while you're walking."

"I'll take your word for it. How's Phillip been since you started seeing the specialist?" her mother said, changing the subject back.

"He's fine. He's actually been pretty supportive and doesn't shy away when I talk about all the tests and possible medical procedures."

"That's good. I have been praying for you both."

"I have been, too. I know prayer works, Mom. He seems so much more like his old self again."

"They haven't found any problems with your tests, have they?"

"No, none so far, which is a relief. Deep down I hope they don't find anything, but I know there must be a problem or else we wouldn't be going through this whole process."

"In its own time and season it will happen. God just has to finish preparing the way, that's all."

"I'm ready; Phillip's ready. We both have good stable jobs and a home big enough for five kids," Shelby reasoned.

"Yes, but for some reason God has not released your gift of children. When He feels you're ready, then He'll give you a child or children."

"I'm trying to be patient."

"Just relax and enjoy the time you have alone with your husband now. Once those children get here, your time will not be your own any more."

"I'm trying Mom, but sometimes I feel like it won't ever happen for us. Maybe it's not God's will for us to have children."

"Shelby," her mother said sternly. "Do you really feel that

way in your heart? Do you really feel like God doesn't want you to have children?"

"No. Not really," Shelby admitted.

"Then don't talk like that. You are God's child. He will give you the desires of your heart. All you have to do is ask."

"But I have asked." Shelby whined, even though she hadn't meant to.

"Yes, baby. But there's often a catch. We don't always get what we want when we want it or how we want it. It's on God's time. And God's time is right on time."

"It can be so hard sometimes, especially when I see all of those pregnant women and teens. I can't understand why I have to be reminded daily of what I don't have. Teenagers come through the office scared and unsure of the future. They get pregnant so easily."

"It's not for us to understand why God does what He does. We cannot spend our lives racking our brains trying to figure it out either. All we can do as His children is trust in Him knowing that He knows what's in our best interest."

"Pray for my strength, Mom. Pray for my strength and patience."

"I will pray for you, baby. And you must pray and trust in God. Don't worry about what He's doing. It's all in His hands."

Shelby felt so blessed to have her mother. "What would I do without you, Mom?"

"That's what Moms are for, baby. One day you'll be doing the same thing for your child, giving him or her words of wisdom to live by."

"I hope so."

"You will. I hate to run, but I've got to finish getting ready for my meeting at church. Everything is going to be fine in the long run. You'll see."

"Okay, Mom. Love you."

"I love you too, sweetheart."

* * *

"Good morning, darling."

Shelby slowly opened her eyes and came out of her restful sleep. Phillip was standing over her, next to the bed. She couldn't remember what time she fell asleep the night before. All she remembered was coming home from work, changing into some comfortable clothes, and eating a snack. Then she had laid down on her bed for a short nap, but didn't wake up until two in the morning. Phillip had been sleeping peacefully beside her.

"Good morning," she said, feeling well rested from the sleep she'd caught up on.

"I brought you something since you've decided to sleep in."

She bolted up into a sitting position suddenly realizing she'd forgotten to set the alarm clock. "What time is it?" she asked in panic.

"It's eleven o'clock," Phillip said coolly.

"I can't believe it's that late. I didn't take my temperature."

"It's okay, calm down. I'm sure missing one morning won't be the end of the world."

She thought about it. "Yeah," she said, allowing herself to relax, "I guess you're right. I've been consistent until now." She slipped back down under the covers.

He kissed her forehead. "The three months is almost up, right?"

"Yeah. I only need to chart for another four days."

"I didn't want to wake you up. You were sleeping so peacefully."

"I was sleeping so good. Lord knows I needed the rest." Shelby smiled with content.

"You were snoring pretty loud."

"I was not," Shelby said in denial.

Phillip shook his head affirming the fact. "Yes, you were."

"Stop picking on me. You know I only do that when I'm really tired."

"And let me tell you honey, I'm glad you aren't tired every night."

She pulled her arm from under the cover and smacked his thigh.

"Ooooh, hit me again, baby. That feels good."

"Oh stop, silly." Shelby stretched her body and sighed. "Guess what?"

"What?"

"I had a really good dream."

"What was it about?"

"I dreamed we were at the park on a blanket having a picnic lunch. All of us were there."

"Who? Our families?"

"*Our* family. Me, you, our son and daughter," Shelby told him. "We were having so much fun. Our son looked just like you and our daughter looked just like me when I was little."

"Sounds like a pretty good dream."

"It was. It seemed so real." Shelby closed her eyes again, remembering the dream. "The food smelled delectable, and its like I can still smell it," Shelby said. "I've never had a dream where food smelled so real before."

"Maybe that's because you're smelling the food I cooked you for breakfast." Phillip turned and picked up the breakfast tray sitting on the nightstand. "Did you smell Belgian waffles, blueberries, whipped cream and hot maple syrup?"

"Come to think of it, yes that's exactly what it was. I couldn't put my finger on what I was smelling were in the dream. All I knew was there were some very sweet smells coming from that basket."

"Here's the source." He placed the tray over her lap as she sat back up.

She sniffed the waffles. "Umm. Hot fluffy Belgian waffles. What brought this on?"

"You are my beautiful queen, and you deserve only the very best."

Shelby bowed her head and said grace before she cut into the waffle. "I think this is the best one you've made so far. You've really outdone yourself, my king," she spoke, even though her mouth was full of waffle.

"Thank you."

"Have you eaten yet?"

"Yeah, I ate while I was cooking. I'm full of blueberries."

"Would you like some?" Shelby cut a piece and put it on her fork. She offered it to him.

"No, I'm fine."

She popped it into her mouth. "Okay, don't say I didn't offer. Don't change your mind later either; it'll be all gone."

"Obviously you've forgotten who you're talking to. I'm the chef, baby. I can whip more up anytime I please."

"Uhh, baby, darling, sweetheart, love, come here a second," Shelby said, trying to sweet talk him. She realized her mistake. She shouldn't bite the hand that was feeding her.

"Yes?" he asked, moving closer to her.

"Closer," she said, pulling his shorts. She kissed him fully on the lips.

"Umm. Sweet. What was that for?" Phillip asked.

"That was your tip for making me such a wonderful breakfast. I have to keep you, the chef-waiter-busboy, happy. I know which side my bread is buttered on."

"Trying to sweeten me up, huh? How do you plead?"

"Guilty."

"I'll be the judge and jury also. The verdict will be in tonight."

"Why tonight? Why not now after I finish my meal?"

"Because I have so many job titles that it will be awhile before sentencing. Besides, you'll like my night job."

Shelby played along with her husband, "Your night job? That sounds seductive. What do you do?"

"I'm a bodyguard."

"You're a bodyguard?" Shelby said, trying to conceal her snorting as she laughed, "Who do you work for?"

"Currently I'm not working, but I plan on auditioning, oops I meant to say, interviewing for a position."

"Do you need a reference?" Shelby asked.

He picked up the fork and fed Shelby a large piece of the waffle. "I might. I've heard this lady I have my interview with is really tough. She's hard-nosed and has a beautiful body, which I'm sure would be hard for anyone to guard." Phillip took his index finger and slid it down Shelby's neck and arm. "I just hope she sees that I'm the perfect candidate to guard her body."

"Ummm." Shelby spoke as she chewed the waffle. "She does sound pretty tough. When's your audition? Oh, I'm sorry, I meant to say interview?"

"Later on tonight," Phillip said.

She took a sip of milk. "Have you prepared for it?"

"Yes, I have. I know she'll want to see my resume, and I'll show it to her. I'll take off my shirt like this." Phillip removed his shirt revealing his pectoral muscles which he flexed for her. "I'll flex my right muscle like this, then the left muscle. If she wants, I'll flex them both at the same time."

Shelby's heart began to beat faster. She fanned herself with her cloth napkin. "Whew, I think she'll like your resume. She'll definitely need someone with muscles like yours."

Phillip continued to flex his muscles intermittently as he spoke. "You think so?"

"I know so." Shelby gulped her milk. "You know what? I might be able to help you out a little."

"How?" he asked, raising an eyebrow.

"I've got some baby oil you can use to polish your body."

"You mean polish my resume, right?"

"Oh yeah, that's what I meant. My mistake," Shelby said, looking his body up and down.

Phillip bent over and picked his shirt up. "I just might take you up on that."

Shelby stroked Phillip's chest with her hand. "I could practice putting the oil on now. You know, to make sure it will go on smoothly when it's time for your interview."

He put his shirt back on. "Nope. Sorry."

"Sorry?" Shelby frowned.

"I have to complete my day job first as the busboy."

"Alright, if you say so."

"I do. Besides, lazy bones, it's time for you to get up."

"I know. I do need to run a few errands. You want me to do the dishes?" Shelby offered.

"No my queen, I've got it. And don't stay out too late running errands. You know you've got your sentencing tonight."

"Is that before or after your interview?"

"Let's make it after. You may be able to persuade the judge to go light on you."

"I can't wait," Shelby grinned.

"But you'll have to."

"Then wait, I will," Shelby moaned.

While in the kitchen washing the breakfast dishes, Phillip heard the doorbell then Goldie's bark to inform him someone was at the door. He wiped his hands and walked towards the foyer. Through the opaque glass, he saw a silhouette.

"Just a minute, I'm coming," he called out. He opened the door and saw the mailman.

"Good afternoon, Mr. Tomlinson. How y'all doing today?" The mailman smiled.

"We're good and you?"

"Fine, just fine. It's a beautiful day. I can't believe it actually got up to seventy degrees today, in mid-December. Can you?"

"No, I can't. I guess we'd better enjoy it while we can," Phillip smiled at the young man who looked to be the same age as him.

"I just needed to bring you your mail," the mailman said.

"Thanks. You could've put it in the box."

He held up an envelope. "Actually sir, I have a certified letter addressed to you. Could you please sign here?"

Phillip took the pen the mailman extended to him and signed. "Oh uh, yes of course," Phillip said, wondering who was sending him a certified letter.

"Thank you, Mr. Tomlinson." The mailman tipped his hat. "Have a good day."

"You, too," Phillip closed the front door.

He flipped through the other mail first. All of it was junk mail except for the bottled water bill and a Christmas card. He then turned the certified letter over. The return address said Lafayette County Superior Court. Still clueless, he opened the letter.

Skimming through he couldn't believe what he read. He saw Jeana Sands vs. Phillip Tomlinson. As he raced through the words he read, "back child support" and "due in court" with a court date. At the bottom of the letter he saw a phone number.

"What in the hel . . ." Phillip started to say, angry that he had obviously gotten the letter by mistake, but Shelby stopped him before he finished his sentence.

"Did you say something, honey?" Shelby said as she descended the stairs.

Phillip quickly put the letter underneath the other mail. "Uh, no. I didn't say anything to you. I was just talking to Goldie."

"Did I hear the doorbell?"

"Yeah, it was the mailman. He decided to bring the mail to the door. Some kind of new thing the post office is doing during the holidays. He said they're trying it out to get to know the people on their routes better." Phillip rambled on. The letter in his hand had him perplexed.

"That was nice. Anything important?" She reached for the mail.

Phillip held on to it, moving it out of her reach. "No, just a lot of junk mail, a Christmas card from my mom and dad, and the bill for the bottled water. I'll take care of it."

"Are you alright?'

"Yeah, why do you ask?"

"I don't know, you just seem to be acting a little strange."

"No, baby. Everything is fine. Why don't you go ahead and get your errands done so you won't be late tonight?" Phillip coaxed.

"Oh, okay. I'll do just that."

"Yeah, baby you do that," Phillip said, trying to hide his mounting confusion over the letter he held behind his back. He wondered why he was getting such a letter, but in the meantime, he definitely didn't want Shelby to know about it.

"Make sure you're on time too," she said.

He pulled her close in an embrace. "Don't worry about me. I'm going to the gym to work on my resume."

"Keep talking, and I'll help you work on your resume right now." She kissed him slowly.

Feeling himself getting excited, he pulled back and said, "You had better go ahead and get dressed then."

"Don't work out too hard, honey," Shelby said and turned to walk back toward the stairs.

"Yes, Dr. Silva. Thank you very much. I am so glad to hear that," Shelby said over the phone. "I'll talk with my husband about it, and we will come in to have his tests done." She was excited to hear the news about her test results. "We'll call back tomorrow to set up an appointment. And again, thanks so much, Dr. Silva."

Shelby hung up the phone in her office feeling like she was on cloud nine. She couldn't wait to tell Phillip the good news. She looked at the picture she and Phillip had taken during the Christmas holidays. They both wore matching Santa hats. She then picked up the phone to call him.

When she heard his voice she immediately began to speak, until she realized she'd gotten the voice mail. *"Hello you have reached Phillip Tomlinson. Today is January the 11th. I will be out of the office until two o'clock. If this is a client and you need to speak with someone else, please press zero for the operator. She will further assist you. Thank you and have a good day."*

Shelby looked at her watch—it was already after four-thirty. Reluctantly she left a brief message, disappointed she couldn't speak to him right then. She told him to call her back as soon a possible. She then hung up and waited for a few minutes hoping the phone would ring.

As she waited, she bowed her head, remembering to pray to God. "Dear God, I just want to thank You so much for the good news I just received. You know how scared I was that something was wrong with me. And I'm so relieved everything is fine. God, I also want to apologize if I lost some of my hope for a while. I understand now that all I really needed to do was to be patient. I also want to thank you, Lord, for all of the blessings You have given me—especially for changing my husband's mind about this whole situation. Again, I say thank You, thank You, thank You. Amen."

She opened her eyes and felt at peace, knowing she had actually told God thank you instead of just thinking it. She was getting better in her prayer life and felt her relationship with God strengthening.

When the phone failed to ring for another few minutes, she tried to occupy her time by completing the rest of her charts for the day. After making a couple of mistakes in the first chart, she realized her concentration was off, so she picked up the phone again, this time dialing her mother's number. She got the answering machine there also, so she left a quick message and hung the phone back up.

Shelby was excited and wanted to tell someone about her good news. She thought about calling her best friend, but remembered she had already left for her vacation to Canada, and Rachel had taken the day off. Looking back at her watch, it was finally time to go. Shelby grabbed her purse and headed to her car.

This evening for her commute, she was going to listen to some up-beat, finger-snapping, toe-tapping songs all the way home.

In his office, Phillip slammed the receiver of his phone down, cracked his knuckles and loosened his tie. After making several phone calls, he was still at square one. Because of the holidays, ice storms, and illnesses, he hadn't been able to get the answers he needed. He wanted to know how there had been a mix up with his name. What caused him to get the certified letter from the court? Phillip wasn't used to getting the run around. Whenever he needed answers, especially in his office, people broke their backs to get him all the information he needed and more. The delay was pissing him off.

He had not seen or heard from Jeana Sands in years. He wondered why she would want to take him to court—especially for back child support—when he had no children with her. Oh yes, it was all a mistake indeed.

He sat at his desk frustrated. Putting his hands on his face he rubbed his forehead hard with the heel of his hand. The phone's message light was blinking, indicating he had a message. He punched in his code to check the message.

Phillip listened as his wife spoke. Even though she sounded excited and like it was urgent, he couldn't call her back right then. He was still too upset from the phone calls he had previously made. Knowing Shelby as he did, he knew she would detect the tension in his voice if he spoke to her. So he decided to give himself some time to cool off during the drive home.

As he stared down at the certified letter in his hand, he got angrier. He had wanted to have the whole mess taken care of by the end of the day. Now he realized that would not be possible. He shoved the papers in a manila folder and placed them all the way in the back of his bottom file drawer.

Even though he hadn't taken a drink in years, this evening he felt the urge to take one.

Shelby got caught up in rush hour traffic. She had failed to check the traffic report when she left work. Phillip was already home when she got there. She pulled into the garage and started unfastening her seat belt even before the car came to a complete stop.

Quickly turning off the ignition, she ran into the kitchen and threw her keys down on the counter. She looked throughout the house for Phillip. Not seeing him, she called his name but didn't get a response. Goldie hadn't even come when she called her.

When she looked out of the bedroom window, she saw Phillip outside sitting in the Jacuzzi. She ran back down the stairs to the French doors of the family room to greet him.

"Phillip," she said, swinging the French doors open.

"Yeah baby? Slow down. Why are you breathing so hard?"

"I've been running through the house looking for you."

"What's going on? I got your message but, I . . ."

She wrapped her arms around her body for warmth. "First, why in the world are you out here in the cold?"

"You can't even feel it once you're in here." He wiped the dripping sweat from his forehead. "I'm hot actually."

Shelby shook her head in disbelief. "Well, anyway, I've got some good news!" She was still breathing hard trying to catch her breath. "I talked to Dr. Silva. After reviewing all of the tests he says he can't find anything wrong with me. He says there aren't any problems. There's nothing wrong with me!" She was so relieved.

"That's great. That's really great, baby. I'm happy to hear that."

Shelby could tell that, again, Phillip's enthusiasm had dwindled. But she didn't let it dampen her spirit this time. "I can't believe it. I am so relieved there is nothing wrong with me."

"That is great, honey. So what else did the doctor say?"

"Now, don't get nervous, okay?" Shelby said apprehensively.

"What?"

She saw his body tense slightly. "Since there aren't any problems with me, the doctor needs to run some tests on you. Not that I think there are any problems with you," Shelby added quickly.

"A few tests?" Phillip said under his breath.

"Yes, a few tests.'

He took a deep breath. "Okay."

"Okay, what?"

"Okay, I'll take the tests."

Shelby couldn't believe what she was hearing. "You will? You're okay with it?"

"Yeah," Phillip said, trying to sound nonchalant.

"Really?" Shelby asked again in disbelief.

"Yes baby, really. I'm fine. I'll take the tests." He shook his head to affirm his statement.

Shelby jumped up and down screaming, "Yes, yes, yes!"

"Whoa, calm down." Phillip lowered his hands as a signal to silence her.

"Calm down? No way. I am so happy right now, I could just hug you." Then she leaned over the Jacuzzi and gave him a hug not caring if she got wet.

"I can't believe you just did that. You're all wet now." Phillip looked at her in disbelief.

"I don't care. It's only a little water. I just got some of the best news of my life. First the news from the doctor, and then the news from you saying you don't mind having the tests done."

"It's good to see you so happy again," Phillip said.

"I am. I really am. I'm going to put my bathing suit on so we can enjoy all this good news together. I'll be right back," she said as she ran back into the house.

Phillip watched Shelby as she ran back inside. He was glad to see how happy she was. He wanted her to stay that way, never wanting to see a frown on her face ever again.

He had agreed to take the tests, knowing it would make her happy. Phillip could only hope that fate would be in his favor and his tests would also turn out fine.

While he waited on Shelby's return, he thought about the phone calls he was going to have to make early the next day. He had to resolve the misunderstanding about the certified letter. The last thing he wanted was for Shelby to find out about the mix-up, if in fact that was all that it was.

Chapter 11

Crystal Shaw

"Hey everyone, the Silvermont Petting Zoo is up on the right," Crystal informed the bus full of screeching 3 and 4-year-olds and their chaperones. "I need everyone to gather your things. Each chaperone needs to make sure your group has on the right colors. And please make sure all of the children in your group have their name tags on."

Crystal gathered her book bag equipped with first aid kit, cell phone, and signed permission slips. Each permission slip was color coded to correspond with the colors of each group. There were four groups in all, each with a different neon color. All of their shirts had Little Angels Daycare Center on the back for easy recognition. Crystal's group wore neon yellow.

Crystal chose the neon colors as an extra safety precaution in case a child wandered off or if someone tried to take one of them. Even though she didn't want to think that way, she knew everyone in the world was not good.

"Can I have your attention again please?" Crystal said loudly, trying to get everyone's attention. "I'd like for everyone to meet over there under that oak tree when we get off the bus." She pointed to the tree. "Please do your head count there."

When they were all assembled by the oak tree, Crystal said, "Parents, please make sure you have your schedules. There is a rotation scheduled every thirty minutes. At noon we'll meet back here for lunch. This afternoon the children will be able to enjoy the train ride, ferris wheel, carrousel, and the ponies. We'll do our last headcount at four o'clock. I'll ask you all to do your own individual head counts throughout the day. Does anyone have any questions?"

"Miss Crystal, am I gonna see a pony?" one of the children asked.

Crystal smiled at the 3-year-old, wondering whether or not he would remember the trip in the years to come. "Yes, Kyle, you will see ponies, goats, ducks, pigs, chickens, bunnies and many more animals. You'll be able to pet them and even feed some of them."

"Yipee," he yelled, and some of the other children followed his lead.

"Children, I want you all to be good little boys and girls. All the good children will get a surprise at the end of the day," Crystal told them. She knew most of them would be good and a few would be their usual rambunctious selves. At the end of the day, they would all get a surprise anyway.

The groups split, all going to their respective areas. Crystal's group visited the duck pond first. The children were amazed at how the ducks would stick their heads under the water and then make them pop back out.

The attendant in charge of the duck pond told the children a short version of the *Ugly Ducking* story. Then he gave them some bread to feed the ducks. The children had fun pretending to walk like ducks in a line.

Crystal took delight in watching the children play. Most of the children in her group were from two parent households. But two of the children, a brother and sister, were currently in foster care. Crystal had put them in her group so that she could give them the extra attention they needed—just as she often did at the daycare center. She wanted to make sure their field trip was an enjoyable one. It made her feel good to give them the love and attention.

Crystal thought about the day when she and Warren would have children. They'd be able to take them to the circus and petting zoo. She longed for the day when they'd be able to chaperone their own children on field trips. She also thought about the day when she'd be able to return to their neighborhood for the annual Labor Day cook out with her children. She could picture them playing with their cousins and the other children. She smiled without realizing it.

Her thoughts then traveled to her next doctor's appointment. She was nervous and excited about it. She and Warren would discuss and set up the procedures for IVF. After talking and praying about it, she and Warren felt that God had opened the door for them, and they should pursue it, even though there was still hope a pregnancy could happen naturally.

Looking at her watch, Crystal moved her group over to the chickens. There they were told the story of the *Little Red Hen*.

Next they visited the potbellied pigs. The attendant at this stop told the children the story of the *Three Little Pigs*. Even though Crystal knew the children had heard the story over and over, they listened intently as he told the story, picking up the squealing pigs as he spoke.

At their last stop for the morning, the children visited the sheep where they were able to sing songs about sheep and Mary's little lamb. By the time they finished with the morning events, the children were hungry.

All the groups returned to the picnic area. Two of the dads who volunteered to help, had their lunch of hot dogs and hamburgers ready fresh off of the grill. The children found seats at tables and were ready to eat.

Crystal sat and imagined Warren next to the grill making hot dogs for their children. Her thoughts were interrupted by one of the parents.

"Mrs. Shaw, Brandon is having such a good time. I'm glad I was able to come on this trip. I'm sorry I missed their trip to the circus."

"I'm glad too, Mrs. McCain. We had a very good time on that trip, but I think they like this trip a little better since they can actually touch some of the animals."

"I know Brandon is going to sleep well tonight with all this excitement," Mrs. McCain said.

"I'm sure all of the children will. This will be a full day of activities. They'll probably knock out on the way back to the center."

"It's worth it. They're all having a good time. I didn't get a chance to do all of these things with Brandice when she was younger. I figured I better do some things with Brandon, especially since I don't plan on having any more children. I don't want to miss out like I already have with my daughter. She doesn't even want to hang out with me any more."

Crystal was glad Mrs. McCain had mentioned Brandice's name. She had wanted to find out how the teenager had been doing. "How's Brandice?"

"She's fine. Your husband is really doing a great job helping her with her grades in algebra."

"I was just wondering, because she seemed a little upset the last time I saw her," Crystal said carefully.

"That girl was probably worried about that algebra class. You know how teenagers can be. Either that or I think she and her boyfriend might not be talking this week. You know how teenage girls can get over these little boys. You remember those days, don't you?"

"That must have been it then," Crystal replied.

"Of course it was. Brandice will have to learn the hard way that everything in life doesn't come so easy. And she doesn't know it yet, but the boy problems have just begun."

"I'm so glad I didn't have to deal with all of those problems," Crystal admitted. "Warren and I have been together since forever."

"Lucky you. I wish I could say the same thing, but I guess you live and you learn."

After lunch the children rode the ponies, train, ferris wheel and carousel. At the end of the day, Crystal gave all the children the surprise she had promised them. Each child received a bag of cotton candy. They all cheered with delight when they received the treat.

Again, Crystal's heart was warmed by the children's happiness. Her soul was touched when both of the foster children hugged her to say thanks.

As soon as Crystal arrived home, she took a shower, removing all the dirt from the day. She was exhausted and knew the children were probably more tired than she had been. They had all probably fallen asleep as soon as they got their baths.

She snuggled down under the covers. Just as she was ready to doze off to sleep, she heard the garage door opening. Peeking over at the clock, she saw it was almost ten o'clock. She struggled to sit back up in the bed to wait for her husband to come in.

Her eyes were heavy, continuing to drift closed. When he finally made it in, she attempted to say hello. "Yeello."

He gave her a kiss, "What was that?" Warren asked.

"It was a cross between a yawn and a hello," Crystal said.

"Oh, I thought it was some sort of new language you were trying out. How was the field trip?"

"It was really fun. The sun was bright. There wasn't a cloud in the sky. All of the children had a great time."

"Sounds like it was fun."

"It was. I'll be glad when we can go on trips with our own children," Crystal said.

"In due time, honey."

"I wonder how long it will be before we can start the procedures."

"I don't know. Don't waste time racking your brain, especially since the doctor will be able to give us all the answers on Friday."

"You're right. I'm just a little eager, that's all."

"Honey, you look so tired. Go ahead and get some sleep."

"But I want to talk," Crystal attempted to protest. "How was your PTA meeting?" she asked through another yawn.

"It was good. I'll tell you all about it tomorrow. Now get some rest," Warren commanded playfully.

"Yes, sir. Goodnight," Crystal said, yawning again.

She was asleep before Warren could remove his tie.

It was Friday afternoon. Once again, Crystal and Warren were back sitting in front of Dr. Evans for their next fertility appointment. In the days prior to their appointment, Crystal found herself giddy with excitement. As the date for the appointment approached, Crystal was paying more attention to advertisements for babies. On her visit to the mall the day before, she had visited the children's section of Hecht's.

She hadn't been able to eat or sleep the day and night before; nervous anticipation made her stomach feel as if a pack of butterflies were congregating. Even now, sitting in front of the doctor, she still felt a quiver in her stomach.

Dr. Evans handed Crystal and Warren each a copy of the IVF manual. "I'm happy you've chosen to pursue the IVF option for conception."

Eager, Crystal said, "We prayed and discussed going ahead with the procedures and we feel we're making the right choice."

"My wife and I feel God wouldn't have led us in this direction if it weren't for a reason." Warren looked at Crystal as he said this. "Like my wife said, we've prayed about it and we feel it's in God's will for us to use medical assistance."

"Good then, I won't delay this process any longer," Dr. Evans said. "I'm sure you want as much information as possible, and as I promised at our last meeting, I'll explain our program from A to Z.

Crystal interrupted her. "Dr. Evans, I'd like to apologize for my actions during my last appointment." She was embarrassed about the way she had spoken to the doctor and could feel her cheeks getting hot.

"Mrs. Shaw . . ."

"You can call me Crystal," Crystal interjected.

"Crystal," the doctor continued, "don't worry about our last meeting. Believe me, I have seen worse. But I understand the reasons for your emotions. So don't worry about it. I've already forgotten."

"Thanks, Dr. Evans." Crystal was relieved. The doctor looked as if their last conversation hadn't fazed her at all. "I just needed to apologize."

"And I thank you." Dr. Evans said. She then continued, "For starters, in front of you are copies of the IVF manual. I'll give you a personal copy to keep before you leave."

Crystal opened her binder looking at the table of contents. Many of the chapter headings were unfamiliar. There were a few words that she did recognize in the glossary of terms, but many she didn't.

"Crystal, I see your eyes getting wider and wider," Dr. Evans said.

"You noticed?" Crystal chuckled.

"Don't worry about all the chapters. We will only be focusing on the main chapter on IVF. That chapter has the information on embryo and blastocyst transfer."

"Good, there is a lot of information here." Warren scanned down the page Crystal had the manual turned to.

"It's easier for me to set up one manual instead of a lot of mini brochures," Dr. Evans said. "First, I'd like to give you an overview on the ART technique we'll be doing. ART stands for Assisted Reproductive Technology. With ART techniques we can help couples achieve pregnancy with medical assistance. Not all couples are the same. Sometimes there are problems with the woman. Other times there are problems with the man. Of course there are also times when there is a problem for both the man and woman."

"And I guess in our case there are times when there isn't a problem for either person, for some unexplained reason," Crystal added.

"Exactly." Dr. Evans confirmed. "So depending on what the problem is or isn't, I then determine the ART procedure needed."

"You said you'd be doing a regular IVF procedure?" Warren asked.

"You are probably more familiar with it than you think. Many people used to refer to this procedure as making a test-tube baby."

"The baby will be made in a test tube?" Warren was confused.

"Not literally. In the procedure, some of Crystal's eggs will be harvested and combined with your sperm. This process takes place outside of the body. After about three to five days, the embryo or embryos which are formed will be placed into Crystal's uterus. Then a pregnancy test can be done in about fifteen days."

"That soon?" Crystal asked with excitement.

"Yes. The hope is the test will be positive. If it is, then we'll later do an ultrasound to see how many babies there are."

"How many babies? What do you mean?" Crystal asked.

"That will depend on the number of embryos that implant after the transfer. I can transfer up to three into the uterus."

"Three?" Crystal's jaw dropped.

"Up to three. You'll be given medication to allow your ovaries to release more than one egg. Normally with nature only one is released each month. There are exceptions and times when a woman's body does release more than one egg. But it isn't usually on a monthly basis."

"Twins run in my family," Warren said.

"That's a whole other story. One day maybe we'll talk about twins running in families," Dr Evans said. "As I was saying, Crystal, we'll give you a medication that will allow you to produce more than one egg. You might release one or you could release twenty-one. We never know until it happens."

"So if I release twenty-one then we would have twenty-one babies?" Crystal asked, sure it couldn't be true.

"Oh no, no. You might release that many, but then we will examine the quality of the eggs. Once we have isolated the best eggs, we then use the collected sperm and combine it with the eggs. Next we watch the mixture to see if a fusion occurs to cause embryos to form."

"The embryo is what's put into my uterus?" Crystal asked.

"Yes."

"Up to three?" Crystal asked for conformation.

"Correct."

"What happens if you only get two good eggs?" Warren asked.

"Then we work with two, hoping a fusion occurs and yields viable embryos," Dr. Evans said.

"What if you get ten good eggs?" Crystal asked.

"Then we have more to work with." Dr. Evans pulled out a

notepad and pen. "Okay let's look at this. Let's say hypothetically that we obtain twenty-one eggs, but only ten are of good quality." The doctor sketched as she spoke. "We attempt to fertilize all ten of them. Out of ten, six of them actually fertilize."

"You'll transfer three of them. What happens to the other three? Do they just end up wasted?" Crystal asked.

"No, they can be frozen for use at a later date. The first transfer may yield triplets, twins or just one baby. There is also a chance even in transferring three that it may not be successful. If that is the case, we can use the frozen embies at a later date to try again."

"Embies?" Warren asked.

"Yes, that is what some of my patients call their embryos."

"What if the first try is successful? Especially if it is successful with triplets or twins?"

"Then it is up to you, as to whether or not you would want to use the others later on or not."

"Or not? Then what would happen to them?"

"That's where moral issues come in. It will be up to you to decide what you want to do with the frozen embryos if you don't use them."

"Why not just fertilize a couple of eggs at a time, instead of more than three?" Crystal asked what she felt was a simple enough question.

"Ideally that would be great. But realistically ART procedures are pretty expensive. It's not an exact science in some aspects. We don't know how many eggs each woman will produce, nor do we know the number that will later fertilize, implant, and actually yield a live baby."

"Oh," was all Crystal could say.

"Plus the costs are just too great to fertilize one or two at a time."

"There's a great deal involved with this whole ART procedure," Warren stated.

"There are a lot of details. That's why I can't express enough how I like for my patients to be well informed."

"I could end up pregnant with triplets?" Crystal asked.

"It could happen, although the chances are low," Dr. Evans said.

Crystal let the information sink in. There was a chance she and Warren could become the parents of triplets. The house could grow from two to five almost overnight. She would be the mother of three.

"If you only want me to transfer one or two I can do that also. Although due to your age, I usually transfer three. Some couples know up front they can't handle triplets and don't even want to entertain the idea from the beginning."

"It could be a big gamble, couldn't it?" Warren asked.

"Yes sir, it could be. But we don't normally practice selective reduction. In other words, if you end up pregnant with triplets, then I want you to know up front, unless there is a valid medical reason, we don't want you to decide that instead of three babies you only want two and you want to terminate the growth of one of the embryos. So once the decision is made you need to stick with it." Dr. Evans said.

"We do understand." Crystal said.

Warren tapped the manual. "I'm glad we will have our own manual to take home."

"It is a wealth of information I'll admit, but you'll find it helpful I'm sure. The diagrams should also help you."

Dr. Evans continued to explain the various aspects of the ART procedure. Crystal and Warren asked questions as she went along.

As they wrapped up the appointment, Dr. Evans was ready to set them up to begin the procedures. "Looking at your LMP, Crystal, I am going to prescribe some birth control pills for you."

"Did you say birth control pills?" Warren asked.

"Yes." Dr. Evans held her hand up. "Don't be alarmed. You

heard me correctly. I know it sounds funny, but the pills will regulate your cycle and allow me to set up the start of the needed medications."

"It just sounds weird to me. Using birth control pills to help someone get pregnant."

"Make sure you read the section about birth control pills and IVF procedures. It is on page 23. We will start the medications in three weeks."

"That soon!" Crystal said with excitement.

"Yes, that soon," the doctor replied.

"That's pretty quick," Warren admitted.

"Compared to five years. Yes, I'd say you're right." Dr. Evans chuckled. She wrote out a prescription for birth control pills. "Here you are." She handed it to Crystal.

Crystal took the prescription. "So are we done?"

"Yes. You'll need to fill out some paper work and pay the first half of the procedure today. The remainder will be due in three weeks when you come back," Dr. Evans said.

"You mean the co-payment right?" Crystal asked.

"No, the first half of the procedure for regular IVF. All the costs are outlined on page thirty-seven."

Flipping to page thirty-seven of the manual Crystal saw the bottom line costs for the IVF procedure, which totaled $10,500. Her mouth dropped again. "That's a great deal of money. How much will my insurance cover?"

"Your insurance will not cover any of the actual IVF procedures."

"I am confused," Crystal said. "I thought my insurance would cover the procedures."

"Sadly, no. Many insurance companies don't cover the procedures, just the preliminary tests," the doctor informed her.

The excitement Crystal had built over the previous days slipped away instantaneously.

"Do people actually pay that much money?" Warren asked in just as much astonishment.

"Yes, some people pay even more. That is the average cost for the procedure you'll be undergoing."

"Where do people get that kind of money?" Crystal asked.

"Some people use money from their savings and others borrow the money."

"Are there any programs that help with the costs?" Warren asked.

"There aren't any that I know about," Dr. Evans said.

Warren placed his arm around his wife's shoulder. "Don't worry about it, Crystal. God will make a way. He didn't bring us this far just to leave us," he tried to reassure her.

Turning his attention back to the doctor he said, "Dr. Evans we'll need to get back with you on that start date. As you can see, we didn't realize the total amount of the costs involved."

"I understand. Just give us a call when you've decided when you want to start." Dr. Evans smiled and shook her head understandingly.

"We'll do that. Thank you again," Warren said, and they stood up to leave.

Chapter 12

Vivian Parker

"Mrs. Parker," Vivian's secretary spoke to her over the phone's intercom.

"Yes, Nikki." Vivian's mouth was full of the turkey and cheese sandwich she had just bit into.

"I called Trace Whitman as you asked, he's on line two."

"Thank you, Nikki," Vivian replied as she chewed more quickly and swallowed. She picked up her bottled water and took a quick sip then wiped her mouth with a napkin and cleared her throat. Then she picked up the receiver, and pressed line two.

"Trace, hi," her voice held the same excitement she knew Trace Whitman would hold as soon as he heard her news.

"Mrs. Parker, I'm glad to hear from you. It's good news I hope?" Trace sounded hopeful.

"It most certainly is. I spoke with the construction manager, and we'll be able to start your project two months ahead of schedule."

"Wonderful, wonderful. That is good news."

Vivian heard Trace clap his hands together as he spoke. "You know we weren't really sure at first, but since the weather has held up so well, the projects ahead of yours have been completed before schedule."

"I'm glad to hear it. I have a meeting with the other associates this afternoon and I'll let them know. Thanks for approving our date to be pushed up."

"No, Trace, thank you for choosing our company and allowing us the chance to make sure your building needs are met."

"I guess we could go back and forth all morning. We'll just have to say that all parties are pleased with the agreement," Trace said.

"I'll let you know the exact date as soon as I find out."

"Again, that will be great," Trace said.

"And if you have any other needs, questions, or concerns, let me know."

"Thank you, Mrs. Parker."

"Trace," Vivian said as if reprimanding him.

"Sorry, thanks Vivian," Trace corrected himself.

"You're more than welcome. As I said, as soon as we have the exact date I'll let you know. Talk with you later," Vivian said and hung up the phone.

She looked up to see her husband staring at her with admiration. "Honey? How long have you been standing there?"

"Long enough. You are something else. I guess hanging around me all of these years has worn off on you. Look at you eating sandwiches at your desk. And I'll just bet you used to feel sorry for me sitting at my desk eating sandwiches alone."

Vivian chuckled. She balled up the wrapper with the remainder of her sandwich and threw it in the trash. "You're right, I did. But this is different. I have a lot of work to do, and to tell you the truth, I didn't want to take an hour break. I really do enjoy being back. I hadn't realized just how much I love doing what I do." She stood and crossed the office towards her sink to wash her hands. After her hands were clean she put on some Juniper Breeze lotion.

"Now do you understand where I was coming from back then?"

Vivian smiled knowingly.

"So, the Whitman project is going to begin early?" Roland asked.

"Yes, next month."

"How did you pull that off?"

"Roland, you know me. I aim to please. It took pulling a few strings and calling in a few favors. But you know, when I really want something I won't stop until I get it."

"That's why I am so glad you are my VP. I am the luckiest CEO in the world to have a woman like you by my side. We are a force to be reckoned with."

Vivian smiled. "We most certainly are. The Whitman project is phenomenal. Everyone in Silvermont will be talking about the skyscraper once it's complete. It'll stand out in the skyline as an easily recognizable landmark."

"It's your baby," Roland said.

"It most certainly is. I can't wait for the construction to begin so I can track its progress."

"Time has been flying," Roland said. "Next month will be here before we know it."

"Time has flown by. I can't believe in just four days we'll be back at the doctor's office to start my procedures for the IVF."

"The twelfth?"

"Yes, the twelfth. Where have the last few weeks gone? It seems like it was just Thanksgiving."

"It does. I guess it's because we've been so busy. Busier than I've seen this company in years."

Sheepishly, Roland looked at Vivian. "What?" she asked.

"I need to ask Renee if she blocked my schedule for the appointments next week. I can't remember if I told her or not."

"It is all taken care of. Renee talked with Nikki, and it's done."

Roland sighed with relief. "I should have known. Renee

and Nikki work well together corresponding things—almost as well as we do."

"They sure do. Speaking of which, I think it's about time for both of them to get a raise, don't you? I mean, they're both invaluable secretaries. If one or both of them quit, it would take us months to get someone up to speed."

"That's a good idea. When's Secretary's Day? Oh never mind. It doesn't matter when it is. We should send them flowers to let them know how much we appreciate them."

Vivian's intercom beeped. "Mrs. Parker?"

"Yes, Nikki."

"Please tell Mr. Parker that Renee just called, and he has an urgent message from the CEO of the Millar Group."

"I sure will, thank you."

"You're welcome," Nikki said and disconnected the intercom.

Roland shook his head in agreement with their previous conversation. "Invaluable. Can you decide on an amount for their raises and send them some roses or something?"

"Yellow roses for Nikki, it's her favorite color. And red carnations for Renee, they're her favorite flowers."

Roland shook his head again. "We're a great duo." He gave her a quick peck on the cheek and left her office to return to his.

"Mr. and Mrs. Parker," Dr. Evans said, "we were able to retrieve eighteen eggs."

"That's good!" Vivian exclaimed.

"Hold on, I'm sorry, only three of the eggs are viable."

"Three is better than none, right?" Roland said with optimism.

"You're right. Because of the small number of eggs we'll be working with, I think it's best to perform the ICSI procedure. I want to ensure the sperm is injected directly into the egg. I can't waste these valuable eggs by doing a regular IVF procedure, putting the eggs in a dish with the sperm hoping they'll produce an embryo on their own."

"When will this all take place?" Vivian asked.

"Within the hour."

"When will we know if it was successful?" Roland asked.

"I should start to see the cells multiplying within the day. If they do multiply successfully, in three days we can transfer the embryos."

"Then we wait again?" Vivian asked.

"Right, in about fifteen days we'll be able to do a pregnancy test."

"You mean in a little over fifteen days from now I could find out I'm pregnant?"

"Yes," Dr. Evans answered.

"Modern science is amazing," Roland said.

"It is," the doctor agreed.

"What do we do now?" Vivian raised her hands slightly and let them fall to her lap.

"Continue taking your progesterone and prenatal vitamins. I am also going to put you on an antibiotic to help prevent infection."

"What about, you know?" Roland asked, his face looking sheepish.

"No sexual activity until I give you the okay," the doctor answered. "You can go home. I'll call you in about twenty-four hours to update you on the progress."

"We'll talk to you then. You have our pager and cell phone numbers. We'll be waiting for your call."

Vivian and Roland waited patiently by the phone the next morning. They had tossed and turned all night and had gotten up at five o'clock. It was now nine, twenty-six hours since the eggs were retrieved.

"It's been over twenty-four hours," Vivian said to Roland as she sat at the computer typing.

Roland placed his hands on her shoulders. "Just a little over twenty-four hours. She'll call soon. Don't worry. No news is good news."

"I wonder who came up with that silly saying. No news is just, no news. Period."

"Vivian," Roland said in a chastising tone.

"Sorry. I'm a little antsy I guess. Look at this." Vivian pointed at the computer screen. "I've been reading a lot about the egg retrieval process and fertilization. We were lucky to have had so many eggs retrieved and blessed to have the number of usable eggs that we ended up with."

"Is this a credible source?"

"It is. I also found out that the embryo, or embryos, can be transferred on day three or five. Some sources say day five is better than day three. But the sources flip flop on which is actually better."

"Dr. Evans wants to do a day three transfer, right?"

"Yeah, she feels it would be better and I trust her judgment," Vivian said.

"At least that way it will cut the wait down by two days."

"Roland, what if all three eggs become embryos? I mean, I know there is a chance that only one or two could develop, but what if all three do? I'd be pregnant with triplets."

"Triplets, a house with four children. Our son would finally get his wish."

"Three times over," Vivian laughed.

"It would be a huge change."

"Hey, I just thought about something."

"What?" Roland asked.

"All our other bedrooms are upstairs away from us."

"What about it?"

"We can't have the babies up here and us downstairs."

Nodding his head in understanding Roland said, "You're right."

"Something will have to change." Vivian thought about it for a few seconds. "I guess we could move up here temporarily."

"Or," Roland said, his mind quickly working. "Come with me." He took her hand and led her down the stairs to the study. "We could convert this room into a nursery."

Vivian looked around, sizing up the idea. "With the right modifications it could be done. It would be perfect, absolutely perfect, and we wouldn't have to move. They would be right next to us."

"Problem solved," Roland said with great satisfaction.

"I'll pull up the blueprints of the house to look for the dimensions of the room. Then we can decide on what kind of modifications will be needed. I'll plan neutral colors that will work for a boy, girl, or both."

"Or three," Roland grinned.

Within the hour Vivian had drafted the projected modifications for the room. If the room was to be changed, it could accommodate three cribs, two dressers, two nightstands, two rocking chairs, and a changing station. She chose the primary colors green and yellow with a hint of pink and blue.

She searched the Internet ordering furniture and accessories. Vivian liked the teddy bear theme and ordered the corresponding lamps, rugs, diaper pails, crib bedding and curtains for the French doors of the study. The French doors would be the babies' window to the world. She found what she thought was the cutest little, white-wicker rocking chair with a matching stool, and she ordered two.

Feeling the room needed more, she searched on for other items she felt would make the nursery complete. She went on to order nursery rhyme CD's, a baby monitor, baby mobiles, books, and toys to fill the shelves of the study.

While she tried to think of what else the nursery might need, she heard the phone ring. After the second ring, she heard Roland ask if she was going to get it.

"No. Can you get it?" she replied.

After a couple of minutes Roland appeared in the doorway of the computer room. "That was the doctor." Vivian stopped cold and held her breath. "She said things look very good so far. All three eggs fertilized and the cells have started to divide."

Vivian started to breathe again, letting out a sigh of relief. "Oh my God, Roland. I can't believe it. It is really going to happen!"

"I told you not to worry."

"I know. It was just hard to believe with all of the factors we were facing."

"She said they'll continue to monitor the progress, and we can come back in for the transfer the day after tomorrow."

"Can you believe it?" Vivian stood up and embraced him.

"Believe it. It's going to happen. Our lives are going to change drastically. In two days our lives will never be the same."

Excited, Vivian turned back to the computer. "Look at what I've come up with so far."

She showed him the modifications and all of the items she ordered off the Internet.

"And you said you weren't sure," Roland mocked.

"I know. I guess I was really on a roll. I figure I can always cancel the orders if we don't need it all. And now if everything continues to go well, we won't have to send anything back."

"It looks that way."

"I also found this list of the top thirty things you need for a new baby. I can start ordering those things also."

"Don't forget about me in all of your excitement. I want to do some things too."

"Guess I did get excited. I'll slow down. We can go out together and shop for everything else after the pregnancy test is confirmed."

"Thank you. I'd like that a lot better," Roland replied, kissing his wife on the forehead.

By nine o'clock the next night, Vivian was exhausted and ready for bed. She was excited and nervous about their appointment at eight the next morning for the embryo transfer.

Once she was in the bed, she reflected on the productive day she had. She woke up early, full of energy, and packed up as much as she could in the study, knowing once she was pregnant she would not be able to lift the heavy boxes. Vivian chuckled, hoping Clea would appreciate the calories she had burned.

Roland told her not to worry about packing the room up. He said that he would hire someone to pack it all instead. But Vivian needed something to do to get her through the day. She hadn't returned to work since the egg retrieval and wasn't planning on returning until after the pregnancy test came back. Vivian was and had always been a hard worker. She deserved a break. She used the time to relax and focus on the family they were about to build.

Now she was back in bed, tired but still very excited. The hot shower she had taken was just what her body needed. Roland was already asleep.

The alarm rang at five-fifteen in the morning. It took Vivian only a few seconds to realize what day it was. She hit the alarm to stop its insistent ringing.

Next to her, Roland stirred. She gently nudged him, "Roland honey, it's time to wake up."

Groggily Roland answered her. "I wasn't asleep."

"You weren't? You never are. The snoring I just heard was your sinuses, right?"

"Yeah," he said, turning over to face her.

"One of these days I'm going to get a tape recorder and tape you."

"I was awake, really. I just had my eyes closed."

"If you say so," Vivian said incredulously. "I was really tired last night. I got most of the study packed up. I guess we'll need to move the desk and chairs into the attic for a while."

"I saw all the boxes you packed. You moved pretty fast." Roland smiled.

"I'm on a mission. In less than three weeks we'll have a confirmed pregnancy test and after today I know you won't tolerate me lifting anything heavy."

"I didn't want you lifting anything heavy today either," Roland said.

"I know, but I just had all of this nervous energy. With each box I packed, I got more and more energized."

"I understand. I've been thinking about our appointment also. It was hard for me to concentrate yesterday." He laughed. "I guess I should have stayed home and helped you out. I couldn't cancel my meeting will the Millar Group, though. It went well but I think they could tell my mind was a little pre-occupied."

"Guess we need to get up and get dressed. I want to get there a little early. I'm so nervous," Vivian admitted.

"Let's get ready," Roland agreed.

The drive to the clinic seemed like a blur to Vivian. She couldn't focus on anything while thinking about the changes about to occur. She thought about the possibility of having three babies. She even looked at the back seat of the SUV trying to picture three car seats—each holding a little baby.

They arrived at the clinic thirty-five minutes early. In the lobby they signed in and took a seat. They nervously made small talk—neither of them really able to concentrate on anything but the excitement about the upcoming procedure.

A few minutes before eight, Vivian saw Dr. Evans walk behind the receptionist's desk. Through the closed glass she couldn't hear anything, but she could see a look of disappointment on the doctor's face.

Taking Roland's hand into hers, she squeezed hard. Feeling his wife tense, Roland looked up in the direction Vivian was still looking and saw the doctor's grim expression.

They watched as the doctor picked up the phone receiver and dropped her head down. Vivian thought she saw the doctor mouth the word "Parker," but she couldn't be quite sure. After a couple of seconds, the doctor put her hand on her forehead and started shaking her head slowly in a negative motion.

They watched as she then hung up the phone and took a deep breath. It was only then that the doctor noticed Vivian and Roland watching her. Vivian made eye contact. The doctor's look of disappointment was quickly replaced with a forced smile.

Even though Vivian saw the smile, she couldn't forget what she had just witnessed. The look in the doctor's eyes and the phony smile confirmed to Vivian that something was very wrong. The feeling returned to her as it had for her first appointment, only this time she felt ten times worse. Before she knew it the doctor had disappeared around the corner.

"Roland, something's wrong," Vivian said. Her stomach started to churn.

Roland patted her hand with his. "Think positive, sweetheart. There could be a number of reasons for what we just witnessed. I'm sure it had nothing to do with us," he answered, sounding doubtful himself.

"You saw the way she looked at us when she realized we were sitting here. I think I saw her mouth our name." Vivian could not only feel her heart beating rapidly in her chest, she could feel the pressure of her heart racing in her ears.

Roland squeezed her hand tighter. "Calm down. Your hands are sweating. Let's see what the doctor has to say before we jump to any conclusions."

Just as Roland finished his sentence, the clinic door opened. With the same forced smile still plastered on her face, Dr. Evans called them to the back.

In her gut, Vivian knew something was wrong. Especially since the doctor was calling them in personally and not one of the nurses.

The doctor led them to her office instead of the exam room, which continued to confirm Vivian's fears. Vivian was glad she had Roland there with her for whatever bombshell the doctor was about to drop.

"Mr. and Mrs. Parker, please have a seat." Dr. Evans motioned to the chairs in front of her desk. After they sat down she continued, "Mr. and Mrs. Parker, I am sorry to tell you that I have some bad news," she paused. "The embryos arrested. They've stopped growing."

"All three?" Vivian asked in disbelief.

"I'm afraid so. The first one stopped a few hours after I phoned you the other day. We continued to monitor the other two. One arrested a few hours ago and the last one about an hour ago." She paused again. "I'm sorry."

Vivian dropped her head and took deep breaths. She had been so close, the closest she had ever been to actually being able to conceive. Deep down she felt as if she had just lost three children. She was speechless for what seemed like an eternity.

Composing herself finally, she mustered enough courage

to ask what could be done. The doctor told them they could try again in about two months, reminding them that the chances were high for the same result to repeat.

Vivian and Roland quickly left the office. They drove in silence all the way home.

Chapter 13

Shelby Tomlinson

Phillip leaned back in his office chair, staring at the clock on his phone. It was almost time for him to meet Shelby at the doctor's office for his appointment. It was his turn to be tested.

His mind hadn't been on the appointment—he'd almost forgotten about it. Instead, his mind was on the certified letter he'd received. He'd finally been able to get in contact with the right person at the child support office, although the information he was given was unwelcome. The child support agent told him that Jeana Sands had reported him as the father of her 9-year-old son, and she was seeking back child support.

Phillip had tried to explain that he didn't have a child, and that he knew a Ms. Sands in college but had not seen the woman in years. The agent disregarded what he said and told him that he was due in court. She also told him he'd need to contact his lawyer to assist in getting the matter resolved.

He couldn't understand why, after all the years that had passed, Jeana was trying to get child support for a child that wasn't his. It was time for him to contact his father's lawyer to see what could be done about the false accusations. Looking at the time on his phone, he realized he wouldn't have time. He'd have to make the calls later and leave right away in order to arrive at the doctor's appointment on time.

"Hey, Phillip," Phillip's friend and co-worker, Will said, as he stepped into his office. "You got a second?"

"Not really, man. I've got to go to an appointment with Shelby, and I am about to run late. Can I call you later?"

Phillip closed his office door. Will walked with him as he headed for the elevator.

"Sure, it's not that important. I just wanted to see if you were going to join us tonight to shoot some hoops. Call me later and let me know."

Phillip pushed the elevator button and looked at his watch. "I don't know. I'll have to see how Shelby is after this appointment of hers. You know it's one of those women things."

"Check you later then." Will turned towards his own office.

Shelby sat in Dr. Silva's office waiting for her husband to return from collecting his semen specimen.

When he did return his face was beet red. She saw sweat beads on his forehead. "Are you okay?" Shelby asked.

He closed the office door behind him before saying, "Yes, I'm fine." He lowered his head and whispered so no one else would hear him. "I'm just not used to doing what I had to just do in cup. It's embarrassing coming out here with people looking at me."

"Only the nurses and doctors know why you went into the back," Shelby whispered back a little louder.

Phillip looked behind them, making sure the doctor wasn't walking in. "You couldn't hear anything could you? I tried to be quiet. Man, that was so embarrassing."

"Don't worry about it. I didn't hear a thing. The room is soundproof, I'm sure."

"I don't ever want to do this again," he stated.

Shelby tried to remain calm saying, "I know you're embarrassed, but look at all the tests I've had to undergo compared to yours." Her whisper continued to escalate. "Many of my tests involved pain to go along with the embarrassment." Even though she tried to keep her composure, her temper mounted.

"It wasn't a pleasure, believe me. Maybe if you could have been in there to help me out, it would have been," Phillip said, trying to make a joke.

"Oh Phillip, stop," Shelby said, not moved by his attempt at humor.

"I'm serious."

No longer whispering she said, "So am I. Just think about how embarrassing it is to see a negative pregnancy test or an ultra sound with no baby to show. Now that's embarrassing. Or how about..."

"Okay honey, I understand. Just bear with me. It's my first time," Phillip pleaded.

Shelby took a deep breath. This was supposed to be a good day. They were making progress in finding out what the cause of their infertility might be. Her husband agreed to have whatever testing he needed to have done. Not wanting to let her temper escalate until she had another anxiety attack she said, "I'm sorry. I didn't mean to get carried away."

"All this stuff can get pretty emotional, can't it?" Phillip said.

"I'm glad you're starting to finally understand."

Phillip looked back towards the office door. "I wonder where Dr. Silva is."

Just as he said, this the doctor walked in. "Ah, Mr. and Mrs. Tomlinson. Sorry to keep you waiting." His Spanish accent was rushed and heavy. "I had a very urgent phone call."

"So how did the test turn out?" Phillip asked.

"It will be a few days before we know the results," Shelby blurted out. "Sorry, Dr. Silva. I guess I'm still in nurse mode."

"That's alright. I'm glad you know something about the process. You are correct. It will be a few days before we have all the test results. I'll have you come back for an appointment to discuss the results. We will need to draw some blood for the hepatitis and HIV tests," Dr. Silva added.

"You want to draw blood for an HIV test? I'm not sick and don't look sick, so you don't have to do any additional tests on me," Phillip said.

"I don't think you are sick. These are the tests we do on all of our infertility patients. It is standard procedure."

Shelby glared at Phillip. She knew he got the point, because he immediately pulled up the sleeve on his shirt and said, "Take all the blood you want!"

One week later Shelby and Phillip returned to Dr. Silva's office for the test results. "Thank you for coming back in, Mr. and Mrs. Tomlinson. The test results are all back. The HIV and hepatitis tests were both negative. The overall results for the semen analysis were good. With an IVF procedure, we will be able to help you conceive," Dr. Silva reported.

"What do you mean by that?" Phillip asked before Shelby had a chance to open her mouth. He had been nervous about the results for a week. He hadn't had an appetite and had gone sleepless most of the nights. He couldn't understand why waiting for the results was affecting him so badly.

"Let me go over the results with you. Like I said, the overall results were good. There are many factors we look at when checking the semen for the analysis. Factors such as appearance, viscosity, color, count, and motility. We also look at the pH and volume of the sample provided."

"Viscosity?" Phillip asked.

"Yes, we need to see how thick the fluid is."

"Is that the problem?" Phillip asked, slightly irritated the doctor was suggesting that he had some sort of problem.

Shelby placed her hand on his arm, "Just listen to what the doctor has to say, Phillip."

"No, Mr. Tomlinson, there are no problems with your viscosity or color. Give me just a moment, and I'll get to the abnormality in your results. First I need to give you the whole picture. One factor can affect another."

Phillip heard the doctor say something about being abnormal and he didn't like it. It made him think the doctor was calling him a freak or something. He clinched his fists as his temper rose. He hoped Shelby had not noticed the gesture.

"The volume of semen you provided was good. It was about 3 ML and anything between 1.5 to 5 ML is a good number. The morphology was normal also." Explaining further the doctor said, "When I say morphology that means the shape. All of your sperm were shaped normally. None of them had two heads or extra tails."

"That's good right?" Phillip asked.

"Yes, it is extremely good."

Phillip felt a little better knowing he didn't have any freaky-looking sperm.

Dr. Silva continued. "The pH was 7.5 and anything between 6 to 9 is also very good."

"Things don't sound all that bad to me, Dr. Silva." Phillip's voice was arrogant. He sat up straighter in his chair.

"What could the problem be? It doesn't sound all that bad to me either." Shelby asked.

"There are two other factors left." The doctor cleared his throat.

"What is it, doc? Just tell us," Phillip said, pressuring the doctor to get it over with.

"Motility and count. The motility tells us how quickly and how many of the sperm are moving. And yours are moving just fine." The doctor paused for a second. "The count is your problem. You have a very low sperm count, Mr. Tomlinson."

Phillip looked at the doctor trying to make sense of what he was saying. He looked over at Shelby, and she looked as if she understood exactly. He figured she must have, because her face seemed relieved to hear the news.

"The count is low, that means the number of sperm you have is very low in the relation to the sample we collected."

"But just a few minutes ago you said the amount." He stopped to correct himself. "Or shall I say, the volume, was good." Phillip knew he wasn't stupid. The doctor had just told him not thirty seconds prior that the amount was good.

"Yes, the amount of seminal fluid is different from the actual amount of sperm. That's why I needed to review all of the results with you. We count the number of sperm per ML, and your numbers are abnormally low."

There he goes again using the word abnormal, Phillip thought.

"As I said when we began, with the use of modern science and IVF, I can help you to conceive."

Phillip knew he wasn't brainless. He knew a little about the sperm and the egg. "But wait a minute. I do know a little about the sperm and egg, and it only takes one sperm to fertilize an egg, so what's the big deal?" Phillip's voice was filled with an air of sarcasm.

"You're right, Mr. Tomlinson. It *does* only take one, but in order for that one to make it there, a normal male starts out with millions per episode. You don't have millions."

Phillip stared at the doctor. As far as he was concerned, what the man was saying didn't make any sense.

"Let me break it down and put it to you like this. Let's say the average male started out with say ten sperm on the journey to the egg. Only one or two may reach the egg. And for the ones that do make it there, they still have to be strong enough to penetrate the egg's outer protective covering in order to fertilize the egg and make a baby."

"It still would only take one, right?" Phillip said.

"Yes, but in your case, Mr. Tomlinson, you would only be starting out with one versus the average of ten."

Phillip sat back in the chair. He felt as if a linebacker had just knocked the wind out of him. He was finally starting to understand.

Shelby kept her hand on his arm but said nothing. He took her silence as a sign; a sign telling him that she could now blame him for their not conceiving. He had been right all along. He was being punished for his lifestyle in college.

He couldn't sit there and let his wife think he wasn't man enough to get her pregnant. "Are you sure that test is right? From what you're saying, the chances are slim to none that my wife and I can get pregnant on our own."

The doctor looked between both of them. "That's what I'm saying."

Phillip wanted to speak again. He wanted to tell the doctor that there was nothing wrong with him, because he had gotten a girl pregnant before, but he couldn't say it with Shelby sitting there. It just wasn't the right time or place. Why hadn't he come clean with her before now?

He wished he hadn't taken the easy way out of his responsibilities all those years ago. The price he was now paying was enormous. He wouldn't be able to get his own wife pregnant. The tests showed his chances to be a father were blown away all because of his irresponsibility years ago. He should have never told Jeana to terminate the pregnancy. He should have been a man about the situation instead of a coward.

After a few seconds of silence, Shelby asked the doctor, "What can be done? What do we do now? What do you suggest?" She asked the questions in rapid succession. To

Phillip it seemed as if she had already formed the questions way before their appointment.

"That's the good thing about modern science. We can do IVF. You are very familiar with IVF procedures, aren't you Shelby?"

"Yes," Shelby replied.

"Good. I'll give you some more information on what we do at this clinic. Basically it should be the same as at Dr. Evans office, but in some instances a little different since my office is a little smaller than hers."

It hurt Phillip to hear that Shelby had already given up on his ability to make her pregnant. She didn't care about his feelings; she was happy that the doctor was giving her answers to her problems.

"When can we do it?" Shelby asked.

"We can start as soon as this month, but I would like for you to go home, read over the materials, and discuss it together first. Then give me a call when you've both made a decision."

"We'll do that, thank you," Shelby said.

"Yeah, we'll do that. Thanks, Doc," Phillip said with no sincerity.

"Very well. I hope to hear from you soon."

Shelby broke the speed limit a couple times trying to get home. She was steaming—appalled by Phillip's demeanor during the doctor's appointment. He left the office with such a smug look on his face that she'd waved him away to get to her car. But now she couldn't wait to get home and confront him. *What is his problem?*

As soon as Shelby walked into the kitchen, she saw Phillip closing the refrigerator door.

After swallowing his mouth full of juice he asked, "Hey, you want some juice?"

"No," Shelby said in exasperation. "What was that all about?"

"What was what all about?" Phillip said innocently.

"Your whole attitude at the doctor's office earlier."

"That doctor just got on my nerves. It was like he had to micro-analyze everything. I really don't think it's as bad as he said it is," Phillip said, taking another gulp of juice.

Shelby took a deep breath, counting to ten in her head before she spoke again. "Phillip," she said her words as calm as possible. "The doctor was just doing his job—what we're paying him to do. You acted as if he had some personal vendetta against us."

"He made it seem like I'm some sort of freak, saying that I was abnormal, and I'd never be able to get you pregnant."

"Hold on. You sound like you are taking all this personally. He didn't say you were a freak. What he *said* was there were some abnormalities in the test results."

"I disagree with him," Phillip said, clearly acting agitated with her.

"Numbers don't lie. If something were wrong, then other factors in the test would have come out skewed. Look at the bright side, at least now we know what the problem is, and he can help us have a child," Shelby said.

Phillip gazed at her. She distinctly got the feeling she had said something to hurt his feelings.

"Look, I know the doctor is wrong about me being able to get you pregnant."

"Phillip, he didn't say you couldn't. He said the chances are very, very slim."

Phillip gazed at her again.

"Why do you keep staring at me like that?"

He set the glass down. "Shelby. There is something I need to tell you." His tone softened. He moved towards her and took her hand, pulling her towards the den.

"What? You sound serious," she asked.

"Let's go have a seat."

"What is it? What's so important that you want to sit down and talk about it?"

"Come on, let's sit." He led her to the couch.

Once they were seated, he faced her, then held both her hands.

"Now you want to hold both my hands. This must be pretty heavy. What are you going to tell me? Did you do something to affect the test results?" Shelby asked, not knowing what to expect.

"Shelby, bear with me please. Allow me to speak." He paused.

"Go ahead. I'm listening. Talk," Shelby coaxed.

He took a deep breath. "There's something I guess I should have told you years ago. It's something that's been on my mind for a while, and lately it's been eating away at me."

He stopped and looked away from her for a moment, unable to meet her eyes.

Shelby squeezed his hands encouraging him to continue. "I'm listening," Shelby said impatiently.

"Something happened years ago before we even met. And because of what happened, God has been punishing me by not allowing us to have children."

Shelby sat back, a quizzical expression on her face. "What? What are you talking about? You're not making any sense. What do you mean you are being punished? What happened?"

"My sophomore year in college I got this girl pregnant."

She pulled her hands away from his. "You did what?" Shelby was bewildered. "Did you just say you got some girl pregnant?"

"Yes."

"What girl? What happened? Do I know who it is?" Shelby asked question after question. "Answer me!" She said, infuriated by the fact that he wasn't answering her questions fast enough.

"She was my girlfriend at the time. And, no, you don't know her."

"What's her name? How do you know I don't know her?" Shelby was livid. Phillip had never said anything about an ex-girlfriend getting pregnant before. She knew the names of his previous girlfriends. Phillip had told her about the only three girls he had ever dated before her.

"Her name is Jeana Sands and you don't know her because she dropped out of school that same semester this all happened.

"When did you date her? You told me about the previous three girlfriends before me. You never mentioned anyone named Janie."

"Jeana," Phillip corrected.

Shelby really didn't care how the girl's name was pronounced. "Whatever! I really don't care what her name is." She waved her hand dismissively. "Just tell me what happened. And why didn't you ever tell me you had a child? Where's the child now?"

"There is no child," Phillip told her.

"Huh? What do you mean? You said you got your girlfriend pregnant."

"I did get her pregnant. But I told Jeana I wasn't ready to be a father and she wasn't ready to be a mother. So I told her she needed to terminate the pregnancy," Phillip confessed.

He looked back into her eyes, letting out a sigh, relieved he had revealed his heavy burden. He attempted to take hold of her hands again, but Shelby wouldn't let him. She snatched her hands away.

Her stare bore into him with fury. Shelby erupted and stood. "You told her to have an abortion? Because it wasn't the right time for you? You ended an innocent child's life for your convenience!"

Phillip obviously hadn't expected the eruption. He sat back with fear in his eyes. Quickly he said, "No. No, Shelby, listen. After thinking about it for a couple of days, I told her not to go through with it. So she didn't."

This was all too much. What was he talking about? He'd just said he'd gotten this girl pregnant. Confused Shelby said, "Phillip you said just a second ago that there wasn't a child." She closed her eyes and shook her head vigorously, trying to make some sense of what she was hearing. "What, happened? It wasn't yours or something?"

"No, Jeana had a miscarriage a couple of weeks later," Phillip said hurriedly.

None of this was making any sense to her. There was silence between the two. Shelby stood against the French doors on the other side of the room—as far away from Phillip as she could get.

She stood speechless looking in Phillip's direction, although she wasn't really looking at him, but through him. She tried to absorb everything he was telling her.

"Phillip, why are you telling me all of this now, of all times? You've kept this secret for so long," Shelby finally said, her fury slightly weakened.

"Because it's been eating away at me, ever since we started talking about having children. I've just felt like I'm being punished for the decision I made, telling her to terminate the pregnancy. I'll admit it was a bad decision, but I did change my mind about it. But I'm still being punished." He paused. "I saw this TV evangelist one morning who said God holds us accountable for our sins. And we will pay for them in one way or another."

"You feel like you were being punished when the miscarriage happened?" Shelby asked.

"Yeah. That's what I mean, and because of what I first told her. I figured all this time we couldn't get pregnant because of my stupid decision."

"I still don't understand why you hadn't told me this before. Why couldn't you come to me? If you were being punished, that means I was being punished also, I had a right to know."

"I know and I'm sorry. I should have told you sooner, but it was just too hard and embarrassing. There was never a right time. Then it didn't seem as important anymore, until recently."

"You should have told me, Phillip. Look at all the time that's already been wasted."

"I know, that's why I had to tell you now." He stood, closing the distance between them. Putting his arms around her shoulders, he said, "I knew the doctor was wrong about me being able to get you pregnant. Especially since I got someone pregnant before. I don't want you thinking I'm not man enough to get you pregnant."

Shelby pushed him away and moved back towards the couch. "So what is this, Phillip? Is this a male ego thing or something? Is that what you're afraid of now? You're afraid I don't think you're man enough to get me pregnant?" Her fury was mounting again.

"Yes, sweetheart. I don't want you thinking that."

"Phillip, I don't think that. I've never thought that. All this time I thought there was something wrong with me. I never thought any less of you. All this time I've been feeling depressed. And when I think of all those unnecessary anxiety attacks . . ." She paused shaking her head. "I can't believe you just sat back and allowed me to go through this for so long."

Phillip put his hands out towards her. "I'm sorry, Shelby."

"That was really selfish of you, Phillip. Did you ever think for once that maybe, just maybe, God wasn't punishing you? Maybe all things happen for a reason. God is a loving God. Maybe it just wasn't meant for that other child to come into this world. God probably knew you weren't ready either. And maybe we haven't been able to conceive our own child because you have been hiding information that is vital to our marriage."

"Shelby, I . . ." Phillip tried to speak, but Shelby quickly cut him off.

Tears welled in her eyes. "Did you ever think for one second that if you had told me the truth about all of this, the burden would have been lifted a long time ago? Perhaps we could have found out about our medical problem sooner! Then, Phillip, we wouldn't be sitting here right now having this conversation. Instead, we could be talking about what kind of toddler bed to buy or what daycare to put our child in," Shelby said, determined to let him know how she really felt.

"Shelby, I'm sorry. I know mere words can't really express how sorry I truly am."

Shelby paced the room as far away from him as she could. She clinched her fists. "I am so angry right now, and in the same instance it hurts to know you've been holding back from me." The tears she was trying to hold back streamed down her cheeks.

"I'm . . ."

"Sorry, I know," Shelby said, finishing his sentence.

"I finally came clean. And I *am* sorry. I hate myself for hurting you. I didn't realize all of this would hurt you this much. Please forgive me. I'm sorry." He walked towards her trying to take her in his arms again. She jerked her body away.

She walked back to the couch and sat down. "You laid this on me like a ton of bricks. Now you want me to forgive you," she snapped her fingers, "just like that? How do I know you aren't keeping anything else from me?"

Phillip looked away. "No. I'm not holding anything else back from you."

"Phillip, I don't know what to do. You've really hurt me.

You have truly broken my trust in you. I thought we had something so special. I thought we knew all the important things we needed to know about one another. Now I don't know if I really know you at all."

"Baby," Phillip sat back on the opposite end of the couch and placed his head in his hands. "I am so sorry. Please forgive me. I'll do whatever you want for me to make it up to you." He looked back up.

He again reached to touch her. His touch felt like hot coals. She winced. His touch repulsed her. He retracted his hand.

"Sweetheart . . ." His voice trailed.

She could hear the pain in his voice and looked directly in his eyes. "Phillip. I . . ." Shelby started to say, but was choked by the lump in her throat. She loved him so much. And deep down she knew Phillip wouldn't hurt her intentionally. Even though she had just been furious at him, she loved him too much to let what he had just revealed come between them.

"I'll make it up to you. I don't care how long it takes. I'll make it up. I feel like a burden has been lifted off of me by telling you all of this. I can start by going back to Dr. Silva and letting him do whatever procedures he needs.

I just want to see a smile on your face again." He moved towards her and began caressing her cheeks. This time she didn't move. "I don't want to see you upset like this. Let's call the doctor first thing in the morning to see when we can get in," Phillip pleaded.

Shelby looked into his eyes; she wanted so desperately to believe his apology. Her need to believe him, outweighed everything else. Even though he said he wanted to move forward with IVF procedures, the joy she would have normally felt had been altered. Finally hearing the words from him was a bittersweet moment.

"Phillip, I need some time alone. I don't want to hear anything else right now." She stood and ran sobbing from the room.

Phillip sat motionless on the couch. He wanted to follow her but didn't. He couldn't have said anything else even if he wanted. His heart beat furiously from the new lies he had just made up and told his wife. Each time he opened his mouth the lies continued to flow. He had not wanted to deceive Shelby but felt he had no other choice. He'd never seen her so enraged. To diffuse her anger, he'd had to make up the lie about the miscarriage.

She looked at him as if he were a murderer on death row when he told her the truth. He had suggested that his ex-girlfriend get an abortion. He never wanted to see that look in Shelby's eyes again.

Worse, he'd kept secret the possibility that the child they were just discussing, might actually exist.

It had been confirmed that Jeana Sands did have a child, which might actually be his. His lawyer had contacted him, giving the child's age and date of birth. Phillip's calculations made him realize the child could be his. But to be sure, he told the lawyer he wanted to have a DNA test done before he would pay anything.

Chapter 14

Crystal Shaw

Crystal tapped her hands on the steering wheel as she bopped her head back and forth. She sang the words to the song "I Came To Magnify the Lord." As she sang, Crystal remembered just a couple of months prior when she had sat stolid in the passenger seat of the car—unable to sing praises to the Lord. It had been a dark and dismal time. Now she smiled at the joy she felt singing praises to the Lord. During that ride home after leaving the doctor's office she had been confused, asking God over and over why He had led them in the direction of having IVF done and why her hopes had been lifted only to have them dropped like hot coals.

She knew there was no way they would be able to come up with $10,000 in three weeks and maybe not even in three years. Their savings account had been depleted and their chances of taking out a loan were shot—they'd already taken out loans for the renovation of the day care. They were just a little above living from paycheck to paycheck. Crystal racked her brain during that ride trying to figure out a way to come up with the money.

When she couldn't think of anything, her thoughts turned to anger with God. She felt as if she was being punished. She wondered why He was being so cruel to her, putting her through this emotional torture. Realizing her thoughts were selfish, her tears formed and flowed so much that she couldn't seem to get them to stop.

Then she felt disappointed with herself, ashamed for the inner struggle she was having. For some reason her faith was weak when it came to trusting in God for a child, which in turn made her angry again—this time with herself. Her emotions ran rampant. She'd no idea how she was going to get through the next few hours much less the days and weeks which were ahead. Then the realization hit her; there was nothing she or Warren could do, except pray and give it all to God.

Praying is what they had done. She and Warren took turns praying to God, asking Him to guide their path and show them a clear way. They prayed for the strength to get through the days ahead, and thanked God for his grace and mercy.

Surprisingly, the next morning she woke up and was unable to shed a tear. The prayer had lifted the burden, which had been laying on her for years. She put it all into Gods hands. The feelings of loss and despair were replaced by a calm she hadn't experienced in a long while. She felt the loving arms of God around her. He had not left her nor had He had not forsaken her. Most importantly, He still loved her, and she still loved Him.

She had hopped out of bed that next morning and immediately got on her knees to pray again and ask God for forgiveness for not trusting in Him completely from the very beginning. She felt so ashamed for her feelings against God. Even as she said that prayer she knew God had forgiven her. She knew He understood and it was just a process—a wilderness experience she had to undergo. She thanked God for His grace and mercy, and deep down she knew God was not the one who was trying to hurt her, God had not been trying to torture her as she had thought the night before.

Crystal decided to go on a five-day fast. She fasted for each of the years she had hoped to become pregnant. And for those next five days she prayed, fasted from food and read Scriptures. She focused her attention on being God's child, not on the fact that she didn't have any children. She hoped the focus would strengthen her relationship with God. From then on, she hadn't worried about getting pregnant, coming up with money for IVF, or having children, because she knew God would take care of everything.

Now two months later her relationship with God was stronger than it had ever been before. She sang along with one of her husband's gospel CD's as she drove to her sister's house for the baby shower.

Crystal turned the volume of the music down and picked her cell phone up off the passenger seat, then flipped it open. Crystal pressed speed dial and called her sister, Marcy.

Marcy picked up on the other end. "Hello, Crys."

"Hey, Marcy. Where are you?"

"I'm on I-40 about to pass the Wallace exit. Where are you?"

"I'm on 40 also. I just passed the Faison exit. We should get there about the same time."

"I just spoke with Mama; she was just leaving her house, so she should be there when we get there. I'll be glad when this thing is over. I hate to say it, but it's really been a nightmare trying to get it all together," Marcy sighed.

"It has been pretty hectic, but I'm glad it's all going to work out for Shanice, and especially for the baby."

"Yeah, because as long as I can help it, my little niece or nephew-to-be isn't going to go without. I just pray Shanice gets her tubes tied after this one." Marcy said.

Crystal laughed. "Only God knows best. And I've come to realize He knows what He's doing, whether we realize it or not."

"You're right as always," Marcy laughed. "I'll see you in a few minutes. I need to call and check on the kids."

"Okay, I'll see you in a few," Crystal said and clicked her cell phone off.

She smiled inwardly at the comment her sister made and the reply she easily gave. It was a relief not to feel any animosity against either of her sisters because of her own childlessness. It felt really good.

She was happy for Shanice. It wasn't her job to judge her sister, nor was it her job to try to figure out why God was doing things the way He was. Life had gotten so much simpler since she'd surrendered her heart and gave it all up to God.

God knew better than anyone else what He was doing when it came to blessing His people. He especially knew what He was doing in Crystal's life.

Crystal smiled as she thought about the previous year's Thanksgiving dinner. Each year her family gathered in a huge circle and said prayer before the meal. After the prayer each person would say what they had been blessed with in the previous months, as well as the blessings they were thankful for overall. As she listened to what each person was thankful for, she could see the joy and fulfillment in their expressions.

When her turn came around, she told everyone what she was thankful for, and her list grew longer and longer. She thanked God for bestowing her with tangible and non-tangible blessings. She thanked Him for life and His love for her. She was thankful for health and well being. God had given her a wonderful family, blessed her with a Godly husband and given her grace and mercy. God blessed her daily by opening her eyes to see, giving her the peace of mind to be of help to others.

He gave her favor many times over when it came to the dream of owning her own daycare. He gave her gifts and tal-ents to help make her dream come true so she could bless many families, providing their children with a clean, safe, nurturing environment when away from home. She thanked God for all these aspects of her life and more.

When Christmas rolled around, Crystal had been true to her word and not allowed her faith to waiver. She bought the usual gifts for family and friends, but she and Warren made a special effort to buy extra gifts for their niece, Malika. Crystal knew Shanice was a good mother who just had her priorities in the wrong place. She felt just like her sister Marcy, not wanting their niece to want for anything. Especially when Malika had family who took care of it's own.

Now it was a new year and Crystal felt like a new person. She made resolutions twenty days prior at the stroke of midnight. One was to make time to exercise and lose some weight. She wanted to feel as good physically as she did spiritually and emotionally.

She pulled into her sister's apartment complex and said a short prayer for everything to go well. She knew how Shanice's so-called friends were, and she knew neither Marcy, or their mother would hold their tongues if someone said something off hand.

Crystal pulled the bouquet of pink and blue balloons out of the backseat. She also grabbed two of the large gift bags out of her trunk. Without knocking on the door she opened it.

"Hey, Malika, Auntie Crystal is here." Crystal smiled down at her little niece who ran around in only a pull-up and a pair of socks.

"Pink and blue balloons, you coulda just saved your money. I ain't even trying to have a hard-headed boy," Shanice said as she waddled over to the couch and sat down. "Come here, Malika, so I can put these bows on your head."

Crystal's mother peeked her head around the corner of the

kitchen. "Hey, sweetheart." She wiped her hands on her apron and crossed through the tiny dining area to hug her. "How was the trip?"

"Good, Mama." Crystal hoped her mother would be on her best behavior.

"I think the balloons are nice, Shanice," Willie Mae said.

Crystal turned her attention back to her sister. "You know you're having a girl? When did you have the ultrasound?" She set the gift bags and the weighted balloons on the dining room table then gave her niece a hug as she ran up and attached herself to Crystal's leg.

"I didn't, but the doctor ain't gotta tell me. I know I'm having another girl."

There was a knock at the door. "Come in!" Shanice yelled.

Marcy stepped in with a sheetcake. "Hello everyone! Ooo, I love the way you've coordinated the pink and blue balloons with the decorations. This cake goes perfectly with it. It looks really good," Marcy said.

"It's nice, but I ain't having a boy," Shanice grumbled.

"And hello to you too, Shanice," Marcy rolled her eyes playfully at her sister.

"Hey Marcy, I'm sorry. And come here, Malika," she yelled at her child. "Where the kids?"

"Home with their dad. They're not feeling too well," Marcy replied.

Marcy had agreed to buy the cake if Crystal would do the decorations and games. Their mother was in charge of the food. Crystal took the sheetcake from her sister and set it in the center of the table next to the balloons. She then untied the balloons and began placing them around the room.

Originally they hadn't planned on giving her a shower. Shanice told them one of her girlfriends was going to do it. During the planning process, Shanice's so called friend was all talk and ended up pulling out. Shanice was in her seventh month and didn't have anything for the baby. She had a habit of giving all of Malika's things away as soon as she didn't need them.

Crystal, Marcy and their mother were left with the task of planning the entire event, sending invitations, supplying the food, decorating, and buying the cake.

There was a heavy knock at the door.

"Shanice, someone's at the door," Willie Mae called out from the kitchen.

"Get it for me. I'm in the bathroom," Shanice said, her voice muffled from behind the bathroom door.

Crystal answered the door. In front of her were two women. One had on what looked like her pajamas with some house-shoes. The other woman wore a tight, faded gray dress show-ing a great deal of her cleavage.

"Hey, is Shanice here? We're here for the baby shower," cleavage woman said.

"Yes, she's here. Come on in," Crystal said.

Crystal moved to the side so they could enter. Even though she didn't see any gifts, Crystal said, "You can put the gifts on the table over there."

"Oh, here's my gift. I didn't have time to wrap it," Pajama woman said, handing Crystal a plastic bag from the local dollar store.

"I have some extra tissue paper. I can wrap it for you if you'd like," Crystal said politely.

"That'll be good. I was running late and didn't have time to wrap it. You understand right?" the woman said, shame-faced.

Out of the corner of her eye, Crystal saw her mother and sister in the kitchen rolling their eyes at the whole display.

"Oh, yeah. I know how that can be," Crystal said, still try-ing her best to sound polite.

"I didn't get a chance to get her anything yet," cleavage

woman said. "I think I'm gonna wait until she has it to see if it's a boy or girl."

Tired of hearing the women's excuses, Crystal showed them to their seats.

As more guests arrived, Crystal continued to keep her polite composure to the women who weren't really Shanice's friends. Her sister only had acquaintances. They had came to the shower to be nosey and get some free food.

In a way, Crystal was glad she, Marcy and their Mama took over the plans for the shower. They had avoided the circus it would have turned out to be.

Within the next thirty minutes all the guests had arrived, which only made them thirty-five minutes late. Except for a couple of people, most of them didn't bring a gift. A few brought cards, which Crystal was sure were empty.

When Shanice finally emerged from the bathroom, Marcy led her to her designated seat. "Shanice, you can have a seat here."

Shanice waddled over.

Crystal started by saying, "Ladies, first we're going to play a few games. Then we'll eat and play a few more games. Then Shanice will open her gifts."

"Sounds good to me," Shanice said.

Crystal handed everyone a sheet of paper to play the first game. "This first game is baby word scramble. You'll have three minutes to see how many words you can unscramble. I'll let you know when to start."

When she finished passing out all the papers and pens, Crystal looked at her watch to time them. When the second hand hit twelve she said, "Okay ladies, you can start . . . now!"

After only a minute had passed, Shanice yelled, "Finished!"

"You finished *all* twenty?" Marcy asked in disbelief.

"Sure did," Shanice answered matter-of-factly.

"Okay, everyone stop," Marcy said. She looked at Shanice's list and saw that she had gotten them all right. "Looks like Shanice won."

"Here's your prize," Crystal said, handing her one of the pre-wrapped prizes.

Crystal heard someone mumble under their breath that it wasn't fair Shanice had won. When she looked up to see who it was, the girl smiled at Crystal like she hadn't said a thing. Crystal couldn't wait for the party to be over.

They played a few more games, ate, then they played another game.

"This game is to see who can guess the size of Shanice's waist and stomach," Crystal instructed. "Who ever is the closest will win. I'm going to give you a ball of yarn. Cut the length you think will be closest to the size of her waist and stomach.

"This should be easy," one woman said, who was also pregnant. "I'll just measure my waist since we are due about the same time."

As Crystal watched the women pass the yarn, she could tell most of them didn't really care how much they were cutting. They were full and ready to leave.

Crystal took each piece of yarn and put them around Shanice's waist. One of the pieces wrapped around Shanice three times. Another piece barely made it past her hips. The closest person was the other woman due about the same time as Shanice.

Knowing the women had had enough games, Crystal and Marcy decided it was time for Shanice to open her gifts.

"Shanice is going to open gifts now," Marcy said.

The first gift Shanice opened was a bib and rattle. "Just what I need, another noise-maker," Shanice said in an unappreciative tone.

Next she opened a gift with a pack of newborn Pampers

and another gift with a pack of sleepers. She received teething rings, pacifiers, bottles, a pack of washcloths, and a couple of stuffed animals.

None of Shanice's associates had given her a full set of anything, just odds and ends. Crystal could tell they hadn't put a strain on their pockets.

The nicest gifts Shanice received were from her family.

Marcy got her a car seat and stroller. Her mother bought her unisex outfits, baby toiletry items, two crib bedding sets, and a mobile. Crystal bought her the crib and mattress along with more clothes, socks, bibs, hats, onesies, receiving blankets, and baby toys.

Crystal had bought so many things and wondered a couple of times if she was going overboard. But with each item she put in her cart, she felt better and better about what she was doing. She knew her Sears charge card bill would be high.

She also knew Shanice didn't have a job and her baby's daddy probably wasn't going to help her out as much as she would need. Crystal felt deep down God had blessed her so much and even though she couldn't buy items for herself, she could for her new niece or nephew.

The child was a blessing, as far as Crystal was concerned.

Crystal saw the looks of jealousy on many of the faces in the room as Shanice opened her gifts. She figured the people who hadn't gotten Shanice anything definitely wouldn't now. Not that they would have any way.

Crystal sat in her office the next week thinking about the baby shower. She felt really good once she left. The usual feelings of depression and self-pity from being childless had not haunted her since she started reflecting on all of the blessings God did give her. She had also ceased to have the nightmares. It had felt good to bless her sister and her new niece or nephew on the way.

That night after the shower she drove down to Marcy's in Wilmington and was able to spend some time with her niece and nephew. They stayed up watching cartoons and eating microwave popcorn while she gave Marcy and her husband a break away from the kids.

Crystal felt better than she had in years. She was still amazed at the way God turned things around emotionally for her. All she had to do was have the faith that He would. The peace she held stayed with her, unwavering.

Crystal looked up when she heard the center's front door open. Through the glass she saw a woman she didn't recognize. Crystal figured she was probably in the wrong place especially since she was carrying an expensive attaché case and dressed in a posh business suit.

Crystal stood up and walked out to greet her. "Yes, how can I help you?"

"I'm looking for Ms. Crystal Shaw," the woman replied.

"I'm Mrs. Crystal Shaw." Crystal corrected. *Why was the woman looking for her?*

"Oh good. Mrs. Shaw, I am Vivian Parker with RPDC. I know you were expecting the regular project manager, but he's not going to be able to finish this project. I'm here in his place."

"Oh," Crystal said. She chuckled, realizing the woman was from the group she had hired to design her daycare. "I thought you might have been lost or something. Most of my parents don't come dressed to the heel like you, especially with a brief case like that. And neither do the social workers." Crystal firmly shook the woman's hand. "Please come in and have a seat."

"Thank you, Mrs. Shaw."

"That's a beautiful suit you have on."

"Thank you. It's a Damonaé."

"Damoné, hum, very nice," Crystal said, wondering if she would ever be able to afford a suit like it.

"Thanks again."

"You're welcome," Crystal said.

"I'd like to talk to you about the progress of your center."

Crystal pulled out her plans with the renovations. "I'm so excited. Are you here to tell me the center is complete and ready for operation?"

"Well, Ms. Shaw, that's why I'm here. I drove by there on my way over here. It looks pretty good, but there are a few adjustments that will need to be made."

"Adjustments?" Crystal asked.

"There are a few things I noticed that are not up to specification and I'd like to change them before the inspector comes out and *makes* us change them."

Hearing the words "specification" and "adjustments" made Crystal's heart speed up. "How much more will it cost?" Crystal said, hoping the woman didn't detect her nervous concern.

"Not a penny more than previously agreed."

"Really?" Crystal asked in disbelief.

"The needed changes are not your fault. We will not change the terms of our agreement."

"Mrs. Parker, are you sure about that? I'd hate to get a bill later saying we owe more money. What if your boss thinks differently?"

"Ms. Shaw, I am the boss. I am the P in RPDC. My husband Roland is the President and CEO of the company. So I assure you, this is from the horse's mouth."

Crystal sighed with relief. "That *is* good. I am really glad to hear there won't be any additional charges." She was surprised the co-owner of the company was actually the one meeting with her.

"You see, I'm a bit of a perfectionist, and I want the work that RPDC produces to continue to be first class, top in the industry."

"Thank you, Mrs. Parker."

"No, Mrs. Shaw, thank *you* for the business."

"Mrs. Parker, you can call me Crystal," Crystal said immediately taking a liking to the woman. Even though this woman was wealthy, Crystal liked the fact that she was so down to earth.

"In that case Crystal, you can call me Vivian." Vivian said with a warm smile.

Chapter 15

Vivian Parker

Vivian reviewed the plans for the renovated center with its owner, Crystal Shaw. She discussed the needed modifications and after about an hour, they wrapped things up.

"Crystal, the modifications shouldn't take very long. I would say about two weeks at most."

"That'll be great. I want to open by the end of next month. I've already placed ads in the paper for employees and enrollment for children."

"We should have everything completed well ahead of your opening date," Vivian said.

"I am so excited. I've wanted to open my own center for years. Now my dream is finally coming true."

"I can understand that. It's good when a person can have their dreams in life come true," Vivian said.

"Especially one I've waited so long for."

"I am glad our company has been an instrumental part of making your dream come true." Vivian said and stood to leave. "I'll stay on top of the changes to make sure everything is on schedule. I'll be at the site pretty often making sure you're ready to operate on time."

"Thanks again, Mrs. Parker. Oh sorry, I mean, Vivian," Crystal corrected herself.

"You're welcome. If you have any questions or concerns, please feel free to call me," Vivian said, pulling out a business card.

"I sure will. Thank you for coming in person. It was nice to meet you."

"I'm glad I took this project over. It's been nice meeting you also. I recently decided to take over some of the company's smaller projects. I really miss working one-on-one with people."

Vivian saw Crystal look past her towards the door.

"Well, come on in sweethearts," Crystal said.

Vivian looked behind her to see who Crystal was speaking to. There were two children in the doorway. Vivian smiled at the bashful children.

"Come on in. This is Mrs. Vivian, she doesn't bite," Crystal said, smiling. The two children inched into the office a little further. "As you can see, they're a little shy. That is at first, but once they warm up to a person, it's hard to keep them away."

"Hi," Vivian said, looking into the big brown eyes of the children. "I'm Vivian. What are your names?"

Timidly the little girl, who looked to be the oldest, spoke. "My name is Kylia."

"Nice to meet you, Miss Kylia," Vivian said. The little girl had pretty, brown eyes and long, thick ponytails. Vivian thought she was the prettiest little girl she had ever seen. "What's your name?" Vivian asked the little boy standing next to her.

He looked up at Vivian and smiled but didn't say a word.

"That's Kylia's little brother, Kyle," Crystal said.

"They're so adorable."

"Sweethearts. It's rare that I have any problems with them."

"How old are you, Kylia?" Vivian asked.

"Four," Kylia said. "Kyle is 3," she added.

"I'll bet you are a smart young lady. Do you know all your colors?"

"Yes," Kylia answered.

"Can you count to ten?" Vivian asked.

"I can count to one hundred," Kylia said with a grin.

"Wow, you are a smart little girl. I'll bet you know all your ABC's too."

"Yes, I do. You wanna hear me say them?" the little girl asked.

"Why sure," Vivian said.

The little girl proceeded to say her ABC's, singing the song all the way through.

Vivian clapped her hands. "That was very good."

Kylia smiled and then walked up to Vivian and gave her a hug.

"Oh my goodness. What a sweet child," Vivian said as she hugged her back.

Seeing his sister, Kyle walked up to Vivian and gave her a hug also.

"Wow. I get two hugs today. One from a sweet little girl and another from a handsome little boy." It warmed Vivian's heart. "Do all the children here have these kind of manners?"

"No, I wish," Crystal said. "These two are exceptional."

"I can see that." Vivian smiled at the children again.

"Okay children, tell Mrs. Vivian goodbye and go out and have a seat on the bench. Your ride should be here any minute."

"Bye, Mrs. Vivian," Kylia said politely.

"Bye, Mrs. Vivian," Kyle said, mimicking his sister.

"Bye children. You both keep being good. I know your parents must be very proud of you," Vivian said.

As Kylia turned to leave the office, Vivian saw a sad, familiar look on the girl's face.

Once the children were out on the bench, Crystal told Vivian in a hushed tone, "The children are in foster care. Their grandmother had been taking care of them until her health started failing her. The grandmother told us their mother has been strung out on drugs and neither of the children's fathers have ever been in the picture."

The information about the children brought back memories of Vivian's own childhood—it paralleled these children's almost exactly. But she had been blessed enough not to have to go into foster care. She heard stories of children being in the foster care system until they turned 18. Considered an adult at 18, they then had to find some way to fend for themselves in the world. It hurt Vivian to think about Kylia and Kyle in a system that would not be able to truly nurture them.

Her aunt and uncle raised her and her younger brother, Daniel, after her grandma died. Their mother hadn't wanted them. At the time Vivian was hurt their own mother hadn't felt a need to raise them, but ultimately she was glad they'd never had to go and live with her.

Vivian still resented her mother in many ways. Deep down Vivian blamed her mother and her mother's dysfunctional ways for her having such low self-esteem all those years as a young girl. Even in the present day she had bouts of insecurity, although she felt she hid it pretty well.

As she looked out towards the bench with the children, she visualized her and Daniel sitting there instead. Time stood still. She stood dazed for a several moments.

"Vivian, are you okay?" Crystal asked.

Coming out of her daze, Vivian answered, "Yes. I just . . . I was just thinking about what you said. It's sad that those children will get caught up in the system."

Even though Vivian was talking to Crystal, she continued to look out towards the bench, now clearly focused on Kylia and Kyle.

"You're right. They're wonderful children inside and out. I think social services is trying to contact the children's fathers to see if he will assume responsibility and custody."

Continuing to look out towards the children, Vivian said, "I hope they can find them so they won't have to stay in foster care. Although you really have to wonder if that will be the best thing for them, especially since their fathers haven't been around all this time." Vivian had said the last part almost under breath.

She watched the children stand up and greet a short woman of Asian decent. The woman came into the office, picked up a clipboard, to sign the children out for the day. Vivian could see from the woman's county badge that she was a social worker.

Once the children were out of sight, Vivian finally turned her attention back to Crystal. "I'm sorry if it seemed like I was ignoring you just now. It's just so sad to me that those children have to be put in that type of situation, even if it does only end up being for a short time."

"I feel the same way. I try to give them as much attention as I can while they're here. I pray for all of the children here each night, especially Kylia and Kyle."

Regaining her composure, Vivian looked at the time. "I didn't mean to take up too much of your time. I'll be in contact soon."

"Alright. I look forward to hearing from you," Crystal said. Vivian left.

On the way back to work, she couldn't take her mind off the children. It was eerie. Those children could have been her and her brother. Would Kyle end up like her brother one day? She hoped not. Would Kylia be able to overcome the odds like Vivian had? She didn't know. The memory of the hugs repeated over and over Vivian's head. Kylia's ponytails smelled like coconuts. Both children had an innocent warmth.

As she drove Vivian reviewed the month and a half which had passed since their last appointment with Dr. Evans. She and Roland had been able to finally talk about their feelings the morning after that appointment.

They discussed trying the procedure again and decided against it. The whole week prior to the embryos' failure, Vivian had been a basket case and she didn't want to go through that kind of uncertainty again.

She and Roland talked about the possibility of donor eggs and adoption. But the discussions led nowhere. Vivian was torn because she wanted badly to be a mother to her own biological children.

They had no idea what way they should go. Then Roland did something unexpected—he asked her to pray about it.

It took Vivian a few moments to agree, hindered by the memories of praying to God as a child. She had prayed so many times for Him to help her and Daniel while they endured the abuse from their mother. Even now as a grown woman, Vivian's physical and emotional scars lingered. For so many years she hadn't felt like she mattered much to God.

He had not answered her prayers.

She shivered thinking of all the nights she laid scared, huddled in her bed with Daniel clutching her for safety, never knowing exactly when and where the next physical or emotional blows might come from. With their mother, there was no way to tell.

Then there were those nights in the last week of her grandma's life when she prayed for God to heal her grandma but He hadn't.

When her brother was shot in a drive-by shooting, Vivian cried next to his bed for two weeks while he lay in a coma. She prayed God would spare Daniel but He hadn't. God took him away—just like her Grandma. The people who mattered the most to her had been taken. For what reason, she could not understand.

She stopped praying after that.

Then she remembered the words her grandma had said to her in the dream. Her grandma told her God takes care of things in His own time Finally it hit her; she understood. Understood that God had done things in His own time and in His own way. She had prayed for God to help her and Daniel and God had done that—in His own time. The *best* time. She prayed for God to save her Grandma and He had already done that. He had also seen the need to take her brother Daniel. The Lord giveth and the Lord taketh away. Who was she to continue to question Him?

She had put off speaking with God too long and it was time she put an end to it. She began to pray. It was awkward at first. Not only did she ask God for guidance, she thanked Him for being such a blessing to her and giving her his grace and mercy even though she had shunned Him. She also asked forgiveness for pushing her emotional door closed on Him for so long. A small seed of hope still lay embedded in her spirit that hadn't truly died. Once she finished praying for God to lead them in the right path, her soul felt different—there was a peace about it. God had heard her and some how she knew it.

The next few days she prayed and fasted for an answer from God. Which path should they take? Even though she hadn't been close to God in a while, she did know about fasting and praying. Her grandma had fasted and prayed about many things. During Vivian's time of fasting and praying, she had never in her life felt so close to God.

Until earlier that day, she had wanted nothing more than to give birth to a child of her own. Now after meeting the two foster children at the daycare, she knew without a shadow of doubt, God was giving her the answer she had prayed days for. Even though she had only spent a few moments in the presence of the foster children, there was a tugging in her heart, which she knew could only be explained by God. He was showing her that her true desire was to love and nurture—a desire which could be accomplished without giving birth.

God was letting her know that if she could connect with those children so quickly, she would be able to bond with another child in need of a good, loving home. She and Roland had more than enough room in their home and the finances to comfortably take care of ten children, if they wanted. Adoption was their answer.

Vivian couldn't wait to get back to the office to talk to her husband in person. The cars in front of her just weren't going fast enough on the freeway. The more she thought about it, Vivian knew she didn't need to have a child physically born from her to love it. She already loved and cared for her stepson who felt like a son.

Vivian was thankful for the answer God had given her. She chuckled to herself at God's unique humor. It was funny the way He was worked things out—with strategic moves.

The first move was her receiving of the unwanted news from the doctor, which caused the second move—deciding to take on the smaller projects. If she hadn't taken on the smaller projects, she wouldn't have met Crystal Shaw and the foster children—God's third move. Vivian knew this couldn't be anything but God's divine intervention. Now, finally, after so much uncertainty and heartache, Vivian felt good.

As soon as she got to her office she picked up the phone. "Roland," she said as soon as she heard his voice. "Come down to my office A.S.A.P!"

"What's wrong?" Roland asked with concern.

"Nothing's wrong. Everything's completely right!" Vivian said, hardly able to contain her excitement.

"I'll be there in just a moment." Roland quickly hung the phone up. Roland was in her office in less than sixty seconds. "What's wrong?"

"Nothing, I told you. You know I've been praying and fasting for God to give us an answer as to what we are supposed to do next."

"Yes, I know. What happened? Did He answer you? What did He say?"

"Don't jump to any conclusions. I am not pregnant. But as I continued to pray for a child, I also continued to ask Him for an answer. You know, attempt another round of IVF, donor eggs or adoption. I was so confused. So I continually asked God for guidance." Excited, Vivian talked non-stop. "Today God gave me the answer we need."

"What happened? When I saw you at lunch you didn't say anything."

First, Vivian explained how she had met one of their clients earlier that afternoon and how she somehow felt as if they had known each other for years. She also told him about the two foster children she'd met at the daycare center. She explained the instant bond she felt, and how she understood God was letting her know that adoption was the way they needed to go.

Roland was relieved to hear what she had to say and welcomed the news. He agreed to pursue adopting a child. They embraced, happy about the decision they were making. Remembering that Dr. Evans also had information on adoption, Vivian immediately picked the phone up and called the doctor's office to find out more about the adoption process. Once she hung up, they had an appointment set up for two weeks later.

* * *

Throughout the next couple of weeks, Vivian thought about their upcoming appointment to discuss the adoption process. She wondered if the child they would end up receiving, would be a boy or girl. She also wondered if they would get an infant or an older child. She didn't know what would happen, but she put her faith in God. She had faith that God would place the right child in their home.

Vivian started praying for the child that would one day be theirs, even though she had no idea whether the child existed or hadn't even been born yet. If the child did already exist, she hoped it was in a safe environment.

Sometimes Vivian thought she might have been excessive in her praying, she prayed for almost everyone, even the baggers at the grocery store. She also included the people she recently met. She prayed for Crystal Shaw and her family, all the children in Crystal's daycare center, and especially Kylia and Kyle, the children who had warmed her heart so much.

Chapter 16

Shelby Tomlinson

Shelby hit the unrelenting alarm. It was five o'clock in the morning. She reached over for Phillip, but he wasn't next to her in the bed. Then she heard the toilet flush and the shower being turned on. She was pleased to see he was already up and hoped it was a good sign.

Every since the afternoon Phillip had come clean about his secrets from the past, he continued to apologize profusely. He had been true to his word, doing everything possible to make it up—breaking his back and bending over backwards doing whatever he was required to do in order for them to carry out their IVF procedures. He had even gone with her to New Hope Church a couple of times.

Phillip had accompanied her to all of her doctors' appointments and even attended the injection class they were both required to take without a fuss. Shelby knew deep down he was a good man who had only tried to look out for her best interests. She'd actually started feeling sorry for him having had to go through that turmoil all those years— scared of how God would make him pay for his sins.

Today was the day Shelby's eggs would be retrieved for

the IVF procedure. She had been injecting herself with medication to get her ovaries' follicles to mature and release more eggs. The egg retrieval would be performed via laparoscopy. She hoped the procedure would go well and yield a significant number of eggs.

After a great deal of nervous anticipation, the date had finally arrived. She was anxious and thrilled at the same time. Shelby couldn't believe four months had already passed since she'd first seen Dr. Silva. And even with all recent emotional roller coasters she'd gone through, she hadn't had any more anxiety attacks.

Shelby pulled the covers off then stretched and headed to the bathroom. She heard the shower turn off and watched as Phillip stepped out, dripping with water.

"Good morning," he said cheerfully and reached for a towel.

"Morning baby." She brushed past him to get to the sink, hand over her mouth.

"What, no kiss?"

"Morning breath," Shelby mumbled. "Let me brush my teeth."

"I don't care about your morning breath," Phillip replied, trying to pull her towards him.

"I do. Give me a minute," Shelby said, pushing him aside.

As she brushed her teeth, Shelby wondered what had gotten into her husband. He wasn't a morning person and had never been. This morning he was walking around with a smile and his voice was jolly. He could have actually passed as a seasoned rooster.

After she finished rinsing her mouth, Phillip said, "Can I have my kiss now?" He blocked the doorway of the bathroom.

Without hesitation, Shelby replied, "Yes. Of course you can."

Phillip kissed her like he hadn't in a long time. It was a kiss full of the passion she was used to when they started dating. Their embrace seemed to last for eternity until Shelby realized he was getting aroused. She moved away from him quickly.

"What did you do that for? Where you going?" Phillip asked. His lips were still slightly parted.

"I'm going to take my shower. We have an appointment we need to get to. Remember?"

"I know, but why don't we just finish what we were about to start?" Phillip pleaded.

"No, sweetheart. We can't. Remember what the doctor said?"

"I know we have to abstain for at least seventy-two hours before the next phase," Phillip said, mocking the Hispanic accent of Dr. Silva.

"Seventy-two hours, we can't mess up now." Shelby said.

"I sure will be glad when this is all finished. It's been three days already. I don't know how much longer I can wait," Phillip teased.

"Hopefully not much longer. In a few hours the doctor will give you a cup and another magazine, then you won't have to wait. You can have at it." Shelby chuckled.

Phillip rolled his eyes at her, "Oh, Shelby. That's cold."

"Sorry, baby. That's about as delicate as I can put it," She said in a sing-song voice.

Phillip put his arms back around her. He whispered in her ear, "When this is all over, we will have this discussion again, and I promise the ending will be different."

"Yeah, okay honey, but for now, picture the cup and magazine," Shelby teased, pulling away from him again.

"Ha, for your information, I won't need a magazine. I'll be playing out in my mind what we should be doing right now."

Shelby turned on the shower knob. "Fine, if that works for you. I've got to take my shower now."

"You want me to come help you? You know I can hand you the shower gel," Phillip coaxed.

"No thanks. I'm perfectly capable of getting the gel myself."

"I know you're capable. I just wanted to help."

"Thanks. How about tonight? You can help me then."

"It's a date!" Phillip said.

"Shelby. Phillip," Dr. Silva greeted them as soon as they walked back into his office. "Please take a seat." They sat holding hands. Phillip squeezed so tightly, the circulation in her hand had nearly stopped. "We were able to retrieve twelve eggs!"

"That is a good thing. Isn't it doctor?" Phillip asked apprehensively.

"That is good!" Shelby said with delight.

The doctor nodded. "It most certainly is. Now we need the collection from you, Mr. Tomlinson."

"Okay. I'm ready. Where's the cup?" Phillip was eager to get it over with.

"Here you are," the doctor said. "Room four is around the corner. There are some magazines in there along with a TV and DVDs."

"No thanks. I don't need either. I have a picture of my wife." He held up a picture of Shelby in her two-piece bathing suit lying on the beach in Mexico. "That's all I need." Phillip stood up quickly, almost dropping the specimen cup. "Oops. Caught it."

When he left the office, Shelby opened up her planner, pretending to be preoccupied. Her face flushed—she was embarrassed by her husband's comment and avoided looking up at the doctor.

The phone rang at about nine-thirty a.m. Shelby's heart began to race. She jumped off the kitchen barstool and picked it up before the phone could ring a second time. "Hello," she said anxiously.

"Hey, Shelby!" Rachel said.

"Rachel?" Shelby said with disappointment. It wasn't the call she wanted.

"Yeah. You sound like you're disappointed that it's me."

"Oh, Rachel, well yeah, sort of," Shelby admitted.

"What's up?"

"I was waiting for Dr. Silva's office to call with an update on the embryos."

"That's one reason I was calling. So they haven't called yet, huh?"

"No, and I've been a nervous wreck sitting here waiting. I almost fell off the stool when I heard the phone ring."

"I'm sorry."

"Oh it's not your fault I'm so nervous." Shelby sat back down on the barstool. "So how's it going so far this morning?"

"Good. The wedding rehearsal will still be at six o'clock p.m. on Friday, then we'll all go to Ginny's for dinner at seven-thirty p.m."

"Do you need any help today?"

"No, I think everything's taken care of. Don't worry about it anyway. Just try to relax, enjoy your day off and try not to fall off the stool every time the phone rings."

Shelby laughed. "I'll try my best not to worry. And I'll even move on to the couch, at least there the fall won't be as bad."

Rachel laughed, too. "You can let me know how everything turns out."

"I sure will."

"Bye." Rachel hung up.

For the next hour, Shelby tried to do things to keep her mind busy and off the expected phone call. She tried to do some laundry but kept forgetting to put the clothes in the washer. After she let two empty cycles run without any clothes, she abandoned that idea.

Next she decided to start the novel she bought a month

before, a new release from one of her favorite authors. Even though she had been waiting for months to find out what would happen to the characters in the current sequel, her mind still wandered. She was unable to focus, and after about thirty minutes of reading the same two pages over and over, she abandoned that idea too.

The more she tried to do to get her mind off of the call, the more she couldn't. She could only think about how many of the eggs would fertilize and what she would do if there were more than three. She thought about having four sets of triplets, even though it was highly unlikely.

Shelby imagined a house, full of children, all looking like her and Phillip. She thought about the children in the various stages of life, being infants, toddlers, and as teenagers. She imagined them playing in the park, at birthday parties, and even their first day at school. Thoughts of children were the only things she could keep her mind on.

Shelby went into the den and picked up her Bible. She'd been reading the Scriptures the pastor gave the congregation during the couple of Sunday services she had started to attend. There were two in particular that gave her hope. She turned to the book of Romans 12:12 and read, *"Let your hope make you glad. Be patient in time of trouble and never stop praying."* She meditated on the word and then turned to Romans 15:13 which read, *"I pray that God, who gives hope, will bless you with complete happiness and peace because of your faith. And may the power of the Holy Spirit fill you with hope."* It was these two verses, which gave her hope. She tried to read them daily. The pastor at New Hope encouraged them to read the word of God and take the Scriptures as God's promises for His people.

Every day since, she'd found an abundance of uplifting inspirational scriptures. The two in Romans gave her the most hope and peace. She meditated further on the scriptures and closed her Bible.

The ringing doorbell startled her. Goldie, asleep next to her feet, was startled too and immediately started barking.

Shelby got up off the couch to answer the door. Through the opaque glass she saw a small figure. She opened the door and greeted her next-door neighbor.

Looking past the lady, Shelby saw a fire truck parked in front of her house. The neighbor told her the fireman wanted permission to put a ladder in her tree so they could retrieve a stranded kitten.

"Of course," she said and followed the neighbor out. For the next few minutes she watched as the firemen put the ladder in the tree and rescued the kitten.

The little girl who had cried and pointed up at the kitten stopped crying when the fireman handed her the fluffy white and black kitten. Shelby's smile matched that of the little girl's mother who was also relieved to see her child happy again.

When all the excitement was over, Shelby returned home. As soon as she stepped in, she thought about the phone and wondered if the doctor had called while she'd been out. She picked up the phone and listened hopefully for the shudder dial tone. Her heart almost stopped as she heard the very sound she'd hoped she would.

She quickly dialed the access number to retrieve the message. Pushing seven, she listened to the message from Dr. Silva.

"Mr. and Mrs. Tomlinson, this is Dr. Silva. I am pleased to say that seven of the twelve eggs have fertilized. Everything looks fine. We'll continue as scheduled. I look forward to seeing you both at eight o'clock tomorrow morning for the embryo transfer. If you have any questions, please feel free to call me."

Shelby pressed the button to save the message before hanging up the phone. Then she jumped up and down, screaming with happiness. "Yes, thank You God. Thank You, thank You, thank You!"

Startled again, Goldie began to bark.

She couldn't wait to tell Phillip. She paced the floor as she dialed his office.

"Hello," Phillip answered. His voice sounded perturbed.

"Hey, baby!" Shelby said.

Phillip's tone immediately adjusted. "Hey, honey. What's up?"

"I've got some great news."

"What is it?" Phillip asked.

"Were you busy?" Shelby asked.

"No. Why?" Phillip knew Shelby had sensed his mood.

"You sound a little preoccupied."

"You know me pretty well don't you? No, baby, I just got a phone call right before you called. It's something I need to handle. Work related. That's all."

"I hope you don't have to deal with it tomorrow," Shelby said, hinting at tomorrow's doctor's visit.

"No? Why? Are we supposed to be doing something special?"

"Because we have to go . . ."

Phillip cut her off. "What? Is it because we have to go to the doctor's office tomorrow? Did the doctor call?"

Now she could hear the excitement in his voice. "Yes. He called while I was outside watching the fireman pull a kitten out of our tree."

"Fireman? Kitten? Huh?"

"I'll explain it all to later. The doctor left a message. He wants us there at eight for the transfer!"

"How many fertilized?"

"Seven."

"Oh, Shelby. That is so good. That's great!" he said, almost shouting. "It's really about to happen!" Finally she heard sincere excitement in his voice.

"I know. I'm so excited!"

"You'll be pregnant on Valentine's Day." Phillip said.

"That would be the best Valentines Day present ever." Shelby smiled, but then let doubt creep into her head, "But wait, Dr. Silva said even if he implants three, they might not all make it. It'll be almost two weeks before we can confirm anything."

"I know. Don't think negatively. You are going to be pregnant. My baby is going to have a baby or two! I know you will."

"I just don't want to get my hopes up and then be disappointed."

"Stop being so negative. We can have a pre-celebration tonight."

"Are you sure, Phillip? It might be bad luck to have a pre-celebration. Besides, don't you need to take care of that business from that other phone call?" Shelby asked.

"No, that business can wait. This conversation is so much more important," Phillip said. "I'm so excited!"

It was encouraging to hear him not only say the words, but Shelby could tell Phillip was indeed excited about the news. "Me too, honey!"

"Hold on a second, baby."

Shelby waited and looked at the time on the Grandfather clock in the corner of their living room. It was 11:45 and she hadn't eaten anything all day.

"I'm back, honey. I need to take care of one of our clients. He is *not* happy, and no one else can handle the matter but me."

"Alright. I'm hungry and I've got a taste for ice cream. I think I'll go to that shop on 9th street and try theirs. Then I need to pick up my shoes for the wedding rehearsal Friday."

"Okay baby, you do that. I'll see you when I get home."

"I love you, sweetheart."

"I love you too, baby."

* * *

That evening while driving home, Phillip reflected on the good news. He was so happy to hear how well everything was going. He was glad Shelby was happier than she had been in many weeks. When he divulged the news about his ex-girlfriend, he hadn't expected Shelby to react the way she had. The anguished look she had on her face still haunted him. Every since that evening, he'd done everything in his power to make her happy again.

The good news couldn't mask the fear he had about the call he'd received just before hers. The lawyer informed him the DNA test, conducted a couple of weeks prior, proved, without a shadow of doubt, he was the father of Jeana Sands' son. He was still trying to let his brain process the information when Shelby's call came in.

He didn't want to deal with the DNA results just then. He'd have to push the information out of his mind. Later he would take care of the back child support and the other matters. Right now, all he wanted to do was to think about their appointment in the morning and get home to his wife so they could celebrate their good news.

The morning of February 14th they were again seated in Dr. Silva's office hoping for more good news. The embryo transfer had just been completed. Phillip had held Shelby's hand throughout the implantation process.

"The transfer went well," Dr. Silva reported. "I was able to transfer three of the seven embryos into your uterus. Now we hope for the best and pray that at least one will implant for a successful pregnancy."

"Is there still a chance for two or three to implant?" Shelby asked.

"Yes. There is still that possibility," Dr. Silva said.

"I can't believe it," Shelby said and reached for Phillip's hand.

"I can't either," Phillip said.

"What about the other embryos? The frozen ones?" Phillip asked.

"They'll be frozen for future transfers—whenever you want them."

The doctor turned his attention back to Shelby. "I want you to take it easy for the next day or so."

Shelby shook her head. "No problem. I'll take it easy."

Phillip nodded in agreement. "I'll make sure she does."

"Very good then. You need to return in ten days. At that time we'll do a pregnancy test. Mrs. Tomlinson, you can return to work on Thursday."

"So that's it for now?" Shelby asked.

"That's it." The doctor said. "Continue to take your prenatal vitamins. I'll see you in ten days."

Chapter 17

Crystal Shaw

Crystal slipped in the back of the church for Bible study. The praise team had just finished singing and Pastor Jordan began to speak. "Thank you praise team, for those uplifting songs. Congregation, I hope those songs have raised your spirits as much as mine. Praise the Lord! Praise the Lord! Praise the Lord!"

The congregation agreed with the pastor, clapping their hands and giving praises to the Lord. Crystal could tell the spirit of the Lord had moved, and she had missed it.

"As you know, a couple of months ago I led you in a series on faith. Tonight I want to do a review of sorts. Lately the subject of faith has been on my mind. Instead of continuing where we left off last week, I'll speak about faith again. The Holy Spirit tells me a few of you need to hear this tonight.

"Everyone please turn to Hebrews 11:1. Without faith, many trials will come and knock us down. Some may even knock us out if we're not careful," Pastor Jordan chuckled.

"In this passage of Scripture we find that faith is the substance of things hoped for and the evidence of things not seen. Even from the very beginning in Genesis 1:1, with the formation of the world. It took faith to believe the formation was not only possible, but that it actually occurred.

"It reads, *"By faith we understand that the worlds were framed by the word of God, so that the things which are seen were not made of things which are visible."* The pastor paused for a moment. "Throughout chapter eleven you can read about the tests of faith that people like Abel, Enoch, Noah, Abraham, Sarah, Isaac, Jacob, Joseph, and Moses, went through."

Crystal's ears perked up when she heard Sarah's name again. She remembered Sarah's story of barrenness and then becoming pregnant in her old age. She listened intently as Pastor Jordan spoke, jotting down notes and scriptures.

The pastor continued, "This chapter also mentions others like Gideon, Barak, Sampson, Jephthan, David, Samuel, and the prophets—even thought the unknown author of this book didn't have time to tell us in detail about the faith each person practiced.

"Just imagine if these people didn't have the amount of faith they did. It was written in verse six that without faith, it is impossible to please God. Anyone who comes to Him must believe that He exists. God will reward those who earnestly seek Him," the pastor said. "And if you notice, this passage does not say God will give you exactly what you want. It says He will reward you. Sometimes what we want is not always in God's plan. Sometimes what we want *is* in His plan, but it isn't given to us on a golden platter.

"Most of the time we have to go through tests before we get our rewards. There are often bumps in the road and pitfalls we don't see ahead. But through it all, you must have faith that God will see you through. He will not leave you nor forsake you."

The pastor's message gave her confirmation. She needed to continue walking in faith, allowing God full control of her life. He would not leave her nor forsake her. And He would give her the desires of her heart but on His terms. She knew God had her best interest in mind.

Crystal heard a knock on her office door. "Come in," she said and saw Vivian entering. "Vivian, hi."

This was the date of Crystal's new day care center's final inspection.

Vivian stepped into the doors of Crystal's new center. "Hey, I hope you don't mind my coming by here early, before the inspector got here."

"No. Like I said earlier, it works out great for me. That way I can shake your hand in person."

"Shake my hand? I should be the one shaking your hand for being so patient with the whole delay."

"I've been walking through this center, and it's exactly as I envisioned. The work your company has done is impeccable," Crystal said.

"Thank you for the compliment," Vivian replied.

"I'll be referring your company to all my friends."

"My husband will be very pleased to hear that," Vivian said.

"You're still planning on staying for the inspection, right?" Crystal asked.

"Yeah, that's why I wanted to come over here a little early. I wanted to review all the completed work with you."

"Good, that way I'll know what he's talking about," Crystal said.

"Alright then, let's go ahead and get started."

Crystal and Vivian did a walk-through, inspecting each room. They checked each outlet, doorframe, window, light fixture and lock for the proper specifications, wiring and measurements. They also checked the children's play equipment inside and outside, making sure they were assembled properly for safety.

Then Vivian checked the water fountains, shelves in the

pantry, and storerooms, measuring them for the proper height. She checked each exit, making sure the signs were affixed and working properly.

Once finished Vivian said, "The inspector shouldn't find anything wrong. If it passes my inspection, it will pass anyone's inspection."

As a bonus for Crystal, Vivian printed out evacuation plans for each of the doors in the center.

Looking them over, Crystal said, "Thanks, Vivian. That was nice of you." They looked way better than the hand sketches she had done using a ruler and pencil.

"You're welcome."

"The inspector shouldn't be here for another hour. Do you want to get something to eat?" Crystal asked.

"Sure. There's no telling how long it'll take the inspector to finish. I'll be famished by then," Vivian said.

"I know this great ice cream shop downtown. They serve lunch."

"The one on 9th Street?" Vivian asked.

"Yeah. Have you been there before?"

"Yes. It's the first place my husband and I ever went to eat. We weren't dating yet, but I remember it like it was yesterday."

"Sounds interesting. You'll have to tell me about it. The only first date I can remember was in elementary school. And I wish I could forget it," Crystal laughed.

"You'll have to tell me about that. Ready? I can drive," Vivian said as the two women headed out.

Vivian laughed as Crystal ended the story she told. She coughed, almost choking on a piece of ice. "That is so funny. He tormented you and then became your protector."

"He sure did," Crystal laughed along with Vivian. "Then one day he asked me to be his girlfriend and the rest is history."

"You dated until you got married?"

Crystal took the last bite of her hamburger. "I do believe this shop makes the best burgers in Silvermont." After she finished chewing she said, "I went on a couple of dates with other guys in college, but they weren't anything serious."

"That is so romantic," Vivian admired.

"Not at first it wasn't. I used to cry every night he picked on me."

"Goes to show, a person never really knows what to expect out of life."

"You're right. If someone told me years ago that I'd be married to that little boy, I would've screamed, 'No!' at the top of my lungs."

Vivian took another sip of tea. "Life can be funny that way."

"Is this your first marriage?" Crystal said. "If you don't mind me asking."

"No, I don't mind. It is my first marriage and my husband's second. I kind of got a late start. I focused on my career first. By the time I started seriously looking for Mr. Right, it wasn't as easy as I thought it would be."

"That must have been frustrating," Crystal said.

"It was. I just figured if it was meant for me to find that special man, it would happen."

"Then you met him?"

"Well, yeah, sort of. He was my boss, and he wasn't looking for love. But I got tired of seeing his solemn face. No light in his eyes. To tell you the truth, I started feeling sorry for him. Everything revolved around work, except for his son."

"You have a stepson?"

"Yes."

"Do you have any more children?"

"No," Vivian said pausing for a second while tracing the rim of her tea glass. "I think putting my career first and waiting on love was a costly mistake. My doctor told us that because of my age, our chances of having a child together biologically are slim."

"But, and I don't mean to get into your business or anything." Crystal said.

"Go ahead. I just put it out there to you," Vivian laughed.

"Have you thought about doing IVF?"

"How does the saying go? 'Been there and done that.' It didn't work. And it was hard emotionally."

"I'm sorry to hear that." Crystal said.

"Don't be. I've prayed about it and I know God knows what's best. My husband and I are actually thinking about adopting," Vivian said with a smile.

"That would be great. Giving a child a good home."

"Our home is certainly large enough. We might even consider adopting more than one."

"That would be such a blessing," Crystal said.

"What about you. Do you have any children?"

"No, not yet. We are waiting on God also. We know one day He'll bless us with children. The reason I mentioned the IVF is because my husband and I were told it could help us have a child."

"It might. Don't let my experience discourage you. Your outcome will probably be totally different."

"We've decided to hold off on the procedure for now."

"Don't wait too long. You know how the biological clock ticks. You don't want to find yourself in my shoes."

"Ladies, would you like some ice cream?" their waiter walked over and asked.

"Of course we would. I know I wouldn't pass up a chance to have some of the best ice cream in Silvermont," Vivian said.

"I'm on a diet, but I've been doing pretty good. I think I'll have some too," Crystal said.

He handed them the ice cream menus.

"I don't need a menu. I am going to have the Peach a' la mode," Crystal said.

Vivian handed her menu back to the waiter, "I want strawberry cheesecake. Thank you."

"I'll be right back," the waiter said, walking away.

"That woman looks like the nurse from my doctor's office," Vivian said looking over Crystal's shoulder.

Crystal looked in the same direction as Vivian. "That's Shelby."

"Yeah, that's her name," Vivian said.

Crystal called her over. "Shelby."

Shelby looked over at the two women. She then smiled and headed their way. "Hey, Crystal. Hi, Mrs. . . ."

"Parker," Vivian answered.

"Vivian Parker, right." Shelby said.

"Yes. You can call me Vivian. It's a small world isn't it? We've been talking about the same doctor's office and didn't even know it."

"It is a small world," Crystal replied and asked, "What brings you here?"

"I had an unexplainable craving for ice cream. I've heard good things about the ice cream here so I thought I'd try it out," Shelby said.

"You've never had their ice cream?" Vivian asked.

Shelby shook her head, "No."

"The best in Silvermont," Vivian said.

"Why don't you sit with us?" Crystal asked.

"Sure." Shelby took a seat next to Crystal.

The waiter returned. "Here you go, ladies." He handed Crystal and Vivian their orders.

"Would you like something Miss?" The waiter asked Shelby.

"Yes, let me get the mocha fudge special you're advertising."

"I'll be right back Miss," the waiter said.

"So you two know each other?" Shelby asked the women.

"Yeah, Vivian's company is renovating my daycare," Crystal answered.

"How is everything coming along?" Shelby asked.

"Pretty good. Vivian and I came here to have lunch before today's final inspection."

"Shelby, you've really never had the ice cream here?" Vivian asked.

"I don't really eat a lot of ice cream, but for some reason today I have a craving for something with chocolate."

"We were sitting here talking about kids. Well, you know our situation being the nurse at Dr. Evan's office. Do you have any children?" Vivian asked Shelby.

"No, not yet. Soon hopefully," Shelby replied.

"We've decided to adopt," Vivian said.

"Really? That's nice. A friend of mine adopted a baby last year. The baby looks just like my friend and her husband. You'd never know he was adopted if they didn't tell you," Shelby said.

"So you won't be seeing me for any infertility procedures. I am done with that. Once was enough," Vivian said.

"I am really glad to hear about the adoption. You can give a child a loving home."

"My husband and I are so excited." Vivian said.

The waiter returned with Shelby's ice cream. "Will there be anything else for you ladies?" he asked.

"No, I think we're fine," Crystal said.

Shelby took a taste of her ice cream. "Umph. This is so good."

"I told you you'd like it," Vivian said.

"You were right." Shelby's eyes rolled back in her head with visible pleasure as she ate. "It's hitting the spot."

"Speaking of good food, Vivian, have you ever had any food from Mama Lula's Restaurant?" Crystal asked.

"Mama Lula's? No, I haven't."

"Girl, now it's *you*, who doesn't know what you're miss-

ing," Shelby said. "If you want some good, down-home cooking like your grandmamma used to make, then Mama Lula's
is the place."

"I haven't had any good down-home cooking in a while,"
Vivian admitted.

"We'll have to go there one day," Crystal said. "I know
you'll like it."

"Just let me know. I'm game." Vivian said.

"Shelby, you should join us," Crystal said.

"Let me know. I wouldn't pass up an invitation to Mama
Lula's. My husband and I went there on our first date."

Crystal and Vivian looked at each other and laughed.

Not getting the joke Shelby asked, "Did I miss something?
What's so funny?"

"Before you came in we were talking about our husbands
and how we met them," Crystal said.

"Yeah, I was telling Crystal that this is the first place my
husband and I ever went to together. It was like a first date."

"So I came right on time," Shelby laughed.

"Yep, join right in," Vivian said.

The three women talked more about their husbands and
their lives. Each found they had a great deal in common.
After they finished their ice cream, Vivian looked at her
watch. "I guess we better head back to the center. It's almost
time for the inspection."

"I need to get out of here too. It was great talking with you
both," Shelby said.

"You too, Shelby. We'll definitely have to get together
again," Vivian said.

"We sure can. One night at Mama Lula's." Shelby said.

"Sounds great to me," Crystal said. "I'll make the arrange-
ments and call both of you." They all paid their tickets and
left.

*   *   *

"The inspection went really well. He didn't find anything. Your inspection was more thorough than his," Crystal said.

"Most inspectors know our work. And they know it's always of the best quality."

"Is that it? Was that the last step in the process?" Crystal asked with glee.

"That's it. Let me be the first to shake your hand and say congratulations. You are now free to open the doors for TLC!" Vivian said, extending her hand.

Full of delight, Crystal hugged Vivian instead. "It's finally happened. My dream has come true. I have my own daycare center!"

Vivian hugged back. "Yes, you've got the official go ahead."

"Oh my goodness. I've got so many things to do. I've got a million phone calls to make!" Crystal said.

"Let me get out of your hair. Be sure to let me know when the grand opening will be. I'd love to come."

"I definitely will."

"You take care, Crystal."

"I will. You too. And I'll set up a date for us to have dinner with Shelby."

"I look forward to it," Vivian said.

Chapter 18

Vivian Parker

Vivian drove around the beltline on her way back to the office. The construction of the Whitman building was a month and a half underway. She was very pleased with its progression, as was Trace Whitman.

She turned on the CD player and listened to Beverly Crawford's song "I'm Still Standing." She thought more about their decision to adopt.

They had already met with one of the social workers at the Department of Social Services. The woman gave them the details about the adoption process in their agency. She was pleasant and informative. Vivian and Roland both left the meeting feeling good about what they were doing.

She gave them some information about private and independent adoptions also, if they had a specific child in mind that was not in the county system. All the information made them even more sure about their decision. After discussing it, they decided to stick with the DSS office, especially since they didn't have a specific child in mind for a private adoption. So they filled out their application and submitted it— that had been a couple weeks prior.

Lost in thought, Vivian heard her mobile phone ring. Looking at its caller ID she recognized the number from her office. "Hello?"

"Hi, Mrs. Parker. This is Nikki."

"Yes, Nikki? What's going on?" Vivian asked, wondering why the secretary was calling. Nikki only called Vivian's cell phone when it was absolutely necessary.

"You wanted me to let you know when the social worker called," the secretary answered.

"Yes. Did she call back?" Vivian asked with anticipation.

"Yes, Mrs. Parker, I just hung up with her. I told her I'd call and give you the message."

"What did she say?"

"She said to give her a call back as soon as possible."

Vivian was glad to hear the news. She wondered what the call might mean. She asked Nikki, "How did she sound? Did she sound positive or indifferent?"

"She sounded really nice. Her tone was cheerful, I guess you could say," the secretary tried to guess.

"Good. Thank you, Nikki. I'm on my way back to the office now. I should be there in about fifteen minutes. Can you transfer me to Roland?"

"Yes, Mrs. Parker."

"Thanks, Nikki."

"You're welcome."

Vivian waited until she heard Roland answer. "Hey Viv. What's going on? Is anything wrong?"

"No, hopefully everything is actually going right."

"What do you mean?"

"Nikki just called and told me the social worker called."

"She did? What did she want?"

"I don't know. She wants me to call her as soon as possible though," Vivian said.

"Where are you now?" Roland asked.

"I'm about to exit. I should be back in about fifteen minutes."

"It's almost five. I wonder if she'll still be in her office." Roland said.

"I don't know. I hope so. I would call her from here, but I'd rather we call her together. I'll come straight to your office. See you in a few minutes."

"Viv?"

"Yes, Roland."

"I love you."

"I love you too sweetheart," Vivian said and pressed the end button.

She wondered if the social worker was calling about their adoption application. Even though the woman said it would only take about a week to process it, two had passed. She'd anticipated the call for several days.

Now they would be able to get an update and find out if their application had been accepted.

They put a great deal of thought and care into filling out their application. It could have easily been completed in a matter of minutes but they had taken the time to sit down and discuss each question extensively.

Especially when it came to the questions about what type of child they'd like to adopt.

When answering the question asking "What age child / children would you accept?" they put from newborn to 5-years old. When asked about race, they decided race didn't matter. What mattered was that a deserving child who needed a good home would get one.

When they were asked the number of children they wanted to adopt and if they would consider a sibling group, they checked, "Yes".

They tried to be as flexible and open-minded as possible even when it came to the question about whether they would accept a child with serious health problems. When asked if they were applying for a specific child already in the DSS system, they checked, "No."

She couldn't wait to get back to the office to make the big call with Roland. Looking back at her watch, she prayed the social worker would still be in her office.

"Hey, I was getting a little worried," Roland said.

"It was just my luck. The city started construction, so I had to take detours. Then I got turned around thinking the street I was taking would parallel the other street," Vivian said.

Roland looked at his watch, "It's two minutes to five."

"Yeah, I know. I guess we could try to call. She might still be there. If not, I guess we'll just have to wait patiently until tomorrow."

She pulled out the business card with the social worker's phone number and dialed it.

"Hello, Christina Ingram speaking," the social worker answered.

Vivian breathed a sigh of relief. "Hello, Ms. Ingram. This is Vivian Parker returning your call."

"Oh yes, Mrs. Parker. You just caught me. I was about to leave."

"I know it's late, and I'm sorry. I just made it back into my office. My secretary told me to call you A.S.A.P."

"Yes. I wanted to let you know that your application has been accepted!"

"That's wonderful!"

"You've completed the first phase in the adoption process. We'll need to set up another appointment for you and your husband so we may speak further. Why don't I call you back in the morning to set up that appointment?"

"That would be great," Vivian said.

"I'll call you in the morning then."

"Okay. Thanks, Ms. Ingram," Vivian said excitedly.

"You're welcome. Bye."

"Bye," Vivian said and hung up.

"Good news I gather?" Roland said.

"Some of the best news. She said our application was accepted. We've completed the first phase of the adoption process."

"That *is* good news!" Roland exclaimed.

"She wants to set up another appointment to further discuss our application and start the next phase."

"When does she want to meet?"

"She's going to call back in the morning."

"Sounds great to me."

"It sounds real good, doesn't it?" Vivian said, hardly able to contain her excitement.

"We definitely have something to celebrate tonight," Roland said, taking Vivian into his arms.

Vivian made sure she was back in the office early the next morning. She'd wanted to get in to tie up some loose ends before the office officially opened.

Neither she nor Roland slept all night. They had tossed and turned excited and anxious about the good news. With William out of the house at a friend's for the night, Vivian and Roland pulled out a vintage wine and celebrated. And even after expending a great deal of energy during their celebration, they still couldn't sleep

Once the loose ends were tied up, Vivian sorted through the mail on her desk. The last envelope in the stack was an invitation. The return address listed Crystal Shaw's name and the address of her daycare. It was an invitation to the grand opening of TLC. Vivian looked at the beautiful invitation, which had children playing around its border. She ran her fingers over the embossed, hunter green letters.

The grand opening was scheduled within a couple of days. Looking at the R.S.V.P. date, Vivian realized the date had already passed. She wondered if it had been correct. Looking at the postmark, she saw it was two weeks old. Vivian figured the invitation must have somehow gotten misdirected on its way to her office.

She made a mental note to call Crystal and tell her what happened. She didn't want to miss the grand opening and hoped it wasn't too late to R.S.V.P.

Just then her phone buzzed. "Mrs. Parker. You have a call on line two. It's Ms. Ingram."

Each time Vivian thought about coming closer to adopting a child she felt elated. Her heart began to race with excitement and her stomach suddenly felt as if she had butterflies fluttering around.

"Thanks, Nikki. Send it through." Vivian cleared her throat and when the call came through she said, "Hello, Ms. Ingram."

"Good morning, Mrs. Parker. Are you ready to schedule our next appointment?"

"Yes. When would you like to meet? We're pretty flexible," Vivian said.

"How's next Monday at nine?"

Vivian looked at her calendar. It was the same day as the grand opening for TLC. "Yes, that will be fine. I'll let my husband know, and we'll see you then."

"Sounds good. I'll see you both Monday morning at nine," the social worker said and hung up.

Vivian immediately called Roland to update him. After she hung up, she picked up the invitation to call Crystal. There was no answer at the number on the invitation, so she pulled up Crystal's old contract to find the phone number for Little Angels Day Care Center. Vivian dialed the center's office. As the phone rang, she hoped they would still know how to contact Crystal.

"Hello. Little Angels Day Care, Darla speaking."

"Hello, Darla, my name is Vivian Parker. I'm trying to contact Crystal Shaw."

"She's here. Hold on a second."

Vivian waited, relieved Crystal was actually there. She
could hear the sounds of laughter and playing coming from
what sounded like a room full of children and adults.

"Hello, this is Crystal."

"Hey, Crystal. It's Vivian Parker. How are you doing?"

"Hi, Vivian! I'm fine. How are you?"

"I'm doing great. I was calling to see if I can still R.S.V.P.
for your grand opening. Is it too late?"

"No, it's fine. I'll add your name to the list."

"Sorry I am contacting you so late. I just got the invitation
this morning. It must have been mixed up in all the mail."

"That has happened to quite a few people. I think because
of the awkward size and shape, they got held up."

"I tried calling the number on the invitation but didn't get
an answer, so I tried you here. I hope you don't mind."

"I don't mind at all. Actually, you're lucky to have caught
me here. My last day was a week ago. I came back to pick up
some things, and the kids surprised me with a going-away
party."

"It sounds like you all are having fun."

"I'm having a great time," Crystal said, laughing.

"I won't hold you. I . . ."

Crystal cut Vivian off. "I'm sorry Vivian, hold on a second."

Vivian heard the phone being placed down and then Crystal's voice speaking to someone else. While she waited for her
to return, Vivian looked over plans for an upcoming project.

"I'm so sorry. That was one of your little friends," Crystal
said.

"My little friend? Who?" Vivian asked curiously.

"It was Kylia coming to give me a hug and a special picture she painted."

"Ah," Vivian said with a smile. The warmth in her heart
she'd felt that first day she met Kylia and Kyle returned instantly. "How is my little friend doing?"

"She and Kyle are doing great. This picture is so pretty. It's a picture of a building, and I think the person in front is supposed to be me. Then next to me are two little people. I guess they're Kylia and her little brother. I'm definitely going to have to frame this and put it in my new office."

"You never know, she may be a famous artist one day. You'll have one of her first pieces of art," Vivian said.

"I hope you're right. I just pray they'll be placed in a good home," Crystal said, her voice turning sad.

"Are they moving them to another foster home?" Vivian asked with concern.

"No, no. They have been cleared for adoption."

Vivian's mouth dropped. She couldn't believe she'd heard Crystal right. Kylia and Kyle were available for adoption. "Did I hear you correctly? Did you just say they are eligible for adoption?" Vivian wondered if her ears were playing tricks on her.

"Yes, I found out today. I just hope and pray they'll find a good home, and they'll be able to be placed together."

Vivian thought she was dreaming. "I can't believe they are actually eligible for adoption. I am going to have to pinch myself." It was all so clear to her now. God was so good. She and Roland could adopt Kylia and Kyle.

"I can't believe it either." Crystal said.

"Crystal, you don't understand. I really can't believe you just told me those two beautiful children can be adopted. You don't know what that means to me."

"What, Vivian? What do you mean?" Crystal asked.

"Isn't it funny how things work? Isn't it so funny how God works things out?" Vivian said.

"Vivian, you're losing me. What do you mean?" Crystal asked with concern.

"I just got off the phone with a social worker at the Department of Social Services," Vivian said, pausing. She pulled out a piece of tissue to wipe her eyes.

"Vivian, are you alright? It sounds like you are crying."

"I am. But these are tears of joy." Vivian paused, sniffing as she cried. "I'm sorry, let me explain." She took a deep breath. "Remember when I told you my husband and I were thinking about adopting?"

"Yes. I remember you telling me the day we had lunch."

"Right. The reason I said this is all fate is because my husband and I didn't decide to adopt until the first day I met you. Remember the day I came by to tell you I'd personally oversee your project?"

"Yeah, and I thought you were lost or something."

"Now I know I wasn't lost. It was all in God's plan to have me meet you, so I could meet Kylia and Kyle. It was meeting them and realizing I could love a child, a child not biologically mine. The hugs Kylia and Kyle gave me warmed my heart so much; they still warm my heart. It was like I had an unexplainable bond with the children. A bond, which happened in such a short period of time, it let me know I didn't have to give birth to a child to love them unconditionally.

"You see, I'd been praying for weeks prior to meeting you. Praying God would give us an answer as to what we should do to have a child. The doctor gave us various options when our attempt at IVF didn't work. We didn't know if we should try the IVF again, use donor eggs, or adopt.

"God was giving us the answer we needed. I called my husband immediately after I left your office and told him God wanted us to adopt. Then we contacted our doctor, who put us in contact with a social worker at DSS."

"Oh, I understand now." Crystal said.

"That's why I said God has worked this whole thing out. Our infertility problems were the reason I even met you in the first place. After the failed IVF I needed a change of pace, so I decided to take on some smaller projects. Yours was the first one I took on.

"Ha." Vivian started laughing. "Now I fully understand. He wasn't just using Kylia and Kyle to send me the message that we needed to adopt. Kylia and Kyle *were* the message. God's plan was for us to adopt Kylia and Kyle. That is why the invitation arrived so late. It was meant for me to call today at this very moment!" Vivian exclaimed, overwhelmed by the revelation. She cried more tears of happiness.

"Oh, my!" Crystal exclaimed. "You would consider adopting Kylia and Kyle?"

"Consider it? It's our answer from God. I don't have to consider it. It's a done deal—our destiny. We are supposed to adopt them. It took a little while, but I finally got the full message from God, now I hear Him loud and clear."

Crystal was speechless for a moment. "Vivian. God is so awesome, and He does work in mysterious ways. I've never seen anything like this before. I'm going to start crying in a minute."

"Go ahead. We all need to cry tears of joy every once in a while," Vivian laughed through her own tears.

"I haven't had a chance to do that in a while. I forgot what tears of joy feel like," Crystal said, also starting to cry. "They actually feel pretty good."

"Yes, they do." Vivian agreed, welcoming the tears, which flowed freely.

"So what are you going to do?" Crystal sniffed and wiped her spilling tears.

"I need to call the social worker back and let her know we have two children in mind."

"Just let me know if there is anything I can help you with." Crystal said.

"I will." Vivian thought about it. "Actually, I do need their names. I'm sure the social worker can take it from there."

Vivian wrote down the children's first and last names as Crystal spelled them for her.

"Thank you so much, Crystal. I'm going to talk with my husband and we'll call our social worker back."

"Good luck, Vivian. Let me know how things turn out. I hope everything works out well. It'll be such a blessing if you are able to adopt them."

"Thank you again. I have faith things will turn out just as God planned. We will adopt Kylia and Kyle. We just have to go through the process. God has given me an answer. I'm taking this answer as His promise and I'm holding on to it!"

Chapter 19

Shelby Tomlinson

"How's it going, baby?" Shelby's mother asked.

"I'm fine, Mom, I know I could be pregnant, but I don't really feel anything," Shelby sighed over the phone.

"I don't know what to say about all this IVF stuff. It's all foreign to me," her Mom admitted.

"It's not totally foreign to me, but this whole pregnancy thing is. I don't know when I am supposed to start feeling sick."

"Don't wish for it. You might get lucky and never get sick."

Doubt crept into Shelby's mind. "Or maybe I don't feel anything because I'm not pregnant. Maybe the procedure didn't work."

"Stop talking like that *right now*. I don't want you to start speaking doubt and get yourself all worked up. Think positive and stay hopeful."

"I am hopeful, but the truth is there's a chance I'm not pregnant."

"But you could be pregnant with triplets, and you're just not feeling any of the signs right now. Stay hopeful and just remain positive. For heaven's sake, don't speak negatively. You know God will work things out."

Shelby sat in a chair looking out of her bedroom window as she spoke. Her mother had always been there for her giving her words of inspiration. So that morning as the feeling of depression started to set in, she quickly picked up the phone and speed-dialed her.

Shelby pulled her legs under body, shifting into a more comfortable position. "I'm trying my best mom. My mind just keeps flipping from positive to negative thoughts. I try to control it, but it's pretty hard. It's been seven days since the transfer, and we still have three more days before we can go back to the doctor for the pregnancy test."

"Patience, Shelby. How is Phillip handling the wait?"

"Better than me. He's got some business deal that's been keeping his mind pretty much preoccupied. He tries to hide it though, but he's just as anxious and excited as me."

"Did he give you any more problems about doing any of the other procedures?"

"No. We talked and he realized how I felt. He just wants me to be happy again."

"Happy again? What do you mean?"

Shelby hadn't told her mother about the secrets Phillip had kept from her. She had been too embarrassed and hadn't meant to let it slip. "I guess I was doing a lot of sulking, and he got tired of it," Shelby cringed as she lied.

"Sulking, Shelby. I remember when you were little and couldn't get your way. You'd sulk all day. Though it wouldn't move me, you did a job on your father. You had him wrapped around your little finger. After only a couple minutes of sulking, he always gave in easily."

"Not all the time. There were times when he wouldn't."

"Of course he had to stand his ground sometimes. Especially that time you went to the zoo and wanted to take the parrot home."

"I remember that," Shelby laughed, snorting so hard she began to cough. "I wanted that parrot so bad." She figured she was laughing hard because she had been so uptight the previous week stressing about the tests results.

"Shelby, you can't sulk when you don't get your way. Phillip isn't your dad. He may not put up with it like your father."

"I know, Mom. I'm starting to understand that. So are you and Daddy still coming fourth Sunday?"

"Yes. You know the Bishop I'm always talking about that comes on TV? He'll be at New Hope. Have you had a chance to go to one of their services yet?"

"Yes, actually we have. Phillip even went with me Sunday before last. One of my patients had been trying to get me to go there also."

"You should come with us on Sunday then. I know the anointing will be all over the church. I wish we were a little closer to New Hope. I would consider becoming a member. That place always makes me so full."

"Full? You and Dad always talk about being so hungry when you come over here."

"Not edible food. I'm talking about spiritual food," her mother replied. "Full of the Holy Spirit."

"Oh," Shelby said, not fully understanding what her mother meant. When she was younger, her mother always made it a point of them going to church. But recently she had stopped going to their old church and found a new church. Since attending this new church, Shelby's mother reminded her of what most people would call a Holy Roller. The woman was always talking about the Lord and church services.

"You should really come with us this Sunday. New Hope reminds me so much of my church here."

"Mom, you used to complain about those churches that kept you in for hours and hours, not letting out until after two or three in the afternoon. You used to love the fact that our old church got out at a decent hour—noon."

"Back then Shelby, for me, it was all about seeing who could out dress the other. Making sure the preacher didn't go too far past noon and being home by one o'clock or one-thirty at the latest, so we would all be eating our Sunday dinner at what I thought was a decent hour.

"It's so different now. Today it's about Christ and His love for us. It's about being saved and a child of God. The outfits and amount of time spent in church for me, are not even factors now. As a matter of fact, we have dress down day at our church once a month.

"I am so glad I've been delivered from the old stinking thinking. I do love my new church. New Hope just reminds me so much of it. I want you to see Christ in the same way. That's why I'm always encouraging you to go."

Shelby knew at times her mother could be relentless when it came to some subjects, especially church. So to save herself another ten minutes of her Mom trying to coax her she said, "Okay mom. I'll go with you."

"It would be nice if Phillip would come also," her Mom said.

"I don't know if he'll come, but I'll ask him. I liked the church the few times I've been. Phillip thought it was okay. They did get a little loud with what I guess you are calling the 'Holy Spirit.'" Shelby wasn't really sure what exactly the Holy Spirit was, but she did feel something different when she visited New Hope. And it seemed as though the pastor's sermon the last Sunday she'd been there, was written just for her. He'd preached about having hope and not giving up on God, especially in the areas of life where people's faith is the weakest.

"Just ask him. You never know, he might come."

Shelby thought about it. She knew Phillip didn't like to go to church and had only gone to please her. He always said the people seemed so phony at many of the churches they had visited. He also didn't like to miss his games on Sunday. With pessimism she said, "I'll ask."

"Well baby, I need to go. I've got to get to church; I have an executive committee in a couple of hours. I need to finish getting dressed and review my agenda before I go."

"Alright, Mom. I'll talk to you later."

"Keep me updated, sweetheart."

"I will. Love you, Mom."

Shelby heard her mother say, "Love you too, baby" just before hanging up.

Phillip leaned back in his office chair and drummed his fingers on his desk calendar as he listened to his lawyer. He was so tense, he feared he'd crush the telephone between his jaw and collarbone.

"It's all set, Phillip. The payments will be sent monthly automatically. The account you asked me to set up is not connected to any of your other bank accounts. The monthly check she'll receive is more than substantial," Phillip's lawyer said.

Phillip nodded his head, "Good, good. What about the back support?"

"It's been taken care of. And her lawyer also knows he can only contact you through me. We shouldn't hear anything from Ms. Sands anytime soon. And she and her lawyer know you don't want any contact with the boy."

"Good. I want it kept that way. Make sure her lawyer knows she's never to contact me. Make sure they don't have any direct contact information for me. Nothing—no phone numbers, no address and no e-mail." Phillip wanted to make sure he covered all the bases. He just wanted the whole nightmare to go away, so he could go back to a normal life.

"It's already done, Phillip, relax," Phillip's lawyer said.

Phillip let out a deep breath. He was so glad the whole

matter of Jeana Sands and the boy was finally resolved. "I am relaxed. I'm just glad all of this is over. I wish you hadn't insisted that I go into the courtroom."

"I explained all of that to you, Phillip." The lawyer sounded impatient.

"I know, but I would rather had not seen her again. I'm just glad she didn't allow the boy to come."

The lawyer agreed. "It was good thinking for all parties concerned."

"Thanks for all your help, especially on such short notice," Phillip said, even though he didn't appreciate the lawyer acting as if he was a bother to him. He was a good lawyer, and Phillip might need him in the future for something else.

"It's fine. I've been your father's lawyer for years, and I'm glad you called me. But just relax now. The automatic transfer to Ms. Sands account will take place at the beginning of each month until the child reaches 18. Or until he is 22, if he remains in college full-time."

The tension Phillip had felt in his body, only a few minutes before the phone call, was slipping away. "Good. Now I can move on with my life."

"If you have any other legal needs, feel free to call me."

"I sure will. Especially for taking care of this mess," Phillip said.

"No problem. I'll talk to you later." The lawyer hung up.

Phillip leaned back in his office chair and propped his feet up on the desk as he thought about the previous weeks. His mind had been preoccupied with getting the proof of paternity and then child support mess out of the way.

He hadn't wanted to go to court, but realized he couldn't avoid it once his lawyer explained the necessity. Once the day arrived and he was standing in court he was actually glad that he had gone. He was slightly curious as to what Jeana looked like after all the years that passed. When he did see her, he couldn't believe how different she looked. No longer did she resemble the naïve freshman he once knew.

Seeing her brought the memories flooding back about the first time he saw her on campus. She was there for her freshman orientation and asked him where the business building was located. Phillip thought she had the prettiest southern drawl he had ever heard. It made him think of something from *Gone with the Wind.*

He saw this as an opportunity for some potential "fresh meat," as the phrase went for new, naïve, women. Phillip took the liberty of walking her all the way to the building. As they walked, Phillip found out her name was Jeana and that she was from some little small town in eastern North Carolina. She tried to explain, but all he knew is that it was somewhere between Wilmington and Jacksonville. Jeana was attending Carson State University on scholarship. She was proud of being the Valedictorian of her class, maintaining a 4.0 GPA throughout high school.

Phillip could tell by the way the girl dressed and acted that she was probably from a family that kept a close watch on their "little girl." Now that Mama and Daddy weren't there to watch her, he wondered what their little girl would do now that she was in the big city alone. He was sure she'd never met anyone as fine as him and she'd probably jump at the chance to go out with a star football player.

Phillip looked forward to the semester's start. Jeana Sands was going to be one of his girls. She just didn't know it. He would smooth talk her, and she wouldn't know what hit her. Once they got to the business building, Phillip gave her his pager number and told her to give him a call when she came back for fall semester.

Just two days into the semester, Phillip's pager beeped with an unfamiliar number. As soon as he heard the pretty southern voice, he knew it was his country girl. After only a few dates, he had talked Jeana into sleeping with him, even though she admitted she was still a virgin and had planned to save herself for her husband.

After sleeping with him a couple more times, Jeana told him she was pregnant. That is when it all hit the fan for him. He had never gotten any of the others pregnant. He heard other guys talking about getting girls pregnant and knew they told the girls to get abortions. It was the only solution. He told her she would have to get an abortion and gave her the money from his savings account. After that she called a few times pleading with him, to let her keep it but he didn't want to hear anything. Then she just stopped calling. He heard she dropped out of school and that was that. The problem had been taken care of.

The woman who had stood in the courtroom was just that—a real woman. Jeana wasn't the timid little girl with the pronounced southern drawl. She was a mature woman who carried herself in a self-assured manner.

He could tell by the way she looked at him that she still had a thing for him. He could see the longing she was desperately trying to hide. He thought it was pathetic and actually felt sorry for her.

He had moved on with his life and hoped she had too. When the court proceedings were over, Phillip quickly left. He didn't want a confrontation with Jeana. Just before exiting the door, he saw her out of the corner of his eye. She tried to make her way over to him, but due to the crowd of people, she was unable. He was relieved.

As he drove passed the front of the courthouse to return home, he saw Jeana looking at him from the top of the steps. She was glaring at him. He knew deep down Jeana still wanted him. He could have sworn she had smoke coming out of her ears. The look in her eyes was that of a woman scorned. At that moment he felt Jeana might kill him if given the chance. It gave him the creepiest feeling. Surely he must have imagined it.

Phillip shook his head as he leaned further back in his office chair, breathing another sigh of relief. Finally he could move on with his life, a life which now included only his wife and the children they would soon have.

He picked up the phone and dialed a local florist. He ordered two dozen, assorted roses with English Ivy and baby's breath. Then he called Ginny's to make reservations for dinner.

That evening, Phillip left work and briskly walked to his car. He felt like jumping up and clicking his heels but thought how silly it would look. He had planned a special night for his wife.

Once in the car, he called her from his cell phone. "Hello, love of my life." He allowed his voice to drop a couple of octaves.

"Hello. What brought that on?" Shelby asked.

"What? I can't tell you you're the love of my life?"

"Of course you can. But you sound a little funny, like Lou Rawls."

"Lou Rawls?" Phillip spoke in his regular tone. "I hope this is better. What are you doing?"

"I just hung up with mom, and I'm just trying to stay busy. I keep thinking about the pregnancy test."

"I'm on my way home. We're going out tonight."

"Where are we going?" Shelby asked.

"It's a surprise. Get dressed."

"I don't really feel like . . ."

"Yes, you do. We're not going to sit around tonight and drive ourselves crazy. We need to get out. Besides, we need to celebrate," Phillip said happily.

"What are we celebrating?"

"I'll tell you when I get there. I'll see you soon."

"Okay, okay. Bye." Shelby gave in.

"Bye."

Phillip turned his SUV into the driveway of Ginny's Restaurant. He smiled over at Shelby.

"Ginny's huh? You really mean to celebrate, don't you?" Shelby said as Phillip pulled up to the valet.

"Tonight we're going to celebrate the positive test results."

"You're pretty confident aren't you?" Shelby said with apprehension.

"I sure am. Today was great, and I know it can only lead to better days ahead. Our reservation is at eight. Let's go in before someone else gets our table."

Phillip led Shelby into the restaurant and whispered something into the hostess' ear.

"Yes, Mr. Tomlinson, your table is ready. Right this way please." The hostess led them to their table. "Here you are."

"Wait," Shelby said. "This must be someone else's table."

"No sweetheart, this is our table," Phillip said as he pulled out Shelby's chair.

"But look at these roses." She touched one of the plump blooms. "They are beautiful. The other tables don't have a centerpiece like this."

"They're for you," Phillip said, grinning. Then he leaned over and kissed her.

"They're beautiful. You planned all this?"

"Guilty as charged."

"This is so sweet." She pulled the roses closer and touched them again. She took in the soft scent they emitted. "You knew exactly what I needed. I'm glad you got me out of the house. I was going crazy thinking about the test results."

"Everything is going to turn out fine. I have a good feeling about it," Phillip said, leaning over to kiss her again.

"You really must've had a great day."

Full of exhilaration Phillip said, "I did. I feel like I'm on top of the world."

"I can see that." Shelby was surprised by Phillip's actions. He had been acting strange for the past few weeks. It wasn't anything she could put her finger on, but she knew his mind was on something pretty heavy. She had been hoping whatever project he was working on would end soon and was hopeful the celebration was a signal for the end.

"I do feel like I am on top of the world. Today kicks off our good fortune. I finally resolved that problem I've been working on. And in a couple of days we'll get the positive results of the pregnancy test."

"I'm glad to have my old Phillip, back. And I'm glad you got that problem at work resolved."

"It's me. I'm back in full-force, baby." Phillip smiled his old confident smile. He was truly back.

They picked up their menus and scanned them. "All of Ginny's food is so good. I think I'll try something new, though," Shelby said.

"I'm easy. Steak and a baked potato."

"We really should come here more often. We haven't been since our anniversary."

"We'll start coming more often," Phillip promised.

The waiter approached the table. "Hello, my name is Kim. I'll be your waitress tonight. Would you like to see our wine list?"

"No, Kim. My wife is expecting. We'll both be drinking something non-alcoholic," Phillip said. "I'll have lemonade." He looked back at Shelby. "Shelby?"

Shelby's eyes popped wide open. She stuttered, "I'll have the same."

"Very well then. I'll return in a few minutes to take your food orders," the waiter said, walking away.

"Phillip!" Shelby said after the waiter left.

"What?" he asked innocently. "You are expecting. Expect-ing a positive pregnancy test. Right?"

"It's just the way you said it. It caught me off guard."

"Get used to it. Life is going to change." Phillip said.

They ordered their food and enjoyed the ambiance of the restaurant. They talked about the future and the excitement the next couple of days would hold.

Phillip mentioned buying an over-the-counter pregnancy test. So on their way home, he stopped at the drug store and picked one up.

Once they were in the house, Shelby said, "I'll take it in the morning."

"Why? You might as well take the test tonight. You know neither of us will be able to sleep thinking about it. Don't you want to sleep with some assurance?"

"I do. But my HCG levels will be higher in the morning."

"But the directions say it can be taken any time during the day."

"Yeah, they do," Shelby said.

"So what are you waiting for?"

"I'm scared, but I do want to take it," Shelby said with hes-itation.

"I know you're nervous. If you don't want to take it right now, I'll understand."

"It couldn't hurt, could it? The directions do say . . ." Shelby was unsure. She wanted to take the test. She wanted to find out. But she was scared.

At work she had performed so many pregnancy tests for her patients that she could do it in her sleep. But this was a different story. She was about to take a pregnancy test for herself. It was another ballgame.

"Go ahead, baby! Take it," Phillip said, continuing to en-courage her.

She finally gave in. "Okay. I'll do it." She went into their bathroom and closed the door. Phillip waited patiently on the bed, anticipating her return. After a few minutes, she returned with a blank look or her face.

"What? What did the test say?" Phillip asked, starting to get worried.

Shelby shook her head negatively. "It was negative."

"No, baby. You must be wrong. Maybe you read it wrong." Phillip ran into the bathroom.

He came out after a couple of minutes. "Shelby, maybe you were right. I should have listened to you and let you test in the morning for higher HGC levels. I shouldn't have pushed you to test tonight." He felt guilty.

"It's alright, Phillip. At least I found out tonight instead of at the doctor's office. It will be all right. We still have frozen embryos. I'll just save my hope for them."

"Are you sure you're alright, baby? I feel so bad. I shouldn't have pressured you."

"Yes. I'm fine," Shelby said. Her voice was strong and definite.

Phillip looked at her in disbelief.

"I am sweetheart. It's funny, but a few months ago I probably wouldn't have been okay. But since I've started reading the Bible more and standing on the scriptures like the pastor says, I truly trust God. Romans 15:4 says, '*The Scriptures were written to teach and encourage us by giving us hope.*'

"Because of the Scriptures, I haven't been feeling sad anymore. Haven't you noticed that I've not had an anxiety attack in months? I trust God is going to take care of everything, even curing my attacks.

I'm not going to let that negative result send me back into doubting God. I'll continue to keep hope and faith that God is going to give us children when the time is right. We just have to be patient."

Phillip continued to look at her in disbelief. "You really are okay, aren't you?"

"Yes, I am. I know with God's help and guidance He is

going to take care of everything." She gave Phillip a tight hug and kiss. "I'm tired. It's been a long week. Let's go ahead and get some rest," Shelby told him.

"I'm tired too. I think that's a good idea," Phillip agreed.

Once they were in bed, Phillip wrapped his arms around her. It wasn't long before Shelby was sleeping peacefully in his arms.

"Good morning," Dr. Silva said, his voice cheerful.

"Good morning, Dr. Silva," Phillip said.

Shelby smiled also. Three days had passed since they had taken the home pregnancy test. They had gone ahead and kept their appointment in order to find out what the next steps would be.

"Today is the big day," Dr. Silva said. "I'd like to talk to you about your pregnancy test." He pulled out the test results.

"It's okay, doctor. You don't have to tell us, we already know," Shelby said.

"Oh you do?" the doctor asked.

"Yes. We did a home pregnancy test the other night, so we know what the results are," Shelby said quickly.

"Oh. Okay. Well then I'd like to schedule you to come back in two weeks so we can continue," the doctor said.

Shelby was surprised at the doctor's statement. She hadn't realized they could start again so quickly. "Will I have to start hormones again that quickly? Don't I need to let my body rest for a little while before we attempt to transfer more embryos? I am anxious, but don't you think it's too soon to start again?" Shelby asked.

"I agree with my wife. I think she needs to wait a little while before we attempt this again," Phillip said.

The doctor raised his eyebrows. He looked back and forth at each of them. "I don't understand."

Phillip took Shelby's hand and squeezed it tight. She knew

his temper was rising. And for her sake, he was probably trying to control it.

"Look, doctor, we're just not ready for another disappointment so soon, that's all. You said the embryos would be
frozen until we are ready to use them. Right?"

Shelby hadn't expected for the appointment to go badly.
She dropped her head again, hoping the ordeal would soon
be over. She wondered why the doctor needed to be con-
vinced about waiting to start procedures again.

Phillip placed his arms around her shoulders.

"Yes, the embryos will remain frozen until you decide you
want to use them," the doctor said.

"Good. Is that all for now? Can my wife and I leave?"
Phillip turned to Shelby, "I'm sorry, honey. Let's go." He
stood.

"We still need to schedule the sonogram," the doctor said
abruptly.

"You just don't quit do you?" Phillip said. "Why on earth
would my wife want to do another sonogram?"

"Remember, I told you I'd schedule a sonogram two
weeks after we found out the results of the pregnancy test."

"Yeah, the negative results," Phillip said. "Shelby told me
how it felt to look at that screen with no baby on it. Why
would you want to put her through that again?" Phillip
shook his head. "You know you need to be reported to the
board of doctors or something. What you are doing can't be
ethical."

"No, no, Mr. Tomlinson. I am not sure exactly what you
are talking about. But the results were positive."

"What?" Phillip asked with disbelief. He fell back into his
seat with his mouth dropped open.

Shelby looked up at Dr. Silva in disbelief also. "What?"

He shook his head in affirmation. "The results were positive. What were you both thinking?"

"We got a negative test result," Phillip said, squeezing Shelby's shoulders.

"The test was positive?" In shock Shelby asked the doctor again.

"Yes. You're pregnant. Congratulations!" the doctor laughed. "Now I understand the reason for our miscommunication."

"Oh my God, baby! Phillip yelled.

"I'm pregnant! I can't believe it. I'm pregnant!" Shelby repeated.

Phillip jumped up and hugged Shelby. "I'm so happy!"

"I just can't believe it." Shelby began crying.

"I'm going to be a father," Phillip said and kneeled down to speak to Shelby's stomach. "Hello in there. This is your daddy. We look forward to meeting you."

"Phillip come on, stop being silly." Shelby playfully pushed him away.

"I'm not being silly, baby. I've been waiting a long time for this. I can't wait to meet my child—or children." He hugged Shelby again.

"Doc, when will we know how many we are having?" Phillip questioned.

"Two weeks from today," the doctor replied cheerfully.

"We will see you in two weeks!" Phillip said with excitement. "See baby, everything is fine. Everything is going to be fine. Our life is going to be perfect from now on. Baby, I love you so much!"

Shelby was stunned beyond belief. It seemed so surreal. Was she dreaming? She couldn't believe she had just heard the words that she was pregnant. The thing she wanted the most in the world was actually a reality. She looked up towards heaven, glad she'd held on to her hope and faith even when it seemed like she shouldn't.

"Honey, I love you!" Phillip said again.

Shelby came out of her stunned daze and said, "I love you too, Phillip."

Chapter 20

Crystal Shaw

Crystal stopped by her new center to look it over again, even though she knew she was cutting it close for tonight's Bible study. She admired the way RPDC had done the landscaping. The silver letters with the center's name stood out in the dusk as she pulled up. It was the most beautiful sight she had ever seen.

She parked her car and walked to the front door. There was just enough light to see the master key. She took a deep breath and turned the key in the lock. Even though she had done this many times before, tonight was special. The building was now complete and ready for business to start the next day. It was perfect.

As soon as she was inside, she flipped on the lights. The first thing she focused on was the center's framed and matted philosophy and her personal letter. Both documents would greet everyone each time they came through the center's doors. Now that she was able to see it suspended from the ceiling, it looked better than she imagined.

The paint didn't smell as strong as it had the week before. From where she stood, she could see the reception area and her new office, which already had her name on the door. To her left was the waiting area with the parents' lounge just beyond it. She continued to walk through each of the areas, pleased with their completion.

Once she finished those areas, she checked the other areas further down the hall. Her first stop was the teachers' section. This area held the teachers' offices, lounge, bathroom, and workroom. She was content with the changes there also.

When she entered the kitchen she was thrilled with the way each piece of equipment fit and looked in their respective areas. The shelves in the pantry were in place. The food and supply trucks had made deliveries earlier that day. The room was stocked with food and supplies.

When she walked back out to the corridor, she checked the janitor's closet and the storage room. Then she inspected each of the classrooms.

The first classroom was designated for the infants. It was equipped with cribs, rocking chairs and changing tables. She wanted the infants' environment to be conducive for learning from the first day they arrived at the center. Whether they were being held, changed, carried, or rocked, Crystal felt there were so many things an infant could learn.

Crystal would stress that employees caring for the infants must use age-appropriate communication skills whenever they were with a child. She wanted the infants' senses continually stimulated for learning.

The next classroom was for the toddlers. Crystal wanted their environment to help them become autonomous. Knowing how active toddlers could be, her center would allow them to engage in imaginative play, age-appropriate art activities, and other games to develop their cognitive and physical skills. She had made sure the room was equipped with blocks, music, and books.

Crystal knew the room would appeal to the children since they would be free to use their tactile skills. Their surroundings would also welcome their walking, climbing, carrying objects, and even dropping objects in the designated areas.

The pre-school-aged children had two separate classrooms, one for the 3-year olds and the other for the 4 and 5-year-olds. Both of those classrooms would expound on the disciplines of language communication, science, math, social studies, music, and art, each subject at the level appropriate for their ages. Preschoolers would also practice using large and fine motor skills. She looked forward to taking these children on educational class trips and having special guests come in to talk with them about different subjects.

She continued checking the rest of the building. The multi-purpose room was exactly as she envisioned it. The arrangement of the room included lunch tables, a mounted screen to project movies, and a stage. She pictured the children eating their lunches, watching movies and walking across the stage for their first graduation.

She stepped on the stage making sure it was stable. The work of RPDC was top notch. As she walked on and even jumped on the stage it didn't sway or creek. It was solid as a rock. Crystal and her center were ready for the grand opening.

Crystal again reflected on all the blessings—there were so many—God had graced her with. She thanked Him for her loving family, good health and the job she loved. She was so blessed to have her dream of owning a learning center come true.

She was also thankful to God for giving her the strength not to dwell on the fact that she didn't have any children. She no longer worried about getting pregnant. Crystal knew she and Warren needed to go on with their lives and let God's will be done. If it was to be God's will that they not have any children, then she would accept it. She knew God only had her best interest in mind, so she continued to put her trust in Him.

Crystal stood outside of her center to welcome everyone for its grand opening. "First of all, I'd like to thank you all for coming, especially my husband, Warren, who's been so great through this whole process. I'd also like to thank my family." She smiled at her mother and sisters. "This day has been a long time coming.

"My mother can easily tell you how long this has been a dream for me. This center is dear to my heart. Today will be the first day of many days in which the halls of this center will be filled with the voices of children. It is and always will be a welcome sound I'll look forward to hearing. But most of all, I'd like to thank God for allowing this dream to come to fruition.

"So without further ado, let's cut the ribbon and officially open The Learning Center, A.K.A TLC, which promises to give all of its children tender loving care!"

With that said, Crystal cut the ribbon and the gathered crowd of friends, parents, and children applauded. "Will everyone please come into the multi-purpose room? We have refreshments for you," Crystal said.

They followed her to the room, which was finely decorated for the guests. Crystal stood in the doorway greeting everyone as they assembled into the multi-purpose room. She had budgeted catering into her grand opening plans.

Once everyone was assembled, she took in the moment, trying to pay close attention to details. She didn't want to forget a thing about this day. Family, friends, parents, children and the new employees she had hired, got acquainted. She especially took pleasure in watching the children run around giggling as they got to know one another.

Everyone admired the spread of heavy hors d'oeuvres and

the ice sculpture, which was shaped like children's learning blocks. Next to the ice sculpture was a fountain, which flowed with sparking apple cider.

"Crystal, honey, I am so proud of you. The center is really beautiful."

Crystal turned to see her mother coming towards her. "Thanks Mama. It's what I've always wanted," Crystal said and smiled.

"That's why I'm so proud of you. You were determined, and you made your dream come true. I admire you for that."

"It really means a lot for you to say that to me. Thank you, Mama." Crystal hugged her mother and fought back the tears as they started to form. "It's been really hard work."

"But it was worth it, right?" her mother said.

"It most certainly has been. I can't explain to you how good it feels."

Marcy joined them. "Crystal, this is too much. I wish I had a center like this for the kids. You make me wish I were a kid again. I'd love to come here."

"Thanks, sis." Crystal said.

"I think Shanice likes it too. I left her in the infant room. She's testing out one of the new rocking chairs," Marcy said.

"Poor thing. She's probably tired. I don't remember her being this big with her first pregnancy," Crystal said.

"Me either," Marcy agreed. "She could go any day now."

"I just pray her doctor didn't look at the ultrasound wrong," their mother said.

"Does she know what she's having?" Crystal asked.

"Not yet. I just pray the doctor didn't miss a baby or something. She don't need no twins," Willie Mae said.

"Mama!" Marcy exclaimed.

"Pray you two. Just pray," their mother said in all seriousness.

"Where's Warren?" Marcy asked.

"He ran to the store to get candles for the cake. The

caterer didn't think we needed candles but you know how kids are. They love candles on a cake."

"Crystal." Someone called out.

Crystal turned around again hearing her name. "Vivian! I'm so glad you could make it." She gave Vivian a hug just as she would have hugged one of her sisters.

"I'm sorry we're late. We've been busy with some very good business." Vivian held her husband's hand as she spoke. "We're coming from a meeting with the social worker."

Crystal extended her hand to Vivian's husband, "Pleased to finally meet you, Mr. Parker."

He shook her hand. "You can call me Roland, Vivian has told me so much about you."

"I am glad you were able to come. Thanks so much."

"I am glad to finally meet you, and I wouldn't have missed the grand opening for the world." He looked around at the walls, ceiling, and floors. "It looks like our company did a good job. I remember coming to this old building before the renovations."

"Your company did an awesome job. Everything is just the way I've envisioned it for years," Crystal said.

"I'm glad we were able to come through for you," Roland said and smiled.

Crystal returned her attention to Vivian. "So how did the meeting go?"

"Thanks to you, it went well."

"What happened?" Crystal asked, as she remembered she hadn't done any introductions. "Forgive me. I'm so rude. Vivian and Roland, this is my mother, Willie Mae and my sister, Marcy."

"Oh I didn't mean to interrupt you. It's nice to meet you both," Vivian said extending her hand.

"My other sister Shanice is around here somewhere," Crystal said looking around.

"Why don't I tell you about the appointment a little later," Vivian said.

"No, no. Mama, Marcy, excuse me for a few minutes. I'll be right back," Crystal said pulling Vivian and Roland to the side.

"Vivian, honey, I'm going to let you two talk. I see an old client of ours by the stage. I'm going to speak to him." He kissed her on her cheek.

"Alright, sweetheart." Vivian smiled. Once they were by themselves Vivian said, "It went very well. We asked our social worker about Kylia and Kyle, and she was able to speak with their social worker. Things look pretty good so far. No one else has expressed interest in adopting them yet, not even their foster parents," Vivian said, excited.

"That's wonderful. It's all going to work out," Crystal said.

"I believe God is in control of this and has placed you, and now these children, in my life for a reason. I have no doubt it's what God wants for us. Roland and I will adopt Kylia and Kyle. Everything else, as far as I am concerned, is just a formality," Vivian said confidently.

"I've been praying for you all every since we first talked about you possibly adopting them."

"Thank you," Vivian said sincerely.

"I'll keep praying. I've even got my husband praying. He's heard me talk so much about the kids. I can't imagine a better home for them."

"Is he here?"

"He should be back by now. You haven't had a chance to meet him yet, have you?" Crystal asked.

"No, not yet."

"I'd love for him to meet Roland also," Vivian stated.

"He should be back soon, but you know we'll have to all get together soon."

"Don't worry, we will, and once we have confirmation that we will be getting Kylia and Kyle, we'll transfer them here to

TLC. I see how much they love you and how wonderful you are with children."

"Thank you." Crystal was touched.

"One day you will make a very good mother," Vivian said out of the blue.

"Thanks again," Crystal said.

Crystal was sincere. She didn't feel any dread or depression set in. She felt the peace of God's love around her. She smiled, and her smile was genuine.

A month had passed since the center's grand opening. Crystal had been busy with the enrollment of new children to fill up the remaining open spots.

The idea of getting up to go to her own business was still new to her. She hadn't taken for granted how blessed she was, and continually thanked God for allowing her dream to come true.

All the children seemed to be adjusting well in their new environments and Crystal was very pleased. She was also satisfied with the staff members she'd hired, especially the retired school cook, who was a blessing.

Things had been smooth sailing for the first four weeks. At the beginning of the fifth week, things changed. One of the teachers knocked on her office door. "Mrs. Shaw?"

Crystal looked up from her paperwork. "Yes, come in."

"I have a small problem. Elijah is sick. He is vomiting and has a fever. One of the volunteers is in the bathroom with him now."

"We'll need to call his parents. You go ahead and see about him, and I'll call his mom and dad."

"Okay. Thanks, Mrs. Shaw," the teacher said, quickly leaving the office.

Crystal shook her head. It was her first sick child. She knew it was bound to happen. She called the child's parents so they could pick him up.

That same afternoon the teacher returned to tell her about another child with the same symptoms. Crystal wondered whether it was a fluke or not. Not wanting to jump to any conclusions, she waited to see if any other children got sick before she'd let her own alarms go up. If it happened again, she'd inform the parents to look out for some of the same symptoms in their children.

The next morning three parents called to say their children were sick and would not be in. And later in the day she got a call from the parents of the first little boy who had gotten sick. The doctor diagnosed him with having a stomach virus.

Once she received the information, Crystal prepared a memo for all of the children's parents warning them about the virus that was going around.

As she proofread the memo, Crystal heard a knock at her door. Before answering she said a quick prayer hoping it wasn't another sick child. "Come in."

The door opened. "Hi, Mrs. Shaw," Brandice McCain said timidly.

"Brandice, come in. What a pleasant surprise," Crystal said glad to see her. "What brings you here?"

Brandice held her stomach. "My mom said I needed to come by early to put the baby on the waiting list."

"Brandice? You're pregnant?" It was obvious the girl was pregnant. Brandice had always been a tall, slim girl with a pretty figure. Crystal couldn't believe Brandice was standing in her office telling her she was pregnant. Crystal thought about the night Brandice was at her house for the tutoring session. Brandice had been crying in the bathroom. Now it all made sense. The girl must have known she was pregnant. Crystal's heart was saddened thinking about how scared Brandice must have been that night.

"Yes. My mom said to come by and talk to you."

"Wow, I am just so surprised." Crystal tried her best to

keep from letting her mouth drop. Brandice was the last person in the world she would have guessed would get pregnant. Brandice was a model student. She was always polite and didn't seem like a girl who would be sexually active.

"I know. I'm getting a lot of that lately. A lot of people are surprised to know I'm pregnant."

"When are you due?"

"June 17th."

"So how are you doing? Do you feel okay?"

"Yes. I'm doing fine. I don't have the morning sickness anymore. I don't know why they call it morning sickness though, I was sick all day long."

"That's good. I'm glad you're feeling better now. You were saying you wanted to get the baby on the waiting list?"

"Yeah. I've decided to stay in Silvermont. I received a full scholarship to CSU, and my parents are going to help until I can get on my feet after I graduate from college."

Crystal was pleased to hear this. She was glad there were still parents who helped their children—even when they made mistakes. "That'll be good."

"It sure is. I thought my chances of going to school were shot. But my parents said it is too important for me not to go."

"They're right. You are really blessed to have parents like them."

"I know, I realize that now," Brandice said.

There was another knock at the door. "Mrs. Shaw, there is another sick little girl in the 4-year-old class," one of the assistants said.

"Another one? I'll need to call her parents," Crystal said to the assistant. "Brandice, we have what looks like an epidemic going on around here. Many of my children are coming down with a stomach virus. You probably need to leave before you get sick too. I have your number. I'll call you and get the rest of the information I need later."

"Okay, Mrs. Shaw," Brandice said, turning to leave.

"And Brandice," Crystal said.

"Yes, Mrs. Shaw?"

"If there is anything you need or I can help you with, just let me know."

"I will. Thank you."

"See you later," Crystal said.

"Thanks."

"You're welcome. I'm sorry I have to rush you out of here. Tell your parents and Brandon I said, Hello, please."

"I will."

A week later over half of the children had become sick. Some were starting to feel better and returned to the center. Others were just starting to stay home.

Crystal hoped neither she nor her employees would get the virus, but had no such luck. One of the teacher assistants had gotten sick. Even though she hoped she wouldn't get sick either, Crystal's worst fear had come true, she was starting to feel queasy. She still held hope that other employees would not all get sick at the same time.

As the week progressed, Crystal felt even worse. First she had stomach pains, and when she tried to eat, the food would come back up. The only thing she could seem to keep down was water and cranberry-grape juice.

She tried her hardest to work through the sickness. But after a couple of days, she knew she'd need to see a doctor. It was the last place she wanted to go. By the time she had made up her mind to get checked, the doctor's office was closed.

That night she went home planning to go first thing in the morning. She lay in bed tossing and turning most of the night.

"Crystal. Are you alright?" Warren asked her.

"I feel pretty sick," Crystal replied.

Warren reprimanded her. "You're so hard headed. You know you should have gone to the doctor by now."

"Warren, please, I know I should have gone, but I have a business to run. I had to complete payroll today, and by the time I finished, the doctor's office was closed. I guess I waited too late."

"You should have gone two days ago."

"It's just a little stomach virus. It just needs to run its . . . ouch!"

"What? What's wrong?" Warren said in panic.

"It's my stomach—a sharp pain," Crystal said, holding her stomach.

"You need to see the doctor."

"I'm going in the morning." Crystal said.

"You're going right now. I'm taking you," Warren said firmly.

"What? You can't trust . . . uhhh!"

"What?"

"My stomach hurts so much."

"That settles it. Come on, we're going to the hospital." Warren jumped out of the bed and headed for his closet.

"I feel like I've got to throw up." Crystal leaned over the bed and barely picked up the wastebasket in time. After dry heaving a couple of times, she put it back down.

"Did you eat anything?" Warren asked her.

"Some ginger ale and crackers."

Warren didn't mask the look of pity on his face. "What do you want me to do?"

"Trade stomachs with me for a few minutes."

"If it was in my power, I'd do whatever I could do to help you."

"Hold that thought," Crystal said, jumping up. This time she stumbled to the bathroom.

When she returned to the bed, Warren had already put his shoes and jacket on. Crystal slipped a jogging suit on, and they went to the emergency room. After waiting two and a half hours, Crystal was finally seen. After another forty-five minutes the doctor returned to give her the diagnosis.

"Mrs. Shaw, you were right about the stomach virus. I guess you caught the same bug that's been going around here lately," the doctor informed her.

"How long before I start to feel better?"

"That's a Catch Twenty-Two question."

"Catch twenty-two?" Warren asked.

"Yes. The stomach virus should go away within a couple of days. But the sickness may take any where from two to seven months," the doctor said.

"Excuse me?" Warren said.

"I don't know if you were planning to have a child, but according to the tests we ran, Mrs. Shaw, you're pregnant. Congratulations!" the doctor said with cheer.

"Doctor, are you sure? You also ran a pregnancy test?" Crystal asked.

"It was very positive. You'd be surprised by the number of women who find out they're pregnant coming to the emergency room," the doctor said light-heartedly.

"Doctor, you don't know how much your words mean to us right now. We've been trying to conceive for over five years without success," Warren said.

"It seems so crazy that we'd come here of all places to find out we're pregnant, especially in the middle of the night," Crystal said, overjoyed to hear the news.

"I've seen enough in my life to know God works in mysterious ways," the doctor said.

Chapter 21

Vivian Parker

Vivian descended her marble staircase. Roland had just answered the door. Christina Ingram, their social worker, was standing in the foyer.

"Ms. Ingram, what a pleasure," Vivian greeted the social worker.

"Mr. and Mrs. Parker, thank you for allowing me to come and take another look at your home. I hope I didn't inconvenience you by calling on such short notice."

"No problem. We don't mind, anything that will help this process to move along." Roland said.

"Did you get everything in you ordered for the children's rooms?" Christina asked.

"We sure did, they're rooms are both ready," Roland replied.

"All we need now is Kylia and Kyle," Vivian smiled with anticipation. "Would you like to take a look at the finished rooms?"

"I'd love to," She shook her had affirmatively. "You've talked so much about the plans for their rooms. I'm just curious to see how it all turned out."

"Well, just follow me." Vivian gestured towards the marble staircase.

Vivian led Christina up the stairs and down the hall towards the children's rooms. Roland followed behind. First they stopped to look in Kylia's room.

Christina stepped in and her mouth dropped. "This is absolutely beautiful. You've really put a lot of obvious thought and love into making those children feel special. When I first saw this room just a few short weeks ago, it was a guest room with a golf motif, right?"

"It sure was," Roland said.

"Oh my goodness, the transformation is miraculous." Christina stepped into the center of Kylia's room, turning around 360 degrees to look at it all. Roland and Vivian watched as she admired all the hard work they had done.

Christina walked to the wall opposite the door and stared up at the picture of a young girl in the wall mural. "That looks like," she paused. "Kylia. Is it?"

"It sure is," Vivian beamed.

Vivian had transformed Kylia's space into a room fit for a little princess. One of Vivian's previous customers custom made all of the furniture, which was cream in color with a champagne trim.

The interior decorating had been designed by Vivian. And on the walls there were murals, each with caricatures of a little girl resembling Kylia.

On the wall Christina was admiring, there was a mural of a castle with a winding path leading up to it. It resembled the castle from the story of *Cinderella*. In the carriage leading to the tower, a pretty little girl dressed ready for the ball looked out and waved.

On the wall over Kylia's headboard was a mural of a tower without doors and only one window. Looking out of the lonesome window was another little girl resembling Kylia.

Extending from the picture of the girl's head were real braids of black twine, making it look as if the two long black braids were hanging from the window of the doorless tower just like in the story of *Rapunzel*.

Ms. Ingram stepped into the walk-in closet where there had been another mural of a little girl in a ballerina outfit putting on pink shimmering slippers. In the closet hung racks of clothing already purchased for Kylia. Vivian had been on several shopping sprees anticipating the children's arrival.

Christina stood in awe. "You two make me wish I was a little girl again. This room is fit for a princess."

"I just hope she likes it," Vivian said. She had never had a little girl and hadn't really been around anyone with a little girl to know exactly what little girls liked.

"I know she'll love it," Christina said.

Warren jumped in, "My wife is so nervous. We're looking forward to having the children here with us."

Christina began to open her mouth to say something but paused. "How about Kyle's room?"

Vivian wondered what the social worker was originally going to say. She thought maybe it was something about their progress in the adoption process.

"Kyle's room is right this way," Roland said. He led Christina through Kylia's bathroom. The second door led to Kyle's bedroom. "You can get into his room through here or out in the hall. We thought it best to put his room next to his big sister's."

Christina admired the transformation, which had taken place in Kyle's room too. It was fit for an active little prince. Vivian had chosen red, yellow, and blue to accent his room. There were murals here also. One was of a little boy playing basketball. A real basketball hoop was mounted on a painted pole so Kyle could practice throwing a ball into the hoop.

On another wall was a little boy playing baseball. And on the wall with Kyle's bed, there was a picture of a little boy sitting in a racecar. Below the picture was a racecar-shaped bed Vivian had custom ordered for him. Just as she had done in Kylia's room, all the little boys in each of the murals resembled Kyle.

And also like Kylia's room, Kyle's had accent rugs, lamps, curtains, a clock, and toys to accompany its theme. His walk-in closet was filled with clothes too.

"Kyle is going to love his room," Christina said. "How did you get so much done in such a short amount of time?"

Roland answered, "It was mostly my wife's doing. It didn't take her long to come up with the ideas, and with the many business contacts we have, it really wasn't hard at all."

"And those murals; They are so lifelike. Who on earth did those?"

"We gave a copy of the pictures you all provided us with of Kylia and Kyle and gave them to our good friend Leroy Gift."

"*The* Leroy Gift?" Christina asked incredulously.

"The one and only," Roland replied.

"LG, well that's what we called him in school," Vivian said, "he and I are good friends. We went to college together. Once I told him our story, he literally dropped everything to come out and paint these murals for us."

"I am so happy for these children. For all of you." Christina took a deep breath. "Okay, I can't hold it in any longer." She smiled at both of them. "I am pleased to say that the adoption has been approved. You have been selected as the new adoptive parents of Kylia and Kyle!" Her smile showed her heartfelt excitement.

"We have!" Vivian exclaimed. She looked at Roland in shock. She hoped she wasn't dreaming.

"Oh my goodness, that's wonderful. We were hoping you'd have good news for us today," Roland said.

"Well, congratulations. I wanted to tell you when I first came in but, I needed to see the completed rooms first," Christina Ingram said. "Rules, you know."

"Thank you so much, Ms. Ingram, for personally bringing us the good news," Vivian said.

"No, thank you for deciding to use our agency. It's always a good day when we can place one of our children. This placement is even better since we're placing the siblings together in what I can truly see is a loving home."

"Oh, Roland." Vivian looked over at him as her heart beat with joy. He took her in his arms, embracing her tightly. She couldn't remember the last time she got news as good as this. "I don't know who'll be happier—them or us."

"Those children are blessed to be able to have you adopt them," Christina said.

"No, Ms. Ingram, it's us who are blessed to have those children allow us to be a part of their lives," Vivian said. She hugged Roland tighter.

"Well, I am going to get out of your hair," the social worker said.

"So where do we go from here?" Vivian asked. "When can we pick up the children?"

"I needed to tell you the news first in order to find out if you would accept the committee's decision."

Anxious Vivian said, "Okay, it's done. You know we accept."

"Yes, we accept," Roland agreed.

"Good then, the transfer will take place within the week. I need to call the foster parents and tell them the news. Then we'll tell Kylia and Kyle. As soon as that is done, we'll set up the exact date."

"Excellent." Vivian clapped her hands together with eagerness. "And after that, how long should it take for everything to be final?"

"Well, after placement there is a ninety day wait, then the

papers can be filed with the court and the final decree of adoption can be issued. Then of course, they'll be legally yours."

"Okay, ninety days or so. I can do that. I've waited years for this moment. Another three months won't be so bad," Vivian said.

"I'll need to make a few more visits over the next few months to see how the children are adjusting, but don't worry, I won't be making any pop visits. The meetings will be scheduled."

"Alright. I guess that's all I need to ask right now," Vivian said.

Christian put her hands together, intertwining her fingers. "I know you are both excited. Let me get out of here, I've got some very important phone calls to make."

"And we need to let William know he will be an official big brother." Roland chuckled.

Roland and Vivian walked hand in hand, leading the social worker to the staircase and back downstairs.

Once at the door, Christina turned to the both of them. "And if you have any other questions, feel free to call me."

"Don't worry, we will," Vivian said, then quickly admitted, "Oh yeah, there is one thing. I know I was planning a little prematurely, but we want to have an adoption party for the children. You know, once everything is finalized."

"That sounds like a great idea. The kids will love it I'm sure. Just let me know when it is, and I'll do my best to come," Christina said.

"We'd love that," Roland said.

"I've already made out the list of guests and your name is on it," Vivian said.

Roland opened the front door.

"And again congratulations!" Christina said and smiled as she left.

"Thank you," Roland and Vivian both said as they waved goodbye to her.

Once they closed the door and were alone again, Roland took the opportunity to embrace Vivian once again. "They are going to be ours." He smiled, touching his forehead to hers looking directly into her eyes.

"I know." Vivian nuzzled his nose. "I'm so excited. It feels like a dream." She closed her eyes, relishing the moment.

Roland pinched her on her butt. "Ouch!" Her eyes flew open, and she pulled away from him. He quickly pulled her back in, embracing her tighter. "Why on earth did you do that?"

"I just want to assure you that you're not dreaming."

Vivian rubbed the spot where he'd pinched her. "Keep it up and I might just pinch you."

"Go ahead, I need to know I'm not dreaming either."

Vivian did so, pinching him much harder than he had pinched her. He exclaimed, "Ouch, that hurt!" Vivian pulled out of his embrace and pinched him again on his arm this time.

Roland lunged towards her, but she was too quick. She ran and he followed down the hall to the master bedroom. Roland closed their door with a click before joining Vivian on the bed.

"We better practice closing the door," he said with a grin.

Rays from the morning sun beamed through the French doors of Vivian and Roland's bedroom. Vivian woke out of a restful sleep. She turned to look over at the clock. It was seven a.m.

Today was the day they'd all waited for. Three and a half months had passed since the day the social worker gave them the news Kylia and Kyle would be theirs. The waiting period was over and the adoption had been finalized. It was now the morning of the adoption party, which was scheduled to start at noon.

Vivian was content with the way her life was turning out.

She'd always wanted to be a successful businesswoman one day working for herself, and that goal had been accomplished. She'd also wanted to be a mother, and even though it hadn't been in a conventional way, she was now the mother of three beautiful children.

Vivian knew there was only one reason for her to have gone through so much disappointment in her life, and yet end up being happy and content. It was nothing but the grace of God. He knew what she had needed way before she did. And all she had to do was let go of her own misgivings and trust Him. She was thankful she now trusted Him. She didn't allow herself to dwell on the fact, that for so many years, she hadn't put all of her trust in Him. Deep down she knew God understood her reasons at the time.

Vivian wanted the children's adoption experience to be a positive and memorable one. The party was planned to assist with their transition. She hoped it would further help them understand they were there to stay permanently.

The list of guests included the children's former foster parents, their daycare teachers, the social workers, the children's friends from daycare and Crystal Shaw, their current daycare director. It also included Shelby Tomlinson, the nurse from her doctor's office.

Shelby, Crystal, and Vivian had become close friends, realizing they all had a common bond. With different circumstances, they all wanted children. And with different answers, God had blessed them all to have children.

Vivian remembered the day when they'd all been out shopping for baby items for Shelby. Shelby confided in her and Crystal telling them that she often prayed for all of her patients but especially the ones who had infertility problems. She said it was as if she were in a "secret sisterhood" with those patients since there was a common sisterly bond, but the secret was never discussed. Vivian chuckled at this thought.

Roland stirred beside her. Tenderly she shook him. "Roland. It's time to get up."

"I'm already awake. The kids are too. I've been listening to them laughing and playing," Roland replied.

Vivian thought about the first day Kylia and Kyle came to their home to be a permanent part of the family. They couldn't believe their eyes when they saw the enormous house. They were especially excited when they saw their new rooms. Kylia adored the pictures on the walls and Kyle started throwing the stuffed basketball in the hoop as soon as he saw it.

Vivian laughed with moist eyes as she rested in Roland's arms, listening to the children, "They've got a long day ahead of them. They'll sleep well tonight."

"I'm sure they won't be the *only* ones tired tonight," Roland said. "Are you ready to party?"

"I've been ready for more than three months," Vivian said. "Longer than that really. A party will do me real good right now."

"Guess we need to get up and complete the decorations. I still don't understand why you didn't just hire someone to do it."

"Because, darling. I told you, I want us to do this ourselves. I want us to be an integral part of the planning and preparation of our children's party."

"If you say so, sweetheart. I just didn't want you to over exert yourself."

"I haven't, and Crystal will be over to help at nine o'clock."

"Good. Is Warren coming with her?"

"Yes, and Shelby. She is bringing her husband Phillip."

"You three have gotten pretty close, haven't you?"

"We sure have over the past few months. They're really nice. I feel as if we have kindred spirits," Vivian said.

"That's pretty deep," Roland replied.

"I know." Vivian had never felt as close to her biological

sisters, as she did to Crystal and Shelby. "They are both expecting."

"Both of them? You told me about Crystal, I didn't know Shelby was expecting too."

"Yes and I'm so happy for them. Both couples had infertility problems. Crystal and Warren had been trying over five years to conceive. And Shelby and Phillip had been trying for over two years."

"Isn't that something?" Roland said.

"We're all so very blessed. God finally blessed us all with children to love and nurture."

Roland smiled. "William, Kylia, and Kyle have all been such a blessing to us. I'm glad God put us all together."

Vivian looked over at the alarm clock. "I'm so excited. Almost everyone we invited will be here, even their grandmother," Vivian said.

"I know she's happy for the kids."

Vivian stepped out of bed and walked to the French doors. She looked out. "I hope it doesn't rain today."

"The weather man didn't say anything about rain. But don't worry, I placed an order for a sunny day."

"You know, Roland, it could rain, snow or even hail, and I don't think it would matter to me. Nothing can put a damper on this day for me."

Roland joined Vivian at the French doors and wrapped his arms around her. "Me either."

Epilogue

Another pain shot through her abdomen.

"This is it. Push! The baby's head is almost out," Dr. Evans said.

She took a deep breath, hoping it would be the last push. The labor pain was like nothing she had ever expected. The look on her helpless husband's face was heart wrenching.

"Ten . . . nine . . . eight . . . seven . . . six . . . five . . . four . . . three . . . two . . . one!" the nurse counted backwards.

She allowed herself to let her breath go.

"Okay, okay. You can stop pushing now," the doctor said. "The baby's head is coming out."

She relaxed as best as she could and looked down to see the head.

"Look at all this curly hair. Try to relax, I'm going to pull your baby out," Dr. Evans said.

"Okay, Dr. Evans," she said, trying to get a closer look down and see the baby.

"Alright. Here it is." The doctor quickly handed the mother the baby.

"It's so beautiful. A girl?" she asked.

"A girl," the doctor confirmed.

"She's so beautiful . . . Congratulations, Dad!" The nurse smiled at the husband.

"Thanks," he said, tears filling his eyes. He looked down lovingly at his new daughter and wife. "She looks just like her mother. I can't believe she's finally here."

Looking down at her new baby, the mom started to cry. She had waited so long for the miracle of a child, and now her daughter was in her arms. Even though the odds had been against her because of her age, God had given her favor. She had gotten pregnant even though the doctor said she was too old.

Originally she had accepted the idea that maybe God hadn't wanted her to have her own child biologically. Her age was a factor, no doubt, that could not be helped. All of the science in the world wasn't going to turn back the hands of time when it came to her age.

But now, as she looked down at her screaming little girl, she knew miracles were possible. The baby was healthy. Early tests showed there were no birth defects. She had all ten fingers and toes. The infant was a blessing only God could grant.

"I think I need to call the kids and tell them their new little sister has arrived," Roland said.

"Tell Kylia the house is even now. Three and three," Vivian said. She smiled and kissed the baby's forehead.

"Viv, let me take her for a moment and clean her off," the nurse said.

"Thank you Shelby," Vivian replied handing her friend Shelby the baby. She was glad Shelby was now employed in the hospital's maternity ward and her friend was able to be a part of the baby's birth.

It had been two years since the adoption of Kylia and Kyle had been finalized. Vivian had been astonished to learn that she was pregnant. When the morning sickness started, she thought she was going through *The Change*.

When the doctor told her she was pregnant, she was in denial for the first couple of months until her first sonogram. The sonogram confirmed it for her.

Vivian had felt a tremendous amount of joy when they adopted Kylia and Kyle. She thought she couldn't have felt any more joy in her life. But now that she was able to hold her new baby, she realized there was so much more love and joy in her heart.

A different kind of joy she thought she would never feel. Vivian closed her eyes and thanked God for the gift her two closest friends, Shelby and Crystal, had experienced themselves; Shelby giving birth to a girl and Crystal giving birth to a boy. The wonderful gift of life!

Secret Sisterhood

Reader's Group Guide

Shelby & Phillip

1. Often people let their pride and ego get in the way of communicating, especially with the ones they love. This is true in Shelby and Phillip's case. Do you think this is typical in most relationships?
2. Do you think the only reason Phillip told Shelby about his ex-girlfriend getting pregnant in the first place was because his male ego was at stake?
3. Shelby seems to have forgiven Phillip pretty quickly after finding out he kept a secret from her. How realistic is this? Do you think she did so out of desperation wanting him to cooperate with the fertility appointments?
4. How do you think things would have turned out if Phillip told Shelby the entire truth? Do you think there are times when a spouse is truly justified in keeping the truth from their significant other?
5. Do you believe what is done in the dark, will come to the light? Phillip didn't disclose all the information to Shelby. In what ways do you think the past could hurt him in the future?
6. Phillip felt he was protecting Shelby's emotions by not telling her the whole truth about the child he fathered. Do you think he made the right decision? What do you think most men would have done in the same situation?

Crystal and Warren

7. Crystal often found herself judging people with children, determining whether or not they were worthy of having them or not. How often do you think people do the same as Crystal in everyday life?
8. After praying about what they should do, Crystal and her husband Warren decide to use medical technology to help them conceive. How do you feel about couples using medical technology like IVF and other Assisted Reproductive Technologies to help with the conception?
9. Crystal was surprised when she found out her insurance wouldn't cover the costs for the major IVF procedures.
10. Crystal has strong faith when it comes to many areas of her life. When it came to the faith she had about having a child, her faith was weak. Ask yourself what areas your faith is strong or weak.

Vivian and Roland

11. Vivian allowed past memories of God to hinder her relationship with Him for years. In the end she returned to God trusting in him, realizing He had been answering her prayers the whole time. How often do you think this happens in real life?
12. Vivian had her life planned out almost to a tee. Vivian is devastated to find out she may have waited to long to start having children. Do you think there are women in this day and age who don't know the true meaning of the biological clock?
13. Vivian and Roland decide to adopt after the IVF fails and Vivian gets what she feels is an answer from God as

to what they should do. Do you think most people use adoption only as what seems like a last resort?

General Questions

14. Did this book enlighten you to the emotional struggles women / men go through when having infertility problems?

15. Each of the main characters end up conceiving a child. When it comes to infertility this is not always the case. Many couples adopt. On television, often times we see people adopting children from other countries. We also get the impression that it takes thousands of dollars to adopt a child or children. Vivian and Roland adopted locally through the Department of Social Services DSS. Are you aware of the local adoption resources where you live?

16. For those of you who would consider yourself a member of the Secret Sisterhood, did this book provide hope and inspiration?

17. Do you know of anyone who might be a part of the Secret Sisterhood? Do you think this book would provide them with hope and inspiration?

*Soul Confessions is the Sequel to
Secret Sisterhood!*

By

Monique Miller

Prologue

Phillip's body tensed as he stared at the name, Jeana Sands, printed on the manila folder he had just retrieved from the back of his bottom file drawer. He had forgotten it was there. It had been years since he'd stuffed it in there in the first place. Years since he thought about Jeana Sands and the child he fathered so many years ago.

He flipped through the pages in the folder. The folder held the certified letter he received informing him that Jeana, an ex-girlfriend from college, wanted child support for her son. It also held a copy of the DNA test, which proved Jeana's son was biologically his and documentation of a bank account not connected with any of his other accounts.

Phillip remembered the day he had gotten the certified letter asking for child support for a child he hadn't known existed. The boy was 9-years-old when he received the letter. After going to court and having a DNA test performed, he found out the test proved he was the father by a 99.97% chance.

It was at that point that a secret account to pay automatic monthly child support payments was created. Soon after the account was set up, Phillip placed all documentation connecting him to Jeana in a manila folder. He scrawled her name on the tab and hid it in the very back of the bottom file drawer.

There was no way he wanted his wife to find out about the child. It wasn't *his* fault that he had told Jeana she needed to terminate the pregnancy and she had gone ahead and had the child without telling him. And it wasn't his fault she waited until the boy was 9-years-old before she contacted him. He had no emotional ties to the boy and didn't even know what the boy looked like.

Legally he would provide the child support payments, but that is where the ties ended. His life was progressing just fine. Soon after setting up the account for the boy, Phillip found out his wife, Shelby, was pregnant. He and his wife had been trying for over two years to conceive and now he had the family he always envisioned and wanted.

Jeana and her son did not fit into his plans. Phillip made it very clear to his lawyer that he didn't want anything whatsoever to do with the boy and did not want any contact from Jeana. Jeana had complied with his wishes and never bothered him again.

There was a knock at his office door. "Hello, anybody in?"

Phillip shoved the file back into the drawer and looked up to see his friend, Will. "Of course I am here. I just got promoted. I can't start disappearing now."

Will placed his hand on one of the moving boxes, which sat on Phillip's desk. "You need any help packing up your things?"

"Naw, thanks man. I just have to finish packing up these files from the file cabinet." Phillip closed the drawer he was looking in.

"Congratulations again, you deserved this promotion." Will said.

"You're dog on straight I deserved it. I should have gotten

it a couple of years ago." He shrugged his shoulders. "But hey, I ain't complaining."

"Everything happens in its own season. This is your time. God had his reasons for you getting this promotion now instead of then."

Phillip pulled one of the filled file boxes off his desk placing it next to the office door, "Well, it is about time, is all I can say."

Will looked at his watch. "Hey I just wanted to step in for a second and see if you needed any help. I've got to check my emails before my meeting in a hour."

Phillip's office phone rang. "Hold on a second." Phillip picked up the receiver. "Hello, Phillip Tomlinson speaking." He waited for a response from the other end of the line, but none came. "Hello, hello." He said again, there was no verbal response but he did hear a distinctive click.

Will looked at him questioningly. "Same crank caller?"

Phillip placed the receiver down harder than he intended, "I guess, it's kind of hard to know when they don't identify themselves."

Will shook his head, "It's crazy. Why would someone waste their time calling someone all day long and not say anything?"

"They must not have anything better to do. I wonder how many other people are having the same problem as me with these crank callers?" Phillip said. "Shelby has even been receiving calls at home."

"I don't know but I'm glad they are not calling me."

Phillip shrugged it off. "Hopefully, when I move to my new office the calls will stop."

"Or maybe the person will get a new hobby." Will looked at his watch again. "Gotta go man. See you later. Maybe we can do lunch or something."

"Sounds good. Give me a call later."

Once Will left the office, Phillip closed and locked his office door. He returned to the file cabinet and pulled the manila folder back out. Looking around his office he spotted the paper shredder he had already unplugged, sitting in the corner of the office next to his fake ficus tree.

He retrieved the shredder and placed it on the desk. After plugging it in, he pulled the contents of the folder back out. One by one he took each sheet and shredded it. Phillip shook his head wondering why he had kept all the information in the first place. His lawyer had copies of everything safely tucked away in his own office. He should have destroyed it all years ago.

Once everything in the folder was shredded, Phillip then shred the manila folder also. Wiping his hands as if he were removing imaginary dust, he said to himself, "Let the past, stay in the past."